2000

MERRY Christmas

D1214313

SIMON & SCHUSTER

New York   London   Toronto   Sydney   Singapore

The Other Side

Kevin McColley

A NOVEL OF THE CIVIL WAR

SIMON & SCHUSTER
Rockefeller Center
1230 Avenue of the Americas
New York, NY 10020

SIMON & SCHUSTER and colophon are registered trademarks
of Simon & Schuster, Inc.

Designed by Carla Bolte

Manufactured in the United States of America

1   3   5   7   9   10   8   6   4   2

Library of Congress Cataloging-in-Publication Data
McColley, Kevin.
The other side : a novel of the Civil War / Kevin McColley.
p. cm.
1. United States—History—Civil War, 1861–1865—Fiction. 2.Teenage boys—Fiction.
I. Title.
PS3563.O34316 O8   2000
813'.54—dc21   00-029161
ISBN 0-684-85762-6

Author's Note

This novel is based on actual events. I have rarely departed from the facts concerning William Quantrill, William Anderson, and the men and boys who followed them, or of the actions they were involved in, where those facts are known. However, in some cases, I have allowed myself the novelist's license of imagination. It has been my intention to write not so much a historical document as an account of the spirit of the characters and their age.

—KEVIN McCOLLEY
La Cruces, New Mexico
February 10, 1997

These are the times. A tall man with head bowed stands beside a desk, his trembling fingers resting upon a newspaper headline. Eyes search the sky, dark eyes lift from heat burdened hills to seek a blinding sight. A wagon wheel groans, wrapped in the scent of sweating horses. Scarred backs glisten in the sun. In the heart of the world a nation cracks like an egg. These are the times.

The Other Side

Prologue

The dark river murmured as the boy crossed the yard and the silver sky turned black. At the barn door he stopped to watch the lamplight coming warmly through the cabin window, to watch a shadow move over the pane. He opened the door, quietly stepped in, and pulled it shut behind him. The warm smells of the animals surrounded him, their sweat, the sound of their breath.

She was waiting in the straw behind the stalls. Her skin was the sky and her eyes were shining.

"Where is he?" the boy asked.

"The outhouse."

"Then he'll be back."

"He'll go to the cabin to read."

He lay beside her and ran his hand down her arm. He studied her face, her eyes, then unbuttoned her dress and reverently touched her breast. She was as dark and warm and soft as the spring night. This was a holy thing.

"Jacob," she said.

"Yes?"

"Jacob."

He kissed her. Her lips trembled. He could hear the river murmuring.

Chapter One

A *man followed* an eagle into the forest because he believed in omens. He believed that the earth contained an eternal heart that beat in all of its children.

He followed the eagle day after day as it flew westward along a river. Every morning when he awoke the eagle would be perched in a tree on the riverbank, watching him silently with silver eyes, and it would lift from the branch in a flash of silver as its wings caught the morning light. One morning when the man awoke the eagle was gone, and the man knew he had come to where he was meant to be. He looked to the sky and the river and the trees gathered thickly around him; he inhaled deeply the smell of the life all around him. He thanked the earth.

With the pain in his hands and the pain in his back he cleared a field on the north bank of the Ohio River in what was to become Brown County, Ohio. He spent the first winter camped in the hollow of a fallen cottonwood; he listened for wolves and ate the remains of their kills and lost one of his fingers and two of his toes to frostbite. He prayed to God and to the earth and, with his teeth chattering, pondered the cold lying deep within him. In the spring he jointed the first logs of his cabin, and in the summer when he finished it and lay on the riverbank with the heat of the day passing, with the pain in his body flowing back into the earth, he looked across the murmuring water to the other side and wondered if he should have cleared his field and built his cabin there. But in the eagle's actions God and the earth had spoken. The man believed in omens.

The man followed the river east before winter and returned to his farm with a seventeen-year-old bride just as the snow was beginning to fall. Through the years they raised crops and children, strong sons, strong and beautiful daughters. The man's hair had thinned and the joints in his hands had knotted by the time he buried his wife in the back corner of the pasture. He spent more and more time staring across the water or searching the western horizon. He would wonder at the beat of his heart within him. He had never forgotten the eagle, the flash of its wings in the morning light.

The sons and daughters drifted away, some east, one west, until only one son remained. As the man lay on his deathbed he gripped his son's hand and transferred through their clasp the knowledge that had always driven him. The son felt it as a heat and a trembling, as brittle bones hot with the last of the old man's life, but after he buried his father he lifted his eyes to the river and the horizon.

The son buried his father's knowledge beneath the farm and its responsibilities, beneath its taming, beneath his own fear. He felt it only in an occasional glance at the river, at the sun at the end of the day. In time he took a wife who had come across the river and they had a son of their own. The birth was difficult, tearing from her the seed for other children.

The boy was like any other, but he carried within him the knowledge of his grandfather, the hidden knowledge of the father whose mule and plow he now plodded behind. His name was Jacob, and as his grandfather had done he would lie on the riverbank in the weathered hollow of the long-ago cottonwood and stare across the water or to the sun. He would wonder as his grandfather had done, though he did not understand the wondering. He had never heard of the earth's heart.

Three miles downriver from the farm was a town named Ripley. Between Ripley and the farm, across a stand of oaks and maples and chestnuts on the farm's western boundary, was a plot of semiwild land owned by a coarse Irish immigrant named McIntyre. His wife had abandoned him, leaving him with a daughter named Mary who had taken upon herself the responsibilities of her mother, a colorless girl with the straight, thin, desiccated body of a reed in winter. Jacob had known her for as long as he had known the river, seventeen years. She had known the river two years longer. He planned to marry her one day, though he didn't know why.

"Jacob," she said.

"What?"

"Do you love me, Jacob?" It was almost spring with the sky overhead threatening a cold rain, with the snow gone but for dirty gray husks hiding in shadows. They were sitting beside her father's skiff on the riverbank. A breeze licked a strand of dull red hair across her freckled pale forehead.

He looked at her hair, at her face, at the colorless dreams in her colorless eyes. Something twisted inside of him that he did not understand. He turned to the river.

"I got to go," he said.

"Jacob."

"I love you. I got to go." He felt her eyes upon him as he rose. Before turning away, he dutifully kissed her forehead. The river whispered quietly.

Jacob followed the bank, winding alongside willows, through oaks, through cottonwoods, and stopped in a straddle over a spring to gaze at the river. Dark water, cold water, impenetrable, whispering. An old, dying cottonwood on the other side cast amorphous shadows that for all of its inexorable power the current could not move. He imagined himself an old man with an old wife, her thin red hair graying. He looked at his hands and saw them knotted as he remembered his grandfather's had been in some inherited memory. He stepped over the stream and hurried to the farm. He shoved his hands into his trousers to hide them.

The two hogs in the sty grunted greetings; hens cackled their twilight gossip. The half dozen nameless cats prowled through shadows and glanced at him furtively. As he walked past the barn toward the cabin, Mabel, the cow, lowed from her stall. Whatever it was he had felt sitting beside Mary was the edge of a blade within him.

"How's Buck?" his father, Cyrus, asked when he went inside. Cyrus was a small man with ropy muscles and thinning hair, the callused hands, the thick fingers, the deep color, the thick smell of a farmer. He was sitting at the table, trying to repair a trace. Buck was Cyrus's mule and his pride, tall, strong, bright-eyed, still young, muscles that bulged beneath the harness, perhaps all that Cyrus wished to be.

"Didn't know I was supposed to check on him."

"Mules need checking on. You were over with that McIntyre girl, weren't you?"

"No."

"The hell."

"Leave him be." Clara was sitting at the table beside a lantern whose flame grew brighter with the thickening darkness, flickering on the panes of the china cabinet against the wall, glowing on the china within it. In her face she held a desperate fervency that Jacob had been told she'd picked up in the battle for his birth. A picture hung behind her of Jesus casting down his eyes. She was reading now her Bible. "You were young once, too."

Cyrus glanced up from the trace. "Huh."

"You used to dote on me. You used to steal away from the fields to bring me flowers."

"And my daddy would wup me." Cyrus looked at Jacob.

"I'll go check on Buck," Jacob said.

He stepped out the door and studied the yard and the naked field beyond it, the pasture beside the river, the new grass shining, even in the dusk. The clouds were heavier, darker. Rain had begun to fall, and small, dark circles peppered the yard. The peeling white fence separating the pasture from the field rose from the earth like bones. He hunched his shoulders against the cold rain and shuffled to the barn.

The mule was stamping in his stall and eyeing the oats impatiently. Mabel lowed quietly, the square box of her haunches protruding starkly and her udder hanging almost obscene. Jacob filled the mangers and watched them eat, smelled them, felt the muggy heat around him from their bodies. He was young, and his ascent to manhood struggled within him. Finally he walked back to the door, trailing his fingers over Buck's withers. It was raining harder now, drops slapping the ground and muttering on the river, and the wind was damp and cold.

Cyrus was still working the trace, and Clara was reading the scriptures to him. Jacob sat at the table. He gnawed at a callus on his palm and studied the fire.

"And it came to pass," Clara read, "when Israel had made an end of slaying all the inhabitants of Ai in the field, in the wilderness wherein they chased them, and when they were all fallen on the edge of the sword, until they were consumed, that all the Israelites returned unto Ai, and smote it with the edge of the sword. And so it was, that all that fell that day, both of men and women, were twelve thousand, even all the men of Ai. For Joshua drew not his hand back, wherewith he stretched out the spear, until he had utterly destroyed all the inhabitants of Ai." She closed the book. "Amen."

"Amen," Cyrus repeated absently. His fingers fumbled with the trace.

"Huh," Jacob said.

"Huh?" Clara asked him. "Do you *huh* the word of the Lord?"

"Seems to me the Lord does an awful lot of smiting."

"He had passed judgment," she said.

"Then it seems to me he does an awful lot of judging. It don't make no sense, him telling Joshua to kill all those people. If something don't make sense, how can it be?"

"The ways of God," Clara answered him. She ran her fingers over the book's cracked leather cover and stared into her son's eyes. "They are beyond men's ways."

"The ways of God and men don't seem much different. One is just an excuse for the other."

Clara's eyes flashed. "Such talk will bring your sins down upon you, Jacob. They will haunt your steps."

"I'm just saying it don't make sense."

"Read the paper," Cyrus said.

"I'm just saying."

"Read the paper." Cyrus settled back into working the trace. "You get to your age and you think you know everything. We don't need a row."

Jacob spread the paper Cyrus had bought in Ripley, laying it in the circle of light thrown by the lantern. He could taste his anger. If God exists, then he is both love and hatred and such a contradiction cannot be and Jacob did not believe in God. God was a word in a book. A justification.

Clara had said that the eye is the mirror of the soul. He had once seen in Ripley a fugitive slave being returned to its master, wrapped in chains, a brand on its shoulder festering. Jacob had looked into its dark, empty eyes. Men are men, are dust. White men are white men, are dust. Black men are black men, are dust and chattel and none of it made any difference. The sanctified choirs of the redeemed sing only in men's longing.

Outside the spring storm grew, a gentle muttering on the roof, a whisper growing with the darkness. The fire sizzled cheerily. Jacob looked from the paper to his father, watched his mother read, watched the fervor in her eyes as they moved almost frantically across the page. She believed.

Cyrus finally sighed and set the trace on the table. It looked little different than it had when Jacob had first come in. "Well. Might just as well turn in."

Clara nodded and set her Bible to the side. She stepped behind the curtain beside the hearth and came out a moment later in her nightdress. Jacob stared at the fire. He looked down at his hands glowing red within its light. He thought of Mary's hair and his youth roiled within him. Were these the hands of a farmer?

"Turn in, Jacob," Cyrus said. "There's work tomorrow."

He nodded and climbed the ladder to the loft where he had slept every night he could remember. The fire's heat was all around him and he lay on top of the blankets, looking up at the rafters, smelling the dusty smell of them. He listened to his parents on the down mattress beside the hearth, listened to the sounds they made, the sighs, the steady breathing. Sometimes they made other sounds, sharper sighs, heavier breathing, and it was nights like those when Jacob stared up into the blackness of the rafters and wished most that he was away from here. Thinking about where he might be, the exotic places, the exotic ladies of every color who would beneath him shout their passion in words he could not understand, aroused him and his hand slipped into his drawers. But his mind kept bending back to the farm and then back to Mary, her narrow, pale, familiar face, her familiar mundane hair flaring, her familiar surety of a future he felt chained to. He took his hand from his drawers.

Lightning flashed and thunder cracked and someone knocked on the door. Jacob sat up and looked down into the flickering darkness.

"What the hell?" Cyrus asked.

"Don't swear," Clara warned.

"What the hell."

"Your sins will come down upon you. Go see who it is."

Jacob listened to Cyrus rise, listened to him shuffle across the rough plank floor. He sat up on the bed and reached for his trousers. The door scraped over the floor and the leather hinges creaked and Jacob felt the wind, smelled the rain on the wind, and when lightning flashed the threshold framed a slope-shouldered silhouette of a man who looked like Tobias from across the river. Tobias's shape attempted to deny the strength in his thick, smooth muscled arms, in his thick fingers. His skull was as smooth and shiny as if he waxed it, and a light brown beard grew down to flare grandly over his chest. Jacob had worked for him with his bees, had worked with him in their fields, since he had been a child. They had shared meals, shared pain, had wept together when Tobias's wife had died. Such are the things neighbors do.

"God damn, Tobias," Cyrus said. Cyrus's shadow looked like a spider beside the bulk of the other man, elbows in angles, knees bent. "What kind of trouble are you in?"

"No trouble." Tobias held out a crock. "I brought you some honey."

"You brought honey at this time of night in a storm? What kind of trouble are you in?"

Tobias wiped the rain from his face, from his beard. "Well," he said.

"Oh, hell."

Thunder cracked behind them, lightning flashed. Jacob climbed down the ladder. Tobias wiped the water from his beard and stood silently. He nodded at Jacob and Clara.

"Don't just stand out in the rain," Cyrus said.

Tobias nodded again and stepped into the room. The water dripping from him stained the wood flooring. He sputtered the rain from his mustache and set the crock on the table. Clara stepped behind the curtain and came out wearing her housecoat. She lit a match and a sudden, tiny light glowed in the corner of the room. She lit the lantern and the light grew.

"I got a problem," Tobias said.

"What kind of problem?" Cyrus asked.

"Well . . ." He removed his slouch hat and wiped his hand over his scalp. The sour smell of his rain-drenched clothing filled the room. "You're good people. I've always known it. I've heard you say that one man is as good as another."

"What kind of trouble are you in?" Cyrus asked.

"Do you know what I do?"

"You're a beekeeper."

"I don't mean that. Do you know what I do?"

"I suspect," Clara said. She pulled a chair back from the table and motioned for Tobias to sit. "Who you got out there with you?"

Tobias looked at her, then dropped his eyes and surrendered to the chair. "There's two of them. I can't keep them with me."

"Two of who?" Jacob asked.

"You're talking about the railroad, ain't you?" Cyrus asked.

"I won't ever come to you again," Tobias said. "I mean that from my heart."

"Oh, Jesus," Cyrus said. "The railroad." He shook his head. "I don't want nothing to do with it. This is the valley."

"It being the valley don't make no difference to them."

"It makes a difference to the neighbors—they'd just as soon shoot the white helping the nigger as the nigger himself. I don't want nothing to do with it. This ain't no railroad station."

"There's a man and his daughter . . ."

"A slave and his daughter," Cyrus said. "And when someone finds out, the government will take half the farm for violating the Fugitive Slave Law and the neighbors will burn down the rest. Maybe somebody gets killed along the way. My daddy built this place; he and my mama are buried out back. That means something to me. Them slaves, they don't mean nothing to me." He wiped his thin face with his thin fingers. "A man's a man and the color don't make no difference. You all know I believe that. But they don't mean nothing to me."

"You're liked. You're respected."

"I'd like to stay that way."

Clara sat beside Tobias. Her long, blond hair had pulled loose in stiff strands that caught the light of the lamp, that stuck up like horns from her scalp. Her corded neck like steel bands. "They got souls. You can't deny that."

"I ain't denying that. But this farm's got a soul, too."

"You never would have placed this farm above a soul when we married."

"There was never a need to. These are different times."

"Right and wrong," Clara said, "don't care about times. God does not change."

She stared at her husband. Tobias again wiped the rain from his scalp and passed his hand down his beard. Jacob leaned against the wall and watched his mother and father. Cyrus sighed and crossed his arms and swore beneath his breath.

Clara rose, handed Tobias a towel, and sat again. "Tell us about them."

Tobias nodded. "There's a man and his daughter, him about forty and her fourteen or so. They brought them to me and I saw that little turd Anders kid hanging around in the bushes. Hell, you know his father. I couldn't keep them there at the house."

"They'll know where you brought them," Cyrus said.

"You've never done this before. And it's the other side of the river."

"Names," Clara said. "Give me their names."

"I don't know them." Tobias wiped the towel over his skull.

"Where they from?"

"I don't know that, either."

The rain was heavy on the roof, heavy dripping from the eaves, spattering in puddles. Jacob looked out the window beside the door into the darkness. He had seen slaves and he had seen free blacks, but he had never seen a fugitive still free. In the faces of slaves he had seen a hopelessness of a world that would never be; in the faces of free blacks he had seen a hopelessness of a world that could not be. He wondered what he would find in the face of a fugitive. They had fled one world and did not yet know the other.

"Where they at?" Clara asked.

"In the willows by the river."

"Good Lord, Tobias," Clara said as she stood. "You left them out in the rain?"

"I wanted to know what you'd say before I let them in your buildings."

Clara wrapped her husband's coat around her shoulders. They stepped out into the chilling rain with bare feet slipping and fingers tugging on hat brims and Tobias leading the way to the river where the raindrops sputtered against the water and the heavier drops rolling off of the branches almost boomed. Long, loose willows on the bank faded up into oaks and maples and chestnuts.

"Are you in there?" Tobias called. No sound came but the wind in the branches and the rain on the water. "It's all right. There's people with me, but they're good people."

Something rustled in the branches. A foot sloshed in water.

"Are you in there?" Tobias asked again.

"Yes," a voice answered. Deep, like the thunder. As steady as rain.

"She in there, too?"

"Yes."

Feet sloshed in mud and bodies jostled. Jacob could smell Tobias, but not the fugitives. Do fugitive slaves hold no scent? He couldn't remember any on that slave in Ripley.

"It's all right," Tobias said. "They agreed to let you stay."

"We thank you," the voice said.

Cyrus cleared his throat, and he spat. "This ain't no place to talk, standing out here in the rain."

Lightning flashed silver on black faces. Then gone. Jacob felt the fervent heat of Clara's body beside him. "To the house."

"To the barn," Cyrus said. "We've had one visitor tonight and if we had another while escaped slaves were at our table there'd be a world of trouble."

"God defends the righteous," Clara said.

"Then let him defend them in the barn."

Now her hand was on Jacob's shoulder. Her grip was tight and trembling, five little points of pain. "Jacob, go fetch the light."

Jacob hurried back to the cabin with the rain in his eyes and his breath hardening within him. He felt only shame for Tobias, for his parents, for himself for saying nothing, for fetching a lantern so docilely. Chattel was not worth this. He drew the shutter around the lantern's chimney to protect its hot glass from the rain, then stepped back outside. Cyrus was standing in the barn with his fists planted on his hips and Tobias was running his hand over his scalp and watching his face. Clara was fawning over the black man and his daughter. The man was as bald as Tobias except for a ring of gray woolly hair that ran from ear to ear and across his dusky face in bushy eyebrows. He was wearing the breeches and waistcoat of a house slave, both mud-spattered and dark with water, torn and frayed at the seams that ran up under his armpits, threads in the fabric briar pulled into feathery loops and circles. A cracked leather book in his pocket. The girl wore a dress printed with tiny blue flowers with no petticoats beneath it. It clung to her body, revealing the narrow hips and high, tight breasts of a girl. Her black hair was tied back and as woolly as her father's. Her nose was slightly flattened, her skin smooth and darkly creamy, and her eyes were wide with fright.

"Poor child." Clara put her arm around her. The girl shrunk and her eyes rolled from Clara's face to her father's. "What's your name?"

"I don't want to know," Tobias said quickly. "You don't want to know, either."

Clara's eyes flashed at him. "People aren't people without names. I want to know their names."

The girl said nothing. Her lips trembled. Buck stamped a hoof; Mabel watched impassively. The black man took the girl from Clara's arms and held her next to him. "This is Sarah Clay," he said, his voice softer now. "My name is Isaac."

"Where are you from?" Clara asked.

"Near Lexington."

"Oh, hell," Tobias said, and he shook his head.

Clara sent Jacob back to the house for blankets, and they made beds for them behind the buckboard and the stalls in the straw. The slaves spoke little, and until Tobias, Jacob, and Cyrus stepped out into the slackening rain, they did little more than watch silently.

Jacob followed the men to the cabin. Together they stood in the thin red light coming through the window from the hearth embers. The rain almost unnoticed.

"I got to get back," Tobias said. "They'll come looking."

"What about that Anders boy?" Cyrus asked.

"He's a liar and everybody knows it. If they come by the house and find no slaves, everyone will call him a liar again. I thank you for this."

"I don't want it to happen again," Cyrus said. "Take them somewhere else next time."

"All right."

Cyrus wiped his hand over his face, over his beard grown more sparse in the rain. "Damn it, Tobias. I never would have thought it."

Tobias pursed his lips. "Sometimes things just come upon you." He settled his big slouch hat on his head and nodded and walked toward the river, disappearing in the darkness.

Jacob listened to Tobias's slogging footsteps. An oar thumped hollowly against a gunwale, then an oarlock creaked and water swirled. The cold rain burst briefly on his shoulders.

Clara came up from the barn. In the hearth light she looked young again. "Is Tobias gone?" she asked.

"Just left," Jacob said.

"I wanted to thank him."

Cyrus grunted. "Thank him for what?"

"For letting us help him."

Cyrus spat. "Hell," he said.

The rain had dwindled to a soft patter. A thin patch worn in the clouds shone dully with moonlight. "They need dry clothes," Clara said. "I'll give Isaac some of Jacob's. The girl I don't know. She's so tiny."

"Give them just what they need," Cyrus answered her. "We got troubles of our own."

She nodded, then strode resolutely into the cabin. The door opened and shut, and her shadow passed over the window.

"You like this?" Jacob asked his father.

"No."

"Never seen two darker niggers," Jacob said. "I bet that old buck pees India ink."

"Buck is a mule," Cyrus said.

Chapter Two

———

The sky was clean the next morning, brittle, the air cool, clear of all but the soft mist on the river. The trees on the far bank were hidden within it but for a few black branches of the dying cottonwood starkly rising. Jacob looked at them from the yard, then studied the barn. He cursed softly, walked back into the trees to use the outhouse, then crossed the yard toward the barn. The cabin door opened and Clara called to him.

"Buck and Mabel got to eat, Ma," Jacob said.

"They can eat in a bit. You let Isaac and Sarah sleep."

Jacob cursed softly again. He walked down to the bank to study the black water. A twisted feeling tied to these two slaves and to his life and to everything else roiled within him. When he went back in the cabin, Clara was fixing two extra plates of biscuits and gravy, the gravy made from the cracklings of the ham they had eaten the night before. Cyrus was sitting with one finger holding his place in the newspaper as his eyes moved between the print and his plate, white gravy on the tuft of beard beneath his lower lip. Finally he sighed and sat back and looked up at his wife. Jacob sat beside him.

"You know what we're in, don't you?" Cyrus asked.

"I know."

"Then why?"

"Inasmuch as ye have done it unto one of the least of these my brethren." Clara covered the two plates with napkins. She nodded at Jacob. "You take them down. You knock before you go in."

"I'd like to eat first."

"They're hungry."

"So am I."

"They've been running. You take them down."

"Do as she tells you," Cyrus said.

Jacob scowled at the plates. "Never had to knock on a barn door before. The animals never cared."

"These aren't animals," Clara said.

Jacob stood roughly and kicked back his chair. He was angry, but as much at the roiling feeling as at his mother. He took the plates and went out the door.

"They sure ain't my brethren," he said.

The sun had already burned the mist from the river. Its reflected brightness caught in his eyes. He turned to study the empty fields, new and dew-glistening, the rickety fence at its boundary. He knocked on the door as his mother had warned him and listened impatiently for the sounds within. Buck shuffled; Mabel lowed in that painful way she did when she needed milking. The awkward rustling of quick and unexpected movement. The man's deep voice said, "Come in."

He opened the door and waited for his eyes to adjust to the shadows. Mabel lowed again, and Buck stamped a hoof. The man was in the back corner in a pair of Jacob's breeches and a faded cotton shirt, his book cradled in his palm. The girl was behind him, darker than the shadows, only her eyes shining. Their slave clothes hung drying in the rafters.

"Breakfast," Jacob said. "Biscuits and gravy. Coffee."

"I thank you," the man said.

Jacob set the tray by the door without speaking and walked back to the cabin. Cyrus and Clara were facing each other across the table, tendons pulled tight in her neck, his eyes and lips set.

"Tonight," Cyrus said.

"Not in front of Jacob."

"He's a part of this, too. Tonight. If somebody sees them . . ."

"They're tired. They need rest."

"They got all day to rest. We got a farm here. We got our lives."

She stared for a moment with only the sound of the breakfast fire snapping. She pushed herself up by clenched knuckles and stared at her husband until his gaze had to drop to the table, then she strode to the door, her legs outlined against her dress, her ardor burning in her face like a flame. Jacob watched her angrily pass the window.

"God damned woman," Cyrus said.

"Fence needs mending," Jacob said.

"God damned woman."

"Mabel needs milking, too. We ought to make that old buck do it."

"His name is Isaac."

"Then we ought to make that old buck named Isaac do it. That's about all niggers are good for."

"We don't need that kind of talk," Cyrus said. "There will be no slaves here."

"There's two out in the barn," Jacob said.

Cyrus studied him silently. The fire crackled; the sun through the window slanted across the floor, dust motes dancing in the beam almost happily. "We raised you better."

"You ain't exactly happy about this."

"I've got different reasons. There ain't no such thing as a man who ought to be a slave." He combed his fingers through his beard, pulling out tangles and crusted gravy. He studied his palm, ran the fingers of one hand over the knuckles of the other. He tapped the newspaper's headline.

"So what do you think of him?" Cyrus asked.

"Think of who?"

"This Lincoln fella."

"I don't think much of him either way."

"You ought to," Cyrus said. "There's a war coming over this; men are going to die over this. A time is coming when you'll live or die by what you're thinking and you got to think right."

"You're talking like Ma. Next you'll be preaching like her."

"We raised you better. What's happened to you?"

Jacob poured himself some coffee. It held the rich, warm scent of the earth. "There comes a time for a man to think for himself. That's in the Bible somewheres, ain't it? A time to be born and a time to die and a time for a man to think for himself."

"A man. You're seventeen."

"I know a few things."

"Like what?"

"Like Lincoln is a fool. Like them slaves out in the barn ain't worth this. I know it like that river is flowing out there. It was flowing a million years ago and it will be flowing a million years from now and what I just said was just as true when it started as it will be when it quits."

Cyrus narrowed his eyes to slits as he drained his coffee; he winced as he set his cup on the table. "I'm going to tell you something you won't know is true until you're my age."

"What?"

"Boys hold knowledge that only boys find unshakable."

Cyrus stared into his cup. Jacob tried to catch his father's eyes, but Cyrus refused to look at him. Jacob thought this a weakness. His words were still strong within him.

"Go milk Mabel," Cyrus said.

"Can't with them in there."

"Why not?"

Jacob had no answer. He went to the door.

The rumble of the black man's voice and the soft music of his mother's reached him before he reached the barn. When he pulled the door open the rumble and music stopped and he looked into their faces, the two black and the one white, into suddenly silent expressions. He understood his father's apprehension. He knew what he knew.

"Got to milk Mabel," he said.

They watched him, Mabel watched him, as he walked by the buckboard and pulled the stool to her side, set the bucket beneath her, and began rolling her teats down, finger by finger, the smell of her and of the milk warm and full, her flank warm and full against his forehead. Milk hissed in the bucket; the cats without names gathered to the side in single file and mewed plaintively. He squirted milk at their mouths and turned his head to look for the slaves. Beneath Mabel he could see the legs of the man and the hem of his mother's skirt. The girl was to his side and wearing a dress too large for her with no underclothes beneath it. As she bent to buckle her shoes, the dress exposed her small breasts, her nipples hanging like dark dew drops about to fall. He watched her until she lifted her head. He turned back to the bucket.

Damn, he thought, and he thought of the nights in the loft with his hand inside of his drawers, dreaming his dreams of exotic places and exotic ladies. He thought of Mary. He thought of loneliness, and he wished he were not lonely; perhaps that was the familiar but unknown emotion that now suddenly twisted within him. He wished that in everyone's mind his life was not so decided. The milk hissed in the bucket. She wasn't bad-looking, this one, he thought. For a nigger.

"You do what it is you think you should do," his mother quietly said.

"I don't wish to put you out," the black man said. "This can't be easy for you."

"You don't talk like no slave," Jacob said over his work, over the twisting emotion.

The black man stepped around Mabel. He didn't walk like a slave, either; his back was too straight, his shoulders too set, there was too much look in his eye. His ring of gray hair smoked around his head, littered with bits of straw and jetsam. "How does a slave talk?"

An uppity nigger, Jacob thought, who does not know his place. "You know how they talk."

"I was born and raised in the home of Henry Clay. I served in the home of John Clay, his son. I have met and entertained dignitaries from Europe and every state in the Union. I have been to London. I have seen Shakespeare performed, and I have read Chaucer. How do you suggest I speak?"

Uppity nigger, Jacob thought. "I was raised here."

"You were."

Jacob hated the man, hated his words. He nodded at the girl. "Don't she ever say anything?"

"When she wishes."

"She talk like you?"

"When she wishes. Is she supposed to talk like a slave, too? Yes massah, no massah? Hoo doggy, gwown get me some o dat cornpone?"

Jacob felt anger flare. God damned niggers. Dust and chattel and nothing more. He wanted to shout the words rising within him, but he didn't know what they were. His mother's glare held him.

"You know how they talk," he said again. He turned to stare into the bucket. Mabel shifted and his forehead pressed into her flank. He concentrated on the feel of her, on the scent and sound of the milk, on the steady rhythm of her breath. On the things he knew.

Footsteps plodded and the door opened and Cyrus came in. Without speaking, Jacob finished the milking and took the bucket to the springhouse, and when he came back to set the animals to pasture his father's eyes and lips held the same setting, his mother's neck the same tightness. The black man stood straight and with his shoulders set, wrapped in a dignity he had somehow acquired as another man's slave. Perhaps he'd stolen it from him.

The girl sat silently on the blankets in the corner, her dark fingers clasped in her lap, her elbows drawn close together, her back bent in a question mark. Nothing like her father. Her dark eyes gleaming. Her skin as dark and smooth as the river had been that morning.

"Take Buck and Mabel on out, Jacob," Clara told him.

"No," Cyrus said. "He's a part of this, too." His eyes were fixed on the black man. "I can't."

"It would be just until I can go and come back. A few days."

"I can't."

"I have a wife. I have a son." The black man's voice wavered. It was a strange thing to hear. "They're thinking of selling him. He might end up in the Carolina cane fields."

"I can't," Cyrus said again.

"There's snakes in those fields. Men die in those fields."

"I know what happens in them fields. I can't." Cyrus studied the black man silently. "How you going to go back? You just escaped. They'll be looking for you."

"I'll have to wait," the black man said. "But only for a day or two."

Cyrus wiped his hand over his beard. He studied Mabel, he studied Buck, he studied the buckboard. "I've got a family, just like you. I've got a farm."

"And if you had to leave it, would you leave them behind?"

Cyrus's gaze drifted to the black man's. "God damn." He threw up his arms in exasperation. "You'll have to stay in the barn while you're here. You'll have to keep as quiet as that girl there."

"We will," the black man said. "I promise you."

Jacob watched the daughter's eyes flit from face to face until she looked at him and he had to look away. The black man had softened, his shoulders relaxed, his head down. The only good thing about this, Jacob thought, is his new subservience.

Clara smiled. She rested her hand on her husband's shoulder, then traced her finger down his arm. "We'll be all right. God smiles on the right-eous."

"Hell," Cyrus said, and he shook his head. "He's laughing."

Another storm came before the week was out, dropping a branch through the outhouse roof. The soil was black and confident, and Cyrus crouched by the side of the field to watch it, as if to learn. He lifted clods to his nose and sniffed them, his fingers trembling. Jacob stood behind him. This was how things had been and were and would always be.

"Just a little warmer." Cyrus stood and let the crumbled clod drop through his fingers. Jacob watched the river flow dark and quiet. The branches of the old cottonwood on the other side reflected off the water.

In the evening darkness with the cool of the new spring still biting Isaac came up to the house with his book in his hand. "Do you mind?" he asked when Cyrus opened the door to him. "It's nice at times to have some adult company."

Cyrus glanced at Clara, at Jacob. Jacob watched Clara smile warmly before he turned to the fire. Isaac came inside. "Get yourself the chair from beside the hearth," Cyrus said. He did. "Where's Sarah?"

Isaac lay his forearms across the table, his gentleman's hands gripping lightly the spine of his book. "She's always been kind of private."

Voices died into the gentle pop and crack of the fire; the darkness gathered at the window. Cyrus stared at the table and Isaac read from his book silently, his lips moving faintly, his eyes glancing up every few seconds to look at the fire, the firelight playing across his inky face. Clara hummed her satisfaction. Jacob studied the black man, studied his eyes, his dull and empty animal eyes, like the eyes of all men. Mud and dust and chattel. There were things going on here he did not understand.

"I'll leave if you want," Isaac said.

Cyrus looked at him. "You going back after your family?"

Isaac's lips trembled as he stared into the fire. "I have been a slave all my life, and now I have run away. I have seen what becomes of runaways."

Cyrus shrugged. "We rest in the palm of the Lord," he said, "and he has even numbered the hairs on our heads. But perhaps that's easy to say with white skin."

"It's easy to say," Isaac said.

Cyrus sighed. "I'm just talking. We haven't had any trouble yet and if we're careful we don't need to have any."

"We want you to stay," Clara said.

"If things were different, we'd want you to stay," Cyrus corrected her. "These are troubled times." Isaac looked up questioningly. Cyrus grunted and stared at the table. "I can't ask you to abandon your family. You stay as long as you need to. Just don't need to very long."

Isaac nodded. His circle of gray hair wrinkled across the ridge of his eyebrows. He opened the book. "I'd like to read, if it's all right. To you."

"What you reading?" Cyrus asked.

Isaac ran his thumb over the edge of the cover, ran his fingers across the pages. "Shakespeare's collected works. I'm rereading *As You Like It* now. The seven ages of man."

"I've heard of that somewhere," Cyrus said.

"We come into this world, and we try to understand it," Isaac said. "We love in it and we fight in it and we think we understand it enough to say that this should be and that shouldn't. But then we realize we're nothing but children, and we leave it as we came."

"Naked came I out of my mother's womb, and naked shall I return thither," Clara said. "I don't need Shakespeare to tell me that."

"There's something in there about a stage, ain't there?" Cyrus asked.

"All the world's a stage," Isaac said, "and all the men and women merely players."

"I knew it was in there somewhere," Cyrus said.

"Read to us," Clara said, and she smiled again.

In his deep, rich voice Isaac read deep, rich words Jacob understood individually, but they were put together in ways he did not understand. He watched the black man's eyes move across the page, line by line, listened to his voice rise and fall. Caught up in his eyes, the words fell into the background with the sound in the hearth, with the gentle spring sounds of the night filtering softly through the window, the beat of the new crickets, the steady murmur of the swollen river. He looked out at the night and felt within him his emotion rise. We come into this world. We live in it and we love in it. We fight in it if we have to. We do what we must. He thought of Sarah and stood. His emotion was raging.

"Where are you going?" Clara asked.

"Can't a man use the outhouse without being harassed?" Jacob asked.

He went out into the night, the darkness cool to the point of discomfort, the stars gleaming so brightly he thought that perhaps he could live among them. Instead of walking to the outhouse he crept to the back corner of the barn where he could hear the quiet sounds that Sarah made, where the light through the separated slats cast edges like knife blades upon the ground. He sat. He held his breath and peered through the slats.

She was sitting with her back to him, her woolly hair tied back, glistening in the light of the lantern. The buttons down the back of her dress were open to the waist, and her dark skin, the sleekness of her back, the gentle curve and line of her spine, the exquisite curve of the nape of her neck, held him. His groin stirred. She seemed to be praying.

Only Mabel sensed his intrusion. Sarah had not moved when a few minutes later he carefully rose and made his way to the river. He watched the heavy current, searched for the light from Tobias's house through the dark trees. He thought keenly of what he had seen. All he was and wanted to be was dancing wildly within him, and his groin filled with a lonely pain. He slipped his suspenders from his shoulders.

Later he followed the bank to the McIntyre farm. A colorless light came through the cabin window. He thought of Mary there washing dishes or mending clothes as she had always done, as she would always do, happy in it. We will grow old and die mending clothes and washing dishes. He looked to the stars and wanted to shout at this God he did not believe in, but he could only stand mutely. He did not have the words to formulate either his curses or his questions.

Chapter Three

Before the week was out, winter's back was broken. The colors that defined the land, that defined the people, intensified, the black blacker, the white more brilliant. A farmer near Cincinnati disappeared after his neighbors burned down his barn because he had been harboring runaway slaves. Cyrus's voice halted and his face grayed as he read the story aloud from the Ripley paper. The edge of the paper trembled in his grip.

"There but for the grace of God," he said.

"The grace of God," Clara answered.

Isaac and Sarah spent their days in the barn or in the house or in the few seconds it took to run from one to the other. Never outside. Sometimes in the safety of the night Isaac would stand in the gray, swollen river with the current roiling around his shins and do nothing but stare across the water.

"Why don't he go?" Jacob asked his father from the cabin door. "I wish he'd go."

"Would you?"

"If it was my wife and son—"

"You see trees when you look across the river," Cyrus said. "He don't see trees."

Isaac came up from the water wiping his eyes and wading through darkness. He met Sarah at the barn, and together they came to the house. They stopped beside Cyrus and Jacob, and Isaac looked up at the stars. The air tinged with spring's coolness. The shadows thick in the trees behind the cabin and the crickets clicking. Clara stepped out of the cabin, wiping her hands with a towel.

"We'd like to earn our keep," Isaac said.

"I don't want you seen," Cyrus said.

"I'm not much on field work, but plowing's coming up and I see you have some harnesses that need repairing. I used to do that as a boy. I can do it in the barn."

"Sarah can help in the house," Clara said.

Cyrus pursed his lips and studied the barn, studied the darkness hiding the water. "I don't want you seen," he said again.

An oar blade slapping water drove the blacks into the trees, drove lies to the faces of the three whites left standing. A keel ground on silt and To-bias came up out of the darkness. He laughed and planted his hands in the small of his back, stretching, a grimace taking the laugh away, the smell of his exertion all around them. "I ain't as young as I used to be. Yanking that thing ashore about kills me." He scanned the yard, suddenly hushed. "Did they move on?"

"No." Cyrus nodded at the trees. "Come out."

Isaac stepped out of the darkness with his eyes and face up as if he were a white man. Sarah followed with her arms crossed beneath her breasts. The dress she wore had been Clara's and was too large for her, hanging from her shoulders, loosely falling over her hips, flowing as she moved, outlining each step she took. Jacob remembered the shape and color of her back in the barn. He thought exotic thoughts that he pushed away to save for another time.

"This ain't what we agreed on," Tobias said.

"I have family," Isaac answered, "still over there."

"You were going north. You're endangering these people. This is the valley."

The black man dropped his eyes. "I have family still over there." His face quivered as he glanced toward the river. He didn't speak.

Tobias removed his slouch hat and ran his palm over his scalp. He studied the darkness in the fields, the darkness over the water, then squinted at Cyrus. "You're all right with this?"

"There ain't nothing to do about it. I can't very well tell a man to leave his family. It don't make no difference who it is."

"What about the farm? You told me once it has a soul."

"The soul of my father. Too damned many things have souls."

"God defends the righteous," Clara said.

Jacob watched the darkness and felt the words rise within him. All this talk of men and God as if niggers had the right to be called the one or de-served the mercy of the nonexistent other. Isaac stared into the darkness. Dull, animal eyes, mud and dust and chattel eyes. Sarah's gaze lay cast upon the ground.

They shared a meal in the cabin. Jacob complained of stomach pains and went out to the smokehouse at the back corner of the barn to filch bacon because he would not eat with niggers. He waited in the trees until Tobias shouted a farewell from the door.

"Where's that boy?" Tobias asked.

"Probably over with Mary," Clara said. "He always makes up some excuse."

The next morning, with Buck pulling the buckboard in front of them, Cyrus and Jacob walked the field, gathering the frost-lifted rocks. It was heavy work that left Jacob's fingers and back aching, blue bruises on his palms, broken nails, knuckles numb and swelling. As he stopped to stretch out some of the soreness Sarah ran up to the house, her skirt gathered in bunches in her fists. He felt the same feeling he had felt that first night he had watched her in the barn, a wild, lonely dancing. Smooth black legs flashed in sunlight.

"I got to go use the outhouse," he said.

Cyrus grunted. "So piss in the field. It won't hurt nothing."

"It ain't that kind of use."

Cyrus nodded and went back to scrabbling after rocks. Jacob crossed the field. He kicked the mud from his shoes and walked around the cabin to the path leading to the outhouse, looking back over his shoulder. Cyrus was struggling with a stone, his back to his son. Jacob hurried back around the cabin and went in through the door.

Sarah was sweeping, the broom kicking up dust in a tickling curl that bent back to surround her. She looked at him and looked down and for just a second stopped sweeping. Jacob climbed to the loft and pretended to be busy with nothing. He watched her.

"Where's Ma?" he asked.

"The springhouse."

Her dress was too large for her. He lay on his stomach and watched the gentle shape of her breasts, the gentle smooth magic of her ebony skin. She swept to the door and came back again. He felt himself harden against the mattress and found himself enjoying this more than the luxury of his exotic ladies. This held possibility.

"So where are you from?" he asked.

She kept sweeping. She didn't look up. "Kentucky."

"I know that. Where are your people from?"

She continued sweeping.

"Where are your people from?" he asked again.

"Africa."

"That's like saying mine are from Europe. It don't mean much." He thrust softly and pleasurably against the mattress. "What part of Africa?"

The broom stopped. Her face was more round than oval, the color of her skin even, and her hair soaked up the light coming through the window. She looked as lovely as the colors in a sunset you believe you will never see again.

"I don't know," she said. Sweat had come out on her forehead. She began to sweep again.

"Everybody comes from somewhere."

"I don't know."

He watched her for a long time, the sight of her and the feeling within him a gentle, teasing pleasure. She had finished sweeping and was leaning over to tend the fire when Cyrus came into the cabin. He looked at her, then looked up into the loft. Jacob had quit moving when the door had opened.

"What are you doing in here?" Cyrus asked him.

"Nothing."

"We don't got time for nothing."

"I was taking a break."

"If you've had time to crawl up there and lie down, you've had more than enough time for a break. We've got stones to move."

Jacob climbed down the ladder and sidled toward the door. Cyrus followed him. Sarah had not turned from the fire.

Jacob stepped outside, the sun heavy upon him, the heat in his groin subsiding. He started for Buck and the wagon, but Cyrus with a hand on his shoulder led him over to the fence delineating the pasture. They leaned on it and stared across the water. Mabel was grazing. The air was warming, and the river muttered softly. The fresh smells of spring, new grass, the trees flowering.

"What are you thinking, going in there and talking to her like that? What are you up to?"

"I ain't up to nothing."

Cyrus pursed his lips and ran his hand over the shreds of his beard. He shook his head at the river. "You don't mess with no black girl."

"I wasn't messing."

"I saw the damned thing. Christ, you looked like a bull about to breed."

Jacob stared at the water. Mabel lifted her head to study him. He didn't say anything.

"You don't mess with no black girl. You got to mess with somebody, sneak over to the McIntyre place."

"It ain't that way between us."

"Between who?"

Jacob glanced at the cabin window. He saw nothing but the day's brightness reflected. "Between me and Mary. Or between me and the nigger."

Cyrus spat, then nodded at Jacob's crotch. "That damned thing has caused more trouble than anything else on the planet. People have died because of it who shouldn't have. People have been born because of it who shouldn't have. The best thing to do is to keep it behind those trousers minding its own business. But might as well ask the river to quit flowing." He wiped sweat off his mustache with his sleeve. "Sometimes I wish we was Catholic. I could sell you off to a monastery or something."

"Then Ma would be a nun."

Cyrus scowled at the water. "And I'd be in the same mess you're in." He wiped his sleeve across his forehead. "Why not ask Mary to marry you? You're on the edge of being old enough."

Why not. Jacob thought of Mary, of the look on her face, of the sure look in her eyes. He glanced at the cabin and felt himself stir again. The question was not why not, but why.

His father was watching him. "You slept with that girl?"

"Which one?"

"Oh, Jesus. If you have to ask . . . Oh, Jesus."

"I ain't slept with her."

"With Mary?"

"With Mary."

"Maybe you ought to. Don't tell your mother I said that." Cyrus glanced back at the cabin, then nodded at Buck waiting in the field. "Those traces are like new. Isaac, he done a good job."

"Sure he done."

"Forget whatever you're thinking," Cyrus said.

"Forgotten," Jacob answered.

But Jacob could not forget lying on his mattress and watching Sarah, could not forget the look of her, and a fetid thought took shape in his mind, developed features, took on hard edges. When the night came and the river was quiet and the only sound was the chirp of the crickets like the beat of the world, like the pulse of its heart, Jacob would make an excuse and leave the cabin. He would walk to the springhouse straddling the spring in the woods or to the outhouse where he would stare up through the crack the branch had made in the roof at the sliver of moon gleaming. He would think about Sarah and his hand would move against his crotch but he would not drop his trousers, would no longer allow himself that pleasure. When he had steeled himself he would work quietly to the back of the barn.

One night, Isaac came up to the cabin with his book in his hand. He sat at the table and thumbed through it as Cyrus watched him from beside the fire.

"How are you with a whetstone and file?" Cyrus asked.

"I'm passable," Isaac said. "Everybody needs to at least be passable."

"Would you mind looking over the tools? Sharpen what needs to be sharpened?"

Isaac looked up. "I'd be honored to."

"I thank you."

"There is no need to thank for what is owed."

"You don't owe," Clara said. "This is freely given."

Jacob rose and walked to the door. His breath was hot on his lips as he muttered something about Mary and stepped out into the darkness. Such an easy excuse. He worked through the trees to the outhouse, stared up at the stars, then made his way to the back of the barn.

Sarah was sitting in the straw half turned toward the slats. He crouched to watch her. Her dress was gathered around her waist and she was working the buttons with a thread and needle. Gooseflesh lay on her arms with the chill of the evening, and her nipples were drawn against it; the muscles in her chest flexed and loosened. Her belly was as smooth as polished wood, as smooth as the lantern light around her.

Damn, Jacob thought. He drew back from his haunches to fall into the brush.

Her head turned and her eyes flashed as she snatched the dress up around her shoulders. He watched her eyes.

"Who's there?" she asked. Jacob did not move. Damn, he thought again.

"Who's there?" she asked.

This could be the time, he thought, this could be the time. But when she came out of the barn with the lantern in her hand he slipped back to the springhouse where the circle of light could not reach. He watched her from there as she searched the darkness. She did not call his name.

He did not return to the barn when she went back inside. He stood in the trees with his breath hammering wildly within him and marveled at what he had seen.

Jacob lay the next night in the loft with Sarah and Isaac at the table. Cyrus sat beside the fire, working his thumbnail with a knife. Clara sat beside Isaac with her hair loose down her back and her narrow chin balanced upon her thin palm, her eyes closed fervently. Isaac's words rose around Jacob like the rich smell of the field captured in his clothing.

"Let me have men about me that are fat," Isaac read, "sleek-headed men and such as sleep o' nights. Yond Cassius has a lean and hungry look; he thinks too much. Such men are dangerous."

Sarah glanced up at the loft with her father's pause. Jacob's eyes fled from hers. He felt an unnerving excitement.

Someone knocked on the door. The knife in Cyrus's hand clattered to the floor as he stood, staring at the door, at Clara, at Isaac and Sarah. Jacob watched the door, feeling the fear of a sordid discovery within him. No one did anything because there was nothing that could be done.

The knock came again, and the latch lifted. Mary stepped through the threshold with a thin smile on her pale face that fell away when she saw the black faces. She stared at them, at Cyrus and Clara. Something in her expression crumbled. Finally her eyes drifted to the loft and came down again. Her chest heaved once, and her eyes rested on Sarah.

"Excuse me," she said. Though more words formed on her lips, no sound accompanied them. Cyrus stood silently with his hands hanging impotently at his sides. The fire spat and crackled.

Jacob climbed down from the loft and strode toward the door. He brushed by Sarah, feeling the heat of her back against his forearm, seeing Mary's eyes still upon her. "Mary," he said, and he took her by the crook of the arm and led her out the door.

The steady beat of the crickets, slow in the spring chill, punctuated the night, wrapped itself in the gentle sounds of the current. A male voice called from the far bank, a mile, two miles downriver. Mabel lowed plaintively. Mary stood at the edge of the light cast through the window, the line of darkness etching her brow and nose and lips. Jacob glanced through the window at Isaac, his book still open but his heavy lips fallen silent, his heavy brow knitted. Sarah sat with her eyes down, her hair a shadow in the lantern light, her skin holding the flickering glow of the hearth.

"They're runaways, ain't they?" Mary asked. Her voice held panic.

"They're free niggers just passing through. They're spending the night in the barn."

"They're runaways, ain't they?"

"They're just free niggers," Jacob said.

"I know your mother. I've heard her abolitionist talk, like niggers are equal to whites. Those two are runaways, ain't they?"

Jacob glanced again at the window. The river mumbled. "You know that if they was runaways, I'd take them back or find someone to take them back. I don't put no stock in them."

"You don't run this place. You don't have no say."

"You know my pa don't put no stock in them, either."

She crossed her arms over her chest. Her shoulders bulged at the joints as if the bones had come out of their sockets. "I heard your pa say once a man is a man. What do you suppose he meant by that?"

Jacob spat into the yard. "Well, he didn't use the word 'nigger,' did he?"

"And your ma and her talk." Mary's lip trembled. "Oh, Jacob. We've got too much going to risk it now."

Jacob searched her face for memories worth remembering. Finally he reached for the door.

"Jacob," she said. "I seen you look at that little bitch nigger."

"I'll see you," he said.

Her arms dropped and her hands locked into fists. "Those niggers are runaways, ain't they?"

Her voice caught in the trees, reflected off the water. Two tear tracks gleamed on her cheeks; her lips had pulled back to show large and yellow-stained teeth. Jacob thought of Sarah.

"They ain't nothing to you," he said.

"Jacob," she repeated as he opened the door.

He went inside and closed the door and leaned his back against it. Even in the coolness he had grown hot and sweaty. He leaned his head back and looked down the length of his nose at his father, his mother, both sitting again, both watching him quietly. Isaac stared at his book, Sarah into her lap.

Finally Jacob went to the window. Mary had left the yard. He walked to the ladder leading up to the loft and sat on the second rung.

"Now they'll all know," Isaac said. "We're endangering you. We better move on."

"You can't," Clara said. "Your family."

"My family is in slavery, and I find I don't have the courage to go back and free them." Isaac's fingers trembled upon the book. His dark eyes filmed. "What is a man made of?"

Cyrus rose and stared into the fire. His shoulders straightened; a hardness came to his features. "The strength will come. You wait."

Jacob glanced first at the black man, then at his father. Isaac studied Cyrus with a different look in his eyes. "That isn't what you once wanted. They'll know now."

Cyrus looked up, looked back at the fire again. He braced his corded arm against the chimney. "Like I told the boy there, there's a war coming over this; men are going to die over this. If you're going to live or die by what you think, you got to be thinking right." He walked to the window, looked out at the farm. "My daddy come here. He carved this farm right out of the trees. He wintered in the hollow of a cottonwood down by the river and almost died in it. Spring flooding would have carried his body to God knows where." He sighed heavily. "His soul is in this land. I can feel it when I work the field. But it's just a farm. You got to be thinking right."

"It won't come," Jacob said.

Cyrus didn't nod. He didn't shake his head. He didn't turn from the window.

Isaac watched Cyrus. Finally his eyes drifted back to the book. "I thank you."

"No need to thank a man for doing what's right."

"God protects the righteous," Clara said.

Cyrus chuckled. He walked to the table and jovially tapped his finger on the book. "Anything in there about God protecting fools?"

"Thy eternal summer shall not fade," Isaac said.

Cyrus grunted and looked again out of the window. His joviality dissipated into the night, into the times. "All things fade," he said.

Chapter Four

With spring came the work of spring, the plowing and harrowing and planting, done by man for so long that it has become a part of him, his foundation. Cyrus then Clara then Jacob worked the plow through the field, its point turning the moist, black, rich-smelling earth, stopping at the end of each furrow with a click of the tongue at Buck and a wrenching of the plow from the soil. As Jacob would lie beside the field and let Buck blow, he would watch the gray swollen river, watch the steamers work down to Cincinnati or up to Portsmouth, its passengers with faces he did not know, with names he did not know, the feeling that he did not know turning sharply within him. He watched Sarah run from the barn to the house and back again, her bare legs flashing beneath her bunched skirt, a hint of fear in her actions, a hint of fear in her animal eyes.

Cyrus spent his evenings with Isaac on the riverbank, staring across the water to the Kentucky side. Tobias would cross the river and stand with them.

"What are they thinking about?" Jacob asked Clara.

"There's killing going on over there," Clara said. "Rebels are killing Federal men; Federal men are killing rebels. Farms are burning, houses are being pillaged, men are left hanging by their necks in trees."

"All this over . . ." Jacob did not finish the sentence.

"For the sin of slavery," Clara said, "God's wrath has fallen upon them. Joshua drew not his hand back."

Jacob looked at her but did not say anything. He slapped at a mosquito humming in his ear. Sarah opened the cabin door to sweep dust over the threshold. Jacob silently watched her.

They harrowed by hitching a log dragging chains to Buck's traces. On a bright, warm morning halfway across the field Buck pulled up lame, lifting his right front fetlock and staring at it curiously. Jacob checked the hoof.

"What do we got?" Cyrus asked.

"Sand crack." Jacob let the hoof drift to the ground. Buck nuzzled his shoulder. "Slit up the middle almost to the coronet."

"Damn." Cyrus spat. "We'll have to take him in to McGown. If there's one thing I hate to do, it's seeing McGown."

Everett McGown was the Ripley blacksmith, a brute of a man: brunt, cruelly large, enormously powerful, his shoulders curved and thick, his fingers curved and thick from a lifetime of bending iron to his will. A black beard covered his heavy, pale face; his hair hung limply into his eyes and glistened in the light of his forge with sweat running down his nose to drip slowly upon the anvil. He came to the door of his shop when Cyrus and Jacob brought Buck up, the streets of Ripley dust ridden even in the spring, and blinked as if he were an animal emerging from a cave.

"Throw a shoe?"

"Sand crack," Cyrus said.

McGown nodded. He blinked in the sunlight and ran his hand over Buck's withers and brisket and down his leg. He braced Buck's knee upon his own and studied the hoof, feeling along the sand crack with his fingers, prying from it and from around the frog and shoe the dirt and stones of the road. He dropped Buck's leg and nodded.

"Bring him in."

The only light the shop held was the orange glow of the forge. The bellows, eight feet long and four wide with an old shoe keg for ballast, waited behind the chimney with the overhead lever reaching to within grasping distance of the anvil. The anvil horn pointed toward the fire, its heel toward a bench littered with hardies and swages, bickerns and twisting bars and hammers. The slack tub squatted beside the forge within reaching distance of the anvil, as all of the shop was, for McGown worked brutally and worked others brutally as well, too brutally to keep a striker in service for more than a few days. Only his son still worked for him, cleaning up and running errands, a boy who skittered silently like a roach from corner to corner. He hid now behind the bellows. Jacob turned from him to look at McGown, and when he turned back the boy was gone.

"How'd he get it?" McGown asked.

"Harrowing," Cyrus said, "somehow."

"It's always somehow—somehow something this or somehow something that." McGown spat unto the dirt floor and fetched his toolbox from the bench. "Nobody ever knows nothing about what's going on."

McGown cradled Buck's split hoof in his lap, his voice rising and falling in the way animals understand. With his buffer iron and hammer he bent out the shoe's clinches, then pulled them with a pincers, starting at the heel and working each nail loose a little at a time. He tossed the shoe into the scrap pile with a stabbing metallic clang, then with his hoof knife he pared down the hoof that had grown around the shoe like lapping water.

When he finished he stood, and with his great fists planted on his hips he watched as Buck tested his hoof. "I hear you have a couple of niggers out there at your place," he said without emotion. "Hard to believe with all that's going on."

Jacob glanced at his father. Cyrus swallowed and straightened his narrow shoulders. "Where'd you hear that?"

"I just heared it."

"Someone don't know what they're talking about," Cyrus said.

"That's what I kind of figured. Someone somehow something." McGown stoked the fire. "We wouldn't have no problems with niggers if we didn't have people like you and that wife of yours. Now we got a war."

"You blaming me for the war?"

"I'm blaming you and people like you."

"You always got something to blame, Everett," Cyrus said. "Always have."

McGown lifted a sledge in his heavy hand and looked at Cyrus. "You and your mouth. You and your high-handed ways." He set the sledge back down again and studied it carefully. "They still out there? I'm talking about your niggers again."

"I ain't never had any niggers."

"They're still out there. You know how I know?" McGown tapped the side of his nose. A mole grew there, dark and ugly. "Niggers got some kind of funny African smell. And there's a funny smell coming from your way."

"I ain't never had any niggers, Everett. That's just another excuse."

"We keep you people around and sweet Jesus, we'll have another Nat Turner. We'll see how much you love the poor nigger when you're kissing his black ass."

"I ain't never," Cyrus said.

"Yeah, well." McGown reached for the bellows lever and gave it a pull. He watched the flame, then with a tong worked a new shoe into the embers. "Your place still has a funny smell."

McGown went to the scrap heap for a flat piece of wrought iron and worked it into the forge beside the shoe. When the shoe had heated from a lemon to a straw yellow McGown took it from the fire and placed it over the anvil horn. With two hard, practiced, ear-cracking raps from his hammer he'd bent it to fit Buck—Jacob marveled at such a brute and subtle power. McGown put it back into the fire. He studied it with his fists on his hips.

"Kentucky's seceding," he said.

"Kentucky ain't seceding."

"You watch. You'll see."

The scrap had turned straw yellow. McGown took it out and rested it over the chipping block on the anvil, just back from the horn. With the hot set he cut off a narrow strip about two inches long, and with a cross peen hammer he rounded its upper edge. With a few light blows from the cross peen, he joint-welded the metal to one side of the shoe, and two hard wraps from the drift punch, one on each side of the scrap, punctured it. He put the shoe back in the fire and spat again.

"Yeah," he said. "You got something to answer for."

When the shoe was ready he did the same to the other side. He quenched it in the slack tub and studied his work. With a rasp he smoothed a burr off the puncture in the left strip.

"What you going to do?" he asked.

"About what?" Cyrus asked.

McGown snorted. "About what, he says. Lincoln and Dennison are calling for troops. What you going to do?"

Cyrus shrugged. "My duty."

"Ain't that the way of it? We all have our duty." McGown worked a bolt through the two holes and screwed a nut over its threading. "Does your duty mean killing white boys for niggers?"

"My duty's something you'd never understand."

"Sure I wouldn't. What about you, Jacob? What's your duty?"

"Don't know," Jacob said.

"Hell, a boy like you must have fire in your blood. Don't you want to fight?"

"Don't know."

"Every girl in town would jump at the chance to lift her skirt to a hero come home. Hell, half the married women, too. Don't you want to fight?"

Jacob thought of Sarah in the barn, her dark eyes, her dark skin shining. He didn't say anything.

"A hot-blooded boy like you," McGown said.

He stared at Jacob before grunting and walking to the door. He blinked at his handiwork in the sunlight, then lumbered back to the hearth, took the bolt out, and worked the shoe into the fire. When it was hot he took it from the embers and fitted it to Buck's hoof—the sharp stench of burning hoof, like the smell of burning hair, made Jacob wince. When the hoof had burned to conformity, McGown inserted and tightened the bolt to cinch up the split, then set the shoe with his shoeing hammer and six nails, crimping them over with a buffer when he'd driven them through the hoof. He stepped back and watched how Buck handled it. Buck lifted his hoof and stomped. He stared down the street back toward the farm.

McGown nodded. "Looks all right. Bring him back when he's ready and we'll shoe that proper. The others will need it, too."

Cyrus nodded and reached into his pocket. "What do I owe you?"

"Your money's nigger-loving blood money and I wouldn't take it. You're bringing this down upon us."

"Then what will you take?"

"I'll take what I need when I need it." McGown's eyes turned to Jacob. "You two would really fight for niggers? My granddaddy lost two fingers at Cowpens when a Tory thrust a bayonet through his hand. But he sure didn't lose them for no niggers."

Cyrus didn't answer. He led Buck from the shop. Buck looked at his new shoe and stamped his hoof again.

"You coming, Jacob?" Cyrus asked.

"I'm coming," Jacob said.

"What duty you got toward niggers?" McGown called after them.

Chapter Five

———

In youthful and innocent exuberance the war came. Bands played and boys with grins on their mouths and stars in their eyes boarded trains and steamboats and worked their way east to Washington. Governor Dennison of Ohio commissioned a dapper young man named George McClellan for an expedition into rebel western Virginia. McClellan called for men, and he assured the western Virginia slaveholders that this war was about restoring the Union. He assured them that he believed black bodies were meant to be owned by white and they had no cause for alarm. Isaac and Sarah stayed. Day after day Cyrus stared across the river, and Clara stood beside him, watching his lined face. Jacob lay beside the water and let the pain of the day seep slowly into the bank.

"If the soldiers find fugitives," Clara said, "he's ordered them to return them."

"I know."

She didn't speak for a long time. She turned from his face to look across the river. "They might kill you."

"I know," he said again.

"So why are you going?"

"My daddy lived on this bank the first winter. He lost a finger and two toes to frostbite."

"So?"

"So maybe if I fight for the Union I can keep the farm. Could they punish their own soldiers?"

The breeze coming up the river lifted his beard, made him blink. He stared across the water. The sweat on his body smelled strangely, different than any Jacob had smelled before.

"Cyrus," she said.

"I don't want to fight. Thou shalt not kill. But it's the only way I can see it."

In the morning Cyrus took his father's old musket from out of the eaves and wiped the cobwebs from its barrel. He slung a grain sack loaded with cornbread and a change of clothes over his shoulder and stepped out into the early morning coolness. He blinked at the sunshine and grimaced into it. Jacob was waiting, and Clara was waiting with tears in her eyes.

"God go with you," she said.

Cyrus held her face in his hands, wiped the tears from her cheeks with the horny pads of his thumbs, kissed each of her eyes. He did not speak. He rested his hand on Jacob's shoulder, the strength of the earth in his hand. Cyrus nodded at his son and walked toward the road leading into Ripley.

"I'll follow you when I can," Jacob called. "I'll kill me some rebels."

Cyrus's step faltered, but he did not turn back. "You got to think right," he said. "There ain't no glory in this." He disappeared heading east.

Clara looked at her son and her lip trembled and she hurried into the cabin. Isaac and Sarah were standing in the barn door. Isaac stared past Jacob to the road Cyrus had taken. Sarah glanced only briefly into Jacob's eyes. The feeling in him turned.

That evening Isaac knocked at the door and stood hesitantly in the threshold before he came inside. His fingers worked on his book's binding. He glanced at Clara where she sat at the table, staring back quizzically.

"Just wanted to make sure before coming in," he said. "Cyrus is gone."

"You're welcome here, Isaac." She settled her hands deeply into her lap. "You're always welcome here."

Jacob rose from where he had been tending the fire. Since his father had left, the feeling in him had grown, his fantasies within him had grown, as if Cyrus had been a restraint to anger and lust and wildness. He thought of Sarah beneath him, her naked body, his hand over her mouth, exotic African words screamed against his fingers, those dark, soulless eyes staring. He rose and hurried to the door.

"Where are you going?" Clara asked.

"The outhouse."

He walked to the outhouse but did not go inside; he worked his way through the thickening underbrush to the back of the barn, where through the slats a lantern light glowed. He glanced up at the dim starlight.

His hand worked hard against his crotch until he could feel the vicious heat of blood through the fabric of his trousers. He let his head fill with wild thoughts. He hurried around the barn, mindless of the brush rustling against his legs. He yanked open the door and pulled it shut behind him.

Briefly he thought of Joshua leading an army across a dusty plain, the ways of God and men. He thought only briefly of the women crying.

She was sitting quietly on a blanket, mending the hem of her dress. When she looked at him her face was smooth and lovely and frightened and he struggled to remember that the release of the heat was the important thing, that wildness that cannot be contained must be set free. He fought to keep in his mind who he knew she was.

He glanced back at the door, then strode toward her past the forlorn faces of Buck and Mabel, slipping down his suspenders as he did. She made a soft, frightened, animal sound and scuttled backward against the wall and stopped there with her knees drawn up and little sounds working in her throat. She did not scream. His pants were open with his swollenness protruding and he threw her down into the straw and ripped open the front of her dress. Her chest quivered beneath him. Her eyes held an acquainted fear.

He pushed his trousers to his knees with one hand, raised her dress with the other. Her lips quivered and her young breasts quivered and in her eyes was a horrible wisdom. A light, a fear, a living, breathing thing leaped into her eyes and he was not staring into the eyes of an animal. The God he had thought nonexistent had kissed her eyes and left a soul within them.

He struggled to hang on to the wildness, to hang on to who he had always believed he was. She lay beneath him with her body trembling and her sweat smelling the same as the sweat he had smelled a day before on his father. The huge, desperate, God-kissed life screamed from her eyes, blazed in them, burned into his own. How can this be when God cannot be? So God must be. This girl must be as God had made her. Jacob felt frightened. In his mind women cried.

"They done this to you before," he said.

"It's why we came north."

He looked from her to the darkness and tried to regain what he knew he had already lost.

"Just get it done," she said, "then leave me be."

The heat drained from him like water. He looked into the soul in her eyes, then backed away down her legs. When his face met her bare lap he dropped his head and cried. The sickness fell from him.

His tears wet her skin, her skin slick against his cheeks. After a few heartbeats he felt her small, soft hands run gently over his hair. Behind them, Mabel ground her cud. Buck stamped a hoof in the straw.

"Jacob," she said softly.

Chapter Six

Something changed inside of him there in the barn, in the deep heat that became a deep longing, a lust, a love. When he dressed and slipped out into the darkness, she was lying on the blanket, her legs together now, her dark skin shining wetly in the soft golden glow of the lantern. She had covered his mouth when the passion had come and the salty taste of her fingers was still on his lips. The night was a remarkable thing.

"Where you been?" Clara asked back in the cabin. She and Isaac were sitting side by side at the table. Isaac's face shone in the firelight.

"I went to the outhouse."

"It doesn't take two hours to use the outhouse."

"I went down to the river to watch the water."

"What were you doing watching the water?"

"Just watching." He glanced at the back of the cabin, as if he could see the woods beyond it and the farm beyond them and Mary McIntyre on it. Clara followed his eyes and dropped her own to the table. She smiled.

Jacob went back to the barn many times, always when Isaac was up at the cabin, and many times in the middle of the night he met Sarah by the springhouse or by the river; he made love to Sarah on the riverbank and afterward watched the dying cottonwood on the other side spread its dark-fingered branches. They talked of many things. This was a new kind of love; this was a watery looseness in his legs, a hair-standing-up-on-the-back-of-his-neck kind of love. A love which accepted no limits, a love that anticipated keenly. When he saw Mary, he saw only a frightened look growing in her eyes.

The country was tense, the valley was tense, the river flowed more haltingly. *Reb* and *secesh* and *yank* replaced the names of neighbors, *johnny* and *copperhead* for supporters of the south; suspicion filled every eye. Faces held a dreaded expectation as they looked across the water to Kentucky; faces studied each other with the same dreaded expectation, a lack of recognition, who was who in this suddenly unrecognizable world. Volunteers in their work clothes marched off to war carrying the same muskets their grandfathers had carried in 1812. Jacob and Clara worked the field, sometimes with Tobias crossing the river to help them. Sometimes Jacob would see Sarah watching him from the cabin window or the barn door, and he would think of the previous night or the night to come, the gentle, smooth, dark curve of her back, the way her eyes dropped when he kissed her, and a warmth would rise in his chest that drained the strength from his joints. He would turn to the sky and smile.

"What are you looking at?" Clara would ask.

"Just looking," he would say, when he answered at all.

Cyrus wrote from Virginia in July to say that he had seen action at a place called Rich Mountain. He said there was a fear there and an exultation, that gunpowder tasted of both. He wrote of musket balls singing in the air, of the taste of that fear, of the blood that filled his voice as he cheered the fleeing of the rebels before the Federal charge. At the end of the letter he said he missed the farm and he missed his family. He did not ask about Isaac and Sarah.

This war is about restoring the Union, Lincoln said, and he said that to lose Kentucky was to lose the whole game, as if the war was a game. The Kentucky slaveholders must be appeased, he said, and, he ordered, their runaways must be returned. The sovereignty of Kentucky would not be violated. Troops moved through the valley, carrying out those orders. A soldier Jacob did not know crossed the field as they were working. He wore a blue woolen uniform too small for him, tight around the throat, the knobs of his thin wrists poking beyond the sleeves. His feet clappered in his boots as the soft earth sucked at their soles. In a thick German accent he announced that his name was Private Klausmann. He saluted smartly.

"I am looking for *der Negers,*" he said.

"What?" Tobias asked.

"*Der Negers.*" The soldier's eyes searched for words. Buck blew and snorted. "Slaves. *Negers.* I am looking for *der Negers.*"

Clara did not look up from the soil. "I haven't seen any," she said.

"*Du zwei?*" the soldier asked Jacob and Tobias. A sparse blond beard grew on his chin and cheeks. Tobias only removed his hat and wiped the sweat from his scalp. He stared at the river.

"No," Jacob said.

The soldier glanced around the farm, then saluted again and stumbled away, his arms occasionally pinwheeling. Tobias watched him until he had cleared the field. "You got to get them out," he said when he could.

"It's not in our hands," Clara answered him.

"It's in that black man's hands and it always has been. He's going to bring something awful down upon you."

"It's in the hands of God."

Three days later with the late July sun blistering and the field dust around Jacob rising in the breeze, Clara came hurrying down the drive on the buckboard with Buck slathered white on the withers. She had gone to Ripley for flour.

"Hide them," she said. "There's soldiers coming."

Jacob ran to the barn with the dust clotted in his throat, with fear clotted in his throat. Sarah and Isaac were inside, Sarah helping her father sharpen a scythe.

"They're coming," Jacob said. "You got to hide."

Isaac's eyes grew wide and the whetstone fell from his trembling fingers. He seemed not to know what to do. Sarah took his hand and led him past Jacob out the door.

Clara was waiting by the river. "We'll run them across to Tobias," she said.

"No time to get ahold of him."

"We'll hide them in the woods. The springhouse, maybe."

"They'll look there."

Her eyes searched wildly. "The privy. Hide them in the privy."

Sounds came from the road, clanking and clattering and cursing, horse hooves pounding on hard-packed earth, horseshoes ringing on stones, harsh curses and laughter. Jacob took Sarah's hand and hurried into the trees. The outhouse squatted in brush like a gnome or an ogre. He led her inside it with Isaac following, and Isaac shut the door. Daylight filtered through the hole in the roof. The smell of the place rising.

"They'll look here," Isaac said.

"There's nowhere else to go."

Isaac's eyes scanned the walls frantically. Finally he kicked loose a corner of the seat board, then pried the board off with his fingers. Flies buzzed sharply, the smells of feces and urine almost solid.

"Get in," he said to Sarah.

"Father . . ."

"Get in. I will not let those men take me."

Jacob lowered her into the hole. Isaac followed. Jacob held her hand longer than he needed to, his eyes on hers. Her face, her eyes, the dusky color of her cheeks and forehead made him think he would weep. He released her and tapped the seat back down; he jumped on it to secure it.

"I'll come back after they've gone," he said.

He hurried back through the trees, the brush whipping his legs and arms and face, the heat heavy upon him, sweat stinging in scratches. He saw a blue uniform moving toward the smokehouse and was surprised to find when he cleared the trees that the soldier was only a boy. The boy carried a musket over his shoulder.

A wagon loaded with knapsacks was parked in the yard, the horse in its traces nickering at Buck. Clara was standing in front of the cabin door, her eyes narrow, the tendons in her neck pulled tight. The blacksmith, Everett McGown, was facing her. He was wearing a blue woolen tunic but had his old shop pants on, the fabric dull with dirt, the knees stained black with cinders; his old work boots, worn almost through at the toes, impatiently tapped the dirt. He was staring across the yard and pasture, blinking in the sunlight, to where Mabel stood watching him. Two other uniformed boys were hurrying across the yard, one toward the springhouse and the other toward the barn. Klausmann the German was going around the far side of the cabin into the woods.

"Name," McGown said to Clara.

"You know my name," Clara said.

"Name, damn it," McGown said.

"Clara Wilson."

"Where's the boy?"

"Here," Jacob said.

"You stay where I can see you. Where's your husband?" he said to Clara.

"Fighting with McClellan."

A smile spread through McGown's black beard, a cruel crack in his ugliness. "Mighty funny, a nigger-loving copperhead fighting for the north. What's he doing? Spying?"

"You know right well we're not copperheads, Everett McGown," Clara said. "Union first and last, and you know it."

"It's Sergeant McGown now. Where's the niggers?"

"We ain't got no niggers," Jacob said.

"Tell the boy to keep quiet unless he's spoken to. Where's the niggers?"

Clara's head went back. Her chin came up. Eyes burning with God's righteous anger. "There are no Negroes on this property."

McGown snorted. Sweat ringed the mole on the side of his nose. He adjusted the strap of the ancient musket slung over his shoulder. On his back it looked like a toy. "We'll see."

The first boy Jacob had seen came out of the smokehouse with two hams slung around his neck. The cats without names mewed up at him and he scattered them with kicks. "You find anything?" McGown asked.

"Nothing," the boy said. His voice cracked with youth.

"Those are our hams," Jacob said.

McGown ignored him. "Check the springhouse." The boy nodded and hurried away.

"Those are our hams," Jacob said again.

McGown looked across the river to Kentucky, then squinted up at the sun. The triangle of skin at his throat gleamed with sweat, black hair curling from it. The smell of him filled the yard. "We have orders to confiscate the goods of any copperhead we come across."

"We're not copperheads," Clara said again.

"You're harboring runaway Kentucky slaves. I have orders to return them. Since you're doing one thing and I'm doing another, we got to be on different sides. That makes you a copperhead, because I know what side I'm on."

"Hell, McGown," Jacob began.

"Tell the boy to keep his mouth shut."

Klausmann came back from the woods shaking his head. "Did you check the outhouse?" McGown asked him.

"*Ya. Umsonst.*"

"Check the cabin," McGown said.

Clara stood in front of the door. "You are not coming in my home."

When McGown pushed her to the dirt, Jacob threw himself at the sergeant. McGown shrugged him off and a heavy fist cracked into Jacob's face. The edges of his vision flashed and the center went black and he didn't know where his feet had gone. When he could see again he was lying on the ground and a thick pain was roaring in his head. Something wet bubbled on his lips and covered his chin and soaked into his shirt, and when he ran his tongue over his lip he tasted blood. Every time he breathed something clicked horribly in his nose. Clara was beside him with her arm around his neck, dust staining the side of her dress, her eyes burning. The pain roared again and again and he thought he would pass out. The sunlight was horribly bright, and the door of the cabin was open.

"Your sins will come down upon you, Everett McGown," Clara said.

"God's a Union man," McGown answered her.

Jacob lay back in his mother's arm and held his shirttail to his nose. The blood backed up in his nostrils and trickled into his throat. A tremor of nausea ran through him. The boy who had gone to the barn was trotting toward them with Isaac's book in his hand. McGown took it from him, blinked at it, and flipped through its pages. He studied its inside cover, but the book was upside down.

"It says *Shakespeare* on the outside." The boy pointed. "And it says *Isaac Clay* right there."

McGown looked from the book to Clara. "Who's Isaac Clay?"

"We don't know."

"Your cow named Isaac Clay? Your cow been reading Shakespeare?" He laughed harshly. The boy dutifully joined him. "There's a nigger named Isaac Clay, ain't there? You got a nigger that can read? There's white folks that can't read. Hell, what are they teaching niggers for?"

"There are no Negroes on this property," Clara answered him. "We bought the book secondhand."

"The book ain't all, Sergeant," the boy said. "They've got two beds in the back of the barn. Somebody's been there awhile."

"It's the god damned niggers." McGown slipped the book into his pocket and studied Clara. "Where they at?"

"There are no Negroes here," she repeated. "And you know I'm not a liar."

McGown spat. "Yeah, well." He pursed his lips and wiped the sweat from the side of his nose. "Maybe they run them over to the other side. That bald bastard abolitionist, I bet. Where's he?"

"I didn't see him," the boy said.

"I'm not talking to you, shit for brains. Where's he at, Clara?"

"I suppose he's working his bees," she said, "like always."

"And you say you ain't a liar."

Klausmann came out of the cabin gnawing on a chicken leg. He shrugged. McGown nodded at him, then at the boy. "I'll take a look at that barn. You guard these two. If they move, shoot them."

"Shoot them?" the boy asked. His voice cracked again.

"Shoot them."

"This gun ain't even loaded. I ain't been issued any ammunition."

McGown spat again. A dark spot in the dust glistened in the harsh sunlight. "Then club them with the stock."

He strode toward the barn with the heat shimmering around him. Klausmann stood watching with chicken breading clinging to his mustache. He looked at the chicken leg, then at Clara and Jacob. He went back into the cabin and came out without it. Finally he hurried off toward the springhouse with a scrambling gait that said he was happy to have thought of something to do.

"I'll get a cloth for your face," Clara told Jacob.

"Ma'am," the boy said, "you got to stay here."

"I'm getting a cloth for my son's face." She stood and went into the cabin with the boy impotently watching.

The boy stood over Jacob, his musket loose on his shoulder. The pain swirled in Jacob's head and he had to lie back on the ground. He could feel blood clotting between his teeth.

"What's your name?" he asked.

"Bartels," the boy said. "Private Benjamin Bartels."

"I heard of you. Ain't you from the other side of Ripley?"

"Three mile out."

"How'd you get enlisted? You ain't any older than I am."

"You just got to get your pap to let you. Or you lie about your age. That's what I done. Hell, Teague is even younger than me."

"Who's Teague?"

"The one with the hams. You're Jacob Wilson, ain't you?"

"I am."

"Proud to know you."

"Wish I could say the same."

Benjamin Bartels smiled a sheepish smile that quickly faded. He had big, brown eyes like Mabel's. "Sorry about this. It's the war and all."

"The hell if it's the war. It's McGown."

"He don't like nigger lovers."

"Do you?"

"Niggers are niggers and they ain't nothing to me. If you love them, that's your own business." The boy squatted confidentially. The butt of his musket cracked hollowly against the dirt. "Where they at, anyway? The niggers. I won't tell."

"You must think I'm a fool."

"That nose of yours looks like some kind of balloon," Benjamin Bartels said.

Clara came back with a towel and knelt beside Jacob. Benjamin Bartels stood and became a soldier again. Jacob lay back in his mother's arms and let the pain take him. He must have been hurt worse than he thought, because his mind clouded and when it cleared again he was leaning against the cabin wall. Clara was squatting beside him with her skirts blowing slightly in the breeze and Benjamin Bartels was gone. The shadows were longer.

"They all right?" Clara whispered.

"They're all right," Jacob said.

McGown had Klausmann and Teague pull the buckboard into the yard and they loaded it with plunder. Buck watched them work from the traces. They loaded the springhouse eggs into wicker baskets and into the wagon bed, loaded the hams, then they caught and decapitated the chickens, plucked them, cleaned them, throwing their innards to the cats, and put them in beside the eggs. When the soldiers had finished searching and found they had nothing to do they searched the house one more time and cleared it of the china and the cabinet the china was stored in and loaded it all into the wagon bed. Benjamin Bartels tied Mabel to the back of the buckboard, and the other boy lifted Buck's lip to check his teeth.

"You're not taking our mule," Clara shouted.

The boy looked up. He had a narrow face and pale blond hair and thin hands that fumbled clumsily. Perhaps a year older than Jacob, perhaps a year younger. "Sorry, ma'am. Orders."

"You're not taking our mule," Clara shouted again. "How are we supposed to live?"

McGown came out of the cabin munching the chicken leg. Isaac's book poked up out of his jacket pocket. He looked first at the boy, then at Clara.

"Everett McGown," she said, "you're not taking our mule."

McGown looked again at the boy. He blinked away sweat and sunlight and swallowed loudly. "Unhook him, Newt."

"Sergeant?"

"We ain't going anywhere until I know about this nigger Isaac fella and the other one they got here. We'll take him when we go."

"Your sins will come down upon you," Clara said.

"God's a Union man," McGown told her again. He scowled up into the incredible blueness of the sky, then back at Newt. "You ever butcher out hogs before?"

Newt nodded. "All the time."

"Then get busy. Take one of the others to help you."

"We'll need boiling water."

"The woman will get it for you." He looked down at Clara. "Get it for him."

"Get it yourself."

"Get it, or I'll beat your boy again."

Clara rose with a heavy, smoldering hatred in her eyes. "You're killing us," she said as she pushed by him into the cabin.

When the afternoon came it lay heavily across the yard, only the dust having the strength to rise against it. Jacob stumbled when he could to the stock pen with the pain in his head leaving him topheavy. Before he reached it the first pig had squealed its death, and the hard splatter of blood on soil sounded like a bucket of discarded water, like a heavy rain. Newt and Benjamin Bartels had strung a shoat up in a tree behind the pen and it was quivering in its dying. Jacob walked to the riverbank and plunged his head into the cool water. He tried to lose himself in its murmuring.

When he came up, he was bleeding again. He lay back against the bank until the blood had congealed, blinking up at the sunshine and listening to the activity behind him. He stood and walked back to the cabin. McGown was standing in front of the door watching him, watching everything, seeing everything, his thick, iron-bending fists resting against his hips. Jacob turned and walked toward the woods.

"Where you going?" McGown called.

"To take a shit."

"You're not taking any shit."

"If I got to, I got to."

McGown thought about this, then nodded. He called for Teague. Teague ran over from the barn, blood on his hands and tunic. "Our boy here has to use the outhouse. Go with him."

Teague looked at Jacob, then he nodded. He followed him into the woods.

They walked until the only sounds around them were the sounds of the woods, of the birds singing and the tree branches soughing. Out here it was just a beautiful summer day.

"Why you doing this?" Jacob asked.

"Orders," Teague said.

"My daddy's fighting with McClellan. You think McClellan would have ordered you to kill those pigs? To be a chicken thief?"

"Sergeant McGown did."

"That's not orders. That's McGown."

"You're hiding niggers."

"You seen any niggers?"

"There was them two beds. And that book."

"Everybody sleeps in beds, and everybody's got books. You seen any niggers?"

Teague shrugged. "Orders," he said again.

When they reached the outhouse, Jacob went inside and Teague stood in the open door with his big, clumsy boot on the threshold. "Do you mind?" Jacob asked. Teague shrugged again and turned away and Jacob shut the door.

He looked up through the hole in the roof at the sky, at the trees. A robin flitted across the blue. He listened to the sounds of Teague's boots trod away. He listened to Isaac and Sarah mucking around below him.

"You all right?" he whispered.

"They've been in here," Isaac whispered back.

"They didn't find you."

"They've just been in here to use it."

"I'll get you out," Jacob said, "when I can."

He waited for what seemed the right amount of time, looking up at the sky, at the walls. He opened the door. Teague was leaning against the oak that had dropped the branch on the roof. Teague grinned.

"Everything come out all right?" He laughed gutturally. "I heard that one in Columbus."

They walked back through the woods. The buckboard was piled high now, the slaughtered shoat eviscerated, the earthy smell of its innards enveloping the yard and leaving the other hog quiet. McGown was standing by the river with his musket cradled in his arms. He was motioning with it toward the cabin.

Tobias was on the water in his skiff, rowing uncertainly, his big shoulders hiding the stern. The drops from the oar blades cut the sunlight.

"Come on," McGown called.

"What's going on?" Tobias called back over his shoulder.

"A war's going on," McGown said.

Tobias removed his ragged slouch hat, wiped his bald pate with his hand, put his hat back on. He nodded. The current had pulled him a few yards downstream.

"Come on," McGown said again.

Tobias pulled on the oars. In a few moments the keel ground against the bank, and Jacob waded into the river to catch the bow. He pulled it ashore with McGown watching.

"You got business here, nigger lover?" McGown asked.

Tobias looked first at Jacob, then at McGown. He carefully turned and stepped over the seat and reached down for a crock in the bow. "Got a crock of honey here."

"Where's the nigger named Isaac?" McGown asked. "And where's the other?"

"I don't know no nigger named Isaac. I don't know what you're talking about."

"You got them niggers somewhere. I got orders to confiscate them."

"All I got here is a crock of honey. I don't know nothing about no niggers."

McGown grunted, then lifted the lid off the crock. He looked inside and grunted again. "Looks like good honey."

"The best in the valley," Tobias said.

McGown stuck his finger in and tasted it. He grunted again, then put the lid back on. "Put it in the buckboard."

Tobias looked at Jacob. His hat brim threw his wondering eyes into shadow. "You all going somewhere?"

"They ain't going nowhere," McGown said.

Clara came out of the cabin with a pot of water, the steam rising to leave her hair damp and lank and falling across her face. She stopped when she saw Tobias, then carried the pot to the stockpen. From beyond the willows lining the riverbank, the other hog began screaming.

Tobias put the crock in the wagon, then came back. "So what's going on here?" he asked McGown.

"We got orders. That's about all you need to know."

"Whose orders?"

"You got a reason for being here?"

"Not no more."

"Then get across the river. And if I find out you have anything to do with them missing niggers, I'll hunt you down and string you up. I swear it."

The hog was still screaming and the boys were jabbering excitedly and Clara was shouting. From behind the stock pen came the rubbery slap of a struggling body against tree bark. "Hell," McGown said, "he said he knew how to butcher." He spat and strode toward the pen.

Jacob steadied the skiff as Tobias climbed in, each hand gripping the gunwale. Tobias took his seat and said very softly, "Tonight?"

Jacob studied his back, curved above the bench, curving down from his shoulders, the man's hands gripping the oars. "You'll do it?"

"Tonight," Tobias said. "We'll get them across the water."

Jacob pushed on the bow. The current and a few oar strokes pulled the boat around and out into the water. Tobias settled into the oars and the boat glided slowly. Jacob tried to catch his eyes, but Tobias kept them fixed on the stern. When he reached the far bank, he pulled the boat up under the old cottonwood, then stepped out and stretched his back and studied the activity on Jacob's side of the river. He disappeared into the trees.

The hog was still screaming and the boys jabbering excitedly, then a shot rang in the dusty summer air and the sound of the hog's struggle ended as if it had been cut off with a cleaver. McGown walked to the buckboard with his musket cradled in the crook of his arm. Blood had splattered onto his jacket and face and the binding of Isaac's book. He leaned against the buckboard and stared at the pen. He shook his head. Acrid smoke drifted to Jacob.

Chapter Seven

Newt and Benjamin Bartels finished the slaughtering by mid-afternoon. They put the clumsy, ill-handled chunks into the buckboard, but McGown ordered the meat and eggs and chicken carcasses transferred to the springhouse because the detachment was going to spend the night. They unloaded the knapsacks in their own wagon into the cabin.

Jacob spent two hours lying in the cabin loft, gently prodding his nose—its bridge had a lump it had not had before, it was angled to the right, and was so swollen now that he could hardly see past it. The night came and the soldiers put up the horse and mule and moved into the cabin, all but Newt, who sat sentry on the porch and occasionally made a round of the buildings. McGown ordered Clara to cook up two of the chickens, and while the soldiers ate, they spoke among themselves in soft grunts and single words. They did not speak to Clara or Jacob. Jacob could not eat and Clara refused to. Instead they watched the window, watched the night grow.

McGown broke out a deck of cards after dinner, and he and Klausmann and the two boys sat around the table to play. Isaac's book weighed down his jacket pocket, its leather glowing softly in the light from the dying cookfire. Clara refused to do the dishes.

"You keep a messy house," McGown told her.

"They're not my dishes no more," she said. "Why should I wash them?"

Jacob lay in the loft, but he was restless with what he knew was coming, and the musky stink of the sweat-soaked woolen uniforms below him rose. He climbed down the ladder, paused to watch the soldiers play, then walked to the door. McGown's eyes flashed up from the cards.

"Where you going?"

"To the outhouse."

"You sure take a lot of shits."

"Swallowing blood will do that to you."

McGown's eyes went back to his cards, and he flicked the queen of hearts out onto the table. "You take Newt out there with you."

Jacob stepped outside. The moon cast a sheen on the river as it rose with a slow, majestic grace. Newt was sitting cross-legged beneath the window, the stock of his musket propped in the space between his legs, his pale, boyish face turned up to the stars, his dark tunic sucking on the darkness. Jacob leaned against the wall beside him. Through the window came the muffled voices of the men and two boys calling out their cards. Tobias would not come before the moon had set.

"Where you from?" Jacob asked Newt.

The boy grunted. "You think I'd tell you? You'd get a couple of fellas together and come do this to my place. I ain't going to tell you."

Jacob squatted. He watched the river just in case and gently prodded his nose. Dull patches of pain. "You'd have it coming."

"I got orders."

"There's wrong and there's right. This ain't right."

"I got orders. You got to follow orders."

"There's wrong and there's right."

Newt sighed. His hand gripped the musket's stock and he caressed his cheek with the barrel. "You got to follow orders. Suppose there's a charge somewhere and one guy follows orders and the rest of the bunch didn't. What would happen then? That one guy would get kilt."

"Maybe it's a bad order."

"That don't make no difference. He'd get kilt."

"He'd get killed anyway if it's a bad order. Maybe the whole bunch of them would if they had followed it."

Newt shook his head. "You ain't a soldier so you don't understand. If I didn't follow orders here, I might not follow them somewhere else and that one guy would get kilt. And I'd have to live with that until the day I died. That's the way it is. You don't follow orders, and someday you'll make a mess of everything. You don't follow orders, and someday maybe it'll be *you* getting kilt."

The current in the moonlight cast flickering shadows that lived and died, then lived and died again. The old cottonwood on the other side rose black, its naked, dying branches flaring as if the night beyond it had fractured. Jacob rose and walked to the middle of the yard. The buckboard was piled high and Mabel stood tethered behind it. She lowed quietly, her big, sorrowful eyes upon him.

He nodded at her. "Ought to set her loose to graze."

"I did while you all was eating."

Jacob watched the water again. Finally he turned and walked to the foot of the trail leading to the outhouse. He could just see the shadow of the boy cast by the moonlight stretching across the yard.

"I'm going to shit," Jacob said. "You coming?"

"Nobody ordered me to no outhouse detail."

Under the leaves and branches little moonlight filtered, and Jacob had to trust his feet to know the way. The outhouse rose like an ancient and mysterious monument, a place of sacrifice. He fumbled with the door and stepped inside and closed it again.

"It's me," he said.

"Is it time?" Isaac whispered.

"The moon's up. It's too bright."

"Can we at least come up?"

"Sure," he said. "You can come up." He pried at the seat board and winced with the nails' screeching. He listened for anyone following him but the wind had risen and the soughing of the branches kept him from hearing anything else. Isaac's head came up through the hole, but Jacob only knew this from the sound of the gasping, from the tiny rushes of a warm breath on the back of his hand.

"I'll help you out," he said. He reached and found an arm and followed it to the hand. It was slick with feces and smelled formidable and was as soft as a girl's. He longed to get beyond it and him to Sarah. "You all right?"

"Intolerable." Isaac grunted as his knees clattered over boards. "Absolutely intolerable."

The pull on the man settled in a dull lump of pain in Jacob's nose and he blinked away sudden tears. Sarah coughed and he reached quickly into the privy and found her hand and lifted her out. He tried to embrace her, but she pushed him away.

"I don't care if he knows," Jacob said. His spirit within him was bursting. He felt like one of the characters out of Isaac's book. "Isaac, I love your daughter."

"My God," Isaac said.

"I know everyone says it ain't right but I know the difference between right and wrong and this ain't neither. This is beyond both."

"My God," Isaac said again. "Do you know what awaits you?"

"I don't care."

Jacob tried to embrace Sarah again. She pushed him away. "The smell," she said.

"I don't care about the smell."

"The smell will get on you. The soldiers will smell you."

He resigned himself to her logic. It was crowded in the outhouse, and the stink was all around him. "They were looking for you, but except for McGown I think they've given up."

"McGown?" Isaac asked.

"The blacksmith from Ripley. He's in charge. They tore the place up and they're taking everything. They butchered out the pigs and chickens. They're taking Buck and Mabel. He took your book."

"The dogs of war," Isaac said.

"Sometimes I don't understand you," Jacob said.

Jacob stuck his head out the door. A faint, silver glow lit the trees, the underbrush. He saw no one and heard only the wind in the branches. He found Sarah's hand and led her outside, Isaac following, noisily swallowing gouts of the freshly scented air. Sarah's hand trembled in Jacob's and he wanted to hold her next to him. He wanted to shout to hell with the stink, that this was too big of a thing now. He took her face in his hands and kissed her.

"You got to stay here. You got to make no sound."

"Where are we going?" she asked.

"Tobias is ferrying you across the river."

"That's slave country," Isaac said.

"This is slave country," Jacob answered.

He kissed her again and then to be safe he wiped his hands clean on the sedge that grew around the base of the outhouse. He again had to trust his feet to the path. The lantern threw a brilliant four-paned square through the cabin window, almost dazzling. Newt was not by the side of the cabin.

A fear thrilled in Jacob that the boy might know. It subsided when he heard a soft singing and Newt came out of the barn towing the musket, its stock dragging across the dirt in a growl. Jacob waited until the boy had gone wearily into the smokehouse, then jogged past the wagon and Mabel to the river.

The moon was lower and cast weird shadows across the water. The old cottonwood was as tall and still as it must have appeared to his grandfather as he crouched in the rotting hollow of its dead brother. Jacob searched the water; he whistled as loudly as he dared. No whistle came back and the far bank was too dark for him to find the skiff. He hurried back to the cabin and crouched there, reaching his hands into the window light as if he were trying to wash them in water. When the smokehouse door creaked open and shut, he rose and stepped into the cabin.

McGown, Klausmann, and the two boys were still playing cards. Clara sat in a chair by the fire, her arms crossed, her fingers gripping tightly each biceps, staring into the glowing embers. McGown was in the middle of a laugh that ended when he saw Jacob. He set his cards down and ran a finger over the mole on the side of his nose.

"Hell, boy, you're supposed to leave the stink in the outhouse. Why'd you bring it with you?"

"Can't help it."

McGown watched him cross the cabin to his mother. Jacob sat on the floor beside the hearth and leaned tiredly against the wall. His nose throbbed. McGown's eyes were still on him, and the fearful thrill came back to his chest.

"Private Bartels," McGown said, "go check the outhouse."

Jacob's eyes flashed up before he could stop them. Benjamin Bartels sighed and shuffled the cards in his hands. "Hell, Sergeant, I done that about a dozen times today."

"Do it again. Go up quiet. If you hear something, you don't do nothing but come back here and tell me."

"Hell, Sergeant."

"And don't swear. Didn't your mama ever teach you not to swear?"

Benjamin Bartels cursed and rose and slapped his cards on the table. "Just when I'm winning, too." He went out the door and shut it and his feet shuffled away into silence. McGown's gaze was like two spikes nailing Jacob's shoulders to the wall. Jacob glanced at Clara to avoid looking at him, but Clara's eyes were set on the fire and the only emotion she showed was in the muscles pumping on each side of her jaw.

"We could play three-handed," Teague suggested.

"We'll wait," McGown said.

The fire popped weakly; the embers were dying. The lantern hissed softly and threw its golden light. Benjamin Bartels kicked open the door and came inside. "Didn't see nothing," he said. "It's too dark out there to see nothing. Nothing out in that outhouse but shit anyway."

"I don't care what you saw," McGown said. "What did you hear?"

"I didn't hear nothing. A owl."

McGown was still watching Jacob. "Bartels, you relieve Newt."

"Damn. I always get stuck on this watch."

"If you swear again, I'll break your nose, just like I did our friend's over there."

Benjamin Bartels said nothing. He went outside and muttering came through the window. McGown was still watching Jacob. "Klausmann, you get your musket and load it and keep it pointed at these two."

"What did they do?"

"You do what I tell you."

Klausmann shrugged and fetched his musket from the corner. He bit a cartridge and rammed it and the ball down the barrel. He sat in his chair with the gun across his knees.

"At them," McGown said. Klausmann lifted the barrel. "I'm going outside to have a listen. If either one of them move, you shoot them."

"If they *bewegen*? I can't . . ." His fingers picked at the air for words. ". . . *schießen* them both."

McGown ran his hand over his beard and spat a wealth of phlegm onto the floor. "Then aim at the woman. If either one of them move, shoot her. Be a god damned soldier for once. And have the courtesy to speak god damned English."

Klausmann looked at McGown. McGown waited for him to nod, then rose and stepped outside. The boy's muttering stopped. McGown's heavy footsteps grew soft in the night.

Newt came inside smiling, but his smile dropped when he saw Klausmann. He sat beside him and stared at the musket barrel.

"The devil's work," Clara said. "That's what this is."

"You please not to move," Klausmann said.

Fifteen minutes went by before McGown came back. He grunted as he sat at the table and picked up the cards. "You can put that down," he told Klausmann.

"Did you find?" Klausmann asked.

"Nothing," McGown said. He studied Jacob again. "A owl."

They tried to play a hand, but there was little in it. Finally McGown gathered the cards and put the deck in his pocket. His fingers fumbled over the book and he took it out and flipped through its pages. "God damned niggers reading." He rose and tossed the book on the fire. It flared briefly. A gout of smoke rose.

"What's going on tomorrow?" Teague asked when the flame had settled.

"We'll see about tomorrow when it comes," McGown said. "I want a man on watch all night. Klausmann, you take the bed in the loft. Newt and Teague will sleep in the barn. I'll take the bed down here."

"Where do we sleep?" Clara asked.

"You can sleep with me," McGown said, "if you like. Otherwise, find a place on the floor."

McGown stared at Teague and Newt until they rose and went outside. Soft muttering came through the window again. McGown went to his knapsack in the corner and threw the blanket lashed to it across the floor. It rolled to the hearth and Clara's feet. She looked down at it disdainfully.

"I'll use my own bedding."

"I'll use your bedding," McGown said. "I ain't slept in a clean bed in a week."

Clara stared again at the fire. McGown turned down the lantern. The last of the embers in the hearth threw a dull red glow into the room, the charred remains of the book curling, its ash pages waving daintily. The faint moonlight through the window grew fainter. Clara kicked the bedroll at her feet and stared into the hearth.

"The wages of sin," she said.

Klausmann stretched and groaned and climbed the ladder to the loft. McGown sat at the table and watched Clara and Jacob until Jacob stretched out on the floor beside the fire and the tenseness in Clara's neck began to loosen and her head to bob. McGown took his musket from the wall and loaded it and walked to the bed. He stripped down to his underdrawers while the smell of him filled the room, then lay on the bed with the musket beside him. From the loft came snoring.

"You still awake, kid?" McGown asked.

"I wasn't," Jacob said. "I am now."

"Throw another log on that there fire."

"It's too hot in here as it is."

"I want to be able to see."

Jacob did as he was told. The embers sent a spark shower up the flume that crackled and popped angrily. The book disintegrated. He lay back down.

"You try anything and I'll shoot you," McGown said. "You try to leave this cabin and the guard will shoot you."

"What if I have to shit?"

"You've shit enough." He studied Jacob for a long time. He yawned. "How's the nose?"

"Sore."

"Where's the niggers? What's the other one named?"

"I don't know nothing about no niggers," Jacob said.

"Sure you don't," McGown answered.

They fell into silence. By the time the log was consumed McGown was asleep. Jacob waited. The rhythmic snoring in the loft weighed down his eyes. He waited. McGown's breath was steady and his mouth had fallen open. Jacob waited and suddenly Clara's eyes opened and her neck pulled tight again. Her hair had fallen loose and two strands of it framed her face, and her eyes were black pits that reflected none of the fire. From beneath her skirts she took out a butcher knife and held it poised in her lap.

"Go," she whispered without turning from the fire. "God go with you."

Jacob rose quietly. He crossed the floor and peered out of the window. He could see Benjamin Bartels's legs sticking out away from the wall. They were crossed and unmoving. He opened the door. McGown did not move and the snoring still came from the loft. Clara had turned to the man in the bed with the knife in her grip trembling.

"Go," she mouthed.

He went outside, the night cool around him. Benjamin Bartels was lying asleep against the cabin with his musket beside him. Jacob hurried past him to the river.

The water was black and murmuring. The moon was down, only a soft glow on the horizon. He couldn't see the far bank or the old cottonwood. He whistled softly. He waited, then whistled again.

Something moved on the far bank, then his whistle returned. Wood ground on silt and a moment later he heard oars dipping as steadily as the chirp of the crickets. Behind him he saw nothing of the cabin but the barely visible glow of the fire through the window. The dip of the oars grew louder, and soon he could hear the drops falling from the uplifted blades, the gentle creak and thump of the shafts in the oarlocks. He could see now a shadow coming across the river. He waded into the water far enough to feel the current tug at his calves. He took the bow and gently guided it onto the bank.

"I've been waiting," Tobias whispered.

"Things been a little tight over here."

"I figured."

Tobias climbed carefully forward from the stern, and Jacob winced with each hollow thud of his boots, with each gentle slap of the water as the boat adjusted. When Tobias was clear of the bow they pulled the skiff up onto the bank.

"You go get them," Tobias said. His big slouch hat left his silhouette misshapen, as if he were a creature who had come out of the river rather than come across it. "I'll wait here."

Jacob nodded, and he crept silently back into the yard. He stopped at the barn to listen and heard nothing. He stopped at the cabin to listen and heard nothing. Benjamin Bartels now lay curled with his musket beside him.

Jacob crept into the woods and whistled softly. He gently called Sarah's name. No one answered and he began to fear and he called her name again. Something rustled behind him and he thought of Benjamin Bartels. He turned with his fists clenched and his lips pulled back and his fear filling him. He could see nothing. He let himself relax when he smelled the smell of the outhouse coming toward him.

"Is he here?" Isaac asked.

"He's here." Jacob sought out Sarah. He ran his hand up her back and down over her waist and hips.

"What's going to happen to us over there?" Sarah asked.

"That's up to Tobias. We'll get you back and get you on north when we can."

"I can't go north without my family," Isaac said.

"Then you better screw yourself up to get them."

Isaac fell silent. The crickets chirped. The breeze muttered in the trees. "What about my book?" he finally asked.

"You best forget about that book."

Tobias was pacing beside the boat, his hat pulled so low that its brim merged with the shadow of his shoulders. He stopped when they approached. Sarah was thin and willowy beneath Jacob's hand.

"You got them both?" Tobias asked. "I can't see a damn thing out here."

"Got them both."

Isaac climbed into the skiff's stern, his feet thumping hollowly. Tobias and Jacob wrestled the boat further into the river. Tobias got in and took the oars and Jacob helped Sarah over the bow.

"Is this the end of it?" she asked. Her voice was as soft as the water.

"This ain't the end of nothing."

When he released her hand Jacob closed his eyes. He rarely prayed but he prayed now that the words he had just spoken held meaning. He wondered if God had ever been in love. He thought of a painting he had once seen of God on a chapel ceiling, and he wondered if God could understand what the touch of a hand could mean.

He pushed the bow into the water hard enough for the strain to leave his nose throbbing. The skiff scraped against the riverbed, then was clear and silent. Oars dipped into water and the black hulk of it blended into the darkness overhanging the river. The moon was gone now. The current muttered softly and the stars were silent.

He stood on the bank and watched the heavy shadow, listened to the dipping oars grow fainter. The sound of boots behind him froze his feelings and left his breath rasping against them.

"Halt." Benjamin Bartels's young, high voice seemed to have to crawl over the word. "Who goes there?"

"It's me." Jacob stepped away from the bank. God, he thought, God. "Who told you to say that?"

"That's what sentries are supposed to say." The boy stepped up to the shore and squatted. He planted the butt of his musket between his feet with its barrel rising in front of him. "What you doing out here?"

"Just watching the water," Jacob said. His fear had amplified the sounds of the skiff to equal Benjamin Bartels's voice, to equal the beat of his own heart. The boy was nothing but a dark lump squatting on the bank. Not even human. "Guess I should go back inside."

"Guess so. I can't figure out how you slipped by me."

Jacob walked past the boy into the yard and glanced back over his shoulder. He could still hear the oars. Benjamin Bartels rose and stretched and stared at the water. He stopped stretching and stepped almost into the current. "Is there something out there?"

Jacob turned. He waited.

"There's something out there," the boy said.

"There's nothing out there," Jacob said.

"Hot damn," the boy said, "there's a boat out there. That's them niggers, ain't it?"

Benjamin Bartels turned and hurried into the yard, hurried toward the cabin. Something rose in Jacob and he grabbed the boy's shirt and threw him across his hip onto the ground. The musket clattered uselessly to the side. Benjamin Bartels grunted and wheezed and Jacob gripped the boy's collar at the throat.

"You better let me up," the boy said.

"Let them go," Jacob said.

"Sergeant McGown, he'll have you shot if you don't let me up."

"Let them go. They ain't done nothing to you."

"You better let me up," the boy said.

Jacob stared down at the shadows hiding Benjamin Bartels's face. Not even human. When he tried to tighten his grip he found that he could not, because the boy had turned his face to the thin light coming through the window and Jacob could see his eyes, the light in his eyes. There is something sacred in all men. He watched his fingers relax. He watched himself slide off of the boy.

"Please," he said.

Benjamin Bartels rose and coughed and scrambled for his gun. He stood in a crouch with the muzzle pointed at Jacob, one hand gripping the barrel and the other closed over the trigger guard.

"It's not even loaded," Jacob said tiredly.

Benjamin Bartels stood for a moment before dropping the musket and sprinting back to the cabin. Jacob looked at the water. The sound of the oars had stopped.

"Go on," he shouted. "Hurry!"

The oars began working the water again, frantic this time. The cabin door slammed open. The sound of a scuffle came from within, McGown cursed, then came a high keening cry that might have belonged to an animal. Something thudded heavily, and a moment later McGown came out of the darkness with his musket clutched in one heavy hand and Clara's knife in the other. Benjamin Bartels was behind him.

"Damned woman," McGown said. "God damned woman." He wiped his forehead with the back of his knife hand. A dark, straight line ran from his hairline down to his left eye. He turned to Benjamin Bartels with the back of his hand pressed against his brow. "Go tell Klausmann to watch her close. Tell him that if she gets up, he's to knock her down again."

"I can't tell him that," Benjamin Bartels said.

"You'll do what I god damn order you to do. Go." The boy ran back toward the cabin. "Take your musket, you damned fool," McGown said.

The boy returned to grab the musket, then ran to the cabin. "Where they at?" McGown asked.

"I don't know what you're talking about," Jacob said.

McGown's fist came down with the knife handle clutched within it. Jacob felt the pain as it crushed his nose, but what consumed him was the light it caused to flash across his eyes, so bright it dazzled. He was lying on the ground and he knew he was screaming because his throat was raw, but his voice had been lost in the light. When he could see beyond it he was lying in the dust on his side. Newt and Teague were watching from the barn door and blood was running heavily from his nostrils. Around the edges of his vision the light still hung, as if he were looking through a silver tube. He grew more afraid as the light receded, because with its recession the pain grew.

A heavy boot kicked his shoulder and he was looking up at the sky and choking on the blood and between him and the stars was McGown's big, black body, its edges melded with darkness, almost ethereal. The warm circle of a musket muzzle was pressed against his forehead.

"Where they at?" McGown demanded.

Jacob tried to get his thoughts past the pain now booming in his head, as solid as the ground on which he lay, as unyielding. "On the river."

McGown cursed and spat and the spittle landed close enough to Jacob for him to feel it splatter almost hot upon his cheek. He groaned and clutched at the blood and pain and the clicking sound in his nose was worse now than before. He rolled on his side and curled into a ball as if becoming a fetus would take the blood and pain away. He watched McGown stride to the water. He cried unto God for vengeance.

He could not hear the sound of the oars through the roaring in his head, but he knew McGown could by the way the black hulk of his shoulders tightened as he stared across the water. Newt and Teague and Benjamin Bartels were standing over Jacob and staring at him with sick looks on their faces. McGown strode back to where he lay with the light of the lantern Teague was holding throwing a circle around them.

"Where's there a boat?" McGown asked.

"We can't go into Kentucky," Newt said.

"You just follow your god damned orders."

"But those are Lincoln's orders."

"Where's there a boat?" McGown demanded again.

Jacob choked. "I don't know."

"Hold his head down," McGown ordered.

Newt dropped and Jacob felt a hand on the side of his head push the opposite cheek into the dust. The pressure made the light come back, and though he cursed himself for doing it, he whimpered. McGown stood in front of Jacob's face and reared back his boot.

"Where's there a boat?" he asked again.

"The McIntyres got one," Jacob said.

"How do we get to the McIntyres?"

"You go through the woods."

"You lead us."

McGown uncocked his foot, then pulled Jacob to his feet by his collar. Jacob stumbled along, lost in the light and the steadily roaring pain. McGown shook him and the pain came in accents that made him whimper again. He wiped his eyes and he wiped at the blood streaming over his lip to drip from his chin. He listened for the river and heard nothing, the first time in his life he could not hear it. He found the empty, silent stock pen with the blood on its ground all shadows and the bank beside it and followed it west along the river.

McGown pushed him along it roughly with Teague and Newt and Benjamin Bartels following. The stars bathed in the light in his head and were so brilliant that with luck Jacob thought he could hide behind one. The McIntyre farm opened before them with the windows of the cabin dark and silent. McGown strode to the door, dragging Jacob now, and banged on it with his fist, making it shiver.

Someone stumbled inside, then the high, thin, devitalized voice of Old Man McIntyre came through the planking. "Who is it?"

"The Fifth Ohio Volunteers," McGown said.

Someone fumbled with the latch and the door opened. Old Man McIntyre stood in his underdrawers, lean and bent and dried to the point of brittleness, his hair like a rust, his thin body as shadowy as a ghost, as a banshee from his homeland. "What do you want?" he asked in a brogue.

"You got a boat?" McGown asked.

"Down on the bank."

McGown jerked his head toward the water. Newt and Teague jogged toward it across the yard. Mary came to the door with a lamp, and when she saw Jacob's face she gasped and stepped back, covering her mouth with her hand and breathing heavily through her fingers.

"What's going on?" McIntyre asked. His eyes gleamed. His mouth twisted as he looked at Jacob.

"Got a couple of runaway niggers trying to get across to Kentucky." The line on McGown's forehead had seeped and hung now in clotted strings.

"Hot damn," McIntyre said. "Hot damn." He rubbed his bony hands together as if they were sticks he was trying to light afire. "Can I go with you?"

"This is a military affair." McGown glanced over his shoulder as something splashed in the river. He turned back to McIntyre. "You got a gun?"

"Sure."

"You got ammunition for it?"

"Sure." McIntyre scuttled inside and scuttled back with an ancient flintlock, powder horn, and ammunition pouch. McGown shook his head at them and glanced at Benjamin Bartels. "You know how to load one of these?"

"I ain't never done it," the boy said.

McGown cursed and spat and loaded the weapon and handed it to the boy. "You take him back to the cabin. You kill him if he does anything but what you say."

"Someone ought to look after him," Mary said. She had slipped her father's coat over her shoulders. Her nightdress lifted slightly in the breeze moving up the river.

"Who are you?"

"His sweetheart. We're gonna be married."

"Then you look after him. Go with the private here back to the Wilson place."

"What do I get to do? What do I get to do?" Old Man McIntyre was rubbing his hands again.

"You stay here," McGown said. He pushed Benjamin Bartels and his big, clumsy flintlock back toward the trail. "Go." He snatched the lantern from Mary and jogged heavily toward the river.

Benjamin Bartels stood by uneasily and Jacob leaned against the threshold as they waited for Mary to dress. Old Man McIntyre cursed and went back inside, and he shouted at Mary as if his inactivity were her doing. When she came back out she was wearing a calico dress and her dull hair lay weedy about her shoulders.

"My God, Jacob," she said, "what have you done?"

He didn't answer her. Benjamin Bartels took his shoulder and guided him toward the trail. Oars slapped clumsily on the water, and McGown cursed.

They walked silently, and Jacob listened to the river. He could not hear the skiff, but he heard the heavy sounds of the McIntyre boat as it worked and the harsh, cursing orders McGown was muttering. The lantern light moved slowly across the water, and in it he could see Newt and Teague straining at the oars. The sounds had muted by the time they reached the farm. They had walked the whole way silently.

"I'm sorry about this," Benjamin Bartels said.

"Sorry don't do nothing," Jacob answered.

Jacob stopped to study the river, but Benjamin Bartels tapped him gently on the shoulder with the flintlock's barrel and he was too tired to resist it. Lantern light shone in the cabin window. Mary took his arm as they walked toward it and rested her head on his shoulder, as if they were young and in love or even at one time had been. They went into the cabin. Klausmann was sitting at the table with his musket lying across it. Clara was sitting beside the hearth, staring down at its dying ashes, one side of her face swollen, her lip twisted, her eye narrowed, her cheek swollen and purple. She looked at Jacob and smiled. Blood lined her teeth.

"I got him," she said. "He stood from the bed and I got him."

"You kill him almost, you coot," Klausmann said.

"You see him?" Clara asked Jacob.

"I seen him."

"You see what I done to him?"

"I seen."

"Is he dead?"

"No."

"Is he blinded?"

"No."

The smile dropped from her swollen features and she turned back toward the hearth. "I thought I was the hand of God. I thought I was the instrument of his vengeance."

"God is with *die Vereinigung*," Klausmann said, "you *rebells.*"

"Hell awaits you, Dutchman," Clara answered him.

Mary forced Jacob down onto a chair opposite Klausmann. She filled a bowl from the water bucket, dipped a rag into it, and wiped Jacob's face. He winced at her touch.

"Oh, Jacob," she said. "I could have told you that niggers is nothing but trouble. Look what they done to you."

"They didn't do this to me."

"They did." She wiped his nose and lip, and when she rinsed the rag the water tinted. Bits of chaff floated on its surface. Klausmann watched silently. Benjamin Bartels had crossed the cabin and was sitting on the second rung of the loft ladder with his chin braced on his hands.

"Where they going?" she asked Jacob.

"I wouldn't tell you if I knew," he said, and he pushed the rag away.

She stepped back with the rag dripping dark circles onto the floor. She dropped her eyes. Jacob thought of Sarah with her dress around her waist in the barn and naked and arched beneath him and in the outhouse, in the skiff, in hiding now with real fear in her eyes, with real love in her eyes. If he had had the strength and if there were not two soldiers so near he would have stood and grabbed Mary around the neck and dashed her brains against the wall.

When Mary again tried to wipe his face he again pushed her away. "You got to let me clean you up," she said.

"You ain't putting down some kind of down payment."

She stood by the window, watching him, then walked to Clara and tried to dab at her cheek, but Clara pushed her away, too. Finally she sat at the table beside Klausmann. "You'll see one day, Jacob. You will. And one day you'll thank me for it."

"I don't see nothing," Jacob said.

"I see the vengeance of God," Clara told the dying fire. "I see it all around me."

"Die Hölle," Klausmann said.

They sat silently. Jacob swallowed blood. Mary's face was drawn and pale in the lantern light.

Chapter Eight

Jacob had fallen asleep. He dreamed he was soaring above the farm, and looking down he watched Sarah running across it. He was dropping to meet her when McGown slammed the cabin door and Jacob awoke to a blood-colored dawn coming through the window. His eyes were swollen nearly shut and he couldn't breathe through his nose. The pain had wrapped dully around his head like smoke. Mary was gone. He didn't care about that.

Newt and Teague followed McGown in and collapsed tiredly at the table. McGown paced, stopping only to blink at the new sunlight. Klausmann was sprawled wearily in his chair. Benjamin Bartels in the loft had not stirred.

"God damn," McGown said. "God damn."

"You didn't find them," Clara said. She smiled. Her cheek had gone a purple-tinged green, and her left eye had closed.

"Hell no." McGown spat. The cut on his forehead was a dried black, bubbled line. "But we found something."

"You found what?" Jacob asked.

McGown smiled.

"You found what?" Jacob repeated.

"Red sky at morning, sailors take warning," McGown said. "You god damned nigger lover."

Jacob hurried outside. A feeling he couldn't identify had lodged in his throat, in the pit of his stomach, had filled his lungs with a coldness that he could feel on his lips when he breathed. The river was still misty and dark and the sound of its water whispering. The harsh, acrid smell of wood smoke filled the air, a cloud of it rising across the water above the trees.

Mabel was still tied to the buckboard, lowing plaintively with milking pain. A yellow tom was sitting on the china cabinet, pawing at its reflection the new sun cast in the glass. Jacob walked past them and the silent barn and stock pen to the water. The McIntyre boat had not been pulled far enough up on the bank and rocked gently, its stern angling downriver.

The trees on the Kentucky side were silent in the early morning, with only a few reverent birds singing. The mist moved over the river, wisps of it riding the current downstream, wisps of it grabbing the underbrush lining the banks as if for anchor. Everything slow like a dream. Through the mist the old cottonwood could not throw a reflection onto the water.

Somehow he knew what he would find, as if a bond existed between his mind and McGown's, his spirit and McGown's, as if the sergeant's fist against his face had also been a transfer of knowing. His eyes searched the mist, then crawled up the cottonwood's thick, black trunk, and before they reached the first branches they caught on a pair of boots. He knew what he was seeing. His eyes climbed to Tobias's body hanging calmly in the tree, still swaying. Tobias's neck was jointed where the noose held it, and his bald head shone redly in the dawn. As the rope twisted, his empty eyes followed the river.

Jacob sank to his knees. He cupped his hands and stared at them, then sunk his whole head into the water. Within it was a world that could take the other away. He thought that perhaps his dream of the night was still going on, and when he would raise his head he would awaken to a darkness full and the stars beaming down and Sarah lying quietly on the bank beside him, her dark eyes, her dark skin, shining. But when he finally had to lift his head the sun was still harsh, and the mist on the river was fleeing. He could not bring himself to look at the dying cottonwood.

Something inside him had broken, and he could feel his emotions seeping. He felt as empty as if the sun had scoured him clean, and when he rose, he knew very clearly what he would do. He strode back toward the cabin. As he walked by the buckboard the sun caught on an ax blade in the bed. He lifted the ax out by the haft. The disturbed tom leaped across the buckboard's cargo, yowling.

Teague came out of the cabin door just as Jacob reached it, stretching and squinting and yawning at the sun. Jacob brought the ax around in a hard, fast swing that met Teague just above the shoulder. It slid up the muscle there until it reached his neck and lodged deep and biting just beneath his jawbone. Teague went down without a sound and in a heavy spurting of blood, a surprised look in his eyes. The blade had gone deep enough so Jacob had to wrench it free. He strode into the cabin.

McGown at the far end of the table had his back to him. As the sergeant turned, Jacob brought the ax around again, but McGown got his arm up and Jacob heard and felt the ax blade catch his wrist. The hand came off neatly, but in taking it the blade had twisted and when it met McGown's skull it hit it with its side. It thudded loud and wetly and McGown fell across the table and rolled onto the floor. He lay on his back and lifted his arm. His stunned eyes stared at the stump of his wrist. The cut on his forehead Clara had given him the night before was again bleeding.

"Jesus," McGown said. "Sweet Jesus."

Jacob kicked the table out of the way and swung the ax again. Somehow the haft had gotten turned around in his hand and the butt end of the blade glanced off of McGown's temple. McGown lay back flat and stared up at Jacob blankly, his lips and body trembling. Jacob swung again, but he tried to check the swing because in that instant before the butt end caved in McGown's skull, before the sergeant's forge-lit, iron-bending life was ended, Jacob saw something in his eyes, a flash there, a bursting of life, and perhaps because of the connection they shared Jacob saw something that should be invisible rise. But then the ax had found its mark with a heavy, thumping crunch and McGown lay still with the blood oozing.

Jacob's breath whistled coldly in his throat, and he dropped the ax as if it were the evil thing. McGown's eyes were bleeding, burst with the blows or with the soul that had fled them. His severed hand had rolled onto the hearth.

There was only silence in the room. Klausmann stood with a piece of bread half chewed and hanging from his lips. Benjamin Bartels still lay in the loft. Newt sat in a chair staring dumbly. The table must have hit him when Jacob had kicked it aside because his cheek was bleeding.

"Jesus," Jacob said. "Sweet Jesus."

No one else spoke. Clara had been studying the severed hand at her feet. She turned in her chair and looked at her son through her one good eye and smiled.

"Jesus," Jacob said. A terror filled him, a wildness. He left the cabin as unthinking as he had entered it. He tripped over Teague's body as he hurried out of the door.

Chapter Nine

*The current when J*acob reached the river had almost yanked the boat free of its mooring. Jacob stumbled into the water, fell, and came up dripping with the river running into the slits of his swollen eyes. He yanked the bow away from the bank and heaved himself over it, his boot heels casting water in slim arcs that caught the sun. By the time he had climbed to the seat, the boat had already drifted far enough downstream for the farm to be hidden behind willows.

He set the oars and pulled on them, feeling the water's resistance in his back, feeling a twinge there that must have come either when he had fallen or when he had swung the ax. His nose throbbed as if all of his fear had gathered there, and his breath came quickly. Floating before him he could see Teague falling into the yard, McGown falling onto the floor. He could see the soul rising from McGown's eyes.

The trees beyond the stern grew smaller, and now through a gap in them he could see the farm, the fence line demarcating the field. The buckboard stood silently with Mabel wisely watching him from behind it. Soon he could see the McIntyre farm, silent and still in the early morning. The water swirled from the oars a muddy summer brown, two vortexes drawing down. He could feel Tobias's dead and empty eyes on his shoulder and a panic took him.

He pulled at the oars as if by the strength of his arms he could pull himself out of sin and judgment. The sun had risen high enough for the tree shadows on the Kentucky side to stripe and dapple the water. The bow ground against the bank. He climbed over it and glanced up at Tobias. The man's bald head gleamed, and the breeze gently lifted his whiskers. Flies had gathered on his lips and eyes. Jacob fled into the trees with a heavy fear in him and around him and his nose throbbing. His crime made visible to the world.

The smoke was thicker in the stillness of the trees, its smell more acrid. He stumbled into it along the path running from the cottonwood toward Tobias's shack. He passed the whitewashed beehives, the bees silent and narcotically indolent in the smoke. The shack was still burning, orange flames licking, the roof rising in bits of ash and falling in blackened timbers, the north wall already collapsed. Tobias's old slouch hat was lying by the doorway, soot-stained and trampled. He picked it up.

He called once for Sarah and received no answer. He started to call again, but then held his voice. The soldiers had crossed the river once and a burning shack and a body in a tree is what had resulted. McGown had forced them, but Jacob was not so sure that enough of McGown did not still remain to force them again. He had seen the sergeant's eyes. He could feel him watching. With only the clothes he was wearing and the boots on his feet, with only Tobias's old slouch hat in his hand, with only his fear, he fled into the trees.

He wandered blindly through hickory and oak, avoiding and even refusing to look at the cottonwoods. In an hour, with the sun already high and hot and accusing, he stumbled onto a dirt road with weeds growing between the wheel ruts. He followed it west, constantly glancing back over his shoulder.

The trees opened in patches to reveal farms like his own across the river. Dusty huts with dusty yards, dusty fields, dusty fences standing weakly. Dusty, half-naked children playing, dusty farmers working behind dusty, bony mules, dusty women working behind their husbands or watching with dull eyes the children. He saw no whipped backs, no black and heavy and scarred faces. He saw no liquid brown eyes lifting to catch his own. He thought of Sarah.

Jacob reached a town named Brooksville about mid-afternoon. Buildings shimmered with the sun at its hottest. Blacks here joined the whites walking down the streets on their business or on someone else's, the same as anyone. He was hungry and tired and penniless and still full of fear and the band of Tobias's hat was slick with the sweat from his forehead. The pain in his nose beat steadily.

A tall, stoop-shouldered black man even blacker than Sarah was shuffling along through the dust, barefoot, holes worn through the knees of his overalls. "I don't suppose you know where a fella could do an odd job," Jacob asked him.

"I don't know." Smallpox had scarred the black man's clean-shaven face, and the pores on his cheeks were deep little pits. "How you get your face so busted up?"

Jacob's hand strayed to his nose, as if by hiding his deformity he could also hide his past. He wondered if this black man knew, if somehow Klausmann or Newt or Benjamin Bartels had crossed the river and told him. Perhaps it had been McGown's spirit hovering in the air. A thrill ran through him.

"Got kicked by a mule," he said.

The black man craned his neck forward and squinted at Jacob's face. "A mule kick a fella full in the face and that fella won't be walking around to tell about it. No, sir. Not near so soon, anyway."

"He didn't kick me very hard."

"You ain't from around here," the black man said.

Jacob turned to the passersby ambling. He imagined big, cruel soldiers swarming out of the hills, out of the trees, crawling out of store windows. His fear thrilled again. "Thanks just the same." He started away.

"You hungry?" the black man asked. "Is that why you're looking for work?"

Jacob stopped and sucked on his cheeks and stared down at the street. His nose hurt. The only thing in his stomach was his fear. He glanced at the black man again.

The black man rubbed his eyes and his leathery, chapped lips. He took a biscuit out of his pocket and held it to Jacob. "Go on. You take it."

"Can't take something without earning it."

The black man smiled. "You think I earned this? Some of the boys got together up by the river and waylaid some Yankee transport. This is the stuff they're feeding their soldiers. Go on. You take it." Jacob hesitated. "Take it. It ain't no prize."

Jacob took the biscuit. It was hard and tasteless and caught in his throat when he swallowed. "This is what they're feeding their soldiers?" He thought of his father.

"That and salt pork. Makes you wonder why anyone would want to be a soldier, don't it? God damned Yankees."

"You a slave?"

The black man drew his chin back as if this was a ridiculous question. "Course I'm a slave."

"They want to free you. Some of them do, anyway."

The black man pursed his lips and shrugged his sloping shoulders. The sun had gathered his shadow around his feet. "Ain't nobody free," he said. "Ain't nobody." He stared until Jacob took another bite, then nodded with satisfaction. "You get hungry, you just ask someone for one of them biscuits. Everybody's got them, but nobody eating them. They ain't hardly fit for it. But you get one, you eat it and don't keep it around. It'll get these big fat white grubs that'll eat it for you. God go with you, son."

Jacob nodded and watched the black man walk away. He wanted to sit and finish the biscuit, but he could feel McGown, and he could feel what he had done to McGown, and the north was only a half dozen miles away. A road headed south out of town, and he took it.

He walked south for three days, through Cynthiana and Paris, sleeping in corn and tobacco fields, drinking from streams, bathing his face in the water. The raw, young corn he stole clenched his stomach. On the second day the swelling of his face began to subside, and as he ran his fingers over his nose he could feel the bump on its bridge and the way it angled to the right. On the third day he reached Lexington. White colonnades in front of vast, red-brick plantation houses, sweeping green lawns, rich men and women in shining buggies behind statuesque trotters. Wooden shacks bleached gray by the sun squatting in evil-smelling clusters, poor men both white and black with rags on their backs, sweat in their eyes, no hope on their faces. He looked for work, but beyond four days of hauling flour sacks in a mill found none. He wandered the streets, stealing food when he could, listening to the talk of the war. The north was coming, they said. Jacob fled again, working west.

He found he could stay for only a few days in any place he entered; he could feel McGown all around him, could see him fall, could see his severed hand rolling onto the hearth, could see his eyes and feel them. The swelling died and his color returned and if people commented at all on how he looked they commented on the strange look in his eyes, or his raggedness, or his drawn face. He worked for a livery in Bloomfield, a dry goods store in Upton, alongside a farmer and his slave in a tobacco field just north of Madisonville. His memory of McGown and his fear of Federal soldiers drove him on to Dawson Springs. He was too tired and hungry to go any farther. He looked for work, but even with the war he found none. He had no money, so he crept behind the livery at night and slept against its wall.

When he awoke one morning, he stood and brushed off his clothes and thought he must look a sight. He walked around the livery to squint up at the new-morning brightness and wondered what he should do. He was hungry.

A carriage was parked in front of a dry goods store, the largest donkey Jacob had ever seen in its traces. A man almost as large as the donkey sat within the carriage, his big hands gently releasing petals he'd pulled from a daisy, his eyes watching them slowly flutter to the street. Jacob rubbed his grumbling belly and crossed the street and stood staring up into the donkey's eyes, half hidden by its blinders. The man watched the petals, then turned to Jacob.

"Awful fine donkey," Jacob said. The man just stared. "I said this here's an awful fine donkey."

The man still just stared. Closer now, Jacob could see the sheen of saliva on the man's chin and his almost toothless mouth. His thinning hair stuck up wildly as he rubbed enormous knuckles over his scalp. Tiny eyes that held no intelligence.

"Can you talk?" Jacob asked.

"Good," the man said.

"Can you say anything else?"

"Good," the man said.

Jacob stood with his palm resting on the donkey's withers. The man scrunched up his face and wormed his little finger around in his ear. When a woman in her mid-forties came out of the dry goods store, the man grinned and stepped out and carried the flour sack she had been struggling with to the carriage as lightly as if it were one of the petals. Jacob stood watching. The woman arched her back and smiled at him. A gray lock growing out of her widow's peak lifted in the morning breeze above her otherwise red hair. She was wearing a dress cut low in the front; she possessed breasts of such perfection and size they defied all known laws of gravitation. Jacob stood watching.

"Mr. Gunderson said there was a boy around looking for work." The woman tucked the lock back toward the bun it must have originally been tied into. "You wouldn't be him?"

Jacob stood watching.

"My tits aren't doing the talking," the woman said. "You wouldn't be him?"

Jacob dropped his gaze to his feet. The toe of his boot began making patterns. "Yes, ma'am."

"Can you work hard?"

"Yes, ma'am."

"How old are you?"

"Seventeen, ma'am."

"No."

"It's the truth."

"You look older."

"Must be the busted-up nose."

She pursed her lips and ran her eyes down Jacob as he wished he felt comfortable doing to her. His glance flitted between the dirt and her face. The big man was sitting in the carriage again. The woman went around its back and climbed in the other side. "Well, get in," she said with a slight smile.

"What kind of work, ma'am?" Jacob asked.

"All kinds. You get in."

Jacob nodded and walked around the front of the donkey, trailing his fingers over its brisket. The woman made room for him as he climbed in beside her. The smell of her perfume was powerful and her chest overwhelming. The rest of her was hardly any bigger than Sarah had been. Was. Is. He shook his head and tried to clear his mind. The man silently turned the carriage and headed north out of town.

"I'm Sue," the woman said.

"Yes, ma'am."

"You call me Sue."

"Yes, Sue."

"This is Abner. You call him Ab. He don't say much beyond 'good' and 'bad.' He's a bit simpleminded."

"There's nothing wrong with that," Jacob said.

She looked at him. Her flushed pink skin was slightly chapped. "There isn't?"

"I mean it don't have nothing to do with if you're good or bad."

"That it doesn't."

"You got a nice donkey there."

She breathed deeply. The cut of her dress outlined a shimmering pool into which Jacob longed to plunge. "It comes from a long and distinguished line. It is a descendant of the donkeys George Washington bred at Mount Vernon."

"You knew George Washington?"

"How old do you think I am?"

"I mean, did your family?"

"I am descended from George Mason, creator of the Bill of Rights and neighbor to our first president. A great man, in his way."

"You must be rich."

"Not anymore. My father never had a head for business. I have a head for business and know that to make the best of what you have is only practicality. He gave me only the house and what you see before you." She ran her fingers down the line of her cleavage and smiled at Jacob when he remembered the rudeness of not speaking to her face.

"My oh my," he said.

Abner drove the team north on a road that Sue said led to a town named Charleston. She talked of her past and the history of the land around them, adding in Latin taxonomic detail the names of the plants they passed when the occasion arose. Her father had left Virginia because he had been a second son with no tie to the family estates beyond servitude to his brother. He moved to Kentucky where he started a tobacco plantation, *Nicotiana tabacum,* before the spirit of manumission came upon him and he set free all of his slaves. He lost what money he didn't have tied up in them and most of his land to gambling, and as Abner turned the carriage onto a narrow dirt lane four miles from Dawson Springs she pointed at a hickory, *Carya ovata,* overhanging the road and said that that was where his creditors had hanged him. Jacob listened respectfully. Abner drove with his spittle shining on his thin grinning lips and his little eyes fixed to the hind end of the donkey. Trees surrounded them. The Latinate cacophony concerning them gradually abated as the lane opened onto a spacious yellow-brick house with a porch in need of painting.

"So what am I going to be doing?" Jacob asked.

"Have you ever worked in a whorehouse, Jacob?"

Jacob stared at her. She studied him. "I ain't really built for it, ma'am."

"Sue."

"I ain't really built for it, Sue."

"I'm not asking you to do that." She mulled the matter silently with her lips pursed and brushed the unruly gray strand away from her face. "Would you mind doing that? You could make some money."

"No ma'am. I mean, yes ma'am, I would mind."

"The giving or the taking?"

"Ma'am?"

"Sue."

"Sue?"

"The giving or the taking? With them giving it to you or you giving it to them? Which would you mind?"

"I think I'd mind either way."

She nodded. "Then I'd like you to keep the place cleaned up and an eye on things."

"I guess I can do that," Jacob said.

Abner pulled the carriage around to the back beside a small barn. Sue and Abner walked into the house, Abner with the sack of flour under his arm, with Jacob following behind. Inside he found a small alcove with a chair in the corner and a parlor beyond it. Girls in various stages of undress were lounging within the parlor, some white, some black, one oriental. Sue and Abner walked through it into the kitchen. Jacob stood uncertainly in the parlor while the girls eyed him and smiled.

"He's not a customer, girls," Sue called back. "He'll be working here."

Some of the girls nodded greetings and others sighed and stood and disappeared either up the stairs or into the back. The oriental girl mutely sat with her eyes flitting uncomprehendingly from face to face. A blond girl dressed only in a man's pair of underdrawers smiled. She tapped the seat beside her just vacated by an obese redhead with fleshy rolls covering most of what Jacob was interested in and teeth stained with tobacco and smelling of rot. She left plenty of room to sit down. Jacob sat with his back straight and his hands on his knees. Abner walked by to sit in the chair in the alcove.

The girl in the underdrawers craned her head so Jacob had to look at her. She seemed about his age. "I'm Rachel."

Jacob nodded. This was one of those places his mother said he would burn in hell for entering. He felt a nervous futility and delight as certain sins came down upon him.

"What's your name?" Rachel asked.

"Jacob Wilson."

"I'll call you Jake."

"All right."

"You know what I do?"

"I can guess."

"All the respectable men of Dawson Springs and Charleston come visit us. The only problem is that the good-looking men aren't the respectable ones."

"Who are the good-looking ones?"

"The ones that don't need to come around here." She sighed. "The mayor, he asks for me all the time. He's got this bulldog face and just about the littlest weenie. He's got this belly that hides it. It's like searching for a needle in a haystack."

"Oh."

"He's my uncle. Once removed."

"Oh."

"On my mother's side. I run away because I like to do this and Mother's religious and don't like me doing this. The mayor, he likes to do this, too. He tells her he sent me out east to finishing school. I write letters telling her about it. The finishing school, I mean. This ain't no finishing school."

"Oh."

"When he does it, he needs all kinds of help because of the size of his weenie. He calls me his little girl, but he's the little one." She lifted the waistband of her shorts, studied herself for a moment, then released it. It snapped against her belly. "I can hardly tell he's in there sometimes."

"Oh."

"So what are you going to do here?"

"I don't know. Not what you're doing."

"Some of those respectable men wouldn't mind."

"Oh," Jacob said again.

Sue came in and led him out to show him what to do. First he had to whitewash the porch. Later when the men started coming he sat with Abner in the alcove in case there was trouble. Sometimes men got drunk and loud, and Abner would pick them up and gently carry them outside. Sometimes men would get rough with the girls, and Abner would pick them up and take them outside and give them a squeeze. Men would whimper and sometimes bones would crack. Abner would set them down and they would leave any way they could manage and would never come back again. The regulars never got rough because they knew Abner.

The old brick house held eight rooms and seven girls. The girls used the rooms in sequence and Jacob was responsible for cleaning whichever room was empty. He would strip off the bedding and put down clean sheets and wipe semen and sweat from the floors and walls. Sometimes the girls would leave him tips because he did a good job. Sunday nights were their nights off and they'd sit in the parlor playing cards or chess. The oriental girl could play a mean game of chess, though she could speak no English. Abner would play with the captured pieces. He liked the knights and would say "Good" any time one was captured.

Jacob slept in the barn. He had only been there a week when after work early one morning Sue came out and took his hand and led him into her bedroom. She made him strip and lie on the bed while from across the room she studied him appraisingly. She crossed to the bed and held him with one hand and unbuttoned her dress with the other.

"Are you a good man, Jacob?" she asked.

"I don't know," he answered. Her hand was warm and kneading and very sure of itself.

"I can tell you're a good man."

"Oh."

She had to release him to remove her underthings. She stripped them off with her back to him, and she was as thin and smooth and lovely as Sarah had been, her ribs outlining her only slightly aged skin when she raised her arms over her head. She didn't look like Sarah when she turned around.

"My oh my," Jacob said.

He quit sleeping in the barn. He had been in Sue's room for two weeks when one night a band of guerrillas stopped by, southern boys from over in Muhlenberg County. Things got rough and a black girl named Annabelle got cut up pretty bad. Sue called Jacob out of the alcove. When he went in the room she was sitting on the mattress with her fingers pinching together Annabelle's cheek and blood flowing between her knuckles. The guerrilla was crouching naked in the corner, brandishing a knife with the girl's blood on the blade and on his hairless chest, with his breath hissing in his teeth, his eyes wild, his blond, dirty hair down over his brow. Annabelle was naked and screaming and clawing at Sue's fingers. The room smelled of sweat and the blood.

"Go get Abner," Sue told Jacob. "Then get a bucket."

Jacob hurried to the alcove and directed Abner to the room. He filled a bucket from the pump in the kitchen. On his way back to the room he passed Abner carrying the cursing naked boy out into the yard. Sue was still tending Annabelle.

"Go out and help Abner," Sue said.

"What am I supposed to do?"

She looked up at his face. "Help him."

"Will he need it?"

"He might."

Jacob hurried out of the room, through the parlor, and out the alcove. He wasn't sure he liked working here. Abner was standing in the yard with his arms still around the boy. The boy screamed and flailed with his head jerking from side to side and his hair snapping. Five or six of the guerrillas were standing in the darkness around them. The sight of their guns caught in Jacob's throat.

Abner grunted and tightened his grip and the air rushed out of the boy as if he were a squeeze box. The boy clawed at Abner's eyes, but Abner shut them and squeezed again. The crack of the boy's ribs sounded like breaking branches and blood bubbled on his lips. His body trembled before going limp. With one arm around the boy's waist and the other pushing against his chest, Abner doubled the boy over backward with a dry snap and dropped him onto the yard. One of the other boys, bigger and cockier than the rest, thick-armed, thick-legged, cursed and jumped on Abner's back. Abner pulled him over his shoulder with one hand and with the other snapped the boy's neck. He dropped the boy on top of the other and studied the rest of them dumbly. The sheen on his lips shone in the light from the alcove. The boys fingered their revolvers.

"Leave him be," a boy who appeared to be the leader said. "They deserved it."

"Jack didn't deserve it," one of the others said.

"Jack got tangled up in more than he could handle."

They stood around sullenly, looking at the corpses. Abner went back into the alcove and sat with his hands in his lap resting limply. Jacob waited by the door, his hands fluttering from his face to his pockets to the cracked ivory door handle. Annabelle's screams had fallen to a whimper.

When the guerrillas still inside came out and joined their sullen comrades, Jacob feared trouble, but when they had all gathered they tied the two dead boys across their saddles and mounted their own horses. Sue came to the door as they rode away. "Come back when you're gentlemen," she called after them.

The tightness within Jacob relaxed, his fidgeting ceased. "I'd hate to mess with them."

"Abner would take care of you. Abner likes you."

"I mean without Abner."

She wiped a hand over her chest and shook her head at the sweat and blood smeared on her palm. "They're nothing but dumb little cusses."

"Sure."

"I'm going to run Annabelle in to the doctor. Can you take care of things?"

"Unless they come back."

"If they come back, Abner will take care of things. Can you clean up that room?"

"Sure."

"And don't let anyone else use it tonight. It's got bad luck."

Jacob nodded and went back inside. Most of the girls were waiting in the lounge with either frightened or bored expressions. The oriental girl sat uncomprehending. He walked back to the room Annabelle had been using and began cleaning blood from the floor. By the wall was the hilt of the dead boy's knife and beside the bed its blade. Jacob had seen too much of this kind of thing and he shut his eyes against it. Then he saw memories.

He had stripped the bed and was dropping the red-speckled sheets into the corner when Rachel came into the room, wearing a man's shirt. Jacob looked over his shoulder at her as she sat on the mattress, then went back to work.

"Where'd you get that?" he asked.

"Get what?"

"The shirt."

"It's my uncle's."

"He's a crazy old coot."

"He's just got his desires. We all got our desires."

Jacob stepped out to the hall closet and came back into the room with clean bedding. Rachel got up from the bed as he began unfolding the sheets. She was such a beautiful girl, long blond hair, blue eyes, her skin the texture of flowers, still after all she had done radiating innocence. "Let me do that," she said.

"It's my job."

"There ain't no customers. It ain't like I got anything else to do."

He shrugged and handed her the sheets. "You ever worry about it?"

"About what?"

"About what happened to Annabelle happening to you."

She wafted a sheet over the mattress and snapped it. "It's just part of it, that's all."

She bent over to tuck the sheet around the mattress and the shirt rode up over her hips. Desire rose in Jacob, but then his eyes caught the knife hilt and the desire soured. As he crossed the room he glimpsed himself in the vanity mirror. He stopped to study his face, to see if his crime was written upon it. A misshapen nose, his face drawn beyond his years. His empty, sunken eyes.

"Rachel," he said.

"What?" She had lain on the bed and was smoothing a blanket across her legs.

"I'm a hell of a thing to look at, ain't I?"

"You ain't so bad, Jake. You ain't."

"I'm a hell of a thing."

"Sue don't think you are. I don't think you are, neither."

He studied her reflection. "Why don't you come away with me?"

"You leaving?"

"When I leave."

"But Jake," she said, "my mother and uncle and all. All my family is here. Did I tell you I got a brother?"

He watched her watching him, then studied himself again. His nose half smashed over his cheek, his lips cracked and flaking. He searched his eyes for the soul he had seen in McGown's, the soul he knew everyone possessed. A cold fear came into him and he closed his eyes and shook his head and opened his eyes again. He passed his fingers down over his face, pulling down the lid and letting it open again as if it were only a stuck shutter.

"Sweet Jesus," he said.

"What?" Rachel asked.

He was staring into the eyes of a corpse—walled, glassy, chilled eyes that showed nothing beyond them. He closed his eyes and scrabbled within for some trace of God-given breath. He opened his eyes again. Fear choked him.

"Where are you?" he asked.

"I'm right here, Jake," Rachel answered.

"Where are you?" he cried.

"Jake," she said, "I'm right here."

Suddenly in the mirror hovering above Rachel were McGown's eyes, black and livid and blown wide open from what they had once possessed that Jacob found now he didn't. Jacob turned with terror from the mirror. The eyes were still there, watching him and accusing. He backed up against the vanity. Bottles clinked and fell. The smell of lilacs surrounded him.

"Jake." Rachel was rising. "Are you all right?"

"Sweet Jesus," Jacob said again.

"Jake, you're scaring me."

His hand searched the vanity for something he didn't know and couldn't find. The eyes floated above the knife blade as if in violence Mc-Gown sought reembodiment. They were punctured and dripping the sergeant's iron-bending will.

"Jake?" Rachel asked.

Jacob turned to her, then ran unthinking from the room. He fled down the hall and through the parlor without seeing the girls, through the alcove without seeing Abner. He reached the lane with his breath hot within him, and he could feel a cold gaze upon his shoulder.

Chapter Ten

Jacob fled to Dawson Springs and beyond. Not until he reached Paducah at the beginning of September did the eyes give him respite. He worked for two days on the docks, unloading cargo off the steamboats working the Mississippi, then was fired. He had trouble working there because he was on a river.

When the Federal army seized Paducah, Jacob fled across the Mississippi into Missouri. He worked his way north on a steamboat, earning his passage and two extra dollars by whitewashing the pilothouse. He worked silently, and the crew and passengers avoided him. He saw that he had grown lean and twisted by the shape of his hands, by the way they gripped the paintbrush. When the boat docked at St. Louis he took his pay and left without a word.

St. Louis was a dirty town, a mile-long line of dirty steamboats along the levee spitting smoke into the sky. Garbage in alleys and rats in gutters; German voices filling the air, German hands hanging laundry on lines strung between the buildings. Jacob tried to find work but the only work in St. Louis involved enlisting in the Federal army and he had no interest in that. He followed the Missouri River west to Jefferson City, then talked a teamster into giving him a ride on the post coach to Camdenton for a dollar. The postal guard spoke in hushed tones of the jayhawkers from Kansas raiding the border, of Doc Jennison and Jim Lane and Jim Montgomery as if they were modern Joshuas riding across Missouri's own dusty plains. Jacob could hardly ponder it.

From Camdenton he wandered west, following first the South Grand River and then the Osage to Osceola. He had heard from the teamster there might be work there, and he was hungry. Osceola was a bustling southern town.

He couldn't afford the ferry to cross the river, so he swam across. He waited before wandering into town until his filthy clothes had dried. It was the largest town he had seen since he left St. Louis, perhaps three thousand inhabitants. He walked down the dusty streets with the sole of his right boot torn and flapping. He wore Tobias's old slouch hat to keep off the viciousness of this alien southern sun. His cheeks were so drawn he could feel them sticking to his teeth.

He stopped to sit in the shadow of a livery, waving away flies. People walked by him, hardly pausing. A black man came out of the livery with a curry brush in his hand and looked down upon him. The man appeared to be in his mid-twenties, though his head was bald and beginning to frizzle gray at the temples. Long legs, long fingers, the muscles in his arms thin and corded.

"Mr. Daniels, he told me to ask you to move on," the black man said.

Jacob studied the black man's face, his eyes as soulless as his own. He thought perhaps he should feel commiseration, but how can there be commiseration between two lumps of dirt? Neither of them would be among the multitudes before the throne that had been reserved for those like Mc-Gown. He couldn't understand it. "Why'd he say that?"

"That ain't my business. I'm just saying what he told me to ask you."

"Why do you suppose he said it?"

"I don't know if I'd like to say that."

Jacob nodded and stood. The black man was over six feet tall and dropped his eyes subserviently when Jacob tried to study them. Dust to dust. "You tell him I just needed some shade. I'll move along."

"I'll tell him," the black man said. He went back inside.

Jacob tugged the slouch hat down tight upon his head and worked back into the sun. He walked down the street tipping his hat to ladies, but they either just perceptibly nodded or ignored him. A stone worked up into his broken boot, and he squatted to pry it loose. A fat man in an apron came out of a shop door to watch him.

"I'm moving along," Jacob said.

The fat man wiped the heavy sweat from his brow. Thinning silver hair, mottled pink scalp, his heavy jowls almost reaching his chest. "You look a fright," he said.

"Been traveling."

"From where?"

"From everywhere."

The fat man nodded. "How old are you?"

"Seventeen."

"My God," the fat man said. "You could pass for thirty."

Jacob stood and tested his foot against the broken sole.

"You ever work dry goods before?" the fat man asked.

"Some."

"You looking for work?"

"Some."

"You do some hauling for me and you stock the shelves and keep the place clean. You unload freight when it comes in. I'll pay you room and board."

"No money?" Jacob asked.

"Room and board for now. We'll see how it goes."

"Hell," Jacob said, "you might as well go buy yourself a slave."

The fat man's chin came up indignantly. "You watch your talk. There's two things I won't tolerate, and one is the bondage of my fellow human beings. I ain't never owned a slave and I ain't about to buy one."

"Seems to me," Jacob said, "you're trying to now."

The fat man pursed his lips. His hands never left his hips. "You can just be on your way then."

"I'll take the work," Jacob said. He hated the desperate servility he was feeling. He was hungry. "If you're still offering."

The fat man studied the matter, then nodded. The sense of his superiority came to his face. "Name is Jim Buchanan."

"Like the president," Jacob said.

"Like the president. What's your name?"

"Jacob Wilson."

"Tell me where you're from. No more stories now."

"Dawson Springs, over in Kentucky," Jacob said.

"What did you do over there, Jacob?"

"Grew up, I guess. What's the other thing?"

"The other thing?"

"The other thing you won't abide."

"Alcohol," Mr. Buchanan said. "You drink and you're on your way. Now come inside, and watch the language. I won't have no swearing in my store."

Jacob followed him inside and took off his hat within the store shadows. He was standing in a large room with a rough plank floor that groaned beneath his feet. Long rows of wooden shelves lined each wall. The dusty sweet smell of cornmeal and the heavy camphor odor of liniment roiled in the air.

Mr. Buchanan squeezed himself in behind a wooden counter where a prim, emaciated young woman was waiting; with a pencil he tallied up what she owed for a small bag of coffee. She paid and looked at Jacob, and his eyes followed her out of the store.

"None of that," Mr. Buchanan said. "I don't need looks like that driving away the few customers I have."

"Business bad?"

"I'm a Union man in a southern town. What do you think?" Jacob was still staring at the door. "None of that, I said."

"Kind of hard for a fella not to look once in a while."

"You're still young enough to believe that everything is possible. Everything ain't possible." Mr. Buchanan set down his pencil and adjusted his glasses. He looked Jacob up and down. "You are a fright. And I bet you ain't got any money for new clothes."

"None."

"I guess I can provide you with a pair of trousers and a shirt and call it part of your board."

"Boots?" Jacob asked.

"You've put up with those awhile. Put up with them awhile longer." He wrote something more on the pad, then stood and nodded at the corner. "Get yourself some clothes off that shelf there. Take the cheap ones. Go in the back and change and come out with a couple of sacks of flour. Comb your hair back or something. You look a fright."

Jacob took what he needed and walked toward the back. Mr. Buchanan cleared his throat and Jacob turned to see what he wanted.

"I want to know something right up front and I want you to give it to me honest." He leaned over the counter, his belly gnawing at its edge like a pair of gums. "You a Union man or a secesh?"

Jacob thought of his father fighting with McClellan. He thought of Clara and Isaac. He thought of Sarah, but he pushed the thought away because it was too painful. He thought of McGown. He could feel McGown. A shadow passed by the window. He shrugged.

"Boy," Mr. Buchanan said, "that there is the biggest question there is. You got to take sides on a question that big. I'm a Union man first and last, even if it means this store fails and my family is begging on the streets. I won't have no secesh working in this store."

"Then I guess I better say I'm a Union man."

"Have you taken the oath?"

"What's the oath?"

Mr. Buchanan shook his head. "You don't know nothing, do you?"

"Been traveling."

"Boy, if you're going to work for me you got to take the oath. You go get cleaned up, then come down to the provost marshal's office with me. We'll set you up."

"Sure." Jacob stepped into the back.

"Boy?" Mr. Buchanan called. "If anyone asks you, you're making fifty cents a day. If you don't like that, give me the clothes and be off."

"Fifty cents a day," Jacob said. He kept the clothes.

"And if I catch you stealing, I'll shoot you. That provost marshal is my sister's brother-in-law, and he'll stand back of me. I'll shoot you dead. I've got no qualms."

"Sure," Jacob said.

The trouser seams chafed badly. The shirt was made of good southern cotton with the smell of spring in the weave, and after he'd buttoned it up and studied its sleeves he guessed he didn't look half bad. He combed back his hair with his fingers and checked his nose with futile hope, as if for the occasion it might have shifted back to where it should be. He hefted two twenty-five pound sacks of flour and struggled with them back into the front.

Mr. Buchanan was nodding sympathetically at a fat woman with colorless hair who was complaining about her corns. Jacob stood in the center of the store with the sacks balanced on his arms. Mr. Buchanan nodded at the shelf where they belonged.

"I'll be with you in a second, boy." Mr. Buchanan turned back to the woman. "We're heading down to see my brother-in-law."

The fat woman looked at Jacob. Her warty lip curled. "New help, Mr. Buchanan?"

"Yes."

"You could have hired my boy."

"I don't think your boy, Mrs. Atchison, would settle for fifty cents a day."

"Is that all you're getting?" the woman asked Jacob.

"That's all," Jacob said.

"Some people will settle for anything."

Jacob heaved the sacks onto their shelf, balanced them, then waited as the woman paid for her liniment. How he wanted to boot her out the door. Mr. Buchanan trundled around the counter and with his hand on Jacob's shoulder and a grim, fatherly smile guided him out into the sun. Jacob went back in to fetch his hat.

The provost marshal's office was three buildings down and across the street. Jacob blinked up at the sun as he waited for a wagon to pass, then crossed the street and walked in to stand before a dark-complected man with an iron gray walrus mustache and large rolling eyes who said his name was Tom Crowder. Jacob raised his hand and swore loyalty to the United States's and Governor Hamilton Gamble's governments. He had never heard of Hamilton Gamble and he thought someone in St. Louis had said Claib Jackson was governor. He puzzled over it as he recited the words they wanted him to say. He signed his name on a sheet Tom Crowder set in front of him, then he left the office amid smiles and handshakes and a dirty joke by Tom about a plantation owner and his Negress. He couldn't remember most of the words he had spoken.

"You break that oath, now," Mr. Buchanan said on their way back down the street, "and the army will hunt you down."

"I won't break it," Jacob said.

Jacob slept on the storeroom floor upon a worn mattress laced with bedbugs, and he took two meals a day from the Buchanans, going to the back door of their house with an old tin plate and spoon like a beggar. He ate mainly bread and beans; he had lived better, but he had also lived worse, and he figured if he could stay on for a while, maybe he would get some trust and with it some pocket money, and maybe he could begin to live the kind of life everyone else seemed to be after. But the life everyone else seemed to be after wasn't haunted by a dead sergeant's empty eyes. The life everyone else seemed to be after involved roots sunk deep and a wife and children and he could not think about that without thinking about Sarah. He wondered where she was. He longed for her in the darkness.

One night he dreamed about the farm. In the dream, Cyrus and Buck worked the field and Clara swept the dust off the cabin threshold into the yard. Tobias crossed the slow, dark river in his skiff with a crock of honey in the bow, and Isaac stood in the river with the current roiling around his shins, watching him. Sarah ran from the barn to the house with her skirts gathered in her fists and her dark legs flashing in the sun like finely polished wood capturing the light of a slow, gentle fire. He awoke from the nip of a bug to find the mattress wet with his tears, filled with a smell like the straw that night in the barn. His longing was a palpable agony.

Tom Crowder, Mr. Buchanan, the emaciated girl Jacob had nicknamed Skeleton, and warty old Mrs. Atchison seemed to be the only Federal supporters in town. And Jacob. Tom spent too many days in the store lounging on the counter, buggy eyes rolling every time a noise came through the window. So few customers entered that Jacob wondered how Mr. Buchanan maintained his girth. With southern success in the war the town was getting boisterous and ugly, and Tom said he was afraid he'd be shot if he spent too much time on the streets. Mr. Buchanan didn't seem to mind, since on most days Tom bought leaf tobacco and he was sometimes his only customer.

"Boys are fighting and dying," Mr. Buchanan said one day. "You've got Wilson Springs here and out east you got Bull Run. I heard wounded boys were lying on that battlefield for a week with the crows picking at their innards. Sad times."

"They is." Tom nodded solemnly. Except when he pursed his lips, his mustache hid his mouth.

Mr. Buchanan lowered his glasses and studied Jacob. "You thought about fighting, Jacob? You took the oath."

"I'm only seventeen," Jacob said.

"In a place like this and a war like this," Mr. Buchanan said, "I'm not so sure that age makes a difference."

Jacob nodded and shrugged and went about his work. The dust curled up from his broom, tickling his nose. Tom Crowder walked to the door and spat and came back again. "I shot a boy the other day. He warn't any older than Jacob."

"Why'd you shoot him?" Mr. Buchanan asked.

"He shot at me first. Some kid who's got dreams of being a bushwhacker."

"You kill him?"

"I did."

"There's going to be hell to pay for that," Mr. Buchanan said.

"They is."

"Sad times," Mr. Buchanan said.

On September twentieth, Sterling Price's rebel army took Lexington on the Missouri. The townspeople of Osceola were jubilant, and Jim Buchanan stood in the door of his failing store with his hands on his heavy hips and his face gray and watched them celebrate. Jacob was wiping down the shelves behind him and stopped to watch him watch the crowd. Catcalls came through the door with the smells of whiskey and beer and unwashed bodies. Mr. Buchanan shook his head.

"It can't last," he said. "It can't."

"Maybe."

Mr. Buchanan turned to study him. "I ain't much of a believing man, but I believe this. There is something holding this earth together, that holds the rocks on it and the people on it and keeps the birds from flying too high. There's something that tells the trees to turn green every spring. I see a justice in that, and what's going on out there ain't justice. It can't last."

"Maybe," Jacob said again.

Jacob was sweeping out the store two mornings after the news came from Lexington. He had been working hard and without complaint and he thought it was time he started getting something beyond the meager room and board he was receiving. Mr. Buchanan was behind the counter, working his pencil on his paper and shaking his head sadly. The day was bright and clear and the heat waited at the door. It smelled of the coming autumn.

"Mr. Buchanan," Jacob said.

"What?"

"I need me some new boots."

"New boots are expensive."

"I ain't asking you to buy them. All I'm asking is that you pay me the wage I deserve and I'll buy them myself."

Mr. Buchanan stopped writing and looked up. The sun through the window caught on the lens of his glasses, hiding his eyes. "If I'm giving you a wage and you're buying the boots, then either way I'm paying for them, ain't I?"

Jacob frowned, and his grip tightened on the broom. "Ain't I doing a good job for you?"

"Sure."

"Ain't it true that a workman is worthy of his hire?"

"Sure. Sometime we'll talk about what wage you deserve."

"This is a time, Mr. Buchanan. This is a time right here and now, and it's as good as any other."

Mr. Buchanan began writing again. "We'll talk about it sometime, boy."

Jacob stared down at the broom, watched the bristles bend beneath his weight, the handle tremble. "Even that nigger down at the livery gets some spending money."

"No."

"I seen him. He bought some whiskey out of the back door of the saloon."

"These god damned secesh don't pay their slaves. I bet he begged for it."

"I ain't going to beg. Maybe I ought to just work somewhere else."

Mr. Buchanan looked up again. "You quit working for me and I'll tell Tom you broke your oath and are running with the rebels. You know he'll shoot you because you know he's done it before. I advise you to keep working."

"I knew you was buying yourself a slave back on that day I come into town," Jacob said.

"You watch your talk," Mr. Buchanan said.

The near empty shelves seemed to vibrate in the silence. A shadow passed by the window and Jacob turned to it. Tom Crowder hurried through the door and Jacob felt for him only hatred. The conspirator of this subservience. How many times had it been done, and how many times would it be done again? Tom blew through his lips and his mustache fluttered.

"They's Union cavalry coming," he said.

Mr. Buchanan looked up, his pencil poised above the paper. "No."

"They is. They's coming up the road, maybe five miles south. They was some shots fired last night, I hear, and now they's coming in."

"Fired at them or by them?"

"Hell if I know. Probably both."

"Militia or regulars?"

"Hell if I know. Probably regulars."

Mr. Buchanan set his pencil down. He nodded at Jacob and smiled. "I told you that there's justice in this world. I told you that there's a reason for everything." He looked at Tom. "They must be chasing up after Price."

"They's after Price," Tom said, "but they ain't chasing. Jim, they's burning everything."

Mr. Buchanan's face grayed, and for a moment Jacob thought with hope he was dying. "Jayhawkers?"

"That's my guess."

"Jennison?"

"Lane and Montgomery, maybe."

"Oh Christ," Mr. Buchanan said. "Oh Christ." His fingers fluttered to his lips, his eyes fluttered around the store. "What you going to do, Tom?"

"Get out of town. Grab the wife and kid and get out of town."

"I thought you was Union men," Jacob said. "You shouldn't have nothing to fear."

"*Shouldn't* is a funny word. It leaves a lot of room for things to happen." Tom Crowder left the store with his big eyes fearfully shining. He hurried down the street.

Mr. Buchanan had begun to sweat heavily, his mottled scalp and his heavy face sheened with it. He squeezed around the counter and looked out the front window, dabbing at his forehead with an already sodden handkerchief. "Jacob, you take everything back into the storeroom and hide it as best you can. Better yet, take it out back and bury it in the storm cellar."

"Am I going to get paid for this? I want them boots."

"You keep them from finding my stores," Mr. Buchanan said, "and you can name your price."

They began hauling the stores out to the back, then out to the storm cellar behind the store, a hole in the ground covered with board planking. Hooves thundered on the street and a shot rang out, a clear crack like thunder in the cloudless blue sky.

"That's trouble," Mr. Buchanan said. "That's big trouble."

The hooves milled, then galloped away. "You think they're leaving?" Jacob asked.

"You keep working," Mr. Buchanan said.

Jacob hauled boxes and canned goods and while he was wrestling a sack of flour from the shelves the hooves came back in a loud continuous roar. He hurried to the window as a shot rang and the window glass shattered. A shard sliced his cheek. He dropped to the floor with his hand to his face, his cheek stinging. Pistol shots were ringing continually and the pounding of the horse hooves galloped up the walls, across the ceiling, up and down the floorboards, his spine. Window glass shattered and rained upon him. Mr. Buchanan was sprawled in front of the counter, his belly splayed beneath him like a frog stepped on by a mule.

"You all right?" Mr. Buchanan asked.

"Don't know." Jacob pulled his hand away from his cheek. A touch of vermilion barely stained them. He thought of Annabelle. "I think."

"They come in here," Mr. Buchanan said, "you tell them we're Union men."

"I'll tell them anything they want to hear," Jacob said.

The dissonance outside the window had rolled further down the street. Jacob rose to his knees and peeked out of a broken pane.

"Where they at?" Mr. Buchanan asked.

"I can't see nothing. There's only smoke and dust."

"You tell them we're Union men," Mr. Buchanan said again.

The shots came again and another pane shattered. A shelf edge on the far side of the store splintered dryly. Jacob threw himself to the floor and lay staring up at the ceiling, listening to the sounds of the horses rolling up and down the street. Men shouting. A woman somewhere screaming.

"Jacob," Mr. Buchanan said. "Let's get out the rest of the stores."

"I ain't moving," Jacob said.

Soon the sound of heavy boots mixed with the clatter of horse hooves. Shadows passed over Jacob and someone kicked in the door. Three men came in grinning, short and wiry and possibly brothers. They were all wearing blue Federal uniforms and the oldest had sergeant's stripes on his thin arms and grizzled dark scruff on his almost chinless face. They all carried muskets.

Mr. Buchanan rose clumsily to his knees. "We're Union men, first and last. You can ask anybody."

"What you got in here?" the sergeant asked.

"We took the oath."

"What you got in here?" the sergeant demanded.

"Stores. Clothing and dry goods. But not much."

The three men grinned at each other. "Pretty empty in here," the sergeant said, "for a store."

"The secesh been driving me out of business."

"Where you got it hidden?"

"Ain't got nothing hidden," Mr. Buchanan said. "All I got is what's on the shelves and what's out back. The secesh been driving me out."

The sergeant nodded at one of the men and that man strode into the storeroom. The third man herded Jacob with the toe of his boot toward the center of the store. The sergeant knelt beside Mr. Buchanan.

"Ain't Missouri the god damnedest state, Will?" he asked.

"The god damnedest," the man standing over Jacob said. "Full of these here god damned pukes." The ammonia stink of his feet flowed out of his boots.

"They own niggers and everything. And they want to secede."

"I'm a Union man first and last," Mr. Buchanan protested. "I ain't never owned a slave. I took the oath. We both took the oath."

"They whip the niggers they own and then they come over into Kansas and try to make us own niggers, too. We don't want no niggers in Kansas." The sergeant grinned up at Will. "You want niggers in Kansas, Will?"

"Not me." Will smiled. "Give me the clap, but don't give me no god damned niggers." His teeth were as brown as a walnut.

The sergeant rasped his knuckles up the scrub on his throat. "I got a cousin that got killed by you god damned pukes back in the fifties when you came over and tried to make us own niggers. He's buried in Lawrence."

"First and last," Mr. Buchanan said.

"One puke is as god damned low as another," the sergeant said. "A puke is a puke."

The other soldier came back. Somewhere he had found a bottle of whiskey. His lips were already wet with it as he grinned.

"What you find?" the sergeant asked.

"They got a hole out back chock full of flour and clothes. Other stuff." He lifted the bottle. "Found this shoved back in a corner."

The sergeant fingered the buttons on Mr. Buchanan's shirt. "I thought you said you was a Union man."

"I am."

"First and last, you said. Why you hiding stores from your own army?"

"Take what you want," Mr. Buchanan said.

"We go off and we get shot at and killed by the god damned secesh and you God damned pukes won't feed us?"

"Take what you want," Mr. Buchanan said again. The sweat ran down his forehead and he blinked it from his eyes. "You take it all."

"One thing I can't stand," the sergeant said, "is some fat puke store-keeper who don't appreciate all we do for him." The edge of his hand flashed out and caught Mr. Buchanan across the bridge of his nose. His glasses folded neatly as his head snapped back and he groaned. Blood flowed from his nostrils. The sergeant stood and grinned and buried his heavy boot in Mr. Buchanan's side. Mr. Buchanan whimpered like a child and curled around the boot. He began to cry.

"God damned puke storekeepers." The sergeant stood back and spat on Mr. Buchanan's cheek, then he looked at Jacob. "That bother you? You want to do something about it?"

"Don't make no difference to me," Jacob said.

The sergeant nodded at the soldier with the whiskey. They grabbed Mr. Buchanan by the crooks of his arms and dragged him outside. Will ordered Jacob to his feet and made him follow. Cavalry were galloping up and down the street with their pistols and carbines shooting at any unbroken window, the dust rising around them thick and choking, smoke beginning to rise from some of the buildings. Infantry were moving from store to store and rolling from them kegs and bolts of cloth and clothing and piling it all into wagons. Mr. Buchanan was in the center of the street and other soldiers had other storekeepers out in the street with him. The livery owner, Mr. Daniels, was sprawled in the dirt with his face turned toward Jacob and blood running from his mouth to leave mud at his lips, his eyes wide and staring and his body locked in a spasm. The black he owned stood in the shade by the livery with his hands in his pockets, watching.

"Why do you suppose this fat puke son of a bitch would be hiding stores?" the sergeant asked.

"He's saving it for the secesh," Will said. "Price will come riding through and drop his drawers and this old boy will be on his knees waiting to kiss his white rebel ass."

"That's as near as I can figure it." The sergeant knelt. "You know the penalty for supporting secesh, fat man?" Mr. Buchanan's lips worked soundlessly and tears streamed from his eyes.

The sergeant grinned and stood, stepped back. The soldier with the whiskey set his bottle down and walked around behind Mr. Buchanan. He brought the butt of his musket down hard between Mr. Buchanan's shoulder blades, and Mr. Buchanan fell forward into the dirt with a sharp-edged gasp that ended in a moan.

The sergeant waved the soldier off before he could hit him again. "Wait. Let's make a show of this." He pointed with a toss of his chin at Jacob. "You tell me where to hit him. If you're too slow, then we'll start hitting you. Got it?"

All of Jacob's joints felt loose. He thought he would fall. "Don't make no difference to me," he said.

"Get him down on his knees there, Will." Jacob felt a kick to the back of his knees and he dropped. Will's shadow loomed over his shoulder. The sergeant was still grinning, his face falling into the scruff of his neck as if his chin had sloughed off. He raised the butt of his musket. "All right, you tell me."

"Don't do it, Jacob," Mr. Buchanan pleaded.

"Hit him," Jacob said.

The sergeant shook his head and nodded at Will. Jacob felt a sharp crack against the back of his neck that flashed on the edge of his vision. He fell forward into the dust. He tasted blood and when he wiped his lips he found he had bitten his tongue. Will was standing over him grinning, the musket butt raised.

"Get him back up, Will."

Will grabbed Jacob's collar and yanked him back to his knees. Jacob wiped his mouth and spit blood. The sergeant stood with his musket poised. "You can do better than that. You tell me where."

"In the back again," Jacob said.

The sergeant cocked his arm an inch higher. Mr. Buchanan wailed and tried to curl into a ball, but the musket butt hard against his spine straightened him out again. His breath cut like a clawed-off stump and he lay in the dirt shivering violently.

Jacob squinted and blinked and turned his face away. Two doves perched on the storefront's eaves and watched the scene below them like gods descended. Between them grew a nebulous shadow that roiled like smoke around McGown's soul burst eyes. Fear rooted Jacob's knees to the street, but he no longer feared the soldiers.

"You tell me," the sergeant said.

Jacob blinked. He looked down at Mr. Buchanan sprawled in the dust.

"You tell me," the sergeant repeated.

"In the back again."

"I'm tired of that. You tell me something else."

"Crush his hand," Jacob said.

"Please," Mr. Buchanan whispered.

The sergeant grinned and planted his boot on Mr. Buchanan's wrist. He brought the butt down smooth and clean and hard as if he were breaking winter ice from a lake, as if he were breaking the back of a turtle. Mr. Buchanan yelped and cried, bright faced and high screeching, bulging eyes overflowing upon his cheeks a wet radiance. The sergeant set his face into hard lines and cocked the rifle again. He brought it down harder and bones snapped like cracking sticks and Mr. Buchanan screamed. The sergeant stepped back. Mr. Buchanan cradled his wrist to his chest and kept screaming. The sergeant spat on his cheek and kicked him hard in the face and more bones snapped and Mr. Buchanan rolled silently onto his back and stared up at the sky. His face glistened with blood and tears and spittle, and his whole body quivered.

"Broken, just like yours," Will said.

The sergeant inspected his handiwork, then nodded at the soldier with the whiskey bottle. "You get busy with that storm cellar." The soldier nodded and walked casually into the store.

The sergeant strolled to where Jacob knelt. He crouched before him, his brutish animality around him like a cloud. Jacob's gaze drifted up to McGown's eyes. The doves were gone.

"Look at me, boy."

Jacob looked at the sergeant. He was an ugly man. The sergeant spat in the dirt beside Jacob's knee. "You like what I done?"

"Don't make no difference to me."

"You like me to do it to you?"

Jacob didn't answer. The sergeant studied him. "You hate me? You fear me?"

Jacob didn't answer. Finally the sergeant stood. "I'll make you hate me, anyway."

The sergeant stepped behind Jacob. Will came around to his front with his musket leveled. A foot prodded Jacob's back and he fell forward into the dust. He lay looking down the street, watching the horses go by and the soldiers working. Mr. Buchanan lay in front of him silently, his fingers twitching.

"I'll make you hate me, boy," the sergeant said.

Fabric rustled as the man's pants dropped. Jacob felt against his back a warm stream, a spattering that came over his shoulders to spot the dirt. Will laughed as the stream went higher to course against Jacob's neck and hair and splatter on his cheeks, his fingers. Jacob gritted his teeth against the stench and the humiliation and felt his fingers curl into the soil. All the power of the earth he felt within him and he started to rise. Will brought the musket butt up and leveled it hard against the small of Jacob's back and Jacob's strength broke. He fell with his cheek in the urine-made mud and closed his eyes. God, he thought. God.

"Damn, August," Will said when the sergeant had finished. "You done pissed on my musket."

"You crossed my artillery line," the sergeant said.

The sergeant stepped around Jacob and kicked him onto his back. Jacob lay with the sun on his face and mud on his cheeks, urine in his eyes, his nose. The sergeant squatted. "You hate me now?"

Jacob wiped his eyes and looked up. He said nothing.

"You hate me now, you god damned puke? You tell me you hate me now."

"I hate you now."

"You think you can hate me forever?"

"I'll hate you forever."

"I don't know if I believe you," the sergeant said, "but I'll fix it so I can. You know how? You're going to hate me because I'm going to let you live and you'll have to remember it with gratitude. You're going to be forced to remember the day I pissed on you with gratitude. That's going to tear you up for the rest of your life." He smiled and spat on Jacob's cheek as he had on Mr. Buchanan's. Jacob felt the spittle run down, felt it gather at the corner of his mouth. He stared into the sergeant's eyes.

"Too bad you're a puke," the sergeant said. "You're a hell of a boy."

The sergeant nodded at Will and Will laughed and together they walked into the store. Jacob crawled to the side of the street where he crouched in the sun and watched the soldiers plunder, watched the horses race by, where he could not see McGown's eyes. The sergeant came out with a sack of flour that he threw into the bed of a wagon drawn up in front of the livery. He laughed at Jacob as he went back inside. Mr. Buchanan lay where the sergeant had left him. He was groaning now.

The black from the livery ambled over and squatted on his haunches beside Jacob. Sweat shone on his inky brow and pate. He nodded at Mr. Buchanan. "You going to help him?"

"To hell with him," Jacob said.

"You want me to help him?"

"To hell with him," Jacob said.

The black man nodded. He leaned back against the wall as twenty cavalry galloped by whooping, pistols firing, acrid smoke trailing behind them. Mr. Buchanan had rolled onto his belly and was crawling toward the opposite side of the street, his broken hand dragging.

"You still got spit on your face," the black man said.

Jacob wiped it off. He watched Mr. Buchanan.

"They gave it to you good," the black man said. "I ain't never seen the likes of it."

"Yeah."

"Mr. Daniels, they gave it to him, too. They beat the hell out of him and took him off somewhere to wait on Jim Lane to get here. I don't know what they're going to do to him, but I believe it will be bad. Yes I do."

Jacob lifted his face and closed his eyes against the sun. The stink of the urine rising. He opened his eyes and craned his neck so he could see the eaves. McGown's eyes were gone. Even in all that had happened he felt release.

"The name is Henry Nolan," the black man said, and he held out his hand.

Jacob stared at it. The black man withdrew it awkwardly and nodded at the rapine around them. "I reckon this makes us equals."

"How's this make us equals?"

"I'm walking out of here—there's freedom in Kansas. And I ain't never been pissed on."

Jacob closed his eyes. "May you rot, you black bastard."

The sun was heavy, the heat heavy on his face, bright figures dancing across his red eyelids. He listened to the sounds around him, soldiers laughing, women screaming, men crying, children crying. With McGown's eyes gone he held nothing within him but an emptiness as heavy against his eyelids as the sun, as strong in his nostrils as the urine stink. This is the way of it, he thought. He felt nothing toward the sergeant, but he knew if he ever got the opportunity he could, and he would, kill him. Because, now, it was nothing.

He opened his eyes. Mr. Buchanan was leaning against the storefront across the street, cradling his broken hand to his chest, blood dripping onto it from his mouth and nose. The black man named Henry Nolan was gone.

Chapter Eleven

Jim Lane was a tall, gaunt man, his head only a skull with parchment stretched over it, a wild, righteous fire in his eyes. From the front of the ruined store Jacob watched him ride into town with a godly air and set up court in the middle of the street. He sentenced to death nine men. Mr. Daniels was shot with his back against his livery, silent, with tears coursing from his eyes.

Laughing men loaded what was left of the plunder into stolen wagons. They broke into saloons and passed bottles that they threw through windows when emptied. Horses, cattle, and slaves were herded out of the north side of town. The soldiers fired all but three houses, black smoke rising, heat like an animal and the hair of the nine dead men lying beside their buildings curled and smoking. Jacob did not leave his place in front of Mr. Buchanan's store until the flames licked his shoulders.

He spent what remained of the day wandering the smoke-filled streets. He watched a stringy Kansas preacher thank God for his bounty before raiding the vestments from the local Methodist church and burning it to the ground. He watched three soldiers shove a pregnant woman into the dirt and tear the clock she was carrying from her arms. He stumbled into a group of soldiers emptying a warehouse who beat him. A child with a red, tear-swollen face screamed for her father and Jacob could not help her.

He found the sergeant as the sun was setting, loading drunken soldiers onto a long line of stolen wagons. The sergeant shoved a drunk's limp leg into a bed and turned. Jacob met his eyes.

"You," the sergeant said.

"Just wanted to see your face."

"Why?"

"I want to remember it."

"It ain't likely you'll forget."

The sergeant grinned his chinless, ugly, stubble-faced grin and played with the buttons on his fly. He laughed before grabbing the nearest drunken hulk and heaving it into the wagon. Jacob watched from the side of the street, standing as close to the burning buildings as their heat allowed. A half hour later the line of wagons began to move behind stolen mules. Jim Lane in a handsome new carriage led the procession, a wagon with a piano in it following. Jacob watched the sergeant until the little man disappeared in the smoke and the dust.

Jacob did not see Jim Buchanan again. He went back to the storm cellar for a pair of boots, but it had been emptied. He left town with the dusk, following Jim Lane's column. With a length of twine Jacob slung a ham he found on the side of the road over his shoulder and kept walking. He found a pair of boots another mile down among other plunder that must have jostled out of one of the overloaded wagons. He shucked off his broken ones and slipped the new ones on and found them only slightly too large. He thought that he had rarely been so lucky.

He walked six miles north to Lowry City. He sat beside a farrier's to gnaw the ham. Acrid smoke scented the air and the sky to the south was blackened. He guessed the stink of urine was on him like a rot, but he had become too accustomed to it to notice. The townspeople stood in the middle of the road and looked to the south with their hands on their hips or clasped as if in prayer. Their faces were gray with the dusk. Eyes flitted to him and back to the south again. When he had his fill he rose and kept walking.

Somehow in the darkness he lost his way and found himself on the banks of what he guessed to be either the Osage or the South Grand River. He did not stop to ponder which. He waded with the water rushing warm against the coolness of the thick night around him and swam when he had to. Toward the middle of the river he stopped from soreness and let the current take him, figuring it knew as much about where he was going as he did. Exhaustion hit him when he reached the far bank and he stretched out wet beneath a willow. He watched the moon rise through black branches. The current had taken the ham.

In the morning he stole two ears of corn from a nearby field and ate them raw. He could see no more smoke to the south, but a gray haze lay to the west and he wondered if he had let the current take him farther downriver than he had suspected. When he finished eating he threw the cobs into the field and started north.

The first town he came to was Clinton where he filched another ham from a smokehouse. He worked his way northeast with a vague desire of returning to Dawson Springs, to Rachel and Sue and Abner and his job of cleaning up semen. The ham lasted three days and by the time he finished it he was sick of both ham and traveling, and he'd forgotten about Dawson Springs. The country became hillier and the trees larger and the fields turned from poor, ragged farmers working corn to poor, ragged slaves working hemp and tobacco, and on the morning of the fifth day he stumbled onto a river so large that he knew it had to be the Missouri. He took off his boots and soaked his raw feet in the water.

He watched a steamboat, a big sidewheeler, work passed him east downriver and disappear around a bend. Its whistle tooted and shouts answered it and the hollow thunk of feet on planking made him realize he must be closer to a town than he appeared to be. He pulled his feet from the water and let them dry in the sun before he put his boots back on. He winced as a blister broke. He limped along the bank toward where the sidewheeler had disappeared.

The sidewheeler across the river had dropped its gangplank upon a dock covered with Federal soldiers and slaves either milling about or lying lazily in the sun. Black men and white men were just beginning to haul kegs and crates out of the hold. A thin, wizened, ancient man with a grotesquely large head was watching the work and writing clumsily with a pencil stub in a ledger. Jacob stood impotently for a moment, then stumbled into the water and swam to the other side. He crawled up the bank onto the dock and stood before the old man, panting and dripping.

"I need work," Jacob said as soon as the old man looked up.

"You're wet." The old man's voice was high, flutey, almost the voice of a woman.

"I need work. I can haul them boxes as well as anyone you got here. You give me a chance and I'll prove it to you. If I can't, you don't have to pay me nothing."

"These ain't my men. I'm just checking off my things. You're wet."

Jacob watched the men work. He had not eaten since he had finished the ham the morning before and hunger had lent a filmy edge to everything he was seeing. He looked at the old man again. "I'm hungry."

"I'm hungry, too," the old man said without looking up.

Jacob nodded and felt he would cry. He wondered how he could go through Osceola with only fear and emptiness and yet a simple thing like this was beyond his control. He tried to casually wipe the wetness from his nose and was reminded of its deformity.

"What kind of work do you do?" he asked. He heard his voice waver.

"I got me a store here," the old man said. "Dry goods and grocery. Well, me and my wife got it. Harriet. You'd like Harriet."

"Where's here?"

The old man looked up. The apparent strain on his feeble, stalk-like neck left his chin wobbling. "You don't know where you're at?"

"I've been wandering."

"Rocheport. Howard County. You do know that's in Missouri, don't you?"

Jacob nodded. He watched the men work and wiped his eyes. A lump had grown in his throat that even if it had been food he couldn't have swallowed. "I done that kind of work before."

The old man's neck gave out and he dropped his gaze to the ledger. "Where at?"

"Upton, Kentucky, first," Jacob said. "Then Osceola."

The old man's pencil quit moving. His head didn't come up, but his eyebrows lifted. He laid his pencil in the ledger's spine, then closed the book and lifted his eyes. "You say Osceola?"

"I was there until about four days ago."

The old man nodded and pursed his lips and sighed. The book fell with his hand. "God almighty, son, you should a said. You should a said!" His thin, fragile hand came up to rest on Jacob's shoulder. Sucked almost dry of the weight of life it might have lifted and fluttered away in the breeze, like a feather. "God damned jayhawkers."

"God damn them."

"You say you're hungry?"

"Ain't ate since yesterday morning."

"I'm kind of hungry myself. You come up to the house for breakfast. Name is Swisby. Alexander Swisby. You call me Swizz."

"Jacob Wilson," Jacob said.

"Let me finish up what I got to do here. Can you wait that long?"

"I can wait."

"Well, I hardly can. I'm hungry." Swizz opened the ledger and made marks on the page when certain boxes and kegs were unloaded.

By the time the work was done, Jacob had dripped almost dry. His stomach had so drawn in on itself that it held a dizzy emptiness. The lounging soldiers smoked pipes or spit tobacco. They looked no older than he was; some looked no older than Teague had been. But Teague was dead and locked in his youth, while these boys with luck would grow out of it. Jacob thought back on his life and marveled that he could really be who he had become. What he had become. He thought of Sarah and his heart ached dryly. Everything seemed so far away.

Swizz slapped his book shut and nodded with satisfaction. "I'll send you down with the wagon to pick this stuff up after Harriet's done fed you."

"You going to hire me?"

"I can't pay you much—I hardly make a living at it myself. I'm about as much of a storekeeper as that jackass we got in the White House is a president." Swizz faltered up the dock toward town, his old legs bent into strange angles. "You coming?"

Swizz led him up a knoll away from the river. Red-brick buildings lined each side of the street. Hickory, ash, and chestnut cast a shade that did nothing about the heat fermenting in Jacob's boots, that flowed up his legs and chest. Sweat stung in his ruptured blister; the edges of his vision flickered like heat lightning each time he inhaled. They turned left at a small corner saloon where a young, bony man watched them warily from his perch by the door. Swizz stopped in front of a small, red-brick house with a wide-spread hickory in the yard and a fence badly in need of paint and repair. The walk's exertion shone wetly down his back and under his arms.

"It ain't much," Swizz said, "but it's something."

"There a boarding house in town?"

"One son died," Swizz answered. "Got the consumption. The other up and left out west or out east or someplace. It's just me and Harriet. You'll like Harriet. The boys' room is empty and you can use it until you get on your feet."

"I thank you," Jacob said.

Swizz nodded jerkily and went up the dirt walk. Inside, the house smelled of bread. It held one large front room dimly lit by the hickory-filtered sunlight coming through the little windows, with a hearth on one wall and empty but for a large, quilt-spread bed against the other. A threshold led to a kitchen on the south side and a door was closed on the north. A pot clanged in the kitchen.

"Harriet," the old man called. "Harriet? We got company."

The kitchen clanging stopped, and a massive woman filled its threshold. Her hair was vividly gray and so haphazardly tied back that spikes of it shot out stiffly in every direction. Her neck and arms and waist were so tremendously thick that the seams of the gray print dress she wore had been altered with six-inch strips of a material less subject to fading. She might have been the ugliest woman Jacob had ever seen.

She looked him up and down with her hands resting on the shelf of her hips. She could have balanced her dishes there.

"Jacob Williams," Swizz explained.

"Wilson," Jacob said.

"Jacob Wilson. He come down the river asking for work." He nudged Jacob with a bony elbow. "This here's Harriet."

"We don't have no money to pay him." Her voice was as huge as she was. Jacob hoped she was angry, because if she was this imposing when she wasn't he had real fear for the future. "You look like you've been through some kind of hell, child," she said. "What happened to your nose?"

"He come up from Osceola," Swizz said.

Harriet's face did not soften, though a piteous edge came to her eyes. Swizz looked up at her hopefully. "We was hoping you could fix up some breakfast? Jacob, he hasn't eaten since he come up."

"You've already had yours."

"For the boy," Swizz said. "And maybe a little for me if there's extra."

Harriet nodded. "We got bacon and eggs and I can fry you up some potatoes. We got butter and bread. Jacob, did you say your name was?"

Jacob nodded.

"Throw in some pancakes, too," Swizz said, "if you would."

The hands on Harriet's hips bunched into fists nearly the size of anvils. Jacob thought of McGown. "Those god damned jayhawkers. If I ever get hold of one I'll pin him down with one hand and run my other up around his neck and pull until his head pops off. I swear."

"I seen her do it," Swizz said, his head nodding precariously with excitement. "I seen her do it to a dog once, and she does it to chickens all the time." He demonstrated the motion.

"I'll get cooking." Harriet nodded at Jacob. "Set there on the bed."

Jacob sat. The bed had no give and when he inched up the quilt he saw that it was only a mattress laid on bricks.

"We used to have a big spring bed," Swizz explained, "but it started to give and we'd roll into the middle. She rolled on me one night and didn't know it until the next morning. I was blue and she broke my wrist." He peeked into the kitchen, then came back and sat beside Jacob on the bed. "So what do you think of her?"

"She's a nice lady."

"You think she's pretty?"

"She's a nice lady."

"She used to be pretty, back when I married her. She was big then, too. Now she's just big."

"She probably was a big baby."

"Her daddy was so happy he'd finally married her off, even if it was to some damned old coot like me, that he bought me my store as the dowry." He paused. "Oh hell, she wasn't pretty then, neither. But you'll like her cooking."

"I ain't about to complain if I don't."

"That thing about the dog," Swizz said, "that's the god honest truth. A cur with the hydrophobia come down the street after the McKelly boy. McKelly, he come out with his musket, but it misfired. Everybody thought he'd end up having to shoot the boy and the dog both until Harriet picked the cur up by the back of the neck and popped its head off slick as a whistle. Never seen nothing like it in my life. It ain't so easy to do, even with a chicken."

"I bet."

"I can't even do it with a chicken."

"I bet," Jacob said again.

Pots and pans clanged and bacon sizzled. The smell of it came into the room, leaving Jacob breathless and his ears singing. The sputter of eggs joined the bacon. Jacob watched Harriet cross the kitchen threshold, pans in her hands, flour up her forearms, the complete enormity of her. He turned away when she looked at him.

"Come on in here," she ordered. "Set yourself down and fill yourself up."

Jacob went into the kitchen and sat obediently at an old, whitewashed table. Harriet set a plate in front of him and shoveled onto it from a set of skillets bacon and eggs, pancakes, and fried potatoes. Swizz cut bread and spread it with butter and handed a slice to him. Jacob tried to eat politely, but ended up emptying his plate about as fast as she could fill it. Swizz ate just as ravenously.

Harriet sat on a large, wide, sturdily built chair at the head of the table, four tree stumps still barked for legs, with her heavy freckled forearms crossed and resting in front of her. She watched silently as Jacob ate. When Jacob had finished he sat back and sighed and felt her eyes upon him. Swizz was still eating, his thin throat working frantically.

"Tell me about Osceola," Harriet said.

Jacob shrugged. There were things he wanted to remember and things he didn't. The yelping cry of Mr. Buchanan and the child crying for her father and McGown's eyes wrapped in their murky cloud. The scrubby, chin-less face of the sergeant, the smell of urine rising in the sun. The fear and the nothing. "Not much to tell. They burned it down."

"You know any of them that got killed?"

"The livery owner. Didn't really know him. He ordered me off of his property once."

She nodded and studied him, then went to the stove for a kettle and poured him a cup of tea. Jacob sipped it silently. Swizz had piled another stack of pancakes onto his plate.

"It's no wonder we ain't got no money," Harriet said, "the way you eat."

"I got me a high-boiling constitution," Swizz said.

She turned again to Jacob. He could smell the heavy scent of lard, of butter, the perfume of late summer flowers. "What did they do to you?"

"They didn't do nothing to me."

"You got a look in your eye. What did they do to you?"

"They busted up his nose," Swizz said around a mouthful.

"They didn't bust up his nose," Harriet said. "It couldn't a healed that fast." She looked at Jacob again, heavy gray eyes, a heavy gray face, the authority of her all around him. "What they do to you?"

"They busted up my boss pretty good," Jacob said. He could see the sergeant's leering face, hear his mocking laugh, feel the foul stream on the back of his neck, the dark spots it made in the dust. His anger and the power of the world both rising and breaking. "They broke his hand. Beat him up. They burned his store down."

"Huh." Harriet wiped her hand over her mouth. Her eyes never left Jacob. "I know that ain't all, but I'll let it go."

"Saw a preacher raid the church," Jacob said. "Saw him tear out everything and thank God for it and then burn the building down."

"That don't surprise me. Religion is only an excuse."

"You all take the oath?" Jacob asked.

Harriet flashed a glance at her husband. Swizz paused in his eating. "Swizz did," Harriet said.

"I did, if you're worried about it."

"You got to take the oath," Swizz said. "Can't hardly do business without it."

Harriet's lips grew thin. "One nice thing about being a woman is they don't come at you with that trash."

"Ain't you for the Union?" Jacob asked.

"Nobody," Harriet said, "forces me to do nothing."

"Ain't that the truth," Swizz said.

They sat in silence while Jacob sipped his tea and reveled as much as he was able in a full stomach. He was suddenly very tired. Swizz finished his pancakes and reached for the ones remaining. "Good God, man," Harriet said, "you ate two breakfasts and now you want a third? Those are for the child."

"He ain't eating them."

"You ain't eating them, neither. Don't you have work to do?"

"That's what I hired him for." Swizz nodded at Jacob as he speared a pancake. "You head on down to the livery for a buckboard and mule. Gather up my stuff sitting down there on the river."

"Get it yourself," Harriet said, "you lazy cuss."

"I hired him, didn't I? He's got to earn his pay, don't he?"

"He's got to rest, and that's what he's going to do." Harriet snatched the pancake off of her husband's fork and bit into it. "He just come from Osceola."

Swizz's mouth dropped open in protest, then snapped shut again. He rose and scuttled into the living room muttering. The front door screeched opened and closed. Harriet shook her head. Jacob drank his tea.

"You can tell me now," she said. "It won't go no further than my two ears. What they do to you down there?"

Jacob wanted to keep it inside, but he couldn't. "They threw me down in the street and pissed on me. That's all."

"That's all." She snorted. "Taking away dignity is a lot more than 'that's all.' Most men don't have much beyond it."

"At least I got a full belly now. I thank you."

Her hand came out to cover his hand and wrist and part of his forearm. "You ain't from Missouri," she said. "Where you from? Why'd you leave your people? You tell me the truth, child."

He stared into his teacup, the tea as dark as a night, as dark as Sarah's skin, as dark as her eyes. The longing inside was fearful. The fear of the knowledge he contained. "Ohio. I killed a man. A couple of men."

"Look at me, Jacob." He turned to her face. Large eyes, large nose, her hair in spikes around her head like a crown. "Was it justified? Did you do it to end an evil?"

Now he could feel McGown's eyes. McGown's ethereal, soulless, blown open eyes were in the house, in the kitchen, his presence a black haunting just over Harriet's shoulder. Harriet's soul was big in her eyes, as big as all heaven, as big as all God.

"They was Union soldiers plundering our farm."

"Why were they plundering?"

"They just was."

She sat back and nodded. Her heavy hand left his and trailed back across the table like some lumbering herd animal. "And so you run." She sighed. "You go into the boys' bedroom and get yourself some sleep."

"They hanged a friend of ours," Jacob said. It was all rising desperately within him. "They crossed the river and there's this cottonwood there and then there was Sarah and Isaac. They strung him up as big as life . . ." He began to cry.

Harriet's hand crossed the table again to rest on his. "You get some sleep, child," she said.

Chapter Twelve

Jacob lived with the Swisbys through the rest of the fall, through the winter, into the spring. He worked at their store two blocks off of the river, doing what he had done for Mr. Buchanan, sweeping and stocking, and he hauled supplies from the landing once a week. He took his meals at the Swisby table and he slept in their sons' bedroom. They could pay him hardly a pittance, but he had no expenses beyond the drinking he started to do at the Liberty Bell, the saloon just above the landing. He would drink just until his head went dizzy and would never drink beyond that. Drinking beyond that made it too easy to think of the farm and the valley, of Cyrus's hands resting on the cabin table, the smell of earth laden with earth's blood, that last, terrifying look in Clara's eyes. Dark skin would shine in lantern light, dark hair, dark eyes, a smile. When he drank beyond he would stumble to the river and stare north into the Perche Hills. He would find himself crying.

The talk in the Liberty Bell throughout the fall and winter was of Mc-Clellan taking command of the Army of the Potomac and Lee the Army of Northern Virginia. The talk was of the guerrilla raids throughout Missouri, uprooted railroads and murdered postal carriers, ripped telegraph lines, Union men killed and southern men killed, bodies hanging in trees like banners, brothers and cousins and neighbors found dead in fields, farmers fleeing penniless, despair framing once proud faces, streams of fugitive slaves heading into Kansas. Guerrillas burned out a one-hundred-and-sixty-foot span over the Little Platte River, and a train carrying ninety passengers plunged into its gorge. A little band of farm boys led by a man from Maryland named Charlie Quantrill was raiding Jackson County. Jacob listened to the stories. It was the first time he had heard the name.

The spring came and the snow lost its grip. Trees budded and flowered and the early summer danced in the scent of blossoms and fields, of earth, memories lingering in the streets. Talk in the bar turned to Jim Lane and

Doc Jennison and their bands of jayhawkers—they'd burned out Dayton in Cass County and Columbus in Johnson and driven off their people. Curtis defeated Price at Pea Ridge in northwest Arkansas and but for the guerrillas ended the Confederate threat in Missouri. Quantrill had dashed into Independence just east of Kansas City and attacked the Federal cavalry there and left two dead guerrillas behind. Jacob thought that perhaps he should be going home. Maybe he and Sarah could head west, maybe to Nebraska or California. He liked to think about her on a farm on the plains, or maybe a ranch beneath the foothills of the Bighorns, or tending a store with the Pacific murmuring in the distance. He didn't like it here; there was too much violence here. He was leaning on the bar only slightly drunk and longing for possible futures when a young man sat beside him.

The young man was as tall as Jacob with a dark beard and long, dark hair that curled against his shoulders. He wore faded denim trousers and a butternut shirt with embroidered flowers running up each side of his chest. He nodded at Jacob, then turned to the barkeep.

"Give me a shot there, bucko, of some whiskey I can afford."

The barkeep was a waif of a man with heavily oiled hair and a garter on a biceps so thin it kept slipping to his elbow. He set a shot glass on the bar and filled it, his eyes jumping between the faces and the glass. The man lifted it to Jacob. "Here's to all things good and eternal," he said as he drained it.

Jacob drank from his beer and studied the man over the edge of the glass. A wild face, wild blue eyes blazing.

"Someone tells me you was at Osceola," the man said.

Jacob set down his glass. He didn't say anything.

"You and me, we got something in common. We know about jay-hawkers."

Jacob glanced at him. "How's that?"

"I just come from Council Grove, Kansas. A jayhawker named Arthur Baker jilted my sister, and when my daddy went to complain about it the bastard blew him down a stairwell with a shotgun." He ordered another whiskey and lifted it to lips that held a smile without humor. "Here's to law and order. To all things good and eternal."

"Hell," Jacob said.

"Name is Bill Anderson," the young man said. He smiled again and held out his hand.

Jacob took it. It was warm and callused and seemed to burn with the heat showing in his eyes. "Jacob Wilson."

"What you do in Rocheport, Jacob?"

"Work in a store."

"Hell, I figure that after Osceola you'd be out in the bush with Quantrill. Burn a few farms, tear up a few railroads, kill a few Yanks and jayhawkers. You appear capable."

"I took the oath," Jacob said.

"Hell, everybody's taken the oath." Bill watched him and drank and swallowed. "I want to show you something." He pulled a cord from his pocket so white that in the bar shadows it glowed. "Stole this out of a church. It's silk."

"Nice."

"You know what it's for?"

"No."

"You see any knots in it?"

"No."

"There will be." Bill put the cord back in his pocket.

"You going to tell me what it's for?"

Bill smiled again, but said nothing.

Jacob drank his beer. He felt uneasy with the way his head was beginning to swim. "Well," he said, "I got to work in the morning." He stood.

Bill Anderson nodded. He lifted the glass the barkeep had just filled. "To all things good and eternal," he said again.

Jacob finished his beer and settled Tobias's old slouch hat on his head.

The warmth and humidity in the night was as heavy as its darkness. The Missouri murmured as the Ohio had done and he thought about home, about Clara and Cyrus and Tobias and Isaac. About Sarah. He studied the stars, so eternally alone, infinite distances from the touch of another. Empathy is a powerful thing and soon they were swimming in his drunken tears. He wiped his eyes with his sleeve and the stars settled back into their eternal places. For some, heaven is unattainable, but perhaps with such loneliness it wasn't worth having.

In each shadow on his stumbling walk back to the house waited the memories, waited Teague lying at the cabin threshold with his neck split open, waited McGown, the glint of his eyes peeking from corners, scuttling along fences, looking down like prowling cats from the trees. Jacob hurried from one shadow to the next with the weight of those eyes on his shoulders, his mind. He stepped quietly into the Swisby house and listened with relief to Swizz snoring feebly—Swizz was an old man who had grown far more frail over the winter, as if in lying in bed each night he transferred his strength to his wife. Jacob went to his bedroom and closed the door behind him.

He had drunk too much and the room when he lay on the bed spun around him. He braced his hand on the wall to steady it. He breathed deeply. The stink of the beer was on his breath, the frigid winter loneliness of the stars within it. Why, he thought, why? He was too young for such a fundamentally simple question.

Toward the end of the month a slave in the Perche Hills found in a cottonwood a Union man strung up by his neck. Like Tobias. Someone shot a soldier in the head just outside of Rocheport. When Jacob mentioned it over breakfast to the Swisbys, Harriet looked up and looked down again and she rose from the table to tend the fire. Swizz just kept eating. Jacob spent the day pondering it.

"You know Harriet Swisby?" he asked Bill that night at the Liberty Bell.

The brilliance in Bill's eyes had somehow tainted. Drink, perhaps. "I do."

"So what do you think of her?"

"She's a fine woman. Have you every killed anyone, Jake?"

"I'm thinking that maybe she . . ."

"Have you ever killed anyone, Jake?"

"No," Jacob said. He stared down into his beer.

"What do you suppose it feels like?"

"To die?"

"To kill."

Jacob fell silent. Why, he thought again. "I guess it feels awful, like something in you died when you killed the fella. Maybe you have to feel haunted for the rest of your life."

"By the fella?"

"I don't know."

"By God?"

"By the fella, I guess."

"You think that's how it is?"

"I'm just guessing."

Bill nodded. "You know what I think about it? I think if you're haunted, you're haunted by your memory. The whole trick is to trick your memory, but that wouldn't likely be something easy to do. But it would be that or go crazy." He drained his glass and sat back to dig from his pants pocket the white silk cord. He studied it silently.

"You got a knot in it," Jacob said.

"What?"

"I said you got a knot in it. On the end."

Bill studied the knot solemnly. The barkeep filled his glass and he drained it. Finally he put the cord back in his pocket. "You want to do me a favor, Jake?"

"Sure," Jacob said.

"It'll take you some time. A couple, three days."

"I got to work."

"Harriet won't mind. She's a fine woman."

Jacob studied him, then nodded. "All right."

"One more drink," Bill said.

Bill ordered a whiskey and Jacob another beer. When they went outside, Jacob looked at the sky thinly overcast, the clouds covering the moon with a sheen.

"You ain't got a horse, do you?" Bill asked.

"About the only thing I got is this busted nose."

"I got one for you. You can keep it. It's a good horse."

"Where'd you get it?"

"I just got it is all."

Jacob followed Bill to the river. They walked past the dock and into the trees and up the river toward where Jacob had first come upon it. An ancient, silent man with only one eye was waiting there with a skiff. He ferried them across, his hands tight on the oars, the water swirling from their blades, his socket a black shadow. He did not speak and they did not speak to him.

"He's an ornery fella," Bill said when they had reached the other side and the man had disappeared back into the darkness.

"Who was he?"

"Just an ornery fella."

The night was warm, the mosquitoes whining. Hidden in the trees were two mares, one piebald and the other a gray. Federal cavalry saddles and saddlebags, Federal cavalry bedrolls and tack. Tall and lean and muscular with a bright alertness in their eyes, not the typical broken-down nags of the Union cavalry.

"The piebald's yours," Bill said as he mounted the gray.

Jacob ran his hand down its warm, trembling withers. He was not familiar with riding horses and he could feel the horse sense it as he mounted. "Where'd you get her, Bill?"

"There's two Navy Colt revolvers in the saddlebag there on your right, compliments of Harriet Swisby."

"She keep you supplied, Bill?"

"Stick them in your belt. Keep them close."

"You with Quantrill?"

"What?"

"You with Quantrill?"

"She's a fine woman," Bill said. "Don't you ever forget that."

Jacob reached back into the saddlebag and took out a heavy pistol, cold even in the summer night. He reached back again and his fingers fumbled upon a powder flask and an ammunition pouch heavy with lead balls. He slung them over his shoulder.

"I ain't much on shooting. I ain't much on riding, neither."

"You will be on both," Bill said, "by the time all is said and done." He turned his horse away from the river and guided it in a walk into the hills.

Jacob had to kick the piebald's ribs to get her going. She followed the gray and looked over her shoulder questioningly. Jacob shrugged and tried to adjust to the saddle. "Where we going?" he asked Bill.

"To Freeman first, over on the border. We're meeting a friend of mine."

"Then where?"

Bill looked back over his shoulder. The thin moonlight shown in his eyes. "To Council Grove, Kansas."

Jacob followed silently. The piebald shifted beneath him and he shifted with it as he thought he should do. The pistols in his belt felt like new-grown appendages. "Why me, Bill? I ain't nothing but a shopkeeper."

"And I ain't nothing but a farmer," Bill said. "I figure we're all more than what we think."

The piebald plodded onward. Jacob looked at the sky, the blank, empty, unseeing, lonely sky. "I lied to you back there, Bill."

"About what?"

"About never having killed nobody. I killed a couple of fellas up in Ohio. Union soldiers. I used an ax, though. I ain't never shot nobody."

"God damn, Jake. I wish you would have told me that before."

"Why?"

"It would have saved me a lot of anguish."

They rode west for over an hour, past the hemp and corn and tobacco fields, through the hills, the trees silent around them, the air silent around them growing cool and cooler in the hollows, the moon behind them casting weird, almost living, shadows. The piebald moved gently, rising and falling, her head down but her ears up, a slight trembling in her sides. The pistols were heavy and uncomfortable. Jacob pulled one free and aimed it at the moon.

They reached a creek heavily grown with willow and oak. Bill stopped and looked up at the stars, at the illimitable blackness they occupied. "What's this here?" Jacob asked.

"This here's the Blackwater. We'll follow it for a while. There's a couple of towns along the way, Nelson and Sweet Springs and Valley City. We just ride through or around and we don't talk to nobody, you understand?"

"Sure," Jacob said.

"If we got to talk, I do the talking."

"Sure. We going to stop anytime?"

"When we need to," Bill said.

The rode in silence up the creek, munching on apples and bacon Bill had stored in one of his saddlebags. Jacob shoved the pistol into his belt and dozed fitfully. With the sound of the water he dreamed he was standing in the yard back home beneath a high moon. Through the four-paned hearth light coming through the window he could see Cyrus sharpening a scythe at the table. Clara crouched by the fire, her misshapen face huge and purple, her eyes burning like coals, blood outlining her teeth. McGown was lying dead on the floor, but staring at him with eyes full of life. Teague was crawling at his feet and the ax was still in his neck and its handle scraped across the floor. Sarah bounding through it all, her skirt bunched in her fists, as lovely as a nymph out of some Grecian tale.

"Jesus," Jacob said.

"Jesus what?" Bill answered.

"Jesus nothing. Just Jesus."

"Keep quiet."

"You expecting somebody out here?"

"Yanks are too fond of their beds to be out this time of night. But I've been wrong before."

All night they rode around or through tiny hamlets, by small farms with shadow buildings and dogs lifting their heads to bark warnings. Once Bill raised his hand and Jacob reined in the piebald and gripped one of the revolvers, but after a minute Bill led him on again. The moon set with them still riding. The stars began to blaze, the constellations flaming. The Milky Way drifted across the sky.

"You know where they say the Milky Way comes from?" Jacob asked.

"Where?"

"The tit of a god."

"Hell," Bill said.

"It's the truth."

"I'd like to see a tit like that."

The sky behind them lightened to silver, and still they rode on. Jacob's legs ached miserably and he thought he might have a blister on his right buttock. The creek grew blacker as the sky lightened, as if the night were draining into it. It was narrower now than it had been when they started.

"We anywhere close to Freeman yet?" Jacob asked.

"We won't reach Freeman until noon."

"Who's this friend of yours?"

"Archie Clement," Bill said. "You'll like him."

The stars faded as the black turned to silver, the silver to blue. The sunlight on the back of Jacob's neck contrasted with the air almost frosty around him. He thought of that semidream he had had during the night. He shivered in the new morning.

"We'll rest the horses a bit," Bill said.

He dismounted. The gray wandered to the water and drank. The piebald followed it without Jacob's approval, and when Jacob stepped down his foot caught in the stirrup and he stumbled. He had been riding for so long that standing again held a stabbing shock. Bill groaned and stretched beneath an oak and watched the horses. Jacob adjusted the pistols and sat in the dewy weeds. He took off Tobias's hat and lay it beside him.

"How long we resting?"

"A half hour or so."

"You sure think strange things riding all night. Almost like dreams."

A breeze had risen with the sun and caught Bill's long curls, lifting them from his shoulder. "What you dream?"

Jacob shrugged. "About my sweetheart."

"You got a sweetheart? Where at?"

Jacob thought for a moment. "Dawson Springs. In Kentucky."

"She pretty?"

"Pretty young. Yeah, she's pretty."

"How old?"

"Sixteen, maybe."

"She's just getting ripe," Bill said. "What's her name?"

He thought about this, too. "Sarah. You got a girlfriend?"

"Nope. I just got my sisters." Bill closed his eyes. "Don't think about girls on a ride. It's misery sitting in a saddle all swollen up. The only thing it does is remind you of what you ain't doing."

The horses ambled over to a patch of bank sedge to graze. Jacob lay on the bank and let the soil take his pain, a sediment Christ. He closed his eyes and studied the shifting reds and yellows on his eyelids. He could hear Bill Anderson breathing beside him.

"What we going to do in Council Grove?" Jacob asked.

"You can probably guess. Let's get going." They stood and stretched and the blister on Jacob's ass was a hot little ember. He mounted carefully. Bill led him up the stream.

The sun was a quarter of the way across the sky by the time they reached Kingsville. They rode among the merchants and women and the farmers preparing for their day in the fields, all staring, all silent. Jacob looked at their faces as he would penned livestock. Bill never turned his gaze from the road. He kept his forearms over the grips of his Colt revolvers.

The land rolled less as they left the river, trees green, fields green and growing, the heat rising like a living thing, crows cawing raucously, the jokesters of this world. Farmers looked away as they passed, or waved or tipped their hats, all with a war-born hesitancy. Jacob rode behind Bill, drowsy in the sun, his eyes drifting aimlessly. He was tired of riding. The land gradually flattened into hummocks and heat-blistered grasslands. So many things he had seen and done; so much he knew or needed to.

"Did you hang that soldier outside of Rocheport?" Jacob asked.

"All things good and eternal," Bill answered.

They reached a tiny hamlet just before noon, a row of houses along each side of the road, a store, a scabby little hotel. Dogs lay in the little shade cast by the buildings; a sow sunned herself in the street. Bill dismounted and hitched his mare to a rail on the shaded side and Jacob followed his example. A blue tick hound lifted its head to study him complacently. The piebald stamped a hoof and closed her eyes.

"Damn," Jacob said. He took off Tobias's hat and wiped a thumbful of sweat from its band. "I can't wait for fall."

Bill smiled. That full-of-life blue in his eyes blazed disconcertingly. "This here's Freeman."

"I kind of figured. Where's this fella you know?"

"Archie. He's around."

Bill planted his hands against the small of his back and stretched. He looked both ways down the empty street and ambled toward the far edge of town. When he tapped the sow with his toe, it grunted its displeasure at being bothered and studied him with a bloodshot eye. He walked to the last building on the street and without knocking opened the door and went inside. Jacob followed.

They were in a front parlor, with a horsehair sofa against a wall and a mirror above it. A strange mix of smells in the air, staleness and apples, perfume and sweat, cooking grease. Bill stepped into the body of the house while Jacob studied his own face in the parlor mirror. He didn't like the look of it. He turned away before looking at his eyes.

Bill suddenly laughed. "Hey, Jake. Come on in here and see this."

"In a minute," Jacob said.

"Come now, before all the fun is done."

Jacob left the mirror and walked into a living room. Bill was grinning from a door on the other side. Inside the door on a bed with the bedsheets scattered lay a boy and a girl. The boy was small with a square face and blond hair and high cheekbones, large ears covering half of each side of his face. He had wide, square, naked shoulders and the first scraggled beginnings of a beard. He groaned and buried his head in his arms and rolled on his side away from the girl.

The girl was curled like a fetus with a sheet tangled around her. Her blond hair was loose and one eye purpled and swollen. She had her hands between her legs and the sheet there was stained maroon, blood in smears on her fingers. She looked at Jacob and Bill and seemed to have no strength to cover her childish breasts. She might have been fourteen years old.

"Hell, Archie," Bill said. "What you been doing?"

"What's it look like I been doing?" the boy asked. His arms muffled his voice.

"You taken to fucking babies?"

"I ain't done nothing she didn't want me to do."

"I'm willing to bet she didn't want that eye or that blood between her legs," Jacob said.

The boy released his head and looked at Jacob from gray eyes soured almost black. "Who the fuck are you?" He rolled onto his belly and reached beneath the bed and came up with a Colt revolver just like the two in Jacob's belt and aimed it at Jacob's head. "Who the fuck are you?"

"Take it easy," Bill said.

"Who the fuck is he?" Archie demanded.

"He's a friend," Bill said. "Tell him you're a friend, Jake."

"I'm a friend," Jacob said.

"The hell if you are," Archie said.

"The hell if I ain't."

Archie sat silent and naked with the gun still aimed at Jacob. His privates were as maroon as the sheet between the girl's legs. Blood in smears on the mattress, on the quilt kicked onto the floor. She moaned again and Archie glanced at her, but he kept his gun aimed at Jacob. "She was a virgin," he said. "Virgins bleed."

"Virgins get black eyes, too?"

"You're pushing your luck about as far as it will go, friend," Archie said.

Jacob didn't say anything more. A hatred rose within him for this boy rapist that was stronger than any he had ever felt but for McGown. In some strange way stronger than even that.

The girl whimpered and rolled onto her belly with her knees tucked up beneath her. Her hair slipped down off her shoulder blades to reveal a thin, rib-striped back and the narrow hips of a girl. Skinny buttocks with the bones showing through. Archie spat on the floor and kicked his leg free of the tangled sheets. "What time is it?" He scratched at his groin with the pistol muzzle.

"About noon," Bill said. "We got to go."

"Yeah." Archie stood and stretched and looked down distastefully at his privates. He muttered some curse beneath his breath. He was a full head shorter than Jacob and except for the hair on his face and between his legs he looked hardly older than the girl. "Look at what she done to me."

"Well, Christ, Archie," Bill said. "Nobody said you had to fuck her."

"She did." He grinned.

"Get dressed."

"I'm getting." Archie reached for his pants.

"We'll wait for you outside," Bill said.

"Well, go get waiting, then." Archie slipped one foot into his pants. He had left the gun on the mattress.

Jacob followed Bill outside. He sat beside the house and let the sun soak into his face, burning him clean of an unseen foulness. The sow lay on the far side of the street. The dogs had retreated with the shadows to press themselves against the foundations.

"Hell, Bill, how do you know this guy?"

"Archie's all right."

"How do you know him?"

"I know him is all."

"He shouldn't a been doing that."

Bill leaned against the house beside him. Across the street, a heavy woman came out of a building, glanced at them, and bustled as fast as the heat allowed toward the store. "That all depends on if she wanted him to or not. Archie, he has a way of making them want him to."

"She wouldn't a wanted that."

"There's funny people in the world," Bill said.

In a few minutes Archie swaggered out in a wide-brimmed black leather hat, a white cotton shirt, and his denim trousers. A pistol shoved into his belt and the wide scabbard of a Bowie knife on the side. "So we going?" he asked.

"Right now," Bill said.

Archie nodded and looked down at Jacob. "What you say your name was?"

"That there's Jake," Bill said.

"Hey, Jake." Archie held out his hand. Jacob took it and Archie pulled him to his feet. "Sorry about that in there. I felt a little ornery sitting there naked."

"You shouldn't do that to women," Jacob said.

"She wasn't no woman. She was just a girl." Archie studied the sky, the street. The air caught the dust and held it. "You ride all night?"

"All night."

"You need sleep."

"We can't sleep in town," Bill said. "You don't know who might come along."

"There's them box elders on the border."

"There is."

"Then I'll meet you there at sundown. Right now I think I'll go in and have another whack at her." Archie grinned and slid his knife into and out of its scabbard. He laughed and stepped back into the house.

"Boys," Bill said. "What you going to do?"

They walked to the hotel where a silent, gray woman served them roast beef and beans. When they mounted again, the piebald walked only with protest. The fat woman had come out of the store, and she and the dogs watched them silently. Bill rode on as he had before, his eyes on the road, his curls resting on his shoulders. Jacob studied the house Archie and the girl were in as they passed it.

They stopped on the prairie at a stand of small box elders. Bill dismounted and took the tack from the gray and hobbled her. She grazed for a minute before closing her eyes. Jacob stripped the piebald and she did the same. He joined Bill in staring across the land to the west that lay opened like a book before them. Grass as tall as he was waving gently, the clean western wind carrying the ripples from miles distant in shades of green and blue and red. The smell of it foreign on the air, the feel of it foreign inside him.

"There she is," Bill said.

"What we going to do in Council Grove?" Jacob asked.

"We'll be riding all night again. Get some sleep."

Jacob took off his hat and studied it, studied his hands, the hands that had held the ax, still cracked and callused with the work of the farm, stained even yet with its soil. He raised his face to the western horizon. These plains were like the plains of Jordan, and Joshua drew not his hand back. These were the ways of God and men and Jacob did not understand them. He was eighteen.

He lay in the shade, but when he awoke the sun was low and in his face and the heat had tightened his skin. He sat and cursed and failed to spit the dryness from his mouth. Someone shoved a canteen in his face and he took it. He looked up as he drank to see Archie smiling down upon him. "Gets a little thirsty," Archie said, "lying in the sun." Jacob nodded. The water was warm and tasted of iron.

"So where you from, Jake?" Archie asked.

Jacob handed back the canteen. "Ohio."

"What's a damned Yankee like you doing in Missouri?"

"I'm in Missouri because I killed a couple of soldiers in Ohio."

Archie squatted beside him. He pulled his knife free of its scabbard and played mumblety-peg in the turf. The blade shone redly. "How'd you kill them? You shoot them?"

"I pretty near cut one private's head off with an ax. I clubbed a Union sergeant to death with the butt side of it. First I cut off his hand."

The knife thunked into the ground. "Damn, Jake." Archie shook his head in admiration. The grin on his face was a gash across his youth. "Damn."

Bill groaned. Archie tapped his shoulder with the canteen as he came up to his knees. Bill took it and rinsed his mouth. He looked up at Archie. "You done with your fun?"

"I'm done with it."

"Then we best get going."

"How you planning on getting there?"

"Follow the Marais des Cygnes."

They rose and stretched and groaned and cursed and freed the horses from their hobbles. Bill saddled the gray, and while Archie took care of the piebald Jacob went into the box elders to relieve himself. The urine came out in a hot, hissing stream, as if the sun's heat had boiled down his spirits. When he came back, Bill and Archie were mounted and waiting for him.

Jacob mounted. The boil on his buttock hissed and he grimaced. Archie grinned his grin that was not a grin. "Saddle sore?"

"A little."

"I'm sore down there, too, but not in the ass." He laughed and slapped the neck of his horse, a blue roan, with his reins.

They moved almost silently into the sunset and the dusk that followed it. The sky faded from red and orange and rose into silver, into gray, the grass and horses and men fading with it, the sun gathering into its arms all colors. They rode southwest, the land gently rolling, treeless hills, the piebald plodding slowly with her head up, the grass in places whispering against her chin. Bill rode as he always did. Archie followed with his head tilted to the right as if seeking his shoulder's support. Jacob watched the first stars come out.

In two hours they reached a winding river, dark and clotted, a scar on the face of the earth. Trees and brush lined its edge which they skirted. "The Marais de Cygnes," Bill said. "We follow this until morning."

"Any fun along the way?" Archie asked. "We could stop in Osawatomie. Have a drink, maybe."

"We ain't stopping in Osawatomie."

"Stanton, then. That little shit town."

"We ain't stopping nowhere. This is business, Arch."

"Let's ask the ax boy back there." Archie turned in his saddle and grinned. "What do you say, Jake? I'll find you a virgin as sweet as what's-her-name back in Freeman. It'll take the edge off you."

"Let's just get this done," Jacob said.

The stream flowed from the west and they followed it, the darkness sliding over them like a lid over a pot, the tree branches grasping beside them. The wind carried western smells that Jacob imagined to come from buffalo, from the war paint on Indians' faces. Before the moon's rising the darkness was complete, and he could only know where he was going by picking from the sound of the wind the plodding of Archie's blue roan in front of him. The stars brilliant above him, the Milky Way a white swath, the dark universe cracked to let in the light beyond it.

They passed through Osawatomie. A lantern in a window cast a yellow light onto the street and Jacob thought of home, of the river, of Clara and Cyrus and Isaac, of Sarah. As they left the town and again entered darkness the thought became so real it floated before him, so real that he heard its mute voices, heard Mabel's lowing and the river, then heard the heavy creak of the rope in the cottonwood beyond it. He cried silently to the stars. He prayed to a God who had no reason to take an interest in him for the moon to rise, and when it did, and its silver light drove away the thoughts, he was thankful. The wind was strong and clean and whispered in the grass. They rode all night, keeping the trees off their left shoulders.

The river turned north. At dawn they worked into the trees and crossed the river. To the west lay rolling hills with scars on their slopes showing the red earth like blood, the sky still black above them, the grass chest-high and studded with red and purple flowers. A trail as old as the scars and the hills it crawled over worked toward the western horizon. "We sleep until dusk," Bill said, "then follow the Santa Fe to Council Grove."

"How much farther?" Jacob asked.

"Three hours."

"It'll be a hell of a long three hours," Archie said.

Jacob freed the piebald of her tack as Bill hobbled his mare. The piebald gamboled to the river like a pony to drink and graze, its coat where the saddle had girdled it wet and slick and steaming in the early morning air. Jacob lay the saddle at the base of a cottonwood and looked up into its branches. He picked the saddle up again and moved out into the grass.

"Don't you like the company?" Archie asked.

Jacob looked back. The boy was grinning. "Don't like the trees."

"Trees never hurt nobody."

Jacob ran his finger along the brim of Tobias's hat and flicked the sweat into the grass. He lay with the saddle under his head and only the pure blue sky above him.

"You're going to get burned all to hell," Archie called.

"Then I'll get burned," Jacob said. He fell to sleep thinking of Sarah.

Chapter Thirteen

Jacob awoke with the sun's dying. It was a fitful sleep and he awoke tired, with his skin pulled tighter across his face, the dry smell of the enveloping grass surrounding him. His nose ached unaccountably. He scowled and sat and spat and looked wearily toward the trees.

Archie and Bill were sitting by the river with their backs against cottonwood trunks, watching the water, Archie playing mumblety-peg in the grass. They were talking low and when Archie looked toward Jacob they stopped and he smiled. "Sleeping Beauty awakes."

"Sleeping Beauty never had a face like this."

"Ugly shows character," Bill said.

"You ain't ugly," Jacob said. "That mean you don't have no character?"

Jacob stood and stretched and studied the sky, the prairie. Clouds moved in scraps across the horizon, shoring up the sun and casting the grass into premature shadow. A whirring cloud rose in the far southern distance, perhaps locusts. He lifted the saddle and carried it to the trees and dropped it beside Archie without looking at him. He went back into the trees and urinated and drank from the river, then plunged his head beneath the water. A different world under there, the water warmer than the Ohio but otherwise the feel of it the same. He came back wiping water from his face, blinking against the familiar ache in his nose and his memories.

Bill and Archie were standing beside the horses, watching the sun grow brilliant as it dropped beneath the clouds. The grass turned orange, the world it covered empty but for long, slithering shadows.

"What's going on?" Jacob asked. He fetched two apples and a sliver of bacon from Bill's saddlebag.

"Three hours west," Bill said. "Baker is a fat guy with his hair just beginning to gray. I get him. You two can split between yourselves whoever might be with him."

"Maybe we can find you a ax, Jake." Archie grinned.

"You ever killed anyone?" Jacob asked.

"I could," Archie said.

"Could ain't the same. You ever killed anyone?"

"Sure. All the time." He paused. "I can kill somebody."

"Hell," Jacob said, and he spat. Archie watched him silently.

Bill pulled the silk cord from his pocket and studied it. The breeze swung it, silver in the sunlight, like a pendulum marking an alien time. He swung the knot up into his palm, studied it, then shoved it back into his pocket.

"Let's get on with it," he said.

They saddled the horses and followed the trail in silence. The night came; the wind died to a soft flutter.

The hours passed. Just as the moon began to rise, Bill reined on a small knoll and waited for the others to join him. His broad back was silhouetted against the moonlight and his hair framed his head. A few house lights glowed yellow below them and Jacob could smell water.

"There she is," Bill said.

"Home sweet home." Archie grinned.

"Which is Baker's?" Jacob asked.

"You just follow me," Bill said.

They descended toward the sleeping town, the horses moving almost silently. The house lights wavered like stars reflecting on water. Jacob rode with his arms tight to his body where he could feel the heavy reassurance of the pistol grips against his forearms.

They dismounted in front of a livery and hitched their horses to the rail. Across the street was a dry goods store and beside it a house with a single light burning. The streets were deserted. Occasional shadows passed in windows. Bill pointed with his chin at the house across the street.

"Looks like he's home," he said.

They quietly studied the house. Jacob ran his hand down the piebald's withers, over its brisket. With the feel of its breath on his shoulder a calmness entered him that faded away to the nothing he had felt at Osceola. Bill patted the gray's flank, then pulled his pistols free from his belt.

"Archie, you go on in that house and tell them you want to buy whiskey. You get them in the store."

"Why don't we just go in the house and kill them?"

"You just do what I say."

Archie shrugged and stepped into the darkness covering the street. Jacob heard him knock and had to step back away from the light that splashed out the door as it opened. Archie muttered with the shadow standing in the door, then two shadows left the house and crossed the yard to the store with Archie's shadow following. The door opened and closed and a lantern light glowed in the window, throwing a four-paned light on the road.

"Let's go, Jake."

They crossed the street. Bill had to put one of his pistols away to open the store door. He went in and Jacob followed.

Two men sat at a table with a whiskey bottle upon it. Archie stood to the side, grinning his black grin. One of the men was heavy with hair just beginning to gray. He looked like Bill said he would. The other was younger and taller with the beginning of jowls and a round, pink face wearing a hint of beard. An odor of horses upon him, even from this distance. Perhaps he ran the livery. They must have been laughing, for smiles were frozen on their faces.

"Bill," the heavy one said.

Bill pulled his second revolver free and aimed both pistol barrels at Baker's belly and fired. The explosion was deafening and the smell of feces and gunpowder was sudden and almost overwhelming. Archie pulled free his Bowie knife, its blade flashing in the lantern light, and moved toward the second man, but Jacob raised his pistol and fired in front of him into the man's face.

Baker was lying on the floor, whimpering like a child. Jacob's shot had knocked the younger man back against his chair with his spine bridged from seat edge to chair back and his arms rigid along his sides. He was trembling. The bullet had entered his mouth and left his skull just behind the right joint of his jaw. White teeth shone on the table like popped buttons. Archie was rubbing his ear.

"Hell, Jake, I wanted to do it."

"He ain't dead yet."

The younger man's eye were wide and staring, his whole body locked in spasm. His face seemed to say that the afterlife from his vantage point was shockingly unpleasant. Perhaps it awaited him. Perhaps those not elected are allowed in that final moment to see what will be denied. Jacob felt nothing about it either way beyond perhaps a faint jealousy. He leveled his pistol again.

"You let Archie finish him, Jake," Bill said. "He needs this."

"Well, Jesus," Archie said with disgust, "he didn't leave me much, did he?"

Archie drew his knife across the man's throat in a thin red line that suddenly erupted to arch and splatter blood on the table and the man's feet. Archie jumped back with a laugh. The man gurgled, then collapsed into the chair and rolled off of it to lie beside Baker. Baker was crying on the floor and looking up at Bill with a string of spit joining the corner of his lip to the rough wood planking. Bill had his revolver pointed at Baker's forehead. Smoke rose from its muzzle in a single acrid curl.

"Can I do him?" Archie asked. "Can I?"

Bill did not speak. He kicked Baker onto his back and pointed the gun at the ridge of bone between the man's eyes. The spittle lay across the man's trembling and sweaty cheek. His eyes were wide and staring. Finally Bill nodded and stepped back. Archie leaped forward delightedly. Bill held him back with a hand on his chest.

"There's a cellar. Throw him down it. Throw the other fella down it, too."

Jacob took the younger man's legs and waited for Archie to take the shoulders.

"Hell," Archie said. "He ain't dead even yet."

"Give him a little time," Bill said.

They stumbled to the dark maw of a door in the back that Bill had opened, and they tossed the bloody hunk down the stairs. It thudded heavily and a gurgling rose from the darkness. Bill kicked Baker in his wounds and Baker, screaming, obeyed the prodding and crawled like a worm to the door. He left a red smear flecked with feces behind him. As he stuck his head over the threshold, Bill pushed him with the flat of his boot down the stairs into the darkness. Body hit body with a sound like two lovers meeting in a strange and forbidden tryst. Baker screamed incoherently. Bill closed the door and slid a box in front of it.

"Get outside. See if anyone's coming."

"Ain't you going to finish him?" Archie asked.

"I'll finish him." Bill picked up the lamp from the table. "Get outside."

Jacob followed Archie out the door. A man was running toward them in underdrawers with their unbuttoned flap hanging loose and slapping against the back of his legs. He held a musket that he dropped when he saw Jacob's pistols. Jacob raised one of them and aimed at the man's forehead. The man's face blanched and he turned and ran, his buttocks flashing. Jacob was about to fire but saw in the thin lamplight coming through the window a shadow above the man's shoulder blacker than the surrounding darkness. In the middle of it were two cold eyes. McGown was squatting in front of the livery, the shadow now possessing a hint of legs, of arms; the foggy hint of the Federal sergeant's coattails were wisps that fled and dissipated down the street. Jacob's hand trembled and the nothingness beneath his breastbone succumbed to a cold, roiling fear. His hand dropped. He looked back at the store. Glass broke inside it. A dull flame glowed in the window that grew brighter as Bill stepped through the door and closed it. Jacob glanced again at McGown.

Bill looked at the man in his underdrawers and raised his pistol but let it fall again.

"Why don't you kill him?" Archie asked. "Hell, why don't you kill him?"

"I ain't never shot a bare-assed man before."

"That ain't no reason."

"We got to leave somebody alive who's seen. I want them to know who I was."

The store flamed rapidly. As they waited, Bill drew the cord from his pocket, tied a second knot in it, and studied it almost sadly. Not five minutes had passed before a windowpane snapped with the heat. A sharp, banshee wail fled through the window with the flames. Agony almost palpable.

"If they come out," Bill said, "don't kill them."

"What do you want us to do?" Jacob asked.

"Push them back in again."

Archie grinned. "Hell, Bill, you're a son of a bitch. A bona fide and true son of a bitch."

"For Joshua drew not his hand back," Jacob said.

The shriek came again. The fire had begun to consume the store's supports, and when something collapsed inside the shriek rose frighteningly before falling into a gibber. Bill waited. Jacob waited beside him. Archie looked down the street in the direction the man had run and wiped his knife blade back and forth across the seam of his trousers. McGown had dissolved back into the night. Perhaps he was made of it. Jacob felt a release.

"They ain't coming out," he said after another five minutes. The heat burned intensely in the sunburn on his face.

"I guess not." Bill shoved the cord back into his pocket. His eyes held the flames. "Might as well head home," he said almost sadly.

Before they left they fired Baker's house. They waited until it was burning gaily before crossing the street and mounting the horses. Jacob shoved one pistol in his belt and rested the other on his thigh with his index finger against the trigger guard. They rode back up the knoll. Behind them doors opened and shadows flitted around the flames. Jacob wondered where the man in the underdrawers had gone.

"Shame to leave that musket behind," Archie said.

"That was nothing but a Harpers Ferry," Bill said. "He'd have been lucky to hit one of us with it from where he was standing."

"Did you smell that fella?" Archie asked. "I bet he hadn't shit in a month."

"Smelled bad," Jacob said.

They followed the trail back east with the light of the moon full upon them. Bill rode as he always rode, looking straight ahead, his shoulders set. Archie kept glancing back at the fires, whose light had ceased any longer to hold their shadows. Jacob kept his eyes on the mane between the piebald's ears.

"I told you I could do it, Jake," Archie said.

"You told me."

"Too bad we didn't find you a ax. That was a store. We should have looked for a ax."

"Should have," Jacob answered.

Chapter Fourteen

They rode through the night, through two nights, through the following morning. Rocheport lay as it had before with the trees blanketing it in shadowy coolness and the river flowing almost silently. They reined at the edge of town above the dock. Bill looked at Jacob and Jacob looked at Bill. "You done me my favor," Bill said. "I can't ask you to do nothing more."

"Can't very well go back to what I was doing."

Bill nodded grimly. "Once it's in you, it don't come out. But you go on in and get something to eat from Harriet."

"I'll tell her you say hello."

"Don't tell her nothing. It's best just to let some things be." Jacob nodded. "You best let me have that horse. One of the Yanks in town might recognize her."

Jacob dismounted. He pulled one of the pistols free of his belt and put it in the saddlebag. He stuck the other in the back of his pants and pulled his shirttail over it.

"You take care, Jake," Archie said.

"We'll be around," Bill said.

Jacob nodded and walked tiredly into town. He had ridden for so long that his legs had conformed to the arcs of the piebald's body and walking was both painful and unnatural. Men were working at the dock, black men and white men, soldiers, slave men and free. The hills beyond the river rose green and blue and gray, patches of yellow, the river murmuring quietly. When he walked into the Swisby house, Harriet and Swizz were sitting at the kitchen table eating dinner, sausage and boiled potatoes, Swizz leaning over his plate with his elbow crooked around it, gobbling ravenously, his wizened throat working.

Harriet looked up as Jacob stepped through the threshold. Her fork dropped to click against her plate. Swizz followed her eyes to Jacob. He worked the potatoes into his cheek to give his tongue some room. "Where the hell you been?" he demanded.

"I had something to do."

"You had something to do here. You're supposed to be down at the store."

"I had something to do," Jacob said again.

"You've got something coming—"

Harriet lifted her big, freckled hand and rested it on her husband's shoulder. He looked at her and the look in her eyes and fell grumbling onto his food. Harriet studied Jacob. Jacob leaned against the threshold tiredly.

"You all right, child?" Her voice wavered.

"Yeah," Jacob said.

"You get done everything you needed to do?"

"I did."

Harriet nodded and sighed and wiped her hands over her face and back across her cheeks, pulling the loose skin tight. "Swizz," she said, "why don't you get on to work?"

"There's a whole nuther sausage on the stove I ain't touched yet." He glared at Jacob. "If a man's got to work all alone, he's got to keep his strength up."

"You've done ate three plates and you've never done three plates' worth of work in your life. Save the sausage for the boy." Her voice caught and she stared out of the window with her chin on the heel of her hand and her knuckles hard against her teeth. She cleared her throat painfully.

"Save it for Jacob," she said.

Swizz rose grumbling, wiping his mouth on his sleeve, and walked toward the door. His legs were bent like Jacob's as if struggling to support the weight of his meal, a man all elbows and knees. "There's plenty to do in the storeroom," he told Jacob when he went by.

"I'll be there after I get something in my belly."

"See that you do."

Harriet was still staring out of the window, so Jacob fetched his own plate and filled it from the stove. It was a pork sausage, thick with spices, and he downed it as if he hadn't eaten since he had left Rocheport. Finally, Harriet turned her eyes on him. He could feel them as he chewed.

"Everybody come back?"

"Everybody came back."

"Nobody hurt?"

"Not any of us."

Harriet nodded. She rose as if in pain from the table and heaped another spoonful of potatoes onto his plate. Her bulk beside him was enormous. "You need anything?"

"This'll do me fine."

She nodded, then sat. She stared again out of the window. "You can't stay here no more," she said.

Jacob stopped chewing and looked up at her. Finally, he went back to his potatoes. "All right."

"It's not that I don't want you here. It's not that Swizz don't want you here. You're like one of our own."

"I understand."

"It's not for us at all. It's for you. It won't help you if the Yanks know where you live."

"I understand," he said again.

"You got anywhere to go?"

"I'll be fine."

Her big hand came out to swallow his. "I can talk to some people. They'll put you up."

"I wouldn't want to get them in trouble."

"You need help finding any of the others?"

"Bill knows his way around."

"Good old Bill," she said. "Funny to think he come from Kansas." She stared again at the window. Her voice came up in a withered little whimper that she had to bite her knuckles to stop. "They done killed my boy, Jacob. They done killed Oscar."

Jacob sat back and pushed his plate to the center of the table. He studied her big, heavy face, studied the way she struggled to hold it as it was. "I thought he was out west or east or somewhere."

"He's been right here."

"What did they do?"

"Caught him pulling down telegraph lines south of Boonville. They just put him against a pole and shot him. Just like that, no trial or nothing."

"Harriet."

"Oh, God!" She brought her fists down hard on the table. Jacob's plate leaped and fell to the floor to shatter. The color had flamed in her face, the muscles in her jaw pulled tight, the cords in her neck standing out like those in a straining draft horse. "God damn Yankees. God damn Yankees. I'd like to get my hands on each and every one of them. I'd like to squeeze the bloody life from out of them all." She banged her fists down again and the end board broke off into her lap. She collapsed onto the damaged table weeping. "God damn them," she said. "God damn them."

Jacob studied her quietly. "Does Swizz know?"

"No." Her arms muffled her voice. Her fists worked and relaxed like great hearts pumping. "You don't tell him. He's too old to take it."

"I'll leave in the morning," Jacob said.

Harriet's arms relaxed; her fingers fell away from her fists like petals dropping. When she looked up, all the color in her face had gathered around her eyes, and she wiped the clots of tears from them. "You forget about going to the store," she said. "You get some sleep."

He nodded, wiped his mouth, and stood. "All right."

"Jacob," she said.

"Yeah."

"Jacob."

"I hear you."

"Hard times are coming. They'll hunt you down like a dog. They'll kill you like they done Oscar."

"I know."

"Maybe you should head back north."

"I can't."

"You ought to, Jacob," she said. "You ought to."

He wiped his mouth awkwardly and stood for a moment as if he had something to say. Finally he nodded and backed through the kitchen door with her eyes upon him. He stepped into his bedroom, closed the door, and shucked off his boots. Not until he lay on the bed did he remember the pistol. Funny how you can carry something like that, remembering what it had done, and forget you're carrying it. He wondered without emotion what awaited him. He couldn't bring himself to feel anything beyond that for Harriet. Something inside him had died.

He rose and rinsed his face in the wash pan and watched the gray water flow back into it. He studied his face in the mirror, his eyes, his empty dead eyes. Why, God? he thought. Why this to Harriet, why this to me? Why?

He dried his face with the towel Harriet had left for him, then stripped off his trousers and shirt and underdrawers and let them fall in a reeking pile to the floor. He looked at himself in the mirror again. Standing straight, the mirror caught only his torso, almost as slight and hairless as the day that he'd been born. The mirror could have held Sarah's features. He saw her eyes, her shining skin, the way she held her face. Sarah, he thought, and he wanted to cry. He wondered why he would think of her now. Perhaps because she was to him one of only two emotions remaining. His love for her and his fear of McGown.

He tucked the pistol beneath the pillow, stretched naked on the bed, and stared up at the ceiling. The curtains were drawn and threw only a gray, melancholy light. He could feel so much around him. He thought he saw McGown at the edge of his vision, but when he looked it was only the curtain lifting lightly in a draft. A slight touch of fear and knowledge.

He closed his eyes, sighed. He opened them only long enough to stare briefly at the ceiling.

He awoke with the revolver against his cheek, the muzzle against his eye. He pushed it away, sat up, and ran his tongue around the inside of his cheek. His clothes were resting neatly at his feet, washed, dried, and folded. Outside, the light held only the eerie gray of the coming dusk.

He sat up and dressed and looked at himself in the mirror. "Damn," he said to the nose smashed across his face, but he said it only as a distraction. He avoided his eyes.

He dressed and slipped the pistol into the back of his trousers, his shirttail over it. In the living room, Swizz was sitting on the bed, mouthing words to his hands lying open in his lap. He looked up at Jacob through bleary but life-filled eyes.

"Harriet says you're leaving."

"Yeah."

"After all that we've done for you."

"It ain't that I don't appreciate it."

"I ain't mad for me, but Harriet . . . well, with the one son dead and the other gone, it was nice to see a strapping boy come out of that room again."

"It was nice of you to let me use it. I owe you."

"I love her so." The old man looked down at his hands. His face folded in the wrinkles of his years, long decades of seeing and living, staring at water, staring at sky, watching things change. "It wasn't just the dowry, you know. I don't and never did give a damn about that store."

"I know."

"I ain't never been no good at it. I love her so."

Jacob sat beside him. The old man did nothing but stare numbly at his hands. Jacob did nothing but stare at his.

"Harriet left a plate of food in there for you. Some fish. Cornbread. Squash pie."

"You eat it."

Swizz looked up. "You don't mind?"

"I got things I need to do. Where's Harriet?"

"Out doing something."

"I'll see you."

"You'll be back? It would be awful nice if you could say goodbye to Harriet."

"I ain't leaving till morning," Jacob said.

"I never liked it, this leaving. I didn't like it in Oscar, neither."

Jacob rose. Swizz's eyes dropped to his withered hands again. They were cupped to hold the unspoken burdens we carry.

"Well," Jacob said. "I'll see you."

"Harriet done broke the table."

"I know."

"She's strong."

"I know."

He looked up proudly, his eyes glinting. "You should have seen her with that dog. Pulled its head clean off. I ain't never seen nothing like it."

"I'll see you."

"I can't even do that to a chicken."

"She's strong," Jacob said.

"She damn well is."

Jacob went out the door into the growing darkness. The branches were black above him, the leaves gray, the sky beyond them a fathomless silver quickly fading. He shivered as the breeze from the river dried his sweat. He could feel the fall, the winter coming, though it was only July. He strode down the walk and turned toward the river.

Two soldiers were lounging in front of the Liberty Bell, each indolently gnawing half a loaf of bread. One leaned on the horse hitch and the other lay collapsed against the building with his legs sticking into the street, a half-empty bottle of something beside him. Their bodies stank of sweat, their breath of bad alcohol. Their uniforms hung from them as if they were children playing in their parents' wardrobe. They grinned as Jacob tried to sidle past them and through the door.

"Hey," the standing soldier said.

"Hey," Jacob answered.

"I hear that if you pour wood alcohol through a loaf of bread you can drink it." The standing soldier studied Jacob thoughtfully. He was just old enough to have a trace of whiskers on his chin.

"Try it and find out," Jacob said.

"You bastard. You're trying to poison me."

Jacob felt everything inside of him empty. He looked at the last of the sun, at the rose-colored sky gathered around it. The Navy Colt revolver in his waistband prodded.

"Why ain't you in uniform?" the prone soldier asked. Jacob didn't answer. "God damn secesh bushwhackers everywhere, and he ain't in uniform."

"I bet he's a god damned secesh hisself." The standing soldier bit a chunk off his half of the bread loaf. His saliva sopped into what remained. "You god damned secesh ain't so tough when you're all alone, is you? You got to pack together like rats, like them fish they got somewhere that eat people. Them what-do-you-call-thems." He spit wet dough on Jacob's boot.

Jacob stared at the boot, at the soldier. He leaned over and brushed the dough off with the edge of his hand, then wiped his hand on the seam of his trousers. The soldier grinned down at him. Jacob stood again.

"I ain't so tough," he said.

"Damn right. God damned right." The soldier laughed. Both soldiers laughed. "You're just some damned god awful ugly kid with a pushed-in nose. How'd you get such a pushed-in nose?"

"A mule kicked me." Jacob went inside.

The blinding, choking smoke of cigars filled the bar. Men sat in the tobacco haze, Union men at their tables, southern men at theirs, talking quietly, casting glances. The hollow ring of tobacco juice against spittoons, the occasional invective. Jacob ordered a beer and stared at the bar's dull wooden surface. He listened for the soldiers' voices. He wondered what lay before him.

He drank the beer, drank another. He had just ordered a third when a commotion arose at the door and he looked to see Bill Anderson coming through it, his long curls lifting with each stride. Archie Clement was behind him, still outside of the door, grinning down at the soldier stretched out beside it. Bill spoke sharply over his shoulder and Archie came inside.

"Hey, Jake," Bill said.

"Hey."

"Hey, Jake," Archie said. Jacob didn't answer him. He did not trust the boy and he had never liked the look in his eyes, that grin. Every time he looked at him he heard the whimper of that girl in Freeman.

"How you feeling?" Bill asked.

"All right. A little sore. How about those two fools at the door?"

Bill looked over his shoulder as he sat beside Jacob. "They're just fools. Bucko, give me the usual."

The barkeep brought it to him meekly and ran the garter back up his arm. He brought another for Archie. They drank them silently while Archie's eyes passed over the men in the bar.

"Got your piebald outside," Bill said.

"I thought you weren't going to bring her in."

Bill shrugged. "What the hell. We'll be out of town before anyone gets up the nerve to do anything about it."

"And it's a Friday night," Archie said. "A little whoring and a little fighting is all in line." He grinned at Jacob and ordered another whiskey. "You much on whoring, Jake?"

"Not much."

"You got a girl?"

"Back in Kentucky."

"Kentucky's a long way to go for a little poontang. You got a girl here?"

"No."

"Hell." Archie shook his head. "So what do you do if you don't whore?"

Jacob studied his face, the angles of his cheekbones, that grin, those dark, dark eyes. He turned back to his beer. "I mount hogs."

The grin fell from Archie's face for only a moment before he laughed. "Hell, Jake, you're something." He drank. Bill drank hunched over the bar, drank glass after glass. Jacob watched him silently. He sipped his beer.

"I done you a favor," he said. "I want you to do one for me."

Bill looked at him. The light in those brilliant blue eyes. "Yeah?"

"You take me in."

"I ain't got nothing to take you in to."

"You take me to him, then," Jacob said, "and you get him to take me in. I don't want to be no danger to Swizz and Harriet."

Bill lifted his glass to his lips. "Lucky we brought the piebald with us." He smiled and drank.

They drank some more, listened to the talk, sat together and fed off of what they knew each of them to be. Finally Bill slapped the bar and stood and tossed a coin onto it. "For you, bucko," he said, then he clasped Jacob's shoulder and guided him to his feet. He led him toward the door.

The soldiers were still outside, the standing one showing less drunkenness with the time, or perhaps only less in relation to Jacob's own. The other lolled helplessly, his head against the wall, his bottle lying on its side.

"Here they come," the standing soldier said. "The god damned secesh bushwhackers."

"We ain't no bushwhackers," Bill said.

The soldier spat. "You ain't in uniform."

"Can't get poontang in uniform," Archie said.

"Hell. I get all I want."

"Then what are you doing standing here?"

"What are you doing standing here?" The soldier spat again. The bread was gone. "Guys like you only fuck nigger women anyway. That's why you want to keep them as slaves."

Jacob emptied again. His fist snapped forward into the soldier's face and a sting came to his knuckles and the soldier dropped without a word. Jacob dropped and groped for his pistol and swung with it low to aim at the prone soldier, but Archie was already working at him with his knife, a quick sweep across the throat, a strangled gurgle. Archie came up grinning. The soldier's toes jerked in the street.

"Hell," Bill said, "we sure don't need this."

Archie wiped the blade off on the prone soldier's pant leg. The soldier was still jerking, his tongue out, his eyes wide and drunken and frightened and already as empty as Jacob's own. "It's just a god damned Yankee. And there ain't no one around."

"There's a whole saloonful of men right behind you."

"They'd a killed us," Archie said. "They knew who we was. Jake?"

"You shouldn't a done that, Archie," Jacob said. "You shouldn't have."

"Well, I did. I'll get the other one." Archie sighed and stepped toward the soldier Jacob had hit as if this were a chore, like milking cows, like chopping wood.

"Leave him be," Bill said.

"Why?"

"They'll think he killed this other one."

Archie stopped and studied the soldier still living and studied the knife. The soldier groaned and rolled his head from side to side. Blood ran along the line of his mouth, and his upper lip was deeply cut. Archie grinned and sheathed the knife. "Hell, Bill, you're always thinking. That's what I like about you. You're always thinking."

"It don't take no thinking. That's what soldiers do."

"Let's get out of here," Jacob said.

"Think some more are around?" Archie asked. "I'd sure like to stick a few of them."

"Let's get out of here," Jacob said.

They walked down the street to where the horses waited. The piebald tossed her head in recognition, and Jacob smiled as he patted her withers. He mounted, then looked back over his shoulder at the two soldiers. The one, of course, had not moved, and the other had rolled onto his side. Jacob felt sorry for the dead one, thrust drunken into eternity and still a fool. But at least the wise and loving and hateful God had offered him the opportunity.

Bill led them north out of town into the hills, then led them west. The sky dark above them, the stars shining. The river in glimpses through the trees moonlit and lovely. It was a good night to be riding.

"Where we going?" Jacob asked.

"Where you said. To find Charlie Quantrill."

"You know where he's at?"

"I'll ask around when we're getting close."

Jacob nodded. He stuck his revolver into his waistband at his hip, reached back into the saddlebag and pulled the other one out. He aimed at the stars. Bang, bang, bang, he thought, and I could put each of you out.

"You hear about Oscar Swisby?" he asked.

"Everyone's heard about Oscar," Bill said.

They rode silently into the dark, the river on their left, the moon on its surface, the gentle sound of it the undercurrent of all Jacob experienced, the whisper of the world. In half an hour they left the river and headed north into the Perche Hills, and just before midnight they stopped on a farm just south of Fayette. Even though he had slept all day, Jacob was tired.

"You two wait here," Bill said. "I'll do some talking."

Bill walked to the farmhouse and knocked on the door. He knocked again and the door swung open, revealing only shadows. Bill nodded and talked and from within a face emerged like a ghost. Jacob watched from the piebald with Archie beside him.

Bill came back and nodded. He took his mare by the reins. "He says we can use the barn. He says he's got some cornbread and cold beans."

"Who was that?" Jacob asked.

"A farmer."

"He got a daughter?" Archie asked.

Bill's eyes flashed. "You get that thought out of your head right now. You don't mess with her."

"I was only funning." Archie shrugged. "Guess I'll have to settle for bread and beans."

They unsaddled the horses and wiped them down, then bedded in barn straw, the sweet-smelling hay, the warmth of the animals a blanket around them. Bill went to the house and came back with a pan of bread and a pot of beans. They ate silently with the pot between them and passed the pan around. The beans were sour, the bread gritty and dry.

"Sleep," Bill said when they finished. "We got a long ride in the morning."

Jacob lay back in the straw and studied the darkness above him, the patterns his imagination made of it. He could not sleep because this reminded him too much of home. The mule would stamp and he would think of Buck. A cat would mew and he would see them lined up and waiting for milk. The cow lowed just as he was drifting off and not until he rubbed his face and felt the shape of his nose did he realize it wasn't Mabel. A happy, warm feeling within him faded. What, he wondered, had become of her? Bill and Archie were already asleep and all Jacob could think of was Sarah, was him and Sarah together back there in the barn, on the riverbank, with their own barn and livestock and house and bed. Their own love. He rolled on his side and covered his head with his arms, but his fantasy was made of the darkness and there was as much darkness within his arms as there had been without them. He closed his eyes and it was the same and he couldn't escape it. The darkness was everywhere. He curled around the hollow, aching coldness within him. God, he thought. God.

Within an hour he heard Archie rise. He listened to him walk toward the door.

"Where you going?" he whispered.

Archie stopped. "It's just a little funning."

"You leave her be."

"It ain't like I'm going to hurt her."

The door creaked open and shut. Thinking about Archie made Jacob think about Sarah again. Thinking about anything made him think about Sarah again. He fell asleep before Archie returned.

He awoke with the first light through the cracks in the rafters, a yellow light thick with the summer. He sat and rubbed his face and stretched the lazy stiffness from his body. He covered his face with his hands and rubbed his cheeks and smelled the leather, horse smell of who he had become. It wasn't unpleasant.

Bill and Archie were still sleeping. Jacob rose and dressed and walked by the mule, which watched him solemnly. Jacob ran his hand down its neck and over its withers and stepped out into the new day.

The sky was a solid silver-blue, no clouds. The air was still cool enough for him to feel it through his clothes, the sun half an orb on the eastern horizon. He walked around to the back of the barn away from the house to relieve himself. When he finished he watched the sunlight on the fields heavy with young corn startling in its greenness. Such a place as this, he thought. He thought again of Sarah.

He went to the sunward side of the barn and squatted there in the warmth. He closed his eyes against the sky, the sun, seeing the brilliant oranges and shifting reds that dreams of the day are made of. He turned toward something clattering at the house. A girl in a flannel housecoat was standing at the door looking toward the barn, one arm wrapped around her chest and her other hand clutching the coat together at her groin. Her hair was long and loose and blond, and her face, the color of oatmeal, was bathed in new knowledge. She should have been playing with dolls in front of the hearth, and perhaps by the end of the day would be doing so. When she saw Jacob watching her, she pulled herself back inside and shut the door.

The animal, Jacob thought. The black-grinning, black-eyed animal. He looked up at the sun and closed his eyes again.

From the barn came the hacking and groaning and cursing that all men awake with. Bill came out with his hat in one hand and the fingers of his other working through his long hair. His beard was unkempt and wild.

"How long you been up?" he asked Jacob.

"An hour."

"You ready to go?"

"I'm ready. We got any breakfast coming?"

"I'll check." Bill pointed with a jerk of his head back into the barn. "Get him up."

Jacob nodded and stood. He watched Bill walk to the house, watched him knock on the door. The girl answered it shyly, looking a child. Beneath his breath Jacob cursed.

The cow was lowing fitfully in the barn for the relief of milking, and the mule was dozing with his head angled so one eye was in the sun. Archie was asleep in the back with the fat body of a lazy old tomcat curled against the top of his head. Jacob kicked his boot. Archie groaned. The boy smelled of sex.

"Get up," Jacob said.

Archie smacked his lips, his eyes still shut. "Hell."

"Get up."

Archie sat and rubbed his face, rubbed his eyes.

"You up?" Jacob asked.

"I'm up."

"I think there's breakfast up at the house."

Jacob went outside before he grew more angry. Bill was crouching beside the door with a spoon in a pot. An emaciated, gray, balding man was standing in the threshold, spiritlessly watching him.

"All I got is cornmeal and water," the man said. "Them Yanks took everything else."

"Cornmeal will do," Jacob said.

Bill lifted the spoon to his lips. "We'll get it back for you."

The farmer's face crinkled, pulled tight, fell loose and lifeless again. The girl was watching the barn door from over his shoulder. "How you going to do that?" the farmer asked. He had a tooth missing in front.

"The Lord giveth and the Lord taketh away," Jacob said, "but vengeance is also the Lord's."

"You a religious man?" the farmer asked.

"I grew up with it."

Archie came out of the barn, buttoning his trousers. The girl's face brightened; Jacob thought she might crawl out the door over her father's shoulder as if she were climbing through tree branches. Archie squatted beside Bill and paid her no mind. "Why don't you give me some of that? I'm a growing boy."

Bill put the spoon into his mouth and pulled it out clean. He handed it and the pot to Archie. Archie stirred the pot with distaste. "Hell, this ain't nothing but cornmeal."

"You'll eat worse before this is all through," Bill said.

Archie grumbled but said no more. Jacob watched the girl desperately watch him eat, then turned to look across the fields, the trees, the hills. When the meal was offered he took a few bites, but it was tasteless and he felt uneasy eating in front of the farmer. He wiped his lips on his sleeve and handed the pot to him. The farmer passed it over his shoulder to his daughter. She looked wildly at Archie, her face filled with promises made and being broken, then disappeared into the darkness of the cabin.

"Where's the wife?" Jacob asked.

"Dead. Got the cholera a few years back."

"Sorry to hear that."

"Well," the farmer said, and he squinted across the fields.

Bill rose. Archie and Jacob followed him back to the barn. They went in and saddled the horses, the piebald stoically suffering Jacob's incompetence. When all were saddled they led them out into the yard. The farmer was standing in the door, staring dully into the pot. Bill called a farewell to him and he looked up. Jacob nodded as they left. The girl was gone.

They rode westward into the hills, the sun behind them casting long shadows. They kept to the creek bottoms and trees when they could, and before an hour had passed and the heat had fully risen, they had sighted a Federal patrol on a hillcrest, twenty of them, starry-eyed boys or old Quixotes in cast-off clothing, sporting firearms of every make and model, some without firearms at all, riding nags and swaybacked geldings whose shoulders stood out starkly in sharp points and angles. They waited until the patrol had passed before continuing. An hour and a half after leaving the farm, they reached a town as small as Ripley clutching a bend in the Missouri River. They rode through in silence, the people staring. A black man ran loping until Bill aimed a revolver at him. The man fell to his knees gaping, sweat glistening on his dark, pitted cheeks. They rode by him with Bill's arm arcing smoothly to keep the pistol aimed at the man's face. He was still on his knees when they left town.

"We got something to worry about with him?" Jacob asked.

"Nothing," Bill said. "The good citizens of Glasgow keep their niggers in line."

Just outside of town they forded the Chariton River and three hours later the Grand. They crossed the Missouri in a stolen skiff with the horses swimming behind them, their reins tied to the stern, and headed into the wild open country, hickories and oaks, scrub brush, pawpaws, a litter of farmhouses, the hills like the earth's furrowed brow. Some farmsteads they avoided and some they didn't and Bill seemed to know how each one stood. Jacob followed silently, his eyes on Bill's back, on Archie's.

They spent that night camped at the foot of a hill overgrown with honeysuckle. The next morning they rode for an hour before coming across a ravaged, burned field, a farmhouse collapsed and smoking in the distance. A man was lying on the cow path they were following, blood on his back, blood in his ear, his cheek in the dirt and his wide, death-emptied eyes staring. His mouth open in an eternal cry. The piebald shied as it stepped around him. A shiny black cluster of flies roiled in his ear.

Archie drew his pistol and shot the man again. The body jerked and the flies scattered. "God damned Yankees."

"How do you know he was a Yankee?" Jacob asked.

"Because all of them Yankees die with that same scared look on their faces."

They rode by the farmhouse. A woman scrabbled through the brambles behind it, her face and movements wild and her hair knotted with sticks and mud. Her eyes showed only the animal she had become, her cracked and bloody lips twisted in ways Jacob had never before seen. Archie did not seem to notice her and though Bill glanced at her he paid her no mind. Jacob rode on silently.

Just before noon they stopped beside a field where an old, hunchbacked farmer was working behind a tired mule. Bill dismounted and talked to the man while Archie and Jacob waited, Jacob with his arms close to his sides where he could feel the comfort of the revolvers. Finally Bill came back smiling. He removed his hat and wiped his brow, then settled his hat on again and led them westward into Jackson County.

Before them lay a deep cut in the land that stretched north and south as far as Jacob could see. Gorges and forests and brush, cliffs lined and weathered like ancient visages. There appeared to be no way in or out.

"The Sni," Bill said. "There ain't a soul in the world who can touch us in there."

He led them down a narrow, nearly hidden trail into a gorge. The piebald snorted as she slipped on shale, her withers trembling. The only sounds were the sighing wind and the birds, the clink of the horseshoes, somewhere below them the sound of running water. They wandered through a bewildering maze until they reached a creek that Bill followed south. The world had become the creek and the cliffs and the hollows and the strip of blue sky above them.

They didn't stop at noon. The piebald blew and flustered. Finally around two they turned off into a valley with a small, clear stream winding along its belly and oaks spreading up each side to form a cathedral. A voice called from somewhere and they stopped.

"Halt. Who goes there?"

"Is that Perry Hoy?" Bill asked.

"Of course it's me, Bill. Now tell me who goes there."

"What you doing, playing army? You know who I am."

"Who are the other two?"

Bill looked back over his shoulder. "The little one is Archie Clement. The one with the broken nose is Jake Wilson. Jake, he shot the brother-in-law of that Baker fella I was telling you about. Archie, he cut his throat."

"I like a knife," Archie said to the trees.

Rustling came from the brush and a man of maybe twenty stepped out from a tangle of sumac. He wore trousers with frayed suspenders and broken boots that reminded Jacob of the ones he had worn in Osceola. His shirt was ornately embroidered, colorful curls, little flowers, big pockets weighed down with what must have been ammunition. Another man followed.

"Hey, Perry," Bill said. "Hey, Dave."

"Hey, Bill," Perry Hoy said. The other man nodded. He was short and thin and had a long goatee that caught the breeze. "You seen any Yanks around?"

"Not since yesterday in Ray County."

"We know about those." Perry grinned. He had black eyes and a voice like a rusty hub. The face of a ghost in search of a haunting. "You head on in."

"He at the house or out in the field?"

"Hell if I know," Perry said.

Bill nodded and kicked the gray mare lightly in the ribs. Jacob followed him, looking down at Perry and Dave. Perry looked up and smiled, but Jacob did not return it. He could see in his eyes the same blood lust he had seen in Archie's.

They rounded a bend in the stream. Ahead of them lay a small, barren field and a cabin struggling to hold itself upright. Smoke snaked up thinly from the chimney. Perhaps fifteen men were loafing about, dirty men, wild men, pistols in belts, horses grazing in a distant pasture. Crows in the trees heckled all. Bill called a few greetings.

"You two stay here," he told Jacob and Archie when they'd dismounted. "Archie, watch your mouth. You say the wrong thing here and someone will put a pistol in it."

"I wouldn't want to say the wrong thing." Archie's eyes flitted across the field. His lips cracked into his grin. "These are my kind of people."

Bill left the gray mare's reins with Jacob and walked into the field. He slapped a man's shoulder, and the man took his hand and smiled. They spoke for a minute, then Bill walked across the yard and into the cabin, knocking first. Jacob waited.

"What you thinking, Jake?" Archie asked.

"I ain't thinking nothing," Jacob said.

Bill came out of the cabin with a thin man in his twenties an inch or two shorter than Jacob. He had sandy hair and a thin mustache, a hooked nose and rounded shoulders, and he didn't look like much. Bill waved them over and Jacob and Archie walked slowly toward them, Jacob leading the horses.

The thin man watched them silently. Bill fawned around him. "Jake? Archie? This here's Charlie Quantrill. Charlie, these are the boys I told you about. They're good boys, Charlie. They are."

Jacob nodded at the man. Charlie studied them silently. No one spoke and the summer sun beat down and the only sounds were the laughing crows and the bustling men behind Jacob.

"Afternoon," Charlie said. His voice was soft and high and refined.

"Afternoon."

"I have to ask you both something. Will you follow orders, be true to your fellows, and kill those who serve and support the Union?"

"Damn right I will," Archie said.

Jacob tried to see into Charlie's eyes, but the man's eyelids drooped too heavily over them. "Sure."

"You're not from around here."

"I grew up in Ohio. But I've moved around some since then."

"What are you doing here?"

"I'm just here is all."

"He killed a couple of Yanks with a ax," Archie boasted.

Charlie studied Jacob silently. "Bill, you go tell Bill Gregg that you're back. Take this little one with you."

"Anything you say, Charlie."

"What did you say your name was, Ohio boy?"

"Jacob Wilson."

"You go out in the field there and help Henry."

"How do I know who's Henry?"

"He's the only nigger you'll see."

Jacob nodded. Charlie watched him for a moment before stepping back toward the cabin. A clean-faced man was leaning against the door frame, wide forehead, vicious, stupid eyes, his mouth a gash like Archie's. "Meet George Todd," Charlie said as he went inside. George nodded and followed Charlie in, closing the door behind him.

Jacob stared at the wood plank door; he looked up at the sky. He turned to Bill, but Bill was no longer there. Archie was gone, too. The smell of the trees in the air, the gurgle of the stream. The land beyond the field danced in the heat.

He led the horses to the pasture and unsaddled them, piled the tack beneath a tree, and walked into the field. He felt vulnerable without Bill and Archie, alien beneath the eyes of the others. A tall, thin black man with his back to him was adjusting a tripod over a pile of firewood, sinewy arms and long spider fingers, shoulder blades working beneath his dark, sweaty skin, bald head almost glowing. Jacob stopped beside him. The black man looked up. He was the slave from the Osceola livery.

"You," Jacob said.

Henry Nolan spat a tobacco-stained line into the dead ashes. They rose in a puff. "Well god damn."

"You remember me?"

"How the hell would I forget you? You told me to rot."

Jacob turned uncomfortably from his face. "Charlie says I'm supposed to help you."

"White boys can't cook."

"I'm just saying what he said."

"Well god damn," Henry said again. "Josiah or Jehosophat or something, wasn't it?"

"Jacob. Wilson."

The black man squinted at Jacob's face. Sweat had beaded on his forehead and he lifted a spider arm to wipe it away. "Go get me some wood, white boy."

"Where's it at?"

"Where do you think? In the god damned trees."

"You ain't got any cut?"

"What, you think with me feeding all these shitbird white boys I got time to cut kindling? There's an ax by the cabin. You fetch it and cut me some firewood before I stripe your ass."

"You wouldn't never of said that in Osceola."

"This ain't Osceola."

Jacob put his hands in his pockets, felt his pistols against his forearms. He stared down into the ashes. "I didn't come here to take no orders from some skinny, bald, loud-mouthed nigger," he said.

Henry's arm came around in a smooth arc and the edge of his hand caught Jacob under the jaw. The blow lifted Jacob off his feet and flashed sharply across his mind. When he could see again he was lying on his back with the sky smiling down upon him. Henry was crouched beside him with a long finger in his face. Two guerrillas were laughing, a big man and a boy who looked like a rat.

"You came here to do what you're told to do," Henry was saying. "By God, you'll do it or I'll wup you to death. In front of all of these white boys I'll wup you to death. By God. This ain't god damned Osceola."

Jacob choked and tasted blood. He rose to spit it away and wiped his palm over his lip.

"You gonna do it, white boy?" Henry asked.

"Sure," Jacob said.

"This ain't god damned Osceola. I don't put up with no mouthing."

"Sure."

"The ax is by the cabin."

Henry went back to fixing the tripod. Jacob stood. He gathered up Tobias's hat and settled it back on his head. His jaw ached almost as much as his nose had and the world swam in his tears. He stumbled toward the cabin.

The man and the boy who had laughed at him snickered as he walked by. The man was a towering lump of decaying fat and rancid skin and rotting clothes. He wore a priest's collar gone as yellow as his face and chewed on the spit-soaked stub of a cigar. The boy had the face of a rat and the manners of a rat and stood beside his companion glancing up with twitching eyes at his soft, lard face.

The man flicked the cigar stub at Jacob's feet. Jacob stopped to stare at it. "There is an irony," the man said, "in being a nigger to a nigger." The boy broke into a high-pitched, squeaking titter. His long, bony hands wrestled with each other in front of his chest.

"You a priest?" Jacob asked.

"Heavens, no." The man fingered his collar. "A priest gave this to me when I demanded it as penance for his apostasy. But I had been a preacher in the tradition of the great Baptist until I found a higher calling."

"What's your name?"

"Larkin Skaggs. The Reverend Larkin Skaggs."

"I'm going to piss in your plate of beans tonight, Reverend Skaggs. I'm going to shit in your bedroll."

The reverend's smile dropped. He fingered at his lips as if the cigar was still between them. The boy's hands fell still and his eyes flickered until finally the reverend laughed loudly, his back arched, his ugly, sallow face to the sky. He clapped a heavy hand on Jacob's shoulder. "You're a good boy, my son."

"I ain't your son."

"You are as innocent as a lamb but as sly as a serpent, just as our good Lord called us to be."

"You take your god damned hand off my shoulder."

Jacob walked on with the reverend still laughing and the boy beginning to mimic him. He found the ax at the corner of the cabin where Henry had said it would be. Too much came back just by looking at it to pick it up and he left it behind. He hurried into the woods as if fleeing.

He worked all afternoon dragging kindling he could break with his hands or with a kick from the woods to the field. With stream water he washed the sweat from his neck and stared up through the trees at the sky. He found a crosscut saw hanging on a peg on the back of the cabin and with it cut what didn't need to be split and took it to Henry. Henry always scowled at him and sometimes shook his head. At sunset Henry started the fire and soon there rose the smell of the beans, of the fatback stewing with them, of griddle bread baking at the side of the fire. Jacob stopped in the firelight to pull splinters from his fingers and to rub at his stomach's grumble.

"You ain't done yet," Henry said. "This ain't no dry goods store."

"Pays about the same," Jacob said.

Jacob worked until the darkness was full and stopped only when Henry shoved a tin plate of bread and beans into his swollen, blistered hands. He collapsed beside the fire among the men and boys who had spent the day loafing. Only Perry and Dave acknowledged him. Larkin Skaggs lifted a blessing that no one paid any mind.

Two boys no older than Jacob had ridden in just as the sun had disappeared. As Jacob ate, they came to the fire where their shadows flickered and danced. One of them had a rag wrapped around his bleeding, limp arm and tears furrowing the grime on his face. Jacob listened to the talk around him, hearing and not hearing it, another strain in the music of the night that mixed with the cricket beat, with the owl call, with the lonely, baleful cry of two doves mourning. He lifted his face to the black sky and tried to remember what he thought this should remind him of.

When he finished his meal he wiped off the plate and set it beside the fire. Henry was sitting aloof on the fire's far side, his black skin shining, his eyes shining, the muscles of his jaw and throat working on bread and catching the firelight. He glanced at Jacob but said nothing, and Jacob took that to mean he didn't have dish-washing duty as well. He rose wearily and stumbled across the pasture to watch the piebald graze. He searched out the tack and found Bill's and Archie's missing. He lay with his head on his hard wooden saddle and contemplated the sky.

He spent the next day collecting wood, and the day after that. He spent his nights flicking into the fire the gray-backed lice he'd picked up somewhere and listening to the guerrillas' stories. Bud Younger was a boy of eighteen with a broad, bland face and hair already thinning whose father had been a wealthy Union magistrate before Federal militia murdered him. Dick Yeager's father was rotting in prison, and his freighting business burned to the ground by Jennison, its horses grazing on Kansas prairies and its wagons hidden in Kansas barns. Frank James was thin and corded with a face like a weasel's. He'd deserted Price after Lexington. Boys from Osceola told stories of Lane. When they asked for Jacob's story, he only muttered a few words before falling silent. He thought of McGown and God. He stared at his hands.

Bill and Archie rode into camp on the evening of the third day just as Jacob was sitting down with his meal, a roasted rabbit breast. He watched them come to the fire. Archie took a plate and ate with gusto. Bill only sat tiredly.

"Hey," Jacob said.

"Hey," Bill answered.

"You hungry?"

"I ain't hungry."

"What you been doing?"

"Some raiding in Cass County. We killed a Yank and his boy. Strung a few others up."

"A boy?" Jacob asked.

"Twelve years old, I guess. We killed the Yank and the boy come at us with a butcher knife. Archie, he took the knife away and done him." Jacob glanced at Archie, who waved a rabbit haunch at him and grinned. "I got a sister that boy's age. Jennie."

"Yeah."

"I wish he hadn't done it, Jake, butcher knife or no. Men fighting you is one thing, but kids . . ."

"Yeah."

"Anyway, I wish he hadn't."

Henry grinned from the far side of the fire. His eyes were on Bill and scraps of rabbit stuck in his teeth. "Poor little Willie," he said. "Poor little Willie suffers so."

Bill stared at the black man's face. "You god damned niggers."

"Killing's killing, Willie. It don't make no difference the age or anything else. You might as well face what you are now and quit whining about it."

"I ain't whining."

"Whining's your excuse. Whining makes everything right. I'm tired of it. Poor little Willie."

"You god damned nigger. You call me that again and I'll kill you."

Henry's face was set, his eyes still shining. "Poor little Willie," he said deliberately.

Bill studied him silently. Finally he turned from Henry and lay back, his face toward Jacob. "God damn, Jake. I thought you would keep better company than niggers."

"I'm just doing what Charlie told me to do."

"Ain't you going to kill him, Bill?" Archie asked. "Ain't you?"

"Not now," Bill said.

They moved the camp the next morning, the men in a column, Charlie leading with George Todd and Bill Gregg behind him, a wiry, long-faced man with sad eyes and a thick black goatee, Bill and Archie in the middle, Perry Hoy and Dave Poole, Jacob and Henry in the back with the cook mess, with the dust. As they left the Sni the land opened onto fields and trees and pastures. They made camp beside the Blackwater River on the farm of a man named Pardee, a beautiful farm with a quaint house, a quaint barn, a mule and three cows, a meadow of green blending with the sky. While Henry unloaded the mess, Jacob searched for firewood. Such a place, he thought. Such a place.

Charlie rode out the next day with George and Gregg and a band of six riders, Archie and Bill among them. Jacob stayed to gather firewood and obey Henry's orders.

The riders returned three days later at dawn, the grass almost dewless in the summer heat, the air like a breath on the neck. There were only six of them now. Two others straggled in around noon, one wounded, one not. Pardee was a man seldom seen, but he came to the field late in the day with a doctor to tend the wounded boy, his eyes darting around him in bemusement or fear or respect. The doctor said he would have to amputate the boy's leg, but he would die anyway. The boy ended up shooting himself in the mouth.

A carriage pulled up to the farm just after sunset. A woman in a black dress and bonnet stepped out of it, dragging a boy behind her. Jacob squatted at the fire and watched the woman bang on the Pardee door. The boy stood awkwardly in the yard as she went inside.

The boy was wearing a man's pair of trousers hitched by suspenders up to the middle of his chest. He had a woman's white cotton blouse on with sleeves rolled nearly to their elbows but still hanging down to his knuckles. He was towheaded with a ringworm scar on the back of his head like a bull's-eye, and one eye almost certainly blind swung independently of the other. Both of his ears were cut off. Jacob pondered him silently, slowly chewing his beans.

The boy scratched at the ringworm scar and turned to Jacob. Eyes as empty as Jacob's own, and Jacob felt commiseration. "Hey!" the boy shouted. He waved his skinny arm wildly above his head. The blouse sleeve slid up to his shoulder.

"Hey," Jacob answered. Such a summation of misfortune he had never before seen.

The woman came out of the house like a thunderstorm with Charlie following her, a thin smile on his face, his hooded eyelids drawn even lower. George was behind him and laughing like a mule.

The woman turned. "Will you take him?" Her face was as hard and pointed as a pick-ax.

Charlie looked the boy up and down. The boy picked at his ass and continued to stare at Jacob. The toes of one bare foot clenched at the toes of the other.

"He isn't much," Charlie said.

"Will you take him?" the woman demanded, her voice rising high and shrill and just about breaking.

Charlie shrugged. "We'll take him." George continued laughing.

The woman spun the boy by his shoulders and shook him. She spoke in a rumble of words made to Jacob incomprehensible by the distance, and, by the look on his face, equally as incomprehensible to the boy. She shook him again and demanded his understanding. The boy either nodded or his head was still bobbing from the shaking. She pulled him to her chest quickly, then shoved him away, the same action she would use to work a pump. The boy watched her stride angrily to the carriage, his head cocked to the side. He waved wildly as she and the carriage pulled away.

Charlie spoke softly to George, who shrugged. The boy had turned back to Jacob, and Charlie followed his gaze. Jacob looked down at his plate. When he looked up again, Charlie was pointing toward him and the fire, and the boy was nodding happily.

"Sweet Jesus," Jacob said.

The boy skipped across the yard to Jacob. He grinned, his bad eye swinging wildly. Both of his front teeth were missing, and his tongue worked around the hole in his smile. Such a summation of misfortune. He rubbed his palm over the stump of one ear.

"Hey," he said. "That Charlie fella says I'm to help you."

"Did he."

"Yep. So I'm going to help you."

Jacob set down his plate. The boy looked at it and him and grinned with the tip of his tongue looking like a pimple on his lip. With the back of his wrist he smeared a swath of snot from his nose across his cheek. "Hey," he said again. "My name is Haywood." His words whistled in the gap in his teeth.

"Haywood what?"

"Haywood Lee, yes sirree, just like the general. You can call me Hay."

"What are you doing here, Haywood?"

"They done killed my pap and done burned us out. Mam says I'm to get revenge. I'm gonna be a gorilla."

"What happened to your teeth?"

The boy smiled vacuously. "This here fella done kicked them in when he caught me mounting his sheep." He pointed at Jacob's plate. "You got any more of those? They burned us out and took all our stuff and I ain't et nothing except a bunch of berries all the way out here. They done give me the skitters. You want to see?" He turned and showed Jacob the brown stain on his trousers. Their waistband reached to his shoulder blades.

"How old are you, Haywood?" Jacob asked.

"Fourteen. Mam, she brought me here to fight, just like the general. I'm gonna be a gorilla. My last name is Lee. I don't know if you caught that."

"What was you doing mounting sheep?"

"It was a nice sheep. It come all the way from Spain, I hear."

"Why don't you just get yourself a girlfriend?"

"Girls don't like this eye. But sheep, they don't care about eyes."

Jacob nodded at the obvious logic. He fetched the boy a plate and watched him ravenously eat. When Haywood finished he asked for more and Jacob got it for him.

Finally the boy burped loudly enough to raise the birds from the trees. The lounging guerrillas stared at him.

"Hey." Haywood wildly waved his skinny arm. "You can call me Hay."

When Haywood finished, he wiped off his plate as he had seen Jacob do and set it by the fire. Jacob didn't know what to do with him, so he took the boy to Henry. Henry only stared incredulously.

"Hey," Haywood said. "My name is Haywood Lee, yes sirree, just like the general. You can call me Hay."

Henry looked him up and down and shook his head sadly. "All hail the superior race." He turned to Jacob. "Put him to work on the dishes. It's about time they got done."

Haywood's good eye went wide. His other seemed indifferent. "I got to do dishes? How is I going to get revenge if I got to do dishes? I ain't never seen no gorilla doing dishes."

Henry tensed and Jacob pulled Haywood away. A blow from Henry would break the boy like a dry stick. "You'll just do it," he said.

"But how . . ."

"Haywood. You'll just do what he said."

Haywood shrugged and scratched at the ringworm scar and smiled. The hole in his teeth was the only part of his mouth that didn't catch the firelight. "I done a lot of dishes. Pap, he'd get all randy after supper and take Mam into the bedroom for a little rutting and I'd have to do the dishes. The whole damn house would shake so the water in the dishpan would wave around and I'd just have to hold the plates there and let it slosh them. That was before they shot him."

"Get yourself busy."

"Pap," Haywood said, "he sure liked his rutting. 'Holy rolling thunder,' he'd shout, 'she's gonna blow!' Sometimes I'd sneak over and watch them sometimes."

"You best get to work."

"You got a horse?" Haywood asked. "I bet you got a horse."

"You leave my horse be, Haywood. It ain't no sheep."

"You can call me Hay." He grinned and set about the dishes. "So how am I going to get my revenge?"

"We'll have to wait and find out."

They slept together that night at the edge of the pasture, under the trees, Bill, Archie, Jacob, and Haywood, Haywood in the bedroll of the boy who had shot himself. Bill and Archie fell asleep and Jacob lay on his back and looked up at the stars, muttering yes or no to or ignoring the steady roll of Haywood's questions. There were things he let himself think about and things that he didn't. He let himself think about Tobias, and with that thought the memories came rolling and he thought about him hanging in that old and dying cottonwood. He thought about Teague lying in front of the door.

McGown suddenly appeared squatting above him in the crown of a hickory. The dead sergeant was more than eyes now, more than shadow. He squatted there full of flesh as dark as the sky above him, so embodied that the branch strained beneath his weight as it would beneath a bloated buzzard. Black eyes staring down from a lifeless face. A heavy sweat smell in his uniform, the side of his skull caved in, the stump of his wrist dripping putrescence that pattered on the leaves. The puckered knife wound across his forehead wriggled with parasites glowing white against the darkness. His eyes as soulless as Jacob's own, for his soul had already fled. What is a living dead man without a soul? Jacob wondered. Do demons have souls? Does the devil? Are angels only souls wrapped in the matter of the kingdom? McGown watched him silently and smiled. Jacob rolled on his side and hid his face. He prayed a futile prayer for safekeeping.

Haywood had fallen asleep, his breath a short, little-boy whistle, his face twisted, young, and ugly in the shadows, the one mutilated ear Jacob could see like a hole in the side of his skull. Jacob closed his eyes. The light from the rising moon filtered through his eyelids. He could feel McGown hovering over him like a black, infernal lover.

Haywood's whistle stopped abruptly around midnight. The boy rustled in his blanket, then Jacob heard him slip down his trousers. The steady, pulsing thump of his masturbation raised within Jacob a feeling he couldn't understand. It drained away like water a few seconds later when the boy drew in his breath and the thumping stopped. "Holy rolling thunder," Haywood whispered. He sighed before he fell asleep again.

Jacob opened his eyes to study the boy in the moonlight, then rolled onto his back. He felt nothing now. McGown was gone.

Chapter Fifteen

A Confederate officer rode into camp the next morning, his uniform weather-stained, mud on his boots, the tip of his scabbard worn as if it had been gnawed by a dog. Round face, soft eyes, his chin held high in his pride. Jacob was gathering wood for the fire and Haywood squatted beside the embers, the waistband of his trousers gathered to his armpits, bits of debris clinging to the blouse. The pale skin within the circled scar on the back of his head showed starkly.

"Who's that?" Haywood asked.

"Don't know."

"Bet it's a general," Haywood said, "just like General Lee." It was the first Confederate officer Jacob had ever seen.

The farmhouse door opened and Charlie, George, and Bill Gregg stepped out. They saluted sloppily, and the officer returned it. He stepped inside and they followed. Bill Anderson walked toward the fire from the pasture, slinging a suspender over his shoulder, pulling his hair loose when it caught beneath it. "Who's that?" he asked.

"Don't know," Jacob said.

"Boy," Bill said to Haywood, "if you want to yank on that thing all night, you sleep somewheres else."

Haywood grinned. His cocked-eye lazily rolled. "You can call me Hay," he said.

Henry came to the fire and sent Haywood after water. Bill stared at the black man with disgust and walked toward the latrine, unslinging his suspenders again as he did. Haywood skipped toward the well with the bucket banging hollowly against his leg. "Strange boy," Henry said, "but not a bad little nigger."

"You seen we got a visitor?"

Henry bit off a chaw from the plug he took from his pocket. "Them god damned officers." He shook his head and worked the chaw deeper into his lip. He nodded at the sleeping forms still strewn around the fire, around the field. "All these white boys are fools."

"Why's that?"

"That damned officer is going to say, 'You ride here and you capture this, or you kill that.' He says it and they does it and a lot of them are going to die trying." He spat tobacco juice into the embers. "These dumb shitbird white boys are more slave than I ever was."

Jacob turned to squint into the rising sun. The house when he looked at it was hidden beneath the tangible brilliance it had left in his eyes. He turned to the hickory where Archie was still sleeping. He thought of McGown.

"You're a northern boy, ain't you?" Henry asked.

"Ohio."

"What are you doing here?"

"I just ended up here, I guess."

"What you fighting for that damned officer for?"

"All I'm doing is gathering firewood," Jacob said.

Fallen wood was getting scarce, and Jacob and Haywood had to work deeper into the trees. They followed a game trail into the forest with the crows and the songbirds and somewhere a rooster calling around them. The mid-morning, mid-August sun heated even the shadows. The whine of mosquitoes, the leaves in the branches whispering. Haywood cocked his head at Jacob with that strange, wild-eyed stare, that strange, gappy grin. "How old are you, Jake?"

"Eighteen."

"You sure look older than that. Must be the busted-up nose."

"Must be a lot of things."

"How'd you get your nose busted up?"

"Got kicked by a mule."

An oak had fallen to the right of the trail and they worked their way through brambles toward it. Haywood hacked with the ax at the dried crown while Jacob gathered up the wood and hauled away the brush. Haywood could hardly swing an ax even feebly, but Jacob wouldn't touch it.

"You got a girlfriend, Jake?"

"I sure don't chase after sheep."

"What's her name?"

"Sarah. She lives over in Dawson Springs, Kentucky."

"What's she look like?"

"She's pretty. Dark hair, dark eyes."

"What's she do over there? She just sit around and pine for you?"

"She works in a whorehouse."

"Whoring?"

"What else would she do in a whorehouse?"

"That ain't much different than mounting sheep, Jake."

"Haywood, you're a fool."

"I wish you'd call me Hay," Haywood said.

Jacob yanked a branch clear and dragged it away. He had been working hard and his breath was hot in his throat and his sweat lay in a sheen upon him. He sat with his back against an oak trunk and looked up into its branches, wondering with a taste of fear at what he might see. Haywood sat cross-legged in front of him, his back so curled he could prop his chin on his hands with his elbows in the moldering leaves in front of his ankles. He squinted at Jacob. His bad eye shone almost completely white, the iris turned in toward his nose.

"Hey, Jake? You ever play hide-and-seek?"

"Not in a long time, Haywood."

"I was playing back around Christmas. With this boy. He wasn't really playing though, because it's hard to get someone to play with you when you got an eye like mine."

"You blame too much on that eye, Haywood."

"So he was going through the woods and I was kinder following behind and then this shot goes off and back at the house Mam screams. And then I hear this running and then this other shot goes off and the back of this boy's head, it's just gone. Just gone. And then these soldiers come and one of them, he shoots at me but he cain't hit me because I'm magic. But then they catch me and this doctor named Jennison from over in Kansas works off my ears with this knife. But they cain't kill me because I'm magic. And then they kill Pap and clean us out and then they come back a few days ago and we don't have much left to clean out and so they burn us down. I just go hide in the trees and they shoot at me but they cain't hit me. Because I'm magic."

"Why do you think you're magic?"

"I got this here spot on the back of my head."

"That's just ringworm."

"And I got this here eye, and I ain't got these two teeth. Mam says I got me the mark of Cain because no one will ever want me around with the way I look, but it makes me magic because nobody cain't never kill me, neither. That's why I'll be such a good gorilla." He cocked his head and studied Jacob. "Hey, Jake?" he asked.

"Yeah?"

"How come you don't call me Hay?"

"It ain't much of a name, Haywood."

"It's better than Booger. That's the name of that boy that got the back of his head blowed off."

It took them a few minutes to gather up the kindling, Haywood with it loaded in his arms and Jacob with it across his back in two leather slings. By the time they reached camp Jacob was tired and light-headed with the sweat soaking his clothes in clinging dark stains, with his ears ringing. The guerrillas were saddling their horses. A buckboard had been pulled to the side of the fire, where a new boy doused the embers, the hissing steam rising. Henry was packing the mess gear into the wagon bed. He kicked the boy in the ass when a tripod leg fell into the ashes.

"What's going on?" Jacob asked.

"God damned officers," Henry said.

"What's going on?"

"Breaking camp." He kicked the boy again. "Douse that right, you dumb white shitbird fool."

"You mean we got all this wood for nothing?"

Henry squinted at him. "You try my patience."

Jacob and Haywood dropped their loads and stretched their backs and helped Henry and the new boy break and stow the mess. The new boy had coarse red hair in patches like mange, a pug nose, muddy green, uncomprehending eyes. He didn't speak; perhaps he couldn't. As they were stowing the tripod, Charlie came out of the house and walked toward them. Henry paused in his work as he watched him.

"Hey, Henry," Charlie said.

"Hey."

"You tired of chopping wood, Ohio boy?"

Jacob stopped working. He wiped at the sweat burning the corners of his eyes. "I never cared for it much to begin with."

"Then why didn't you run home to Ohio?"

"Because this is what Henry told me to do."

"You like taking orders from a nigger?"

Jacob looked at Henry. Henry glanced back. "Don't make no difference to me."

Jacob went back to work. Charlie stopped him with a hand on his shoulder. He was a slight man, but had the strength of a horseman in his grip. "You a Yankee?"

"I used to be."

"Why should I trust you?"

"Because Bud Younger used to be a Yankee, too."

Charlie pursed his lips. He seemed to approve of the answer. He looked at Haywood, who had stopped working when the man had come over and stood staring at him with his head cocked to the side and the toes of one foot working the toes of the other. "What's your name again?"

"Haywood Lee, yes sirree, just like the general. You can call me Hay."

"Will you follow orders, be true to your fellows, and kill those who serve and support the Union?"

"Mam just told me to get revenge. Is that the same thing?"

"It is. Will you do it?"

Haywood grinned. "Sure."

Charlie nodded. He watched Henry work. "You about ready here, Henry?"

"About."

"We leave when you are."

"I'll be ready by the time you get in column."

Charlie walked back toward the house. Henry watched him go. The heat was heavy upon him and sweat in rivulets ran over his scalp. The sun filled his eyes when he turned to Jacob and he squinted. "No more wood chopping for you."

"I guess."

"You're in for it now."

"I guess."

"Me, too," Haywood said happily.

Henry worked his lips. Tobacco juice stained them. "I'm losing my little nigger."

Haywood poked Jacob in the ribs. "He calls me his little nigger, Jake." He grinned.

They rode north the rest of the morning through the hills and the heat and the trees, crossing narrow creeks and pastures, the road dust rising. Farms burned out or still standing with farmers either waving from their fields or fleeing into the trees. Single riders or boys in groups of three or four joined them, and other riders rode out to scout. The mess was again in the back of the column and the men rode before them four abreast fading into the clouded, choking, limitless dust. Ghost riders. Dave Poole rode just ahead of them. Jacob could see neither Bill nor Archie. Haywood rode an old Morgan mare, the horse of the boy who had shot himself, and he sat upon it stiffly, the reins in his hands and his fingers tangled in the mane, trying to hold himself up from the jolt of the horse as it trotted. His eyes were red and his face caked with the dust. Snot threatened to drop from his nose.

"It would work better if you just sat on the saddle," Jacob told him.

"I done tried that. My balls are too big and when I bounce I end up squarshing them."

"It ain't that your balls are too big. Your stirrups are too long."

"My balls are too big. They keep getting squarshed."

"Haywood."

"Yeah?"

"It comes from mounting sheep."

"A fella's got to do something, don't he?" Haywood asked.

They stopped at noon to rest the horses. They numbered now perhaps forty. Flies and heat were all around them and mosquitoes whined in the air. Jacob adjusted Haywood's stirrups with a warm satisfaction at his growing equine proficiency. The boy mounted and sat easier, though he still rode with both hands tangled in the Morgan's mane and a grimace on his already deformed features.

They stopped two hours later with the sun beating down. Henry handed around to those who hadn't left to raid meals from farms, old griddle bread and stolen Federal army rations. The Confederate officer refused to accept it from Henry's hand. The men ate silently, eyes glancing into the trees, into the hills, at the sun, jaws working. The land around them lifeless. A Union home burned with its chimney pointing starkly at the sky; a southern home burned with its chimney pointing starkly at the sky.

"Hell of a thing to see," Henry said as he chewed.

"For Joshua drew not his hand back," Jacob said.

"If that ain't a dumb-assed thing to say."

Jacob watched the black man eat, watched the sweat and dust clump, watched his sinewy throat work as he swallowed. "Let me ask you a question."

"All right."

"I thought when you left Osceola you said you was going to Kansas."

"That ain't no question."

"Wasn't you going to Kansas?"

"I went to Kansas. Lawrence, Kansas. Lawrence is full of niggers all living in shacks with the rats down by the river. All the white folks live in nice big houses. Same as here. White folks, they're the same, no matter what side of some border they draw. You go look at one of them borders. You won't see nothing."

"You could go somewheres else."

"I hear that Lincoln fella wants to send all us niggers to Africa or South America or someplace. I don't want to go to Africa or South America or someplace. I was born in Missouri."

"You could go out west somewheres."

"I don't want to go out west somewheres. Ain't I got a right to stay here?"

"With Quantrill?"

"Sure."

"Why do you want to?"

"The other day when I knocked you down. Could I have done that anywheres else?"

"No."

"Not in this world and not in this lifetime. But I can knock you down as long as I'm with Quantrill, because men got to eat and white men can't cook. And here there ain't no rules that say white men don't have to be scared of me." He grinned. "You know Poor Little Willie Anderson."

"Came in with him."

"You know Georgie?"

"George Todd? Sure."

"They're both as dumb as shit. But they're mean. Before the war, Georgie'd catch runaway niggers and slit them open. He'd load them with rocks and dump them in rivers. But me, I call them shitbird white boys to their faces and they don't do nothing about it. You know why? Because they got to eat. And because they're scared of me." He forced a plug of tobacco leaves behind his lip with a snakelike tongue. "There ain't a nigger that can do that anywheres else. Not one."

"It can't last," Jacob said.

"Course it can't. Nothing does."

"What do you think of that officer not taking your food like that?"

"Maybe I'll kill him one day."

When the riders returned from the farms and Charlie gave the order, the column mounted, the clatter of firearms, the creak of leather. They rode through the late afternoon, picking up more boys, stopping at creeks to water the horses, the riders. The sun grew heavy in the west, its yellow light in the whispering leaves, in the call of the birds. They neither saw nor heard any sign of Federal soldiers. They rode silently.

They stopped to camp just outside of Strother, fifteen miles south of the Missouri River. The day's heat was just beginning to lift. The men unsaddled and rested and when Jacob tried to gather wood for the cookfire, Henry pushed him to the side.

"What's going on?" Jacob asked.

"You just unsaddle your horse."

"What's going on?"

The black man's eyes flashed. "You do as I say. You want me to knock you down again?"

Jacob unsaddled the piebald and took off her bit and bridle. He hobbled her and left her to graze. As Haywood tried to pull the saddle off the Morgan, it stepped deftly to the side and he pulled it down onto himself.

"Holy rolling thunder!" the boy shouted.

He collapsed to the ground with the saddle upon him, squirming like a lizard beneath a horse hoof. Jacob helped him out from under, with the boy spitting and grinning. Haywood tried to work loose the bridle, but the Morgan stomped on his toes. Jacob had to get it for him. Henry watched them silently, leaning against an apple tree.

"You're going to raid Independence in the morning," Henry said.

Jacob wiped horse sweat from his hands onto his trousers. "How do you know that?"

"I got eyes. I got ears. We got a Confederate officer at the head of this column and we're camped a few miles from there. We've been picking up bushwhackers all day. I ain't some stupid white fool."

"Holy rolling thunder," Haywood said again.

Henry studied the boy and shook his head. He spat a heavy brown stream that the boy had to jump away from. "If you ain't blessed, little nigger, you're dead."

Haywood grinned and poked at Jacob. "He called me his little nigger."

Henry sent the mangy redheaded mute after wood and began to set up the tripod. Jacob watched him work, then started forward up the column. "You looking for Bill Anderson?" Henry called after him.

Jacob turned. The black man was watching him. "Whatever's between you and Bill is between you and Bill. I ain't got nothing to do with it."

"You give Poor Little Willie my regards."

"I'll do it for you, Henry," Haywood said.

Jacob walked up through the men with Haywood following. Halfway up the column he came across Bill and Archie sitting at the edge of a field munching on just ripening apples.

"Hey," Jacob said.

"Hey."

"What?" Haywood asked.

Bill looked at him. "No one was talking to you."

"But I told you to call me Hay."

"Good Christ, can't I even greet a fella without confusion?"

Haywood scrunched up his face and scratched at the back of his head. "Well, you can call me Hay."

"I'll call you any damn thing I please."

"Don't call me late for supper!" The boy screeched a laugh like a mating tomcat. Even the birds quit singing. "Henry sends his regards, Bill."

"That god damned nigger," Bill said.

Jacob sat silently beside Bill, enjoying the coolness coming with the evening. Haywood sat beside him with his chin propped on his hands and his elbows in the dirt. The ringworm scar on the back of his head was the only part of him not covered with dust, and it shone brightly.

"What you thinking about?" Bill asked.

"I ain't thinking about nothing," Jacob said.

Archie was playing mumblety-peg with his Bowie knife in the turf, its big blade flashing, the turf accepting its violation without a whimper. "I hear you're coming in with us tomorrow."

"I'm coming, too." Haywood grinned.

"Oh, hell."

"Mam says I got to get my revenge."

"You even got a gun?" Bill asked.

"My pap used to have a musket. I was hunting squirrels this time and shot his toe off."

"You shot your pap's toe off?"

"Only one of his little ones."

"You ever fire a pistol?"

"They'd be easier than my pap's musket. I could hardly pick that son of a bitch up."

Somewhere in Bill's traveling, he had found two more .36 caliber Navy Colt revolvers, and he leaned back to get at one of them in his belt. He aimed the pistol at the sun, the trees, then handed it to Haywood. "You see that dead branch sticking out of that burr oak over there?"

Haywood squinted. His lip pulled back from the hole in his teeth. "With my good eye I can."

"See if you can come anywhere close to hitting it."

Haywood raised the pistol and without aiming fired. The pistol cracked and Haywood jumped back with a yelp, dropping it to the ground. Archie laughed. Bill didn't laugh.

"God damned cross eye," Archie said. "God damned sheep fucker."

"Look what he done." Jacob nodded toward the tree. A neat, round hole had appeared on the branch, now shivering.

"Hellfire," Archie said.

"You couldn't hit that."

"Hellfire."

Haywood was grinning. "Give me another one."

Bill studied the child. "You look out over the pasture and shoot me the first swallow you see."

"Nobody can hit a swallow without a shotgun," Archie said.

"You just let him be."

Haywood picked up the pistol with excitement dancing on his distorted features. He raised it into the sun and his hand jerked as he fired and he dropped the gun again. "Did I get him?" he asked, dancing from foot to foot. "Did I? I seen him go by and I cain't see him no more."

"He didn't get nothing," Archie said, but the grin had not risen again on his face. "Nobody can shoot a swallow with a revolver."

Jacob rose and walked into the pasture, the smell of the new hay, its greenery, around him. He thought he had seen a swallow and he thought he had seen it drop. He walked until he saw feathers. A minute later he found the bloody stump of a swallow wing down among the hay stems. He hefted it and carried it back to the guerrillas. More had gathered. He tossed it at Archie's feet.

"Well, he ain't much good if he keeps dropping the pistol," Archie protested.

"I'll rig up a lanyard so he can tie it to his wrist," Dick Yeager said.

"Twenty dollars says he can't do that again."

"Find yourself another swallow, Haywood," Jacob said.

Haywood hefted the gun. He cocked his head to the side and squinted with his good eye at the sky above the pasture. The muzzle jerked and the report echoed and Haywood dropped the revolver as if it had bit him. Jacob didn't need to go into the hay because they all had seen it, a bit of black exploded, a few feathers fluttering down.

Some of the guerrillas clapped and some of them swore and Frank James slapped Haywood on the back and called him a little fucker. Haywood grinned. Jacob accepted a twenty dollar gold piece from Archie and gave it back in payment for a second revolver. Haywood slung the two of them in his waistband as he had seen the other guerrillas do; with the pants pulled up to his armpits, the grips stuck out like malformed ears sprouted to replace the ones Jennison had taken. He sat between Jacob and Bill and accepted the apple that Bill offered and gnawed on it with his back teeth. He had to remove a pistol to eat. His lazy eye swung in a long, unnerving arc.

Archie swore softly and wandered off toward the cookfire, from where the rich scent of beans and bacon was just beginning to waft. Bill patted Haywood's shoulder and rose to follow Archie. Haywood squinted happily after them.

"I won't never shoot no toe off with one of these."

"Unless you want to."

"You getting some beans, Jake? I sure could use some beans."

"You go ahead."

"You want me to bring you some beans, Jake?"

"I'm all right."

"You think Henry will call me his little nigger again?"

"He might," Jacob said.

Haywood nodded and rose and skipped toward the cookfire. He stopped long enough to pull his brown-stained trousers free of his ass. He had left one of his revolvers on the turf beside Jacob. Jacob covered it carefully with his hand.

Chapter Sixteen

They spent the next day loafing in trees and heavily brushed gulches, out of sight of the road. Two more Confederate officers rode into camp with perhaps seventy-five farm boys either unarmed or hefting ancient muskets from Doniphan's command in the Mexican War or carrying pitchforks. The three Confederate officers saluted each other smartly and seemed to take pride in doing so. They conferred in the brush with Charlie, squatting on their haunches, drawing elaborate lines and arrows with sticks in the dirt. Jacob remembered Henry's words about the danger of officers' orders and the boys who would die following them. He felt uneasy about the next morning.

Jacob rolled over in his blanket in the middle of the night and groaned. He winced at a bite and pulled a grayback from his armpit and crushed it between his fingernails. He had been dreaming of Sarah, but the dream's memory was fleeting and when it was gone he found within him only a strange, aching longing. He flicked the dead louse away. Henry was walking by, banging together two frying pans. Jacob nodded a greeting that Henry would not return. He walked back toward the fire, the flames silhouetting him, black against light against the black of the still heavy night.

Haywood was lying beside Jacob. He'd kicked his blanket off and his father's pants were gathered around his knees. His frail little hand was gripping his stunningly developed privates. He sat up without relieving his grip, blinking.

"Oh damn." Haywood studied his crotch with dismay. "I got all skeeter-bit."

"Pull up your damn pants when you're finished."

"I must have fallen asleep."

"Or don't do it at all."

Haywood lay back and lifted his skinny hips and skootched his pants over them. "A man's got to do something."

"You don't see me with a skeeter-bit dick."

"But you got you a girlfriend. I got me the mark of Cain."

Bill and Archie were lying under the trees. Archie cursed at the noise and curled beneath his blanket. Bill lay propped against an oak, staring up into the moonlight. Jacob remembered him lying just that way when the sun had set the day before.

"Hey, Bill," Jacob said.

"Hey."

"You ready?"

"I guess."

Jacob rose and stretched the stiffness from his back and shoulders. He gathered up his pistols from where he had placed them beneath his saddle. Haywood stood and stuffed the blouse into the waist of his pants, then slung his suspenders over his shoulders. He stuffed his pistols, with their new lanyards, into his waistband.

"You going to get some breakfast, Jake?"

"Ain't really hungry."

"I am. I ain't eating no more of these apples. They give me the squirts. My dick itches."

"Pull up your pants next time."

Haywood grinned his cockeyed, gap-toothed grin and skipped toward the fire. Jacob pondered this boy and his mother and how she was not allowing him to be the way he ought to be. Boys should play hide-and-seek in the woods; boys should do the dishes while their parents are in the bedroom. Boys should lie in lofts and dream exotic dreams. But perhaps that was no longer the way of this world.

Archie pulled his blanket down from his face and squinted at the cookfire. "What time is it?"

"Hell if I know," Bill said. "God damned early."

"I'm hungry."

"Then go eat."

Archie grinned. He was uglier now than he normally was, as if the night had allowed the ugliness within him to seep. "I do believe I will. I'd hate to kill somebody when I got an appetite." He sat and rubbed his face and grinned again. "How you doing, Jake?"

"Fine."

"You ought to find you a ax so you can ride into town lopping Yankees' heads off. Didn't some old king used to do that?"

"Don't know."

"I wish I could think of his name. I'd start calling you that."

"You call me Jake."

"And I can call Haywood Hay." Archie loaded his waistband with pistols. The Bowie knife hung in its scabbard. "I do believe I'll track me down some breakfast."

He walked to the fire, mixed with the men gathering around it, dark backs, fire-lit faces, eyes solemn or excited or anxious. Jacob turned to Bill, who was still staring up at the stars, his long hair falling in shadows. "You going to eat something, Bill?"

"No."

"Why not?"

"My sisters are up on the Kansas River. You ought to see them. They're about as pretty as three sisters could be."

"Your sisters don't have nothing to do with this, Bill."

"They got everything to do with this. Every single damned thing." He closed his eyes, left them closed, then opened them with a sigh. "You?"

"I ain't hungry either."

"No. I mean do you have any family."

"No."

"No parents even?"

"No."

"But you got that girlfriend in Kentucky. What was her name?"

"Sarah." It was a word from his childhood, his innocence, but he held no innocence and the name only floated in darkness. McGown was squatting in the oak above them, looking down and grinning, scratching the stump of his black-scabbed wrist with his thick, iron-bending fingers. The mole on his nose like a tear, the cut on his forehead festering, the dead flesh, the white bone beneath, bloated parasites dropping like rain that evaporated before reaching the ground. He spilled into Jacob's fear.

"Bill, do you believe in ghosts?"

"I don't believe nothing I ain't seen."

"Do you believe in God?"

"I ain't never seen God."

"I bet you believe in Paris. You ain't never seen Paris."

"Paris is different. Somebody's seen Paris. Ain't nobody ever seen God."

Jacob thought of his mother and what she had seen. What she knew and what she didn't.

They waited silently. The dawn came closer but was still distant and suddenly McGown was gone. The men who had finished eating milled about restlessly, checking horses, checking weapons, searching the sky or staring at the ground as if seeking in the dust answers. Haywood skipped over, wiping his mouth on the sleeve of his mother's blouse. He squatted beside Jacob.

"Today I get my revenge," he said.

"Hope so."

"Mam will be so happy."

It must have been the third hour when the three officers appeared out of nowhere with Charlie beside them. They talked softly by the fire as they ate, then handed their plates to the mangy mute who skittered around them like an abused dog. Archie had come back and began playing mumblety-peg with his knife. "What do you suppose they're talking about, Bill?" he asked.

"Figuring out the best way to kill a lot of them without getting killed, I guess," Bill said.

Within fifteen minutes the order went out and they mounted. Those with revolvers went to the front of the column with Charlie while the rest gathered at the back behind one of the officers. Jacob leaned forward to whisper into the piebald's ear of the day he thought awaited them. She nickered, the white speckles on her withers looking like the sky above them. Haywood sat mounted on the Morgan beside him.

"You string those lanyards around your wrists," Jacob said.

Haywood did. "I still say my balls are too big. And I'm all skeeter-bit."

"You just keep your mind on not getting shot."

"I wasn't planning on it," Haywood said.

The column moved forward slowly. The night was thick enough to leave to Jacob only the black hulk of McGown now visible, somehow floating above the head of the column, his legs trailing like a stork's, his jacket flapping. The piebald's ears lifted and she tossed her head and shivers ran down her flanks. For almost an hour the column rode without words among the creak of leather, the soft clatter of hooves on hard-packed earth, a few coughs and curses and spitting, the early morning chill. Jacob kept his head down and his eyes away from McGown. He wondered if this would ever end.

They came up a rise. Below them lay darkness. Charlie galloped back along the column and galloped forward again.

"Let's give them hell, boys," he said.

Suddenly all was wildness, with the men riding silently with their drawn pistols in the air. The horses plunged into the darkness, like coins dropped into a well, eyes reflecting wildness on glinting edges, wildness passing over Jacob and leaving him untouched. Everything had drained from him. Even McGown was gone.

Bill's eyes were wild, his face gray in the darkness. Archie grinned orgasmically. Haywood rode beside Jacob with his mouth gaping and both hands tangled in the Morgan's mane. The pistols hung from his wrists and slapped impotently against the saddle. "Holy rolling thunder!" he shouted.

"Pick up your guns, Haywood!"

"My balls are done near squarshed!"

Now only the rumble of the hooves, the horses blowing. Buildings now around them and wild savageness sparking in the air and Jacob rode into it as if it were falling water. He shot at a window and watched it break before the horses swept him beyond it toward a wide, tree-lined town square. A boy in a blue uniform was crawling at the side of the street, and Jacob aimed around Haywood and shot him. The boy's head jerked. Jacob was better at shooting from a horse than he had thought he would be. It gave him a strange pleasure and pride.

The riders milled in the square in confusion; there was nothing to shoot at and all was silent. Charlie mumbled something to George, and George nodded and took five men with him to the north side of the square. Some of the men dismounted and Jacob sat in the saddle uncertainly, glancing at the dark buildings. He couldn't find McGown. A young voice from the southwest corner of the square shouted "Halt!" as if they hadn't already done so. Someone fired a rifle from a brick building at that southwest corner. The piebald's ears pricked and she shivered. Charlie held up his hand.

"For God's sake, don't shoot," he shouted. "It's your own men!"

They waited anxiously. One of the officers was marching his farm boys north through the square. Suddenly men in long underwear burst out of the building the rifle shot had come from. They saw the officer and ran back in again. More shots echoed and the guerrillas returned the fire and suddenly all was madness. A blood-filled rebel yell lifted from the milling horses. Archie picked it up and dashed past Jacob toward the southwest corner. Now all the riders were yelling and shooting and the horses were galloping in circles around the square. Jacob raised his pistol and kicked at the piebald's ribs. He studied his actions with a detached, analytic curiosity.

Darkness and gunsmoke everywhere, its acrid smell burning, stinging Jacob's eyes. He fired at windows when he could see them and he fired blindly when he couldn't. Bullets whistled around him and a rider Jacob didn't know threw up his arms and fell backward off of his saddle. His toes caught in the stirrup and the piebald rode over his chest as it surged ahead through the smoke. In front of Jacob in the slow-growing dawn Charlie fired at a second-story window in a bank across the street from the building the men in their underwear were shooting from. Jacob fired at it, too.

The riders were sweeping in circles around the square and Jacob on the second pass could see that the soldiers firing at him weren't men but teenaged boys. Like himself. Some were trying to run across the street to the bank, their underdrawers almost glowing in the half light. Others had gathered in front of their building and were firing steadily into the horses. Another rider went down. Another rider went down. It shouldn't have been like this but it was and Jacob cursed all Confederate officers.

The horses milled and jostled as one by one their riders fell. Jacob glanced up at the night; he wasn't sure, but he could have been praying. McGown was perched on the top of the bank, squatting and smiling and pointing with his good hand at a towheaded boy who had broken in a run across the square. Jacob kicked the piebald and she leaped forward savagely, foam flecking back from her mouth over her flanks, her eyes rolling in hatred. The boy looked over his shoulder and even in the darkness Jacob could see that his eyes were insane with fright. The boy dropped his musket and ran with his arms pinwheeling. Jacob rode him down and the piebald knocked him over and the boy rolled onto his back and Jacob, leaning back, put a bullet in his smooth throat. The boy jerked and stared up at the coming morning. Jacob's empty feeling did not obscure what he saw, but rather clarified it; even in the darkness all was black and white with the distinct edges of ink on paper. A gift of sight given where the gift of soul had been denied. He wondered if Joshua in his own mad dashes had taken the time to pray.

The Morgan was standing calmly in the middle of the square. Each time Haywood reached for his revolvers they slipped down on their lanyards and he had to grab for the horse again to keep from tumbling. Jacob galloped toward him, bullets like rain. He wheeled into the bullets and fired into the white-shadowed line of boys firing at him. Holes opened on backs and chests and in faces. The boys broke before him and ran for the bank. Jacob kicked the piebald and it opened into a gallop. He fired deliberately. He looked to his right and saw Charlie beside him with a black fire smoldering in the slits beneath his eyelids. A hint of a grin on his face.

Most of the soldiers had entered the bank and were firing steadily from the windows. More guerrillas were dropping. Jacob rode in a hard gallop across the face of the building and fired twice into windows. When he had finished his pass he paused to check the square. Haywood was still grabbing for pistols with the Morgan standing calmly. Guerrillas lay motionless or twisting spastically or hiding behind trees. Three or four horses were screaming hellishly with blood pumping in great gouts from their necks and chests and flanks. His pistols were empty.

Charlie was studying the bank from across the square. Jacob dashed toward him with bullets whistling past his face. He fetched Haywood's Morgan by the bridle as he went by.

"Hell, Jake, this is something, ain't it?" Haywood's good eye was wide and his face pale in the early dusk.

"Get yourself your damned pistols, Haywood."

"I keep grabbing for them and they keep slipping away. I try to reach across and grab them with the other hand but then my balls get more squarshed."

"Do you want squashed balls, or do you want to be dead?"

"I don't really care for the choice."

Jacob reined the horses up beside Charlie. The sudden stop caused Haywood to half tumble over the Morgan's neck and he dropped the pistol. Charlie nodded at Jacob.

"You're a devil, Ohio boy."

"I ain't a devil," Jacob said.

"You and the boy there go help George over at the jail."

"Where's the jail?"

Charlie pointed north. Jacob nodded and rode off in that direction, still leading the Morgan. Rifles and pistols and muskets cracked and echoed. Through the smoke and darkness behind him, Jacob watched the guerrillas take cover in the abandoned brick building the soldiers had used as a bivouac. The firing became sporadic and mixed with the sounds of the wounded and dying.

"Hell, Jake, horses sure can scream, cain't they?"

"You just watch yourself, Haywood."

George was beating on the jail's front door with a blacksmith sledge. Bill was there with his eyes wide and darting, screaming wildness; Archie was coiled beside him and grinning, a cold, black spot in the heat and passion around him. The door cracked beneath the blows as Jacob and Haywood dismounted and gave way as they reached it. Frank James followed George inside with six other guerrillas in a cursing, screaming wave, Jacob and Haywood in its wake. The jailer dropped a musket and backed away from his desk with his hands raised. Sweat lay in a sheen across his pale features. He was in the process of wetting himself.

"Where's the keys?" George demanded. "You give me the keys and we'll let you go unharmed."

The jailer reached eagerly forward to the desk and opened a drawer. He handed a ring of keys to George, then backed away again. George hefted the keys and grinned and shot the jailer in the belly. The jailer curled forward and George kneed him in the chin, then shot him in the forehead as his head snapped back. George handed the keys to Frank as the man slid almost soundlessly down the wall.

"You let everybody out," George said.

Frank nodded and opened the jail cells one by one and the prisoners fled. Two of them grinned and slapped Frank on the back as they left. Frank unlocked the last cell and hurried away, but the prisoner didn't come out. Archie stopped in front of the door and grinned.

"Hey, Bill," he said. "Ain't that there the town marshal?"

Bill stepped over to study the man in the cage. "Hell if it ain't. Knowles, what are you doing in jail?"

"I killed somebody." The man was tall with a black beard and closely cropped, thinning hair. Dark eyes, a face gone as gray as the cold brick around him. "But it wasn't no secesh," he added quickly. "I swear to God it wasn't no secesh."

Bill spat into the cell, then looked over his shoulder at Haywood. Haywood stood with one bare foot on top of the other and his head cocked to the side. His lazy eye swung wildly. One pistol hung from its lanyard and the other he cradled to his chest.

"Haywood."

"Yeah?"

"You kill him."

"I want to kill him," Archie protested.

"Let the boy do it."

"I want to kill him."

"Let Haywood."

"He can kill him," Haywood said, "if he wants to."

Bill sighed and studied Haywood and shook his head and Archie leveled his pistol through the bars. Knowles whimpered and collapsed against the back wall. Archie grinned.

"Beg me not to kill you," Archie said.

"You'll kill me anyway. I seen what you all done to Wally."

"Beg me not to kill you, and maybe I won't."

"Don't kill me," the man said.

Archie cocked the pistol. "You get on your knees and beg me."

The man dropped to his knees. "Don't kill me," he said again.

Archie fired. The explosion echoed off the walls but did not cover the cracking thud of the man's skull against the back wall as the bullet drove him into it.

They left him in the cell and went back out into the street. Jacob stopped Haywood at the door.

"What?" Haywood asked.

"You ever get a chance to do that again, you kill him. You don't let Archie kill no one if you can beat him to it."

"Why?"

"Because he takes a pleasure in it. There's something wrong with a fella who takes a pleasure in it."

The street around the jail was silent until a mockingbird trilled somewhere above. The occasional crack of a pistol or the heavier boom of a musket came from the square, the bloody scream of a horse. More shots and screams and voices of men dying from the dusk north of town. Archie and Bill were hurrying for the square, Jacob and Haywood after them. The sun was rising.

They sprinted into the brick building where the boys in their underwear had bivouacked. Boots lay scattered across the floor and the stairs leading up to the second floor in the back; trousers lay over tables, and Federal uniforms hung from pegs on the wall. Bill was going from uniform to uniform, trying each one on. Archie was crouched by one of the shattered windows, levering charges into his revolver's cylinders. Jacob reloaded and crouched beside him, and Haywood beside Jacob. A musky smell rose from Archie as he leveled his pistol through the window at the bank and fired. The smell of the girl back in Freeman. Jacob hated him.

"What you shooting at, Archie?" Haywood asked.

"What the hell you think I'm shooting at? I'm shooting at windows."

"You hitting them?"

"The hell if I know. Why don't you shoot at them?"

"Well, maybe I will." Haywood pointed his pistol out of the window. "All the glass is already busted up."

"Bullets will do that."

"What fun is it if all the glass is already busted up?" He sighted again with his tongue poking out of the gap in his teeth. "I bet I can hit that little chink there in that window on the second floor, third one over. I bet I can hit it."

"Well hit it, then," Archie said.

Without waiting to aim Haywood fired. He fell backward as he dropped the gun out of the window. The lanyard yanked his arm and the pistol grip caught on the sill. When the smoke cleared Jacob saw that the chink was gone.

Haywood rubbed his shoulder. "Did I get it?"

"You got it."

"I told you I could do it, Archie. What was the bet?"

"The bet wasn't nothing. It was just a bet."

"Hell," Haywood said. "If I'd a known that I wouldn't a bet you."

The firing kept up for two hours. Boys on the bank roof tried to tie a Union flag to the chimney, but someone shot them down. In the lulls Charlie would holler from the second floor above Jacob and a thick, clotted voice from the bank would holler back. Will you surrender; no I will not. You will die; you are Quantrill and I will die anyway. In the lulls came the sharp cough of firing from the north side of town where the Confederate officers, the farm boys, and the guerrillas without pistols had gone. The firing lessened and boys began straggling toward the square, some with bloody spots on their shoulders, on their thighs, grins or scowls or tears of pain on their faces. One of the officers limped in a crouch toward the bivouac. A fresh volley came from the bank. His big, soft eyes were bright with pain and the top of his right boot was swathed in blood that caught the dawn.

"Where's Captain Quantrill?" he demanded.

"He's a captain?" Jacob asked.

"Where is he?"

"Second floor," Bill said.

The officer limped to the back and up the stairs without further comment. Another volley came from the bank. Parts of the sill splintered, bullets whined; Haywood grinned happily and shot bits of glass from the windows. Archie ducked his head and chuckled. "Them gray uniforms draw fire. Bill, why don't you get me one of them blue ones?"

"Get one your own damn self," Bill said. He had joined them at the window with two pistols drawn and a Federal jacket over his shoulders. His long hair fell over its collar and blood flecked in his beard had dried to clots. The wildness in his eyes had grown.

"There any officer ones?" Archie asked. "I don't want one if it ain't from a dead officer."

"Looky there," Haywood shouted. "I got me another chink!"

A minute after the officer had gone up the stairs, Charlie called for a cease-fire. The air grew quiet but for the moans from the square of one or two boys who hadn't yet died, who hadn't yet been shot a second or a third or a fourth time, the scream of one tortured horse, the others having died or run off in their madness. A morning breeze had risen with the sun and whispered in the trees, carrying the smell of the trees, the coolness of the dawn. A beautiful summer day had begun that reminded Jacob of that farm a lifetime ago. He thought briefly of Cyrus and Clara and Tobias, of Isaac. He thought of Sarah until the feeling lumped in his throat too large for him to swallow. He tried to push the thought away, but it kept returning. The smooth coffee skin, the soft skin of her throat. The gentle curves as her waist fell to her hips. Her eyes.

McGown was crouching on the bank roof, bouncing lightly on his toes, his mouth as dark a maw as his eyes had become. His uniform in tatters, the skin on his forehead in tatters, the bone beneath it glinting thinly. Jacob watched him silently, then aimed his pistol at him. McGown grinned.

"What's going on?" Archie asked.

Bill shrugged. "Hell if I know."

"Something's going on," Jacob said.

Charlie shouted the order to fire and shots began ringing. Bud Younger and a boy perhaps a year younger than he was came in a run around the corner of the bivouac and sprinted for a carpenter shop just beyond the bank. The firing from the bank was sporadic, puffs of white like clouds being chased across a sky. Jacob did not fire. He still aimed at McGown. McGown only grinned with his secret knowledge.

"What are we shooting for?" Haywood asked.

"This is a war, you damned fool," Archie said.

Bud and the boy came out of the carpenter shop with their arms loaded with shavings. In a crouch they broke toward a wooden store leaning against the west side of the bank. The gunfire from the guerrillas grew to a continuous barking roar and McGown danced on the roof like a child at play. Bud and the boy piled the shavings in front of the store's front door and lit them. Flames were already licking the eaves by the time they'd sprinted across the street, the boy's face wild, Bud's as bland as always. Dirt leaped in spurts around their feet. Bud dove through the window into the building beside the bivouac and the boy went through the door.

Charlie called for another cease-fire. "Surrender, Buel," he shouted, "or you will surely roast!"

The only answer from the bank was the boom of a musket and a cloud of white smoke and the gentle click and whisper of the growing flames. A musket ball thudded into the wall behind Jacob. The fire was burning gaily now, the store and the bank shimmering in the heat. The sun was higher, mid-morning on a bright, late-summer day. As if to escape the flames, McGown was gone.

"So now what do we do?" Haywood asked.

"They got to come out," Archie said. "We shoot them as they come out."

"We do what Charlie tells us to do," Bill said.

"When did he become a captain?" Archie asked.

"The hell if I know," Bill said.

Black smoke rose from the bank in gouts. The firing ceased. It must have been nine o'clock when a blue elbow knocked the crosspieces out of a window on the bank's second floor and hung a white sheet from it. The guerrillas cheered. Jacob felt no emotion beyond a low growing anger and he cheered only hollowly. He looked at the dead men lying in the square, at the dead horses.

"God damned officers," he muttered.

Bill looked at him. "What?"

"God damned officers. Me and you and Archie and a couple of others could have done all of this just like we done in Council Grove and not one of us would have been hurt. We would have sneaked in and sneaked out. Instead we got to come in like some band marching down the street. And look at this."

Bill spat out the window. "It's an officer's job to get some of us killed."

"The hell."

"Why would we need them otherwise?"

"I ain't never fighting under one again."

When the cheering died, one of the other Confederate officers stepped out of the building Bud and the boy had fled into—how he'd gotten there, Jacob didn't know. He ignored the blood seeping from his knee as he cupped his hands around his lips and shouted into the bank through the growing rumble of the fire.

"You surrender?" he asked.

"I want to know if me and my men will be turned over to Quantrill," the clotted voice asked.

"You'll be turned over to me," the officer shouted.

"And who are you?"

"Colonel Gideon Thompson, army of the Confederate States of America."

"I want to know if we'll be treated as prisoners of war. I want to know that we won't be executed."

"You have my word," Colonel Thompson said.

"Then we won't be turned over to Quantrill."

"You won't be turned over to Captain Quantrill."

The parley ended and the colonel stood waiting. The front door of the bank opened and the Federal soldiers filed out amid great black billows, led by a stout man in full military uniform, his face flushed with his embarrassed foolishness, soot on his cheeks. Most of the men behind him were still in their underwear, gray with smoke and splotched red in places, hair mussed, soot in eyes, thin chests clenched with their coughing. The soldiers lined up in the square and the colonel strode formally toward them and accepted the stout man's sword. The guerrillas poured out of the buildings.

"Get to work, boys," Charlie said.

The guerrillas cheered again and went to work on the stores. What doors were locked were broken open, and the goods inside were hauled out and loaded on wagons. The soldiers watched silently. Larkin Skaggs with his priest's collar and his rat boy lackey headed straight for the saloon, quoting to the smoke-hazy skies great eloquations of scripture in praise of blood and victory. Soon bottles were being passed around and bottles emptied and the air around the guerrillas stank of whiskey and their voices were full of it. The looting became more disordered and spread wider. Guerrillas went into houses and came out with draperies and dresses. Windows shattered and women cried and their men watched silently with lips and hands trembling. Jacob walked among the chaos. A shadow passed overhead, and he looked up to see McGown flying like a giant bat or carrion eater. The dead sergeant landed on the roof of a house a block off of the square. He scratched the stump of his wrist, then pointed down at the house's front door.

Jacob left the square and walked toward the house. He didn't know what to think of McGown. His fear of him was a huge thing, but so great a fear left little room to fear anything else and perhaps that was the reason he was not lying dead in the square. He had something to ponder.

He reached the front yard without figuring it out. By the time he had reached the porch he'd heard McGown's boots scrabble across shingles and the dead sergeant was no longer there. Jacob went up the creaking steps and knocked on the door. No one answered, so he drew a pistol and knocked again. A desiccated old man opened it and looked at him with fearful dignity.

"You take what you want," the old man said. "I don't want any trouble."

"I'll just take what I need. I don't want no trouble neither."

Jacob stepped over the threshold. An old woman with a hunch to her back as if she carried her years upon it was standing just inside of the door. A young girl who must have been a great-granddaughter clutched the old woman's skirts, dark pigtails that shown like mahogany. Jacob tipped Tobias's hat to both of them. "You got a blanket, ma'am? Winter's coming, and it's going to get cold out there. I can't hardly remember the last time I slept in a house."

"We're southern people, come up from Georgia," the woman said, peering up from the angle her deformity had forced upon her. "We always have been. Our son is with Price right now."

"North, south, it doesn't make any difference," the old man said. "First it was Jennison and now it's Quantrill and soon it will be Jennison again. Maybe Lane. It doesn't make any difference."

"I got experience with Jim Lane," Jacob said. "I was at Osceola."

The old woman nodded, but her voice held no sympathy. "The blankets are in the hall closet."

"Can you show me? It'll save me from looking and maybe tearing things up."

The old woman tore the girl's grip away, and the girl whined and clawed at her rosy little lips with her idle fingers. Jacob followed the old woman's faltering steps down the hall. He turned to the old man, who stood at the door with his long, bony hands gripping the girl's shoulders. "You don't move from there, all right? I'd hate to have to do something I wouldn't want to."

The old man did not move. The woman was at the closet, her hunch hiding her neck and half of the iron gray bun she kept her hair in on the back of her head. She opened the door and with tortured graspings took from a shelf a heavy wool blanket. Jacob hefted it and nodded. "I thank you."

"There is no need to thank me for what I'm forced to do."

"You got any guns here?"

"Senator," the woman called over Jacob's shoulder, "he wants the guns."

"You a senator?" Jacob asked the old man.

The old man straightened his shoulders. "A state senator. Retired. I have an old flintlock of my father's that isn't much use. I have a pistol my son sent me."

"What kind of pistol?"

"A Mexican dragoon."

"I'd like to see a pistol like that."

"See it or take it?"

"Well."

"Ah."

Jacob shrugged. "I'm fighting and you're not."

The old senator nodded as if this was enough of an answer. He walked into the living room and Jacob followed him. As Jacob walked by the girl she cowered by the door and he smiled at her. Her eyes never left his face and were round and bright with fear and her breath rushed in and out of the little O of her mouth. Was he so fearful a thing to see?

The old senator handed him a polished walnut case from the fireplace mantel. Jacob opened it. It held a pistol and powder flask and a silver-studded ammunition pouch, ornately tooled. He took them out of the case and put the case back. The pistol was heavier than his Colts with a checkered rosewood grip. Six cylinders and a bore as big around as his index finger. He aimed it at the window.

"Sweet Jesus, you could bring down a moose with this."

"It isn't made for moose."

"You ever fire it?"

"Once. It takes half-ounce balls and a rifle charge. I shot through a tree as big around as your thigh."

"Clean through?"

"Clean through."

"Damn." Jacob tried to heft his goods under one arm and still leave his pistol hand free. The pistol felt good there and he liked the weight and look of it. Finally he shifted it under his arm so he could carry in his hand one of the loaded Colts. "Ma'am," he asked the old woman, "I don't suppose you have something for me to carry all of this in?"

"A gunnysack out back."

"You get it quick."

"I can't get it quick. I'm an old woman."

"Then you do it as quick as you can."

They waited silently for the old woman. The senator swayed gently on his feet and watched Jacob. Only his hands trembled now. The child still stood by the door. Guerrillas passed in front of the windows, laughing drunkenly and occasionally firing pistols into the air. One went by with a piano leg over his shoulder. They waited. Suddenly the girl bolted toward the drapes and Jacob's pistol rose automatically to point at her and the old senator moaned softly. She hid behind the drapes with only the polished toes of her shoes sticking out. Jacob stood with the pistol pointed at where her head would be, then lowered it slowly. The old senator's mouth was a circle and his breath whistled through it. So like his great-granddaughter. He had to lean on the mantel. His face had gone pale to the point of the death that years would soon no longer withhold from him. Whatever had stiffened him had now broken.

"Sorry," Jacob said.

Somewhere in back a door opened and the Colt rose again, but it was only the old woman's clicking, faltering step. She came around the corner peering up at him with arsenic eyes and with a potato sack hugged to her chest. She thrust it at him and he loaded his booty into it.

The old woman's eyes flashed frantically around the room. "Where's Jenny?"

"Behind the curtain," Jacob said.

He nodded to the senator and his wife and started for the door. He stopped to look back at them. On the mantel above the senator's shoulder was a ceramic figurine of a black woman dancing, one thin arm raised over her head, the other around her waist and her face tilted back and laughing. Her skin was chocolate smooth and shone in the light coming through the window. He walked back and lifted it from the mantel. It was warm to his touch from the sun.

"This is awful nice," he said.

"Are you going to tell me you need that, too?" the woman asked bitterly.

He hefted the figurine's weight in his palm. So delicate, that smile; an arm he could snap with his fingers. A dread he did not understand filled him and he put it back on the mantel. "No. I won't."

He walked across the living room to the door, opened it, and looked out at the morning. He closed it again. The old couple watched him, the woman glaring, the man's chin trembling. The girl was still hiding; the figurine danced.

"I ain't taken nothing that will cause you hardship. But I'll pay you for what I took." He fished in his pocket for a coin. "I got here twenty dollars."

"The pistol itself is worth more than twenty dollars," the old woman snapped.

"Just please take it," the old man said.

Jacob walked back and put the coin in the old man's palm. It was cool and trembling and his face was flushed and he would not meet Jacob's eyes. Jacob tipped Tobias's hat to the woman and the girl still hidden behind the drapery and went out into the morning. He was glad to be out of there.

He spent the next hour walking the streets and watching for McGown. He didn't find him. He walked to the north side of town, to a bloody cow pasture holding what remained of a battle and found scattered among bivouac tents and behind a stone wall on the west side boys in their underwear with holes in their backs and cold grimaces on their faces, cold eyes staring blindly. Two dead horses lay with their lips twisted back, the third Confederate officer beneath one of them with a bullet hole in his forehead. One boy was stuck to a tree with a pitchfork and big, black flies were crawling on his lips and around his eyes. Hogs rooted in what the sun was already festering. So it must have been on the plains of Jordan when Joshua carried out the Good Lord's commands. Our maker unmaking.

More soldiers had gathered back at the square; boys, Jacob imagined, from the battle on the north side. They sat or squatted and watched impassively the rapine around them. Twenty wagons had been lined up across the square from the burning bank; the first officer sat in a chair with his bandaged foot propped up and directed their loading. Dry goods, ammunition, muskets. Flour and cornmeal and bacon. Dresses and furniture and other finery. Some of the guerrillas had remounted and were riding around the square with Union flags tied to their horses' tails, whooping and heaving empty bottles through windows. Dick Yeager was tying a bolt of blue gingham across the back of his saddle. Charlie sat mounted on a beautiful brown gelding outfitted with Federal cavalry tack, watching all impassively.

Archie came out of the bivouac wearing a Federal officer's uniform with long blue tails and a polished black belt with a large gold buckle, polished black boots. He grinned at Jacob and waved, jogging toward him across the square.

"Hey, Jake, look what I found."

"Where'd you find it?"

"Hell if I remember, I been everywhere. What you got in the sack?"

"A few things."

"You seen Haywood? You ought to see Haywood."

"Where is he?"

"Around. Hell if I know. This is one big party, ain't it? We ought to have done this in Council Grove."

Jacob nodded. He searched the square for the boy and found instead Bill sitting beneath a hickory a few yards from the soldiers. Jacob walked over to him as Archie danced off to the saloon. Bill looked up, then back down at his hands lying in his lap, playing with the knotted silver cord. A leather pouch closed with a drawstring lay by his side.

"Hey, Bill."

"Hey, Jake. What you got there?"

"A couple of things. What you got?"

Bill glanced at the pouch. "My tithe."

"What's that mean?"

"My penance."

"What's that mean, Bill?"

"Maybe I don't know." Bill studied the soldiers. "Tell me about the first time, Jake."

"The first time for what?"

"The first time you did something you got to do penance for."

"I ain't Catholic, Bill."

"Tell me about the first time you killed somebody. Tell me about killing those two soldiers."

"You don't want to hear about it."

"What did it feel like?"

"It felt damned bad."

"Does it feel any different now? When you kill somebody now?"

He thought of McGown watching him from the top of the bank. Did it? "I don't know."

"Here's the way I see it," Bill said. "It's like when you're a kid stealing pennies. The first time you do it you think God is watching you and you know you're going to burn in hell for doing it. But pretty soon you're stealing dollars and it don't feel as bad as them pennies because maybe God ain't really watching. Does it feel that way to you?"

"I don't know."

"It feels that way to me. Or I'd like it to, anyway."

Jacob squatted beside him and watched the guerrillas. Bill sat with his head bowed and didn't speak again.

Finally Jacob rose and walked north to the jail. It was empty but for the dead men; he enjoyed the coolness and the way the thick brick walls muffled the racket. The jailer still lay on the floor and Knowles still lay in his cell, though his body was now bullet-riddled and someone had pinned one of his shoulders to the floorboards with a kitchen knife. He had obviously had enemies.

Jacob sat at the desk and pretended to order prisoners to their fates, his finger guiding judicially each imaginary convict from their cells out the door toward either freedom or an illusory gallows. He opened the desk drawer, and in the back found a small strongbox. He set it on the desk and went to the door for the blacksmith sledge George had dropped there.

Two blows opened the box. Inside he found five hundred dollars, two hundred in coin and three hundred in scrip. He whistled softly, cursed beneath his breath, and stuffed the money into his pockets. He studied the jailer on the floor and for a reason he did not understand reached down and put a twenty dollar note into his mouth. Perhaps in consolation; perhaps so the man could pay the piper or the boatman or whoever awaited him, if anyone did. He left the jail with the intention of going back to the senator's and paying those good people properly for what he had taken. By the time he reached the square he had convinced himself that they would just as soon not see him.

Colonel Thompson was standing in the center of the square, propped on a crutch, talking to the Federal officer. Some of the soldiers around them were leaving, most heading west on the road Jacob guessed led to Kansas City. Haywood was standing by Bill, and when the boy saw Jacob he grinned and waved and walked toward him. He was wearing a Federal forage cap that had settled over his mutilated ears and caught on the ridge of his eyebrows. His pistols were stuck in the waist of his trousers and his trousers were pulled up to his armpits. He'd buckled a Federal light cavalry saber around his waist, and one of the buttons in his fly had caught on it. The tip of the saber's scabbard dragged in the dust.

"Hey, Jake. Looky what all I found."

"You ought to find yourself some pants that fit, Haywood."

"They don't make none that fit. But I got me some underwear. Looky at this." With a flourish he tried to draw the saber from its scabbard, but his arm was too short and the blade tip wouldn't clear. He slid it back in sheepishly. "I got to practice."

Jacob pointed with his chin at the boys leaving. "What's going on?"

Haywood squinted his good eye and studied them, then cocked his head back as the bill of his cap dropped further. "That officer back there done told them that if they promised not to fight no more they could go home. Archie, he ain't happy about it."

"I bet."

"He says that if it was the other way around they'd shoot or hang us all. He says so we ought to do the same."

"I bet."

"I didn't kill no one, Jake." Haywood's voice grew serious. His twisted lips did not form either a smile or a frown. "I didn't. I just kilt a couple of chinks in them bank windows."

"I know you didn't, Haywood."

"Mam, she won't like it."

"She don't have to know."

"So what do I tell her?"

"You tell her anything you please."

"I cain't lie to my mam, Jake. I cain't. She's my mam."

"Then another day, Haywood."

Haywood's lazy eye swung wildly. He shrugged and grinned and tried to draw the saber again. "I guess I got to practice." The bill of his forage cap slipped over his face.

By the middle of the afternoon the officers had grown satisfied with their booty and were anxious to leave. They gathered together the farm boys and marched off southeast on the Blue Springs road toward the Sni. It took longer for Charlie to gather the guerrillas—too many were drunk and had difficulty mounting, and too many others were still hungry for plunder. Finally he rode out of town without them, with fifteen guerrillas in column.

"That wasn't so bad," Haywood said. He was riding beside Jacob. Somewhere he had found another Colt that poked out of the front of his waistband like an exaggerated phallus. The saber slapped gently against the saddle as the Morgan walked, its head down. "I thought it would be a lot badder than that."

"Haywood, you could a been killed. At any time you could a been killed."

"I cain't be killed, Jake." He grinned. "I got me the mark of Cain."

Jacob stared straight ahead at Archie's slumped, alcohol-reeking blue-uniformed back. Beside him rode this grinning child like an ancient fertility god, spouting a faith that could not penetrate the clear blue veil over this world.

They made camp at the farm of a balding man named Morgan Walker, seven miles south of Independence, a quarter mile off of the road. A big, stone farmhouse with the slave quarters in back. The smells of manure and urine and pasture. Henry was already there, sitting beside his kettle and tripod, the slaves watching him warily and he scowling at the slaves, the mangy mute waiting servilely beside him. George and Gregg did not even get off of their horses, but led bands of two and three into the hills, leaving behind only ten guerrillas. Jacob dismounted and opened his sack. He loaded and stuffed the Mexican dragoon pistol into his belt and draped the wool blanket over his shoulders to ward off the already approaching chill of the night. Each was getting colder. He thought about that figurine on the senator's mantel and wondered what that little girl he had almost shot had named it. Children have such games. He didn't understand why he felt about to cry.

"What's the matter, Jake?" Bill asked.

"Ain't nothing the matter," Jacob said. He wiped his eyes.

The autumn was a wild thing; dead Union men, dead Southern men, dead guerrillas, captured guerrillas, Perry Hoy among them. Jacob rode to Independence with Charlie to collect some of the plundered gunpowder, and while they were gone some of the boys rode to a battle in Lone Jack where over a hundred and fifty men were killed, brothers and neighbors and churchmates driving lead into each other's chests and faces in the name of country and in the name of God. Federal Brigadier General James G. Blunt hanged Perry at Fort Leavenworth, and in revenge Charlie shot four Lone Jack prisoners and led a raid into the Kansas town of Olathe, shooting over twenty men and leaving them squealing in the streets like wounded hogs. The militia hunted them then like animals, and they lay in the grass and looked up at the night with their breath rising silver and trembling in the sharp crack of rifles and the pleadings and whimpers of the men dying around them. In October they burned Shawneetown on the Kansas side of Kansas City to the ground.

Jacob, Bill, Archie, and Haywood ambushed a mail coach just south of Pink Hill in Jackson County. Bill killed a private and Archie a sergeant who could have been the private's grandfather. Both soldiers had been armed only with shotguns and afterward Jacob found that the boy's hadn't even been loaded. He'd been careful to drop the lieutenant in charge of the guard from his horse with a shot to his thigh before coolly finishing him with a bullet in his forehead, leaving the lieutenant's single-breasted frock coat undamaged. McGown had perched in an oak beside the road and had seemed to approve of the coat's fit.

Through it all Bill Anderson tied knots in his cord and dropped coins belonging to dead men into his pouch. Through it all Archie Clement's eyes grew wilder and his grin uglier, and Jacob's hatred of him as he raped more girls grew deeper. Through it all Haywood rode into battle gripping the Morgan's mane with his pistols flopping impotently from their lanyards. Through it all Jacob killed more old men than the stars, more young boys than the years. With the coming winter the nights grew blacker.

When the leaves began to fall, Charlie called the guerrillas together at the Morgan Walker farm. He mounted the porch like a preacher, flanked by George and Gregg, while Morgan Walker peeked his bald head out of the window behind him. Slaves slunk around the edges of the men or hid in their quarters. Beside Jacob and Haywood, wrapped in his scent and his sanctity, stood Larkin Skaggs. He was alone because the rat boy had been shot in the bowels after Olathe and had died from the poison he contained. An evil soul flickered now in the preacher's eyes. His neck billowed over his collar.

"We're heading south," Charlie said. "Arkansas."

"What we going to do in Arkansas?" Archie asked. "There ain't enough Yankees in Arkansas."

"We're going to fight with the Confederate army for the winter. There isn't enough cover around here with the leaves down, and it's too damned cold."

"Hell," Bill muttered, and he spat. Jacob spat but didn't say anything.

They spent the night on the farm huddled around fires to fend off the chill. Jacob sat beside Haywood, the boy drawing pictures in the dust with his saber and whispering loudly the stories they contained. Archie and Bill sat across the fire from them, their faces flashing orange and shadow in the flames. Jacob looked up at the sky, the stars, holes in the veil showing tiny glimpses of an eternity denied. He cursed and stood and spat into the fire. He walked to the piebald's tack and began putting it on her.

"Where you going, Jake?" Haywood asked. The saber rested against his knee, catching the firelight.

"Don't know. But I ain't fighting for no damned Confederate officer."

Bill studied him silently. "Why's that, Jake?" he finally said.

"I ain't forgotten Independence. If we'd a done that right without no damned officers, ain't nobody would a been hurt. Instead we lost a bunch. That didn't happen in Council Grove. That didn't happen at Olathe or Shawneetown. When we try to play army somebody gets killed. I don't want to get killed."

"What you going to do, Jake?" Archie asked. He was wiping his knife blade back and forth across his trousers.

"Don't know." He shrugged. "Maybe head over to Kentucky."

"Or go back to Ohio. You god damned Yankee. I ought to shoot you now."

Jacob tightened the cinch and studied Archie. Finally he spat on the dark cold ground and finished adjusting the saddle. The piebald nickered. He mounted her and rode close enough to Archie to force him to look up into his face. "You know what you are, Arch?"

"What?"

"A baby-fucking, murderous fool."

Archie's hand went for a pistol as Jacob slipped his boot free of the stirrup. When the hand came forward Jacob kicked it and sent the pistol skittering into the darkness. Archie stared at him with rage working at the corners of his eyes. Jacob's hatred for this little animal twisted within him like a white-hot worm.

"I'll see you in the spring, Bill," Jacob said.

Bill grinned slightly. "See you in the spring, Jake."

"I'll kill you in the spring, Jake," Archie said.

"You won't do nothing, Archie," Bill told him.

"I'll kill you in the spring, Jake," Archie said again.

Jacob nodded. He shrugged off some of the cold. "You do what you will. I ain't fighting under no Confederate officer."

He wheeled the piebald and started east. Someone behind him stood and his back tensed as he waited for the shot. "You stop and say hello to Harriet for me," he heard Bill say.

"I will."

"See you in the spring."

"See you." He looked back at Haywood. The boy was sitting with the saber point between his bare feet and his hands on the hilt and his cheek against the blade. "You want to come along?"

"I cain't, Jake. I ain't got my revenge yet."

He left the farm with the moon just rising, riding northeast toward the Missouri. His breath rising moonlit in the coolness reminded him too much of the soul he had seen when McGown had died on the cabin floor. And now McGown accompanied him, flapping grotesquely from tree to tree, the branches groaning as he settled upon them, flitting ponderously ahead, falling ponderously behind. His fingers were beginning to rot, and as he flew he dropped teeth from putrid gums. Maggots worked at open places.

"What does it mean?" Jacob asked him.

McGown only stared. Black eyes blacker than the night, cold eyes colder than the night, black stars sucking heat and light instead of shedding them. The flesh around the wound on his forehead was gone.

Jacob reached the river by three in the morning. The chill was heavy and wet and he rode with the blanket he had taken from the senator draped over his shoulders. He ate bacon and biscuits he took from his saddlebag and slept through the next day and rode only at night to avoid the Federal soldiers. The following morning with the piebald standing over him he slept in a patch of black shriveled pawpaws growing on the bank. Once the piebald nudged his shoulder and he awoke to the harsh voices of soldiers. He drew the dragoon pistol and watched through the brush as four soldiers came down to the river to water. He aimed the pistol at the chest of the sergeant and held his breath and waited. They watered their horses and left, cursing the brush and bragging of the guerrillas they had killed.

After the sun had set on his third night out from the Walker farm he found a skiff tucked away in the brush and used it to cross the river, the piebald swimming behind with her reins tied to the stern. When he reached the other side he dried her off with one side of the blanket and draped the other over his shoulders. He mounted shivering, his joints aching with the cold. He was hungry. He hadn't seen McGown since that first night.

He rode into Rocheport at about two in the morning. The moon had set and the buildings were dark, silent shadows. He rode by the Liberty Bell and looked down at the spot where the soldier had died and he wondered what had happened to the other one. He tried to think of that as a beginning and failed.

He only had to knock twice on the Swisby front door before Harriet opened it. Even in the darkness, even though he could not see her face, he could sense that it was drawn and gray.

"Yes?" she asked.

"It's Jacob."

"Jacob?"

"Yeah."

"They done killed Oscar, Jacob. They done killed him."

"I know."

"My boy," she said.

"I know."

A light came on behind her, and old Swizz scuttled forward with a lantern raised. The lines in his face, the shadows the lantern cast, were almost frightening, reminding Jacob of McGown.

"Who's there?" the old man demanded.

"Ain't nobody but me," Jacob said.

"We ain't got nothing left, god damn it. You come again and I swear to the heavens I'll shoot you."

"It's me," Jacob said.

"I swear to the heavens I will. You boys come around—"

"It's Jacob," Harriet said.

Swizz lifted the light higher. "God damn, that there's Jacob, Harriet."

"I can see him, you old fool."

Swizz's old face cracked into a grin. The lines, the shadows, shifted. "Well god damn."

"Hey, Swizz."

"Come on in and get something to eat. I could kinder use a snack myself."

"I ought to put the horse out back, in case some Yankee comes by."

"You got yourself a horse?"

"Of course he's got himself a horse," Harriet said tiredly. "How could he be doing what he's doing without a horse?"

"He's got himself a Union jacket on there, too."

"I ain't no Union soldier," Jacob said.

"I didn't figure you were."

Jacob led the piebald out back. He unsaddled her and rubbed her down and left her to graze in the yard. He went around to the front of the house, pausing at the door to listen to the night's silence. The lantern had moved to the kitchen and Harriet was shoving kindling into the stove. Swizz was sitting at the broken end of the table with an empty tin plate in front of him and a fork in his fist, watching his wife's massive behind.

"Ain't got much for you, Jacob," Harriet said. "Fried dough is about it."

"I don't need much."

"The Yankees ruined the store because they said we was secesh. They come in here a week ago and left us with nothing but this table, two plates, the stove, and a fork."

"They didn't take the bed because they said it was too hard," Swizz said. "God damned Yankees. They'd take my pizzle if they could get at it." He nodded vigorously. "But Harriet, she done got one of them. Some snot-nosed Yankee soldier kid gave her some lip and she give him a punch in the nose. Broke his neck like a old stick."

"Don't be talking about that, Swizz," Harriet said.

"It's only Jacob. Broke his neck just like a old stick. Left him lying there out in the woods with his nose splattered all over his face. Kind of like yourn."

"They ain't come get you over that?" Jacob asked.

"The papers said that four bushwhackers tied him up to a tree and bashed his face in with the butt of a carbine," Harriet said. "They say there was witnesses."

"Damned Yankee papers."

"They do what they got to do to make their enemies. You got to have enemies in a war." She lay a dirty griddle on the stove. Soon it was spattering. "We had to steal this from the neighbors. I ain't never stole a thing in my life."

"They Yankees?" Jacob asked.

"And proud of it."

"It ain't stealing if they took it from you first."

"That's one way to look at it," she said. "I saved their child from a rabid dog once."

She mixed up water and flour and set it to frying, then leaned heavily on the table, her great fists planted and her gray head down. Finally she smiled at Jacob and covered his hand with her own. "We appreciate all you're doing for us."

"I ain't doing much."

"You're doing more than you know. Price, he's sitting down in Dixie somewhere on his fat ass doing nothing. You're up here doing something."

"Ain't that griddle bread ready yet?" Swizz demanded.

They ate silently with the lantern glowing and the kindling popping, the smell of the wood around them. Swizz belched and went to bed as soon as he finished. He snored softly as Jacob and Harriet stared at each other, the lantern glowing on the table and faces.

"You need anything?" Harriet asked.

"No."

"You need powder charges? Blankets? I can get you some Federal uniforms."

"Take care of yourself first, Harriet."

"Myself." She sighed. "I ain't got myself no more. Myself was Oscar and they put him against a pole and shot him. Now it's you and the others.

Taking care of you is taking care of myself. There ain't no other myself. And you're all so far away, over there on the border. It's like I can't hardly see who I am anymore."

"You can see fine, Harriet. You can."

"You need anything?"

"I don't need nothing."

"What are you going to do for the winter?"

"Head back over to Kentucky. I'll come back in the spring."

"What about Bill and Charlie?"

"They're heading south. There's no cover here in the winter."

"The thing about being a man," she said, "is that you can leave this."

They sat for a long time staring at the fire. Harriet turned down the lantern flame. "The neighbors," she said. "They might be wondering." The fire burned down to only a glow.

"You ought to sleep," Jacob said.

"I don't sleep no more. I ain't slept in three months."

"You ought to sleep," he said again.

"I'll try. You can have the boys' bedroom if you like."

"All right."

She smiled a soft, unhappy smile. She rose as slowly as an old woman and rested her hand on Jacob's shoulder. Her grip tightened to pain.

"Just trying to feel it," she whispered. "I'm just trying to feel it again. Oh my God, Jacob. I never thought I could miss anyone so."

Jacob didn't say anything. She released him and trudged slowly into the living room. He stared into the last glow of the fire and felt the darkness grow around him. When Harriet had quieted, he left the house and went around to the back and from his saddlebags took all of the biscuits and bacon he had remaining and left them inside the door. She was breathing steadily. He saddled and cinched the piebald. She nuzzled his shoulder.

He led the horse around to the front and mounted. He glanced at the house, then dismounted again. He took from the saddlebag a hundred dollars in gold and a hundred in scrip and set them inside the door. He left town heading east and did not see McGown until just before dawn.

Chapter Seventeen

Jacob made camp in the brush just outside of Easley. While the piebald dozed he shaved his face and cut his hair, using the river as a mirror. He changed out of the dead lieutenant's frock coat into civilian clothes he kept in a saddlebag and stowed the Colts, the powder flask, and the tooled ammunition pouch in the bag. He spent the day sleeping with the saddle as a pillow and the dragoon pistol beneath the saddle.

St. Louis was much as he had left it, bustling and stinking, German soldiers in Federal uniforms crawling in street gutters, proclaiming loudly about God and country and *scher dicht zum* the secesh and the bushwhackers. He followed the Mississippi south to Paducah and crossed into Kentucky. Leaving Missouri behind made it seem as if none of the last two years had even happened. It seemed as if he were just a boy again. But when he reached back into his saddlebags and felt the pistols, or when McGown floated nightmarishly in front of him, or when he remembered boys rotting in brush or dying on town squares, when he imagined Haywood with his head held to the ground by rough jayhawker hands and a knife working at his ears he knew he was not a boy. The piebald shifted too easily between his legs. He swore to the sky that he would never go back to Missouri again.

He rode east through Livingston and Lyon and Caldwell counties, the hills and the sky dark and gray and wet around him, the air cold, the wind bitter. He passed through Dawson Springs early one morning, just another man on a horse, and the people paid him no mind. Only the piebald knew and Jacob could feel that knowledge within her. A trembling.

He left town heading north on the Charleston road and turned onto the narrow dirt lane at the hanging hickory. He tried to remember the Latinate name Sue had used for it as he passed beneath its branches. The morning was still young and the mud beneath the piebald's hooves hard enough for her shoes to clatter. She walked with her head up and her ears twitching.

The house had not changed. There were no customers, no carriages beyond Sue's, no horses. He unbridled the piebald and left her free to graze. He knocked on the old door and turned the cracked ivory handle. Abner was sitting on his chair in the alcove as if he had never moved. He looked up, showing his tiny, dull eyes.

"Hey, Ab," Jacob said.

Abner smiled. All his teeth were gone. His lower lip was wet with drool and a line of it shone at the corner of his mouth. He clapped his hands delightedly.

"How have you been, Ab?"

"Good," Abner said. He stood and hugged Jacob, lifting him off of the floor, and when he set him down, the ache in Jacob's ribs left him hardly able to breathe. He remembered almost nostalgically the Kentucky guerrillas dying. "Good," Abner said again.

"You're looking fine, Ab."

"Good."

Jacob patted Abner's huge shoulder. Abner sat again and scratched his knuckles through his thinning thatch of hair and stared ecstatically at Jacob. He had not stopped grinning, and with his mouth open the drool was free to run in a rivulet to hang from his chin. "Good!" he shouted.

Heels clicked on floorboards. "We got a customer already, Ab?" Jacob heard Sue say. "It's awful early."

She bustled into the parlor. Her hair was loose with strands of it falling, the gray one curling around the underside of her chin. Her hand rose to tuck it back and she lifted her eyes. "Why, Jacob," she said.

"Hey, Sue."

"Why, Jacob, where have you been?"

"Around."

"Not around here."

"No, not around here."

"You come back to work?"

He shrugged. "I can't stay."

"It's so hard to find a good man."

"Ab is a good man."

She laughed. "You know what I mean." She wiped her hand down her bared, irresistible, impossible breasts, then stared at her palm. She looked up at him smiling.

"My, oh my," Jacob said.

She laughed again. "Such times. Such times." She took his hand and led him through the parlor into the kitchen. She had not changed, and he was surprised he felt no desire for her. "You want some breakfast?" she asked.

"Sure."

"Biscuits and gravy and bacon?"

"Sure." He leaned against the wall and watched her light the stove. "Where's all the girls?"

"Gone. It's a whole lot more profitable for a girl to follow Grant's army than it is to wait around for the cheap sons of bitches that pass for upstanding citizens in Dawson Springs."

"All of them?"

"Most."

"Is Rachel still around?"

Sue brushed dust bark off her palms and lit a match. She bent to nestle it beneath the kindling, then looked back past her hips at him. "You sweet on her?"

"I was never sweet on her."

"It's all right, Jacob. I know too much about life to be jealous."

"I was never sweet on her."

"She's back in her room."

"Which is her room?"

"The same room Annabelle got cut up in." She shook her head as she stood and stretched out her back. "God, what a night that was."

"Sleeping?" he asked.

"Sleeping. I've only got three girls now and they have to work extra duty. Sometimes when things are busy, I have to jump into the sack myself."

"I'll wait until she gets up," Jacob said.

She began the breakfast, and the sizzling bacon brought Abner into the room. He sat at the table grinning and watching Sue's hands as she kneaded the flour. Jacob was about to tell her all that he knew and all that he had done, but as she was turning the bacon Rachel came into the kitchen rubbing her eyes. She was wearing only a man's shirt, her legs bare and her hair loose around her shoulders. She stopped when she saw Jacob.

"Jake," she said.

"Hey, Rachel."

"You come back?"

"Just on my way through."

"He's sweet on you, Rachel," Sue said.

Sue set the breakfast on the table. Abner loaded a biscuit in each fist and gummed them happily. Jacob waited for the gravy and watched Rachel. He wanted to hold her, to bury his face in her long, blond hair, to kiss her and run his hands up those pearly thighs, her dark skin, her dark eyes shining. She said they had done it to her before and he loved her anyway or maybe even because of it. Her beautiful, woolly hair had soaked up the light.

"So what have you been doing, Jake?" Rachel asked.

If he wasn't careful, he knew he would cry. "Working the steamers out of Paducah. First I was just unloading freight. Now I'm tending boilers up to Louisville."

"For the army?"

"When I have to."

Sue sat with her plate. She peppered it heavily and looked at Jacob with a small smile. "So you're not a soldier, Jacob?"

"Not when I can help it."

"Good," Abner said, and he grabbed another biscuit.

They ate with Rachel asking questions about Paducah. Jacob made up lies and felt uncomfortable beneath Sue's smile. Abner fell asleep with his head on the table and half a biscuit hanging from his mouth. Rachel rubbed her eyes when she finished and said she was going back to sleep. She rose using Jacob's shoulder as a brace and left with him staring at the remains of the gravy on his plate. Never did he not feel Sue's eyes upon him.

"That's all lies about Paducah," she said.

"Well."

"Where have you been?"

"I haven't been much of anywhere."

"You can tell me what's been going on."

"Ain't nothing to tell," Jacob said.

He could still feel her stare upon him. Finally she sighed and rose and walked around the table and kissed him hard on the mouth, her tongue working. He felt nothing. She ran her hand down over his chest and waist and cupped him.

"You want to go to bed?" she asked.

"I'm sorry, Sue."

"I'd kind of like to go to bed."

"It's just not in me."

"You sure?"

"I'm sure."

She sighed and smiled and withdrew her hand. "I got things that need to be done anyway." She patted his shoulder. She woke Abner and told him to get the carriage. Abner left the kitchen with his knuckles scrubbing at his hair and she went to her room and came back wearing a shawl over her shoulders. The hem formed a V over her chest. Everything she wore formed a V over her chest.

"If you're sweet on her, Jacob, don't let it go."

"You just don't know, Sue. You just don't know."

She smiled and patted his shoulder. "If you get tired, you know where my bed is. I won't bother you when I get back unless you want me to. Will you want me to?"

"I don't know," he said. "I don't think so."

She left briskly. He listened for the carriage to roll away, then sat for a long time at the table. So many things to think about here, so many things to remember. So long ago.

He went outside into the cool morning air and led the piebald back to the barn. He unsaddled her and checked her shoes. The act reminded him of McGown back in his shop in Ripley. His eyes flitted to the rafters, but McGown was not there. Jacob wondered what awaited him in the coming winter.

When he finished with the shoes, he loaded a manger with oats and watched the piebald eat. He pondered souls and the lack of them and the purpose of things. He went back in the house and walked quietly to Rachel's room, cracking open the door and hissing at the squeak of the hinges. She lay on the bed with dirty bedsheets coiled around her and did not even stir. The shirt had ridden up to her hips.

He crossed the room quietly and stared into the mirror. It had been so long since he had seen himself clearly that his ugliness shocked him. His nose was a tangle, he had picked up a scar on his right cheek, and his ear had a nick that he could only guess at. His glassy, empty eyes contained a knowledge too hard to carry. He almost wished he were back in Missouri; he wished more that he was back on the farm, and McGown and Dawson Springs and this war and this mirror had never happened. Is it possible to return to what we have been? The ways of things were beyond him.

"Jake?"

He glanced over his reflection's shoulder. Rachel was lying with her hair loose around her shoulders, one thin, smooth arm hugging her pillow. Her hips were bare and the bedsheets snaked between her legs. She was watching him.

"Yeah?"

"Are you all right?"

He looked himself in the eyes again and passed his hand over his face. He felt its rough, twisted features. "Sure."

"Are you really?"

"Yeah."

"Do you want to sleep with me? It won't cost you nothing."

In his memory, he could smell her skin. In his memory, he ran his fingers over its coffee smoothness. "I can't."

"Do you love me, Jake?"

"I don't know."

"Is that why you can't sleep with me?"

"I don't know. Maybe."

"Did you love Sue when you was working for her?"

"No. Or not like that."

"But you slept with her."

He shrugged. "I was different then."

"What made you different, Jake?"

"I don't know. That was a while ago."

"Jake?" she asked. "Love costs money, don't it?"

"Not always, Rachel."

"It always costs something." She pulled the pillow more tightly to her and curled her bare legs around it. "I sure wish the world was different," she said.

"I do, too. But it ain't."

He suddenly felt very tired. He crossed the room and lay on the bed beside her. She held him as she had the pillow. "Jake?"

"Yeah?"

"I'm awful tired of this."

"So quit doing it."

"All right. Can I come with you?"

"You don't want to come with me."

"But can I?"

"No," he said, "you can't."

"Oh, Jake," she said. "Oh, Jacob."

He fell asleep with the warmth of her arm and leg encircling him. He dreamed of birds soaring in blue skies with rivers and forests and fields far beneath them. He dreamed he was a young bird possessed of all knowledge looking down on a man with dirty hands grubbing in the hollow of a fallen tree like a worm. He dreamed he was an old bird looking down on the farm of a father with a black girl dancing in front of the cabin, one arm above her head, one curled around her waist, her head back and laughing. He dreamed he was a dying bird plummeting to the yard of a farm with a man with unbroken features working the fields, and the man's wife with just a hint of gray in her shadow-black hair twirling happily in her dance. She lifted both arms to receive him. He plunged into the heart of all he wished to be.

He awoke but kept his eyes closed to hang on to the dream, his cheeks and the sheet wet and cool, his eyes hot and stinging. Rachel had released him, and he listened to her steady breathing. He thought that perhaps she was someone else, that he was lying somewhere else. He could still feel the rush of wind through feathers.

He opened his eyes and sat. He watched her sleep. I was a child, he thought. How did I become so old?

He left the room with a panic growing within him that he might not be able to leave the house before Sue and Abner returned. He hurried out into the mid-morning to saddle the piebald. When he reached the hanging hickory he could hear on the road back toward Dawson Springs the clip of hooves and the creak of traces. The panic overcame him, and he kicked the piebald into a gallop heading north toward Charleston. He was still crying.

Chapter Eighteen

He rode in a gallop all the way to Charleston, where his wits returned and he let the piebald blow. He did not stop there, but went on to Louisville. He did not stop there, but went on to Lexington. He did not stop there.

Nine days after he left Dawson Springs, he spent the night camped outside of Brooksville just south of the Ohio River. Snow had fallen during the night and he awoke to see dark, wet footprints leading from the woods into the clearing he was camped in. Behind him the piebald nickered and something fumbled with leather. In one liquid motion his hand went beneath the saddle and came out with the dragoon pistol and he found himself aiming at a boy of twelve or thirteen, a boy even younger than Rachel or Haywood. The boy had been digging in his saddlebags and was fondling one of Jacob's Colt revolvers. His eyes went wide when he saw Jacob and he dropped the pistol into the snow.

"What you doing?" Jacob asked.

The boy didn't answer. Urine dripped from his trouser leg, melting and staining the snow. His eyes, buried in bloodless skin, were full of fright and life.

"Go," Jacob said.

The boy stumbled backward two steps before sprinting into the woods, dodging trunks, tripping on brush, slipping on the new snow. Jacob followed his flight with the pistol until he was out of sight. Now Jacob was staring down the barrel into the silent trees. He lowered the pistol and felt an emptiness within him, almost as if he were riding again into Independence. He thought of the bird he had become in his dream.

Each tree he could remember along the river was still in its place. Tobias's cabin was a collapsed clutter of ash-darkened timbers with the chimney rising bleakly. Jacob's eyes followed it into the sky. He expected to see

McGown, but didn't. A dusty smell in the air, even with the new snow. So much like Missouri.

He studied the cabin; he walked among the ashes. Someone had picked the ruins clean and had broken up the beehives farther down the trail. He listened to the river murmur against its banks. I've come home, he thought. Why have I come home?

He led the piebald silently down to the water. Whoever had cut down Tobias had left the frayed end of the rope hanging. He studied the scars the rope had cut into the bark and the way the frayed end swayed in the breeze. He studied it because it kept him from looking across the water.

Finally, he dropped his eyes. Everything was as he remembered it, though he could see no evidence of livestock. Through naked black tree trunks the springhouse straddled the icy stream and a half-starved cat picking its way across it. The barn stood forlornly and the cabin beyond it the same. No footprints littered the new-fallen snow, and until he noticed the wisp of smoke rising from the chimney he thought the farm was abandoned. But the smoke was there like the soul of the farm, like the soul he had been denied, like the soul of McGown on that first dark morning rising. He squatted and let his eyes drop to the thin shelf of ice along the water's edge. Beneath the iron gray sky the river had blackened. He listened for sounds from the other side of the river.

He stood without looking across and led the piebald back through the trees to the burned-out ruins, then unbridled and hobbled her. He walked back to the river, slipping in the new, slick snow, and searched the bank for Tobias's skiff. It had been pulled away from the river, and the stern was full of ice-crusted, stagnant water. He heaved it up and tipped it to dump the water over the gunwale. It was cold on his hands, numbing. He pushed it far enough into the river for the stern to angle downstream, in the direction where so long ago his boyhood dreams had flowed. He was only seventeen.

He stood on the bank and looked again at the farm. All was still silent with the silent smoke rising. My life, he thought.

McGown was crouching on the cabin roof. His skin hung in green-edged strips; the maggots had spread from the wound on his forehead to the empty black pits of both eyes, to the skin retreating up his forearm from his wrist's blackened, shriveled stump. He rose and flapped ponderously over the barn, over the water, his heavy, black-booted feet trailing impotently behind him. Jacob followed him with his eyes until his neck had craned back with McGown sitting heavily on the branch above him where the sergeant on his last living night had left Tobias hanging. The rotting, cold, dead, evil smell of him was almost overpowering.

McGown grinned. Frayed tatters of his soiled uniform fell around Jacob in black bits that stained the snow. Bits of rancid flesh rained down.

"What do you want?" Jacob asked.

McGown lifted his head toward the grayness above him. He raised his arms and lifted almost gently off the branch. He circled once over the river and once over the cabin beyond the river and flapped southward like a carrion-bloated buzzard seeking warmth. The chimney smoke swirled wildly in his wake, then settled again into its slow rising.

The current had pulled the skiff free from the bank and was carrying it downriver toward the McIntyres'. Jacob let his gaze follow it, then looked again at the farm. It had not changed. He tapped with his toe the thin sheet of ice gripping the bank and studied the cracks he made as if he was seeking portents. Finally he followed the path back to where he had left the piebald. He felt a surety, a finality, a cold, grim comfort. We cannot know the road before us and we cannot retreat down the one we have traveled. He would not have crossed, anyway.

He ordered a meal at the hotel in Brooksville. The boy from the morning was clearing the tables; he must have been the proprietor's son. When the boy saw Jacob he hurried into the kitchen and a middle-aged man with a wave of wrinkles across his forehead like grass on the Kansas prairie poked his head into the dining room, his eyes moving anxiously from table to table. Jacob wiped his mouth though he hadn't eaten and went outside. He mounted the piebald and left town, heading south toward Lexington. He rode with the comforting weight of the Mexican dragoon pistol pressing into the small of his back.

He took a room in a Lexington hotel and put up the piebald in the livery. With the money from Independence he didn't have to work, so he drank at night and gambled a little and tried to find ways to fill up his time. He got himself deloused. He stole a Bible from a Methodist church and read the book of Joshua, hoping to find something in it he did not already know. He read the story of Cain and Abel. He liked to read on Sunday mornings with his feet propped on the windowsill and the church bells ringing. He never went to church again. He never saw McGown.

As spring approached, he spent more of his time cleaning his already sparkling pistols, looking out of the window at the passing people, white and black, each with their own little world. His thoughts spiraled wildly, and he read the Bible from cover to cover and tried to keep track of those who were killed and those who were saved as if he were counting punches in a street fight. When he wasn't reading, he was thinking about Missouri and Kansas and Bill and Archie and Haywood; he was thinking about souls and God. He was wondering what the truth was or wasn't. When the snow finally melted and the buds finally swelled and the air lost its biting crispness, every day he bought a newspaper and eagerly read it. It disappointed him until the first part of May when he read a headline describing a raid by Dick Yeager along the Santa Fe Road into Kansas even past Council Grove. He slapped the back of his hand against the headline.

"Damn," he said. His spirit leaped within him.

He did not finish the article. Instead he packed his things and paid his bill and fetched and saddled the piebald. Within a half hour he was on his way back to Missouri. He had left the Bible with the illiterate slave who worked in the livery.

Chapter Nineteen

Eastern Missouri was wrapped in the spring's newness, the new green on the trees, the newly plowed fields, the new grass, the new water flowing in the creeks and rivers, the new smell and promise filling the air. Each morning as he headed west he would study the newness and see its promise passing. The fields more and more were left untended, the land abandoned and desolate. The newness of the leaves was coated with the black and rust red of ashes and blood and dust. Smoke in the wind offered a different kind of promise. He rode with all of his pistols in his waistband.

He reached Rocheport on the last Tuesday in May. He waited outside of town beyond the landing, watching from the trees the distant loading and unloading of steamboats. Black men working, white men working, some soldiers, some not, loading hemp bales and tobacco and unloading dry goods and guns. The colors blurred together through the trees and the distance until it was hard to tell who was slave and who wasn't. He bedded down for the day with the piebald keeping watch over him. Somewhere beyond like a memory floated McGown.

He awoke with the sunset and ate a slice of ham he had stolen from a farm near Jefferson City. When the sounds of the town had died he led the piebald by the reins to the riverbank, then to the landing. He sat on his haunches in the shadows and watched the lights at the Liberty Bell. Once a drunken Federal soldier came down to the landing to urinate off of the dock. Jacob watched him with the dragoon pistol between his legs and his index finger resting alongside the trigger guard.

When the streets were silent he led the piebald into town. He turned at the Liberty Bell and walked quietly to the Swisby house. All the windows were dark. He put the piebald in the back before he went to the door.

He knocked once and got no answer. He waited and knocked again and again got no answer. He opened the door and slipped inside. The sour smells of sweat and rotten food assaulted him. One round lump in the bed snored loudly and when his eyes adjusted he saw that it was Swizz. Jacob sat on the edge of the bed and watched the old man. He wondered where Harriet was.

"Swizz," he said quietly, then more loudly, "Swizz."

The old man stirred in his sleep and smacked his lips and muttered. Jacob reached out and touched his withered shoulder. The skin beneath the underdrawers burned. "Swizz. It's Jacob."

The old man cursed and brushed at Jacob's hand. Jacob shook his shoulder. The old man's eyes opened and he stared at Jacob and suddenly he came to wild, exploding life. He lurched at Jacob with his fingers in claws groping for his eyes. Jacob caught his wrists and pinned them to the bed. The old man had no strength left at all.

"Damn you Yankees." Swizz's voice was a curse and a cry and a sob. He struggled against Jacob before collapsing weakly onto the bed, weeping loudly. "Damn you Yankees. Leave me be."

"Swizz, it's Jacob."

"Damn all of you."

"It's Jacob, Swizz. Jacob."

Swizz lay sobbing. His mouth, his eyes, were open black shadows. "Jacob? You come back?"

"I come back. Where's Harriet?"

"Oh, Jacob," Swizz said. "Oh, Jacob."

"Where is she, Swizz?"

"They done took her."

"Who done took her?"

"The god damned Yanks."

"Took her where?"

"They're arresting all the women helping the boys. They come and they done took her."

Jacob released the old man's wrists. Swizz's hands came up to cover his face and muffle his words and his weeping. "They come a few weeks ago saying they knowed she'd killed that soldier last year and to come along peaceable or they'd make it rough on us both. I grabbed at one of them and he hit me in the chest with a musket butt and I crumpled down. Harriet brought up her elbow clean and hard and busted his jaw. He laid there howling with blood all over and then the officer clubbed her over the head with his pistol. She went down and come up again and had him by the throat and he was just all quiet with his eyes bugging out and he kept clubbing her. Her head was all red with it and then she went down, bringing him with her. There was her blood everywhere and she was moaning for Oscar and I couldn't do nothing." He wept. "I couldn't do nothing but lie there all crumpled up, Jacob. I couldn't do nothing but lie there."

"Where they got her?"

"I couldn't do nothing. I'm just a feeble old man who couldn't do nothing. Oh, Jacob. Oh, Jacob."

"Where they got her, Swizz?"

"I should a done something, Jacob. I should have grabbed that god damned pistol and shot them all but I couldn't. But I couldn't."

"They got her here in town?"

"In Kansas City with a bunch of others."

"Maybe me and some of the boys—"

"You can't get her, Jacob. If she could be got, they would have got them all by now." He wiped his nose with the edge of his hand, sniffling. "Oh, Jacob. I should a done something."

Jacob breathed the heat of his lungs into his hands. The silver light of the setting moon through the window cast the bed and the old man into grotesque relief. Swizz wept. Finally Jacob rested his hand on the old man's shoulder.

"You hungry, Swizz?"

"I ain't hungry."

"I'll fix you something if you're hungry."

"I ain't hungry, Jacob. I ain't never going to be hungry again."

"You got to keep your strength up, Swizz."

The old man looked up. The moonlight caught in the tears overwhelming his eyes. "What for? You tell me what for."

"It ain't all done just yet, Swizz."

The old man worked his lips, then nodded resolutely and swung his skinny legs out of the bed. He look like a malformed spider. "You take me with you, Jacob. I ain't much on riding, but you wasn't neither. You learned and I'll learn."

"You're too old, Swizz."

"I bet I can handle a pistol, too. I bet I can get some of them."

"You're too old, Swizz. Riding a horse would just bust you up."

"I got to do something, Jacob. They killed my Harriet and you just said it ain't all done just yet."

"She ain't dead, Swizz. You told me yourself she's in Kansas City."

The wizened face watched him in the moonlight. "A fella gets old and he gets on the edge of eternity and he starts to see over that edge. Harriet, she ain't dead yet but she's dead. I can see her arms reaching up out of her grave, throwing the soil back, just like I see you sitting there."

"She ain't dead, Swizz."

"You're young, so you don't know. You don't see. Me, I know and I see. I ain't never in this life going to see her again."

Swizz's thin neck lost its strength and his head fell forward. Jacob let him cry. They waited in the night for whatever would come.

Swizz's weeping fell into an exhausted series of snuffles and sobs. Finally the old man looked up again. "There's a Federal garrison down by the river."

"I seen one of them."

"I want you to give me a pistol."

"I can't."

"Jacob, we done clothed you and fed you and gave you a place to stay. I want you to give me a pistol."

Jacob studied him silently. He pulled free one of his Navy revolvers, hefted it, and examined it in the moonlight. Finally he stuffed it back in his waistband. "I can't, Swizz. She ain't dead yet."

The old man let his head fall forward. The moonlight caught in the crags in his face. Jacob sat watching him as he watched the floor. Finally Swizz looked up. "You still got that horse?"

"Out back."

"Fine horse."

"She is."

"You best leave while you can. There's that garrison down by the river."

"All right. I'll come check on you."

"You do that."

They stood. Swizz wrapped his arms around Jacob's waist and buried his damp face against his shoulder. Jacob stood uncertainly with the smell of the old man rising. Finally Swizz turned and stood with his back to Jacob, facing the bed and window.

"You best go."

"You ought to eat something, Swizz. I can cook a little."

"But not like Harriet."

There are things that cannot be argued. Jacob nodded. "I'll see you."

The old man's face turned. "Jacob, I want you to know something. I seen over the edge of eternity. I seen everything just like I was God."

"All right, Swizz."

Jacob left the house, went around to the back, and mounted the piebald. He rode past the Liberty Bell and turned west. Just as he passed the steamboat landing a Navy Colt revolver cracked sharply three times behind him. A pause followed before it cracked again and almost immediately following it came the heavy boom of an Enfield musket. Men were shouting and one man was howling in pain. Something cut the howl off and all fell silent. Jacob ran his elbow against his side and was not surprised to find one of his revolvers missing. He'd known that from the start.

He looked up at the sky, at the moon. A speck moved across it like the silhouette of a faraway bat or vulture. He dropped his eyes and let the piebald find her own way. She came across a skiff two miles upriver and he used it to cross to the southern bank.

Jacob found Charlie in the depths of the Sni. Federal militia had been pursuing them closely and the band had split into groups of four and five and smaller. Charlie had with him only Dave Poole and Henry Nolan.

"How was your winter, Ohio boy?" Charlie asked. He wore a scruffy beard, and his heavily lidded eyes still kept Jacob wondering. He looked older than he had in the fall. "Did you head back to Ohio?"

"Kentucky."

"To that girl of yours over there?"

"Rachel."

"I thought you said she was named something else. I could have sworn it."

"Rachel. And you?"

"I spent most of the winter in Richmond. I got Jeff Davis to give me a commission. You can call me Colonel now." He smiled.

"Colonel, huh?" And Jacob spat to the side.

Dave Poole rode off the next day. Charlie spent the evening studying a map, tilting it toward the fire. Henry worked slivers he carved from a piece of fatback into his mouth, his tongue curling out to snatch them from the blade. Jacob had tried to talk to him, but the black man had only looked at him with disdain.

"What you looking at, Charlie?" Jacob asked.

"Colonel."

"What you looking at?"

"A map of Kansas." Charlie looked up. "What would you think, Jake, about a raid on Lawrence?"

"Lawrence is a long way in."

"But Dick Yeager proved it can be done."

"Well," Jacob said, and that was all he would say.

Charlie studied him. The fire snapped. "You don't think we should do it."

"I'm just saying it's a long way in."

"Let me tell you something about Lawrence. My brother and I came out here from Maryland. We were camped on the prairie just south of Lawrence when a band of jayhawkers came out of town. They killed my brother and left me for dead and I spent two days bleeding on his body, trying to keep the buzzards away."

"Damn, Charlie," Jacob said.

"So I'm going to Lawrence, with or without you or anyone else. Everything I've done so far has been leading up to it. There's nothing else for me."

"Damn, Charlie," Jacob said again.

"I've been to Lawrence, too," Henry said. His knife blade slid a white curl of fat onto his tongue. "Rats and shacks and rivers."

Word came from one of Morgan Walker's sons that Bill Anderson was up in Clay County, north of the river. Jacob left the Sni the following evening. He stopped at a farm on the Missouri, where a woman gave him a meal of beef and potatoes and questioned him about Charlie. Her husband had lost a hand to Jennison and an eight-year-old boy had to row Jacob across the river.

It took him three days of wandering before he found Bill with Haywood and Archie in a gorge on the land of a man named Southwick. When Jacob rode into camp, Haywood grinned his gap-toothed grin from beneath the bill of his forage cap and waved his skinny arm wildly. "Hey, Jake. You remember me?" His saber stuck out behind him like a tail.

"How would I forget you?"

"Haywood Lee, yes sirree, just like the general. You can call me Hay."

"How was your winter? You get your revenge?"

"Well," Haywood said philosophically, "I still have to hang on when I ride. But I busted up a few windows."

"Why didn't you get yourself some new clothes? You could have come back dressed like a southern gentleman."

Haywood looked down at his father's trousers. With his chin against his chest, his nose brushed one of his pistols. He shrugged and grinned and cocked his head, his lazy eye swinging. "These here is about all I got left of my pap. I guess I oughter remember him." The boy was still barefoot; the ringworm scar on the back of his head had taken another turn.

Bill and Archie were sitting under a wide-spread cottonwood, Bill watching expressionless and Archie grinning his ugly grin as he played mumblety-peg with his knife. Jacob thought about Freeman and the farm south of Fayette and wondered if Southwick had a daughter. His feelings drained away but for a dull hatred and with his eyes on Archie he dismounted. He kept the piebald between them, pulling free the dragoon pistol and keeping it behind her flank.

"Hey, boys," he said.

"Hey, Jake," said Bill.

"You still want to kill me, Archie?" Jacob asked.

Archie shrugged, still grinning. "Hell, Jake, that was way last fall. And I sure as hell ain't about to try when you got that big old cannon in your hand."

"You about to try when I put it away?"

"Leave it be, Jake. That's all in the past."

Jacob patted the piebald and with the pistol still drawn warily walked around her. He'd so tuned his senses that the pistol muzzle twitched toward the chirp of a robin. Haywood bounded toward him like a puppy, and Jacob had to push him away to keep his line of fire clear. He squatted beside Bill. Archie made no move and looked as if he would make none. Jacob lay the pistol beside his boot. Perhaps everything but his hatred of this little rapist and grinning killer really was in the past.

"What you do all winter?" Jacob asked.

"Got our asses kicked by some nigger lover named Blunt," Bill said. "The same bastard that hanged Perry Hoy."

"I warned you. Confederate officers."

"You hear about old Swizz?"

"I heard. How many of them did he get?"

"Not a one. He hit one in the hand, then they shot him in the chest and ran a bayonet through his throat."

"Hell," Jacob said.

"Pity for an old man to go that way."

Jacob picked up a stick and drew with it in the dust. Lines and circles, a script of hidden meanings. "Pity."

"Them damn Yankees arrested Harriet," Archie said.

"That's what I hear."

"They got the McCorkle girls, too."

"I heard they had others."

Bill nodded. "It makes me worry about my sisters."

"They still on the Kansas River?"

"They're safer there. All the damn Kansans are over here jayhawking."

"They're a long way from their people."

"Who's Swizz?" Haywood asked.

They stared at the dirt and wondered vaguely at what Jacob's stick was drawing. Archie's knife made a sound like a sigh as it entered the turf. Sharp blade. Sharp face. Sharp eyes. Jacob turned from his face to the sky. The blue was impenetrable and dazzled his eyes. He picked up the dragoon pistol and shoved it into his waistband.

"Well," he said.

"Well what?"

"Well I guess I'll go unsaddle my horse."

He rose and walked toward the piebald. He was relieved when he reached her and could turn to face Archie, but Archie's eyes were on his knife and the only sound beyond the birds and the wind in the gulch was the steady thump of the blade into the soil. Jacob thought that perhaps he should kill him but he found no provocation for it now. Bill lay back against the trunk with his eyes closed. Haywood sat cross-legged with his elbows in the dirt and his chin in his hands, watching Jacob intently. He grinned.

"It's sure good to have you back, Jake. It just wasn't hardly the same without you."

The piebald nuzzled Jacob's shoulder, her breath warm and sweet upon it. He patted her, undid the cinches, and lifted off the saddle. As she grazed he lay in the shade of the tree with his head on his saddle and the dragoon pistol beneath it. He looked up at the branches and shifted the saddle out into the sun.

"You got some kind of fear about trees, don't you?" Archie asked.

"Don't like to imagine hanging in one."

Jacob lay with the sun on his face, his hand on the dragoon pistol's checkered grip. He thought as his eyes drifted closed that, sleeping, the pistol would make no difference if Archie wanted to kill him. He ought to kill the little murdering rapist first. But he was tired.

He awoke with the sun just setting. He wiped his hands over his tight, burning face and studied the tree. He settled Tobias's hat on his head and welcomed the way its brim cut off his vision. He was alone.

The piebald was grazing peacefully and nickered when she saw him watching her. He rose to pat her withers and lean his face against the warm, sweat-filled, comfortable smell of her flank, the only steady thing in this world. He walked back to the tree and sat against it and watched the twilight come on. It was a peaceful evening with the birds singing sweetly and a cool breeze on his face. This life, he thought. How beautiful at times it could be. He closed his eyes again.

Hooves thudding down the gully made his eyes pop open and he leaped to his feet. He looked at the dragoon pistol beneath the saddle and decided he didn't have time to fetch it. He drew his Colt revolver and crouched behind the tree and aimed three feet over from the edge of an outcrop at the gully's entrance and about seven feet up. His emotion had drained and he felt nothing. He glanced at the sky for McGown. He saw only a sliver of the moon.

A gray mare came around the outcrop and he found himself aiming at Bill Anderson's chest. He lowered the pistol. Archie and Haywood were following, Haywood grimacing as his crotch slapped against the saddle.

"We went out to find us some supper," Bill said. "You want some supper?"

"What do you got?"

"Potatoes and cold beef."

"Good beef?"

"What's left in Missouri but cows too stringy for the jayhawkers or army to eat?"

They reined and dismounted. Jacob put his pistol away and accepted his dinner from Archie. He held a potato in one hand and a chunk of beef in the other. The beef was from the hind of an old cow; it was spiced strangely and sucked all the moisture from his mouth.

"We got something going with Dave Poole," Bill said as he unsaddled.

"I saw him with Charlie down on the Sni. What you got going?"

"You like the Dutch?"

Jacob thought of Klausmann. Klausmann made him think of Teague, and Teague of McGown. "What you going to do to the Dutch?"

Archie grinned. "Have a little fun." He loosened his knife in its scabbard. Jacob said nothing to him.

Bill watched Jacob eat. "Well?"

"Where?"

"Lafayette County. You coming?"

"When?"

"Your horse rested?"

"She's rested. When?"

"Tomorrow night. We'll meet up with Dave outside of Lexington." He grinned. His brilliant blue eyes blazed, collecting the color of the dying day.

"You used to say things like this deserved penance, Bill."

"Well," Bill said, "it grows on you."

They slept that night beneath the stars, Jacob out on the pasture near the horses and the others beneath the tree. He studied the sky and the darkness. When he fell asleep, he dreamed the dream of the birds.

Chapter Twenty

They left the gully the next day only to raid farms for meals. They rode to different farms, passing burned-out fields and houses, graves new and old, fear and despair new and old, once an old man with a trailing white beard shuffling down the road who refused to look up at them. At sunset they broke camp and rode southeast until three in the morning. A farmer ferried them across the Missouri, letting them dry their horses with a quilt his wife had made while alive, and he nodded as Bill tossed it into the skiff's bow and thanked him. They mounted again and rode through the trees and brush and gullies and fields toward Lexington. The burn wasn't as bad here as it was closer to the border. McGown in awkward flight led them, though only Jacob and perhaps the piebald noticed. His presence portended what was to come, and Jacob rested in that knowledge.

They camped until dawn near Levasy, the chill upon them, the mist from the river around them, then rode in the morning around the outskirts of Lexington. Two miles beyond the town they came across a stream they followed south to a small stone farmhouse with a burned-out barn beside it. Four horses in saddle waited in front of it, and a man curled and hardened as if annealed answered the door immediately when Bill knocked. They shook hands.

"You all come on in," the man said with a lilt just like Klausmann's. "Get yourself some breakfast."

Jacob dismounted. McGown squatted in an oak in the windbreak, the black sockets of his eyes on Jacob, a finger pointing at the threshold. Haywood dismounted, grimacing, and rubbed at his crotch.

"Don't do that."

Haywood peered up from beneath the brim of his forage cap. "My balls are done busted out. One of these days they'll pop like blisters—poof, poof, and then what'll I do?"

"No more sheep," Archie said.

Haywood pondered this solemnly.

"You'll ride easier," Jacob offered.

"It sure couldn't be no worse."

The farmer stood in the door, his arm as curled as the rest of him and beckoning. Jacob stepped inside doubtfully and tipped his hat to the farmer's cow-faced wife and pale, paunchy daughter. The others did the same.

Dave Poole was sitting at the table with egg yolk in his goatee. He stood and smiled and greeted them. Larkin Skaggs and two young blond-haired brothers who Jacob had never seen before were too busy chewing to speak. The newcomers sat while the wife plodded between the stove and the wood pile, frying bacon and eggs. The daughter served them. Archie grinned and ran his eyes over her. She blushed as she set out the plates.

"So what all do you got going on?" the farmer asked.

Dave Poole swallowed. "Well now, there's a tale." He told a story about a German farmer who because of his sexual proclivities stuck his head up the ass of a donkey and found Frederick the Great inside. They all laughed except Haywood, then they all began to eat except the farmer, who sat at the head of the table with his elbows upon it and his fingers working at the cuff of the opposite sleeve. Larkin Skaggs stood and lifted his hands and led them in a great, expostulatory prayer to Jehovah or Elohim, whichever name the listener preferred, explaining to our Lord and Master the mercy of His own ways. He finished with an intricate discourse on man as the dust of the earth and how in doing the Lord's will we walk on the bones of our brothers. His listeners sat silently in either boredom or awe. He finished with his head back and his hands in the air and the smell of the fungus beneath his arms rolling foully across the table.

"So be it," he said as he sat.

The farmer watched him quietly throughout the meal. When they had nearly finished, he tapped Skaggs's forearm with a finger. The reverend drew back violently.

"No man touches me."

"You gonna kill some Dutch?"

"God damn you to hell, no man touches me."

"You gonna kill some Dutch?" the farmer asked around the table. "In-human, abolitionist bastards. The god damned Dutch neighbors is the ones who burned my barn. Victor what's-his-name and his boys."

"Where's he live?" Bill asked.

"A quarter mile past the stream. They come here one night last fall and took a horse and burned the barn and then come in here and stole my daddy's silver watch. Scared Martha there half to death."

"They scared you half to death, too," the woman said.

"And then they threatened to rape Becky. God damned animal bastards. Victor what's-his-name and his boys. Three boys, all with that god damned Dutch blond hair. They farm just past the stream."

"You're Dutch," Jacob said.

"I ain't."

"Your accent says you are. What's your name?"

"Dietrich. That's a Dutch name, and I might speak like it, but I ain't no god damned Dutch. My granddaddy came over here before the Revolutionary War to Carolina. I ain't no god damned Dutch. He fought at Cowpens and he would have owned slaves but he never had the money. Hell, I would, too, but you try scraping enough for a nigger out of this soil. You just try."

"I know somebody else whose granddaddy fought at Cowpens," Jacob said.

"Who?"

"You wouldn't know him."

They finished the meal. Larkin Skaggs belched loudly and farted and explained to his listeners the sanctity of natural functions. The two boys chuckled and poked each other's ribs. Bill rose when he was ready and the others followed him outside. The farmer stood in the yard while his wife and daughter waited at the door, blinking like a species of cave animal unaccustomed to the light. The guerrillas thanked them and tipped their hats and mounted. McGown was gone.

"About a quarter mile past the stream." The farmer pointed. "With the boys, there'll be four of them. All blond-haired Dutch animal abolitionist bastards."

Larkin tapped his heels into his sorrel's flanks and walked it toward the farmer. "Hey, Dietrich, you god damned Dutch son of a bitch sauerkraut piece of shit." He shouted though the man stood only three feet away.

Dietrich looked up. "There ain't no call for language like that."

"Dietrich, you god damned Dutch son of a bitch sauerkraut piece of shit. Don't you know that in the time of the patriarchs the penalty for touching a man of the cloth was to die, was to be stoned to death with the pieces of the tablets Moses had broken upon seeing the golden calf, to be stoned to death with the very pieces upon which the Lord's finger had written?"

Dietrich stared at him dumbly. "I ain't never heard that."

"Read your Bible, you god damned Dutch sauerkraut piece of shit."

"I wouldn't have done it if I had known it. Hell, I shake preachers' hands all the time."

The reverend shook his head at the man's ignorance. "Did you ever get another watch?"

"Sure did. It cost me twenty dollars."

"If God had meant for us to know the time, he would have put a clock in the sky. You god damned Dutch son of a bitch sauerkraut piece of shits are so god damned sauerkraut punctual."

"There ain't no call for language like that," Dietrich said again.

"Give me the watch," the reverend demanded.

"Why?"

"In lieu of the fact that you are fortunate enough that I don't happen to have the pieces of the tablets with me."

"I don't see—"

"Give me your god damned watch or I'll put a bullet in your god damned sauerkraut face."

Dietrich stared up at the reverend without moving. Skaggs drew a pistol and aimed it at the man's forehead. The women stood in the doorway silently with the morning sun upon them. Finally Dietrich fished from his pocket a worn, silver-plated pocket watch. The reverend yanked it away before he had detached the chain and tore the man's trousers. "Nice watch." The reverend put it in his pocket. "Perhaps in his great plan our Lord and Savior will find within his heart the mercy to forgive you."

"I'm for the south, you know," Dietrich said.

"Correct your ignorance," the reverend instructed as he rode away. "Read your god damned Bible."

Jacob looked back at the man standing in his yard with his fists balled furiously at his sides. Larkin Skaggs was admiring the watch. The guerrillas were watching him. He looked from it to them with surprise. "What?" he asked.

"You shouldn't have done that, Larkin," Bill said.

"Oh hell. A Dutch is a Dutch. And he lied about this watch. It ain't worth no twenty dollars."

"We might need a meal there sometime. We might need someone to warn us about the Yankees."

"He'll feed us again or I'll shoot him. He'll do all I ask him or I'll shoot him. Even God's mercy knows limits. Second Thessalonians, chapter fifteen, verse twelve."

"You and your Bible, Larkin," Bill said. "There ain't no fifteenth chapter to Second Thessalonians."

The reverend lifted his face to the sky. "When will they see, O Lord? When will mortal man understand that your ways are beyond him?"

They rode on. "I bet you were something to hear from a pulpit," Jacob said.

"I've saved a few souls in my time."

They crossed the stream with the hooves of eight horses splashing. A hayfield opened before them as they came over the crest of the bank. On its far side in the mid-morning sun was a mule hitched to a wagon standing to its belly in the hay. Three men were mowing with long-bladed scythes, triangles of sweat on their straining backs. Two women with scarves hiding their hair were shocking in the men's wake. One woman paused to pass her sleeve over her brow. When she saw the guerrillas, she stopped with her arm raised and forgotten.

"Let's get them, boys," Bill said.

He kicked his mare and she leaped into the field. Jacob followed with Haywood just ahead of him to his right, the boy's hands tangled in the mane and his revolvers flapping on their lanyards, his saber tapping the Morgan's hip. The reverend and Poole and the two brothers brought up the rear. The farmers looked up and stared for a moment before dropping their scythes and fleeing. Jacob fired once at the oldest of them. The man yelped and grabbed at his hamstring. The youngest of the women stood by the wagon with her hands on her cheeks and screamed. The other woman still stood with her arm raised in the air.

The man Jacob shot had fallen behind and was crawling. Bill ran him down with the shoes of his mare clicking smartly against his skull. Bill reined and fired and the man stretched on the ground silently. Larkin Skaggs and the two brothers rode after one of the other men, who had almost reached the trees. The reverend fired and bark flew from an oak. He cursed and fired again and again missed. Archie ran the man down and knocked him into a tree trunk with the flank of his blue roan. The man smacked hard enough to bounce back and fall onto his back with his legs in spasms and his eyes wide and blood lacing his forehead. Archie swung his leg over the horse and drew his knife from its sheath.

"He's a bloody one!" he called up to Jacob after he had finished him. Jacob nodded and turned back toward the field. He felt nothing. The screaming girl's nails had riven deep red scratches into her face.

The third man was sprinting wildly toward the stream, his arms flailing as his legs caught in the hay. He was younger than the others and smaller. Jacob started after him, but Bill called him back. Bill nodded at Haywood.

"Haywood, you take him."

"I cain't hit nothing from horseback."

"Then you dismount and you take him. You show the new boys here how you can shoot."

Haywood cocked his head at Bill. He squinted his good eye as his lazy eye swung to stare at the bill of his forage cap, as if it could see the sky beyond it and God beyond the sky. "You sure, Bill?"

"You get off that god damned horse," Bill said, "and you shoot that god damned Dutch."

Haywood swallowed and dismounted. He cocked his head and lifted a pistol.

Suddenly the girl screamed even louder and threw herself at Haywood, her fingers bent into red-rimmed claws and a wild, savage, animality distorting her features, blood flowing back in runnels with the tears on her cheeks to her earlobes. "Holy rolling thunder!" Haywood shouted as he skittered like a bug between the Morgan's legs. The girl crawled after him screaming. He came up on the other side, wild eyed, with her right behind him. The Morgan watched calmly. The guerrillas laughed, the two brothers snickering and throwing glances at each other.

"Holy rolling thunder!" Haywood shouted again. The girl's fingers had reached his blouse and had popped loose a button. One hand gripped the saber scabbard and was trying to drag him to the ground. "Somebody get this crazy woman off a me!"

The guerrillas bellowed at the hilarity. Haywood broke into a panicked dance around the horses with the screaming girl clawing him and the saber wagging. Bill dismounted and chased after the girl and the guerrillas laughed even harder. The youngest farmer was more than halfway across the field, and Jacob cursed and kicked the piebald in the ribs and chased after him. He caught him just as he reached the road, running toward the Dietrich farm. He dropped him there and reined in his horse and headed back across the field. He remembered Klausmann, and everything seemed just.

Bill had the screaming woman around the waist while Haywood cowered by the trees, desperately trying to draw free his saber. Dave Poole was laughing so hard he fell from his horse. The woman who had first seen them stood silently with her hand still in the air.

The girl collapsed over Bill's arm and settled into hysterical weeping.

Bill laid her gently in the pasture on a spot the farmers had cleared where she would be more comfortable. The other woman stared impassively. The roaring laughter had descended to chuckles and mirth wiped from eyes. Dave Poole lay on his back beside his horse and grinned up at the sky, his little chest heaving. Bill mounted the gray mare.

"Haywood," he said, "you mount up."

"Someone bring me my horse. There ain't no way I'm going near that crazy woman."

"You mount up."

"Will someone bring me my horse?"

Larkin Skaggs, still laughing, fetched the Morgan's reins and led the horse to Haywood. Haywood mounted carefully, keeping his eyes on the girl now weeping into the field with her fingers clawing the earth and her face smeared red and glistening. Jacob reined up beside him and looked down at the man he had shot in the leg. His skull wasn't a skull anymore. It wasn't much of anything.

"Dave," Bill said. "Mount up."

"Oh hell, Bill," Dave said. "I ain't never seen nothing funnier than that."

"Mount up," Bill said again.

He turned his horse and headed toward the road. The riders straggled after him with the reverend and Jacob and Haywood bringing up the rear. "You ought to get her some help," Haywood told the woman with her hand in the air. "A brain doctor or something."

The woman stared silent and unblinking. The reverend tipped his hat to her. "You ladies go with God," he said before his horse walked away.

Jacob rode away silently. In the hickories lining the far side of the road squatted McGown. One of his boots had fallen from a withered foot gone black and green with separating blood and mold and decay; the toes of that foot clung to the branch like bird talons. He pointed toward the Dietrich farm.

"Bill," Jacob said.

"Yeah?"

"We ought to go back and take care of that Dietrich."

"Why?"

"He lied."

"Hell, Jake, it's just a watch."

"He ain't just lied about the watch. Why would that fella run toward his house? Because he's a Union man."

"It's kind of out of the way, Jake. We're heading the other direction."

Jacob glanced at McGown. The dead sergeant was watching him from the black, empty pits of his eyes. "I think we ought to take care of him, Bill. I really think we ought to."

Bill watched him silently. His long hair curled up at his shoulders like ladles to catch the sunlight.

"I think we ought to, Bill."

Bill pursed his lips and pulled his horse around. "Come on, boys. We're going to pay Dietrich another visit."

"What for?" one of the brothers asked.

"Because we ought to."

Archie grinned. "I wouldn't mind having a shot at that daughter."

"You don't touch her, Archie."

"Then I get to kill her daddy."

They headed back toward the stream. The young farmer Jacob had shot was lying across the road, limbs bent in crazy angles. The two women were still in the field, the younger one still weeping into the pasture. The older woman's arm had dropped, perhaps from exhaustion. McGown lifted from the branch to lead Jacob.

"She done tore my shirt, Jake," Haywood said.

"Well," Jacob answered him. He kept his eyes on the sergeant.

The riders dropped down and crossed the streambed. Dietrich's farmyard looked deserted, the stone house's front door shut, the shutters drawn.

"He's got her all boarded up, Bill," Jacob called.

"Looks like a damned fortress."

One of the shutters cracked open and from it jutted a shotgun barrel and a guttural German shout, "*Gott verdammen* you bushwhackers *zum Teufel!*" The barrel bucked and spit and the guerrillas scattered. Jacob dove from the piebald's back to lie behind the ruins of the barn beside Bill and Archie. The piebald trotted into the brush. Back on the road the Morgan was still standing, Haywood on its back trying to grab one of his revolvers.

"Haywood," Jacob shouted, "get your ass over here!"

"What did he say, Jake? I ain't never heard talk like that before."

"Just get your ass over here!"

The barrel came out from between the shutters again. "*Gott verdammen* you bushwhackers *zum Teufel!*" Dietrich shouted, and the barrel bucked and spit right at Haywood. The leaves in the branches above him rattled and rained in scraps about his shoulders; little dust jets rose around the Morgan's hooves. Haywood had given up on his revolvers and was trying to draw the saber. The scabbard poked the Morgan's hind and it took a hop toward the house. Haywood tottered and grabbed for the mane as the Morgan came to a stop between Dietrich's window and the barn.

"Haywood, you damn fool!"

"Zum Teufel!" Dietrich shouted. *"Zum Teufel!"* The shotgun spit again with the barrel hardly ten feet from Haywood. Jacob, Bill, and Archie ducked as pellets bit into the blackened cinders around them. The Morgan stood impassively, the reins running from its bridle to Haywood's hand riddled with one broken. Haywood sat wide eyed with his breath whistling through the gap in his teeth. As he struggled with his saber again, his forage cap slumped over the stumps of his ears and the bill covered his eyes.

"Holy rolling thunder," Haywood shouted. "I cain't see a damn thing!"

"Get over here!"

"Who's doing all the shooting?"

"Get over here!"

The Morgan cast a bored look over its shoulder at the struggling boy on its back. It must have seen the piebald, for it turned and walked tiredly toward her. Dietrich cursed again and fired at Haywood's back. Jacob hissed as a pellet grazed his wrist and ducked as another went through the brim of Tobias's hat. Bill and Archie were lying flattened against the ground. Haywood had gotten his hand caught in the saber hilt as the other tried to clear his eyes. The Morgan stopped beside Jacob and looked through dull eyes back at the house.

"Haywood, get off!"

"You down there, Jake? My damn hat fell down."

Jacob reached up and grabbed the hem of the boy's trousers. Dietrich fired again and a pellet punctured the meat of Jacob's thumb and when he jerked his hand down, Haywood came with it. The boy tumbled on top of Jacob and finally his cap came off. His trousers were peppered with pellet holes from his ankles to his chest. The Morgan walked nonchalantly off to the trees where the piebald was waiting, its tattered reins hanging uselessly. The piebald nickered greetings.

Haywood worked his hand free of the saber and sucked on a knuckle. "Damn," he said. "I hurt myself." He looked at his trousers and his good eye went wide. The other was blindly contemplating the sky. "Holy rolling thunder, look at these pants. My mam'll kill me."

"You're god damned lucky she'll get the chance," Bill said.

"He cain't shoot me. I got me the mark of Cain."

From across the road one of the brothers made a dash for the house. Dietrich waited until he had almost reached the door to drop him. The blast knocked the boy back off his feet and left him crawling toward the road, leaving a red stain and his foolish bravado behind him. The breeze carried the smell of his ruptured innards and his cruel moaning as the high noon sunlight caught in his hair. The other brother yelped and rose gibbering and Dietrich dropped him with a blast to his chest. Soon they both lay still. A hoot of triumph came through the crack in the window.

"They were my god damned neighbors," Larkin Skaggs called from somewhere in the brush.

"I got the pieces of the holy tablets loaded up special for you," Dietrich called back. He fired again.

Bill rolled on his back and sighed. "So what do you think?"

"I say let's get out of here," Archie said. "We done lost two. This ain't any fun anymore."

"What do you think, Jake?"

"It would have been different if we just come across him milking or something, Bill. We can't hardly shoot through stone walls."

Bill rolled back onto his stomach and studied the house. "You think you could shoot through the crack in them shutters, Haywood?"

Haywood nodded excitedly. "Oh sure. I shot swallows out of the sky once. Twice, I mean."

"Why don't you give it a try. You duck if you see a barrel come out."

"He cain't hit me," Haywood said. "I got me the mark of Cain."

"What the hell does that mean?"

"It's like in the Bible. I got me the mark of Cain."

"You're the sorriest son of a bitch I ever knew, Haywood," Archie said.

"See, Bill?" Haywood nodded at Archie. "He knows what I mean."

Haywood stood with his head cocked to the side and his lazy eye rolling. He raised his revolver and without aiming fired it at the window. As he dropped the revolver, the edge of the right shutter splintered and glass shattered.

Haywood grinned happily. "I got some glass! I did! I got some glass! Let me try her again."

He hauled the pistol up by its lanyard. The shotgun barrel came out between the shutters and fired. Pellets whistled and Haywood fired back. This time there was no splintering. More glass broke and the shotgun fell toward them, its stock forcing open the shutters. From within the house a woman screamed.

"Dietrich?" Bill called. The woman screamed again, and now the high-pitched scream of the girl joined hers. "Dietrich?"

"I think you got your revenge, Haywood," Jacob said.

He stood and brushed off his pants. The pellet wound in his thumb hurt abominably. Haywood cocked his head and reached back to scratch his ringworm scar. His face betrayed only incomprehension.

From out of the brush lumbered the reverend. He kicked at the door once, twice, and was inside before anyone else reached the house. The woman's scream took a different pitch, then the sound of clothing being torn came through the window. Bill and Archie sprinted into the house and harsh voices came out, the reverend following them with Bill kicking him in the behind. Dave Poole stood at the roadside watching with a grin. The reverend's hat fell off and he called the plagues of Moses down upon Bill as he picked it up.

Jacob stood beside Haywood. The boy's revolver hung limply by its lanyard nearly to his ankle. The boy's eyes, his nose, all glistened.

"You can be all done with this now, Haywood."

"Can I?" Haywood asked.

They looted the house with the woman and daughter clutching each other by the stove and crying, the woman's blouse torn open. They found little worth keeping, but when Archie threatened to slit open the girl if the mother didn't tell him where their money was buried, the mother led them to the back yard and dug up on the edge of the garden a glass jar containing five hundred dollars. Bill stuffed half of it into his pouch.

"Why you saving that, Bill?" Jacob asked him.

"I told you. It's a tithe."

"You don't believe in God."

"So maybe one day I will."

They buried the two brothers in the family plot, left Dietrich lying in the yard, then all mounted except Reverend Skaggs, who tried to fire the house with embers left over from breakfast. Stone doesn't burn. Finally he cursed and mounted and as they left he tipped his hat to the ladies and told them to go with God. It was just after noon and they spent the rest of the day raiding.

That night Jacob sat by the fire beside Bill. Archie was sleeping and Haywood was on picket and the Reverend Skaggs with Dave Poole had ridden off to convey the sad news of the brothers' deaths to their family. Jacob bit a powder charge in half to lessen its kick and jammed it and a ball into one of his Colt's cylinders with the revolver's levered piston. He loaded the second as he had the first, then cleaned and loaded the dragoon pistol, covering each chamber with grease to keep out moisture. Bill studied the knots on his silk cord and shoved it into his pocket. He seemed satisfied, and he smiled at the fire.

"You've changed since last year, Bill," Jacob said quietly.

Bill flicked a gray-backed louse into the fire. It popped. The light caught in his hair and beard, his eyes. "We all change, Jake. That's the nature of living."

Jacob stared into the embers. The wound on his thumb and the acrid smell of the wood smoke both stung. The night lay black on his shoulders. He had not seen McGown since before the Dietrich farm, and he wondered at that. He stood, shoving the Mexican dragoon pistol into his waistband.

"You going somewhere, Jake?"

"Thought I'd check on Haywood."

"He don't need a relief already."

"I'm just checking on him. It's a nice night for a walk."

"It kind of reminds you of the old days." Bill smiled. "Back in Ohio."

"I try not to think about them," Jacob said.

He walked through the trees to a rock outcropping overlooking the trail. Haywood was sitting with his cap on the rock beside him, the scar on the back of his shorn head glowing dimly in the moonlight. His back was slouched and his elbows in the dirt and his mutilated face wept into his hands. The saber pointed out behind him.

"If I was a Yankee," Jacob said, "you'd be dead."

Haywood looked up. He sucked a load of snot from his nose into his throat and swallowed. "Oh hell, Jake, I almost wouldn't mind."

"What's that supposed to mean?"

"I killed somebody, Jake. I done killed somebody."

Jacob squatted beside him. The crickets chirped; the night was cool and clear. "He was trying to kill you."

"But he cain't kill me so that's different."

Jacob spat over the outcropping. "You forget about it."

"How am I supposed to do that? You tell me how I'm supposed to do that."

"You just go home to your mam and forget about it. You done all she can expect from you."

"Hell, Jake," Haywood said.

"What?"

"I cain't go home. I'm a gorilla now. How do you get something like that out of you?"

"You just forget about it, Haywood."

"She wouldn't let me. The Yankees wouldn't let me. They'd try to kill me and they wouldn't kill me. They'd put me in jail somewheres instead and maybe after a while God would let them cut my head off."

"What are you talking about?"

"It's like in that Bible story. Cain wandered around and then they put him in jail and some girl danced and she danced so good they chopped his head off. I guess God let them because he liked her dancing."

"That's a different story, Haywood."

"No it ain't."

"That was a different fella. Matthew or Luke or somebody."

"It was Cain, Jake. Pap read it right there in his Bible. I done heard it a million times."

Jacob looked at the stars. He dropped his eyes to his hands and was surprised to find them finger to finger, palm to palm, as if in prayer. "I'll tell you something, Haywood. God, he don't care about fellas like you and me. We're just here and then we're gone and there ain't nothing waiting for us."

"You believe that, Jake?"

"I believe that."

"Then why cain't nobody shoot me?"

"Maybe he feels sorry for you."

"Well, then."

"Feeling sorry for a fella ain't the same as caring about him. I feel sorry for some of the fellas I've killed, but that don't mean I care about them. Hell. I feel sorry for them all. They're dead."

Haywood wiped his nose on the sleeve of his mother's blouse. "I'll tell you what I believe, Jake. There's a reason for everything. That's what I believe."

"That may be so, Haywood. But that don't mean he cares about you."

They stared down into the darkness. Finally Haywood lay back and looked up at the stars. "Jake?" he asked.

"Yeah?"

"You're my friend, ain't you?"

"I'm your friend, Haywood."

"The others, they ain't my friends. They're only friends like Booger was my friend, but Booger wasn't really my friend. But you're my friend, Jake. You are. I know it."

"I'm your friend, Haywood."

"Jake?"

"Yeah?"

"When this is all over, let's go out west somewheres. Let's go dig for gold or something. Or let's be lumberjacks." He sat up and again looked silently down into the shadows. "I sure like trees."

"I like some of them."

"Jake?"

"Yeah, Haywood."

"Those first guys we shot this morning? Remember how that Dietrich said they'd all be blond?"

"Yeah."

"Not one of them was blond, Jake. Not one."

"I didn't notice."

"That'll be the first thing I'll notice from now on. Because I'll remember."

"It's best not to remember," Jacob said.

The moon dropped a few degrees and their shadows grew to fall into the blackness into which they were staring. Haywood wiped his nose again. He yawned and rubbed his eyes.

"You get some sleep," Jacob said. "I'll watch things."

"Jake?"

"Yeah?"

"Is it all right for men to love each other?"

"I ain't no sheep, Haywood."

"I don't mean like that. I mean like friends."

"Then it's all right."

"Do you suppose Cain loved Abel?"

"I don't know."

"Do you suppose he loved that girl that got his head cut off?"

"That was a different fella, Haywood. Go get some sleep."

"Jake?" Haywood asked again.

"Yeah?"

"Booger used to love me. But not like friends. He used to bend me over this here log out in the woods and rut inside me."

"Oh hell, Haywood."

"It hurt, Jake. It hurt bad. Am I evil now?"

"If it wasn't your fault, it don't make no difference."

"It don't?"

"Not a bit."

"You know something, Jake? A sheep's just a sheep. That's all it is."

"I know."

"It ain't a girl. I'd never do that to a girl."

"It don't hurt a girl," Jacob said. He thought of Sarah, then of Archie. "If you do it right."

"I don't do much right, Jake."

"Sure you do."

"I killed that Dietrich fella today."

"Go get some sleep."

"I killed him dead. You like that Skaggs fella, Jake?"

"No, I don't."

"You think he's really a preacher?"

"He says he was. Go get some sleep and quit thinking about it."

"All right." Haywood stood. He shuffled back toward the clearing, his saber scabbard dragging. Jacob watched him until he blended in shadow. He looked down toward the trail, up into the sky.

"Jake?"

"Damn it, Haywood."

"You know why I want you to call me Hay?"

"Go get some sleep."

"Because Booger, he called me Haywood while he was rutting. I'm glad they killed him, Jake. I really am. You think I'll go to hell for that?"

"That ain't nothing you got to worry about, Haywood. Go get some sleep."

"Call me Hay, Jake. Will you call me Hay?"

"Go get some sleep, Hay."

The crickets were settling into a slower rhythm as the night cooled. Jacob studied the stars. Why do you let such things be, he thought.

"Thanks, Jake," Haywood said.

"All right."

"Jake?"

"Yeah?"

"It's like I couldn't see nothing before, and now I can see it all."

"Go to sleep, Hay."

Jacob kept the picket the rest of the night. When the sun rose he walked back to camp and stared into what was left of the fire and rubbed his burning eyes. Bill was waking. Haywood lay in a curl beside Archie. Jacob studied the child. Instead of letting him die in a shotgun blast, God was taking him away in pieces. His teeth, his ears, his blind, swinging eye. His future lost to a bitter old woman, his dignity to a dead pervert. Even his hair to a worm. God is cruel and man is cruel and God is love and man is love and none of it makes any god damned sense. He rubbed his eyes again. They felt as if they sizzled.

"Morning," Bill said.

Jacob looked up. Bill was watching him through sleep-burdened eyes. "Morning."

"You should have woken me a few hours ago. You should have got yourself some sleep."

"I had a lot to think about."

"You get it all thought through?"

"Does anybody ever really get anything thought through?"

"It's best just to forget about it."

"That's what I told Haywood last night."

When the others had awakened they broke camp and rode west. From a good southern woman who gave them breakfast they learned that the Federals were extending their arrests of women associated with the guerrillas into Kansas. She told them of a Federal garrison west of her farm at Odessa and of the slaughter of the local Germans, which they didn't admit to. They left her farm wiping crumbs from their faces, heading northwest along a sow path, keeping away from the roads. Bill rode in front with his back straight and still and his head resting slightly on his right shoulder. Archie rode behind him. Jacob rode just ahead of Haywood, who clutched the Morgan's mane.

"Where we going, Bill?" Jacob asked.

"Up the Kansas River," Bill said.

Archie spat. "What the hell for?"

"To get my sisters. I don't like them out there with the jayhawkers."

"Hell." Archie spat again.

"I ain't never been to Kansas," Haywood said. He shifted uncomfortably on his saddle and grimaced. "Is it a long way?"

They rode north to Mayview to avoid the Odessa soldiers. In less than an hour they reached the town and rode through the quiet streets; scattered, sullen faces watched from vacant lots or broken windows. Wild looks from wild eyes. All of the houses deserted with doors removed and mantels missing and anything that could be taken gone. Pigs rutting in yards, a dead, bloated dog on the street. In a weed-ravaged yard on the far edge of town a young girl playing with a doll stopped to watch them pass. Archie tipped his hat to her and smiled.

They crossed the Lafayette County line and reached the Sni in less than three hours. They continued riding west. By early afternoon with the high summer sun beating down and the flies buzzing and the flick of the horses' tails whispering against their hides, with Kansas City almost in sight to the north, in a flush of willows growing along a sluggish stream, Bill finally called a halt. He looked back at Archie and Jacob and Haywood with a blue glittering in his eyes.

"We wait here until tonight before we cross the border."

"Can I see Kansas from here?" Haywood asked. "I ain't never seen Kansas."

"You'll see it tonight."

"It'll be dark tonight," the boy muttered.

They dismounted and let the horses graze. They tried to sleep but the sun and the flies were too heavy and they were too close to the garrison at Kansas City. They crawled into the pawpaw brush beneath the willows and waited. No one spoke or joked or laughed and the one time Archie tried Bill turned his steady blue gaze upon him and Archie had to satisfy himself with thrusting his knife into the soil. By three o'clock the sun was almost intolerable, and Jacob crawled out to wash his face in the stream. Haywood followed. The water smelled of rot.

"Jake?" Haywood whispered.

"Yeah, Hay?"

"Why are we being so quiet?"

"Bill's worried about his sisters."

"Oh." Haywood stared at the water. "So why are we being so quiet?"

Jacob wet his face and glanced at Haywood and finally he shrugged. Haywood smiled as if this was answer enough and went back into the brush. Bill's gray mare had come down to the water to drink. The piebald was dozing.

Bill was pacing before sunset. He kept pulling free his pistols and sighting down their barrels at the sky, at the northern or western horizon, kept checking the charges in their cylinders. By the time the sky in the east was gray and the sky over Kansas a blood red, all the horses were saddled. They waited. The night slid over them, with just a thin line of fire to the west. All the color had drained from the world, all the color had drained from Bill, but for the surreal glow in his eyes. He was possessed of a barely controlled and barely controllable wildness.

"Let's go," he said.

They rode west onto the prairie. This was familiar to Jacob, a world re-visited. They were the only things moving in the vast colorless sea but for the gentle wave of the grass.

"Where we going?" Archie asked.

"We'll follow the Kansas River to a farm owned by a man named Tinsdale, just this side of Bonner Springs. They're staying there."

"Will you be able to find it?"

"Just have to follow the river."

They rode west with the grass parting around the horses' chests, then closing behind them. In a few miles they reached the river. Within minutes the darkness was so complete it was frightening, so complete that even McGown was only a black lump. The river jogged south and they followed it. It murmured beside them, the smell of it, its coolness rising, darkness below and above. Jacob was wrapped in darkness and was breathing darkness. It was filling the empty space within him. It frightened him and he struggled to think of other things.

His grandfather had followed an eagle into the forest because he had believed in omens. He had slept in a cottonwood's hollow in darkness like this. Without the eagle he must have felt so alone. Jacob had lain in the loft in darkness like this and listened to the love of his parents. He had slept with Sarah, oh God, he thought, Sarah, smooth, polished skin, the way her ribs fell into her waist and her waist into her hips and the gentle line of her backbone in darkness like this. She was in his arms as he rode, but beyond her floated McGown. Teague going down and McGown going down and those eyes, those black eyes whose brilliance overwhelmed all the eyes that had followed of the men who had fallen to Jacob's bloody hands. He was holding Sarah but not feeling her because beyond her in that darkness were those eyes. He wanted to tear it away and see beyond it. He wanted to scream and weep like a child. Why? he wanted to cry. Why?

"Spooky as hell out here," Haywood whispered.

They rode for an hour, for two, the night, the grass almost mesmerizing. They skirted a few small, nameless homesteads and a few small, nameless towns. Always ahead of them Jacob could feel McGown wrapped in his darkness. The river flowed before them, and McGown followed the river.

They rode for another half hour. Bill's head moved side to side as he studied the murky landscape. "Can't make out a damn thing," he muttered. "I'd hate to go right by them."

"We ought to stop and ask somebody," Archie said.

They rode on to the next farm, a small frame house with a shed outlined behind it. A horse whinnied as they approached. Bill dismounted, but before he could knock on the door someone within lit a lantern. He knocked anyway. A young man, hardly more than a boy, answered the door, holding his thin shoulders as if he enjoyed carrying upon them the full weight of that heavy, black night. A girl with skin so fair that even in only the lantern light the blue veins in her temples stood out watched Bill from over the boy's shoulder. She held a bald, round-faced baby in her arms.

"Yes?" the boy asked.

"We're trying to find the Tinsdale farm," Bill said.

"A couple miles upriver. You got dealings with them?"

"Yeah."

"This time of night?"

"Yeah."

"Then you watch out. They'll take every god damned thing you own."

"Why's that?"

"They ain't got no morals. They're god damned secesh."

"You a Union man?" Bill asked.

"And proud of it," the boy said.

"Shoot him, Arch," Bill called over his shoulder.

Archie grinned and drew his revolver. The muzzle flash was shockingly brilliant in the darkness and the boy slammed back against the door and rolled onto the floor. He had a bullet hole in his throat and he was choking. The girl screamed. Only the baby kept its wits, watching all with its tiny wise eyes.

Bill went inside and came out with the lantern. He tossed it back in over the boy's body. Flames rose.

"You better get out of there," Bill advised the girl, "before you get roasted."

The girl was still screaming. Bill mounted and they followed McGown upriver. Jacob looked back to see Haywood staring back at the girl. She was trying to drag the boy's body out of the fire with one hand and was clutching the baby with the other. The baby's hand was raised in the air as the German woman's had been in Lafayette County.

"To hell with them, boys," Archie said. "They're just god damned Yankee scum."

The flames rising behind them grew almost cheery in the distance. When they'd gone a mile or so they came across another farm and they halted. Bill had to knock on the door twice before a balding man perhaps in his thirties with a fleshy growth over one eye answered the door. A strange combination of loose paunch and work-hardened hands.

"There's a fire down the valley," Bill said.

The man looked. "My Jesus," he said. "My Jesus." He disappeared back into the darkness, then came out into the yard pulling a pair of trousers up to his waist. His boots he had tucked under his arm. "That's the Bell place."

"Where's the Tinsdale's?"

"The next place upriver."

"You got a carriage?"

"Sure I do."

"Haywood, can you drive a carriage?"

"Sure I can."

"You go fetch it. Is it in the barn?" Bill asked the man.

"Yeah." The man had finished pulling up his trousers and was slipping on one boot. "What do you need the carriage for?"

"You got a wife? Kids?"

"They're back in New Hampshire." He stopped in the middle of pulling on his boot. He watched Haywood scamper to the barn, then turned to stare at Bill. "Who are you?"

"Your turn, Jake," Bill said.

Jacob let himself empty. He pulled the dragoon pistol free and aimed it at the man. The man stumbled as he backed toward the door, the boot flopping around his ankle. When Jacob shot him a huge black hole opened in his chest, and the force of the ball made him somersault. McGown crouched on the eaves and watched. The eye sockets empty now, the skin around them falling back to show the white glimmering bone beneath. His forehead completely devoid now of skin and the bone almost glowing. Archie laughed.

"God damn, Jake. God damn."

"Archie," Bill said, "you go help Haywood with the traces."

Archie nodded and dismounted and walked by the man's body, shaking his head and grinning. He disappeared into shadow. Bill went into the house. A small but growing flame appeared through the window. When Bill came back outside he stepped over the man's body.

"Ain't they back with the carriage yet?"

"Not yet."

"Hell." The growing light through the window caught his features, caught the glint in his eyes. A breeze carrying the smells of the grass and the water came downriver and gently lifted the curls around his shoulders. A soft summer night. Smoke rose around McGown. "Never send boys to do a man's job."

"Hitching up a carriage is a boy's job."

"I can't get nothing by you, Jake."

In a few minutes they heard hooves stamping. Archie was standing on the side of the carriage and Haywood was sitting in it, driving a mule. "This is more like it," Haywood said. "Nothing gets squarshed like this."

"Let's go then," Bill said.

Jacob gathered up the Morgan's reins. Archie mounted, and he and Bill went on ahead. Jacob waited for the carriage to go by.

Lanterns had already been lit at the Tinsdales'. Bill dismounted in front of the house. The door opened and a teenaged girl laughed and bounded toward Bill, throwing herself into his arms. She was young and slim and looked like her brother, except her hair was blond. She had the same eyes.

"Jennie," Bill said. He held her for a long time and she cried happily on his shoulder. Jacob looked back at the burning farms and waited. He didn't like this. McGown was gone.

"Where's Joe and Mary?" Bill asked.

"Getting dressed," the girl said. "We seen the farms burning and I said it was you but they said it couldn't be you. But I knew it was you, Bill. I can always tell when you're coming."

"You all right, Jennie?"

"I'm all right. Yankees come around sometimes, but only for scaring."

"You get in the carriage."

The girl wouldn't let him go. Finally when he pulled her loose she skipped to the carriage happily. She stared at Haywood, who grinned back and scratched at the scar on the back of his head. She sat well away from him. Archie brought his blue roan around to her, leaned over and tipped his hat. "Hello, Miss Jennie," he said.

"Don't you even think it, Archie," Bill warned him.

"Think what?"

"Don't you even think it. I'll string you up by the armpits in some tree and gut you just right so you live long enough to see the hogs eat your innards. I swear to God I will."

"I don't know what you're talking about, Bill."

"The hell you don't. I swear to God, Archie, I'll do it."

Archie looked into his eyes and the grin dropped from his face. He backed the horse away. Two more girls came out of the door, a few years older than the first, long and sinewy, and threw themselves at Bill. He hugged them both. He was crying, love and joy showing in his face in the lamplight, tear tracks glowing on his cheeks. Jacob had never seen him this way. He didn't like this. He let them hug for a moment before he cleared his throat.

"They'll be coming, Bill."

Bill ignored him. Jacob waited uncomfortably for a minute more.

"Bill, they'll be coming."

Bill looked up. "Right," he said. "Right." He hugged the girls again briefly, then hustled them to the carriage and mounted his mare. A barrel-chested man with a silky gray mane was standing in the door. A gray woman stood behind him.

"I owe you anything you can name, Harold," Bill told him.

"Just get a couple of those bastards for me."

"We already did."

"Well, get a couple more. Don't head back down the valley."

"I ain't dumb, Harold."

"Then forget that damned carriage. Head south across the prairie until you reach Olathe. Don't take the Santa Fe Road. Just head east. In a couple of hours you'll reach the border."

"I thank you," Bill said.

"Just get a couple of them bastards for me." The man shook his head at the fires. He crossed his thick forearms over his chest. "I suppose I ought to go help with those. It would be the neighborly thing to do."

"I figured it would keep people busy until it was too late to bother chasing us."

"You're wasting what time you have," the man said. "I'll see you."

The girls climbed out of the carriage and mounted up behind Jacob and Bill and Haywood—Bill wouldn't let Archie carry any of them. With the tallest girl behind him, with her warm arms clutching his waist and the feel of her breasts against his back, Jacob followed Bill south between the house and the barn, up the gentle slope of the valley into the grass, into the darkness. They rode quickly and silently, always keeping the north star behind them. The moon was a slit and a smile and the edge of a knife, just light enough to hint at the vast rolling land around them. The grass whispered. The piebald looked back over her shoulder at the strange arrangements on her back. She didn't seem to approve.

"Which one are you?" Jacob asked.

"Mary," the girl behind him said. Her voice was low with a hint of wildness, just like Bill's.

"You the one who got jilted?"

"That ain't none of your god damned business."

"I got a pretty one," Haywood said happily.

"You haven't got nothing," the girl he was carrying told him.

"Do your balls get squarshed when you ride?" Haywood asked her.

"What are you talking about?"

"Oh," Haywood said. "You probably don't have none."

"Bill?" the girl asked. "Can I ride behind you?"

"This is kind of like a party," Haywood said.

They rode for two hours, almost three, stopping twice to let the girls stretch, to let the horses rest. As the moon descended, the night grew blind. Jacob crouched in the grass and looked out back behind them at each stop. He heard nothing but the grass, he smelled nothing but the grass. The girls and Bill gathered in a clump and talked among themselves quietly, sometimes laughing. It was always Jacob who broke up the resting and pushed them on.

The moon had set by the time they reached Olathe. Buildings with empty faces, silence, a few charred wrecks, new crosses in the graveyard pointing at the sky. They headed east out of town. The blackness on the horizon before them was fading to gray, and the girl's arms around his waist and her cheek against his shoulder reminded Jacob too much of Sarah.

Before dawn they reached the border. The girl behind Jacob was sleeping, with Jacob holding her wrists around his waist to keep her on the horse. Seven miles into Missouri, halfway to Strother, Bill reined at the door of a farm that Jacob thought he recognized—perhaps he had spent a night or two or had a meal or two here the previous year. The new sun cast long shadows over the hills, over the trees on the hills. The air was crisp and would have been refreshing if not for bone-aching weariness. The piebald faltered as Jacob dismounted and helped Mary off of her back. A farmer came to the door without anyone knocking. Jacob didn't know him.

"You made it," the farmer said.

Bill helped Jennie down. "I take it you got the word."

"We got a grapevine faster than the telegraph. Any trouble?"

"None to speak of."

The farmer pursed his lips and nodded. He was a big man of about fifty with wild gray hair and the beginning of jowls, a hard set to his thick shoulders. He studied the girls. "Which is Jennie and which is Joe and which is Mary?" They introduced themselves. "You'll be all right here."

"I thank you for this, Roger," Bill said.

"There's right and there's wrong, Bill," the farmer answered. "I can't just stand by."

They went inside. A woman about the same age as the man was fixing a breakfast of pancakes and stewed fruit. She had the wide shoulders and square hips, the callused hands, of a farmer's wife. Jacob's need for sleep made the meal taste like dust. When he finished he sat numbly and watched as the woman herded the girls off to bed.

The farmer sat at the head of the table, his thick fingers picking at an overgrown cuticle. He pursed his lips again. "You all are wanted on the Blackwater."

Archie cursed. "What the hell for? I'm tired."

"The word's gone out from Charlie Quantrill. You're wanted on the Blackwater at the Pardee farm." He sipped coffee. "Do you know what for, Bill?"

"I got an idea."

"Can you tell me your idea?"

"No." Bill sighed. "Charlie wants to get us all killed."

"He ain't done you wrong yet, Bill."

"No he ain't. But this I don't like."

"Well," the farmer said. "The word's gone out."

The woman came back and gathered up dishes. Not even the heavy, bitter taste of the coffee could keep Jacob's eyes from drifting shut. Someone shook his shoulder, and when he looked up Haywood was grinning down at him.

"Hey, Jake."

"Hey, Hay."

"We got to move on. I guess there's a creek somewheres we're gonna sleep beside."

"We going to the Blackwater?"

"Bill says there's no way in hell we're going to the Blackwater." Haywood glanced at the door the girls had gone through. "I think that girl I was carrying likes me."

"Why do you think that?"

"She kept putting her arms around me."

"She was trying to keep from falling off."

The corners of Haywood's grin dropped. "You think so?"

Jacob rubbed his eyes. "No, Hay. Maybe she likes you." He stood and stumbled toward the door. Outside, Archie and Bill were already mounted. "Just so you know, Haywood. There ain't a girl in this world that has balls."

"I bet there's some somewheres."

"Not a one, Haywood."

"Have you seen them all?"

"No."

"Well then."

Jacob was too tired for this. He pulled himself up on the piebald, who stamped her foot with displeasure. He followed Bill out of the farmyard into the willows and hickories and pawpaws north of the farm. Not a hundred yards from the house a lazy stream flowed silently. Bill dismounted. Jacob dismounted gratefully and managed to unsaddle the piebald before he fell asleep.

Chapter Twenty-one

Jacob awoke and cursed as he passed his hands over his scruffy, burning cheeks and rubbed his eyes. He was lying out away from the others as if even his sleeping self did not like to look up at the trees.

He went to the stream to drink. The others were still sleeping, Bill with his head cradled on his arm, Haywood curled into a ball, Archie lying with his mouth open and a fly sampling the moisture at its corner. The horses dozed peacefully. He drank from the tepid water and contemplated an oak leaf driven by the current, swirling, bucking in the eddies. He was still too tired to be aware of what he was thinking. The oak leaf was only an oak leaf, the sky only the sky, no hidden portents, or none that he could discern or would admit. It was only a lovely summer afternoon.

When he finished drinking he rose and with his hands planted against his back, with a grimace pulling his sleep-slackened cheeks, he turned to study the farm. A column of blue-clad riders was moving away from it and the day turned dark and his stomach cold and he dropped on his belly into the grass hard enough to leave him gasping. He scuttled like a crab to where Bill lay.

"Bill." He shook his shoulder. "Bill."

Bill opened his eyes. Sleep had swollen them to slits. "What?"

"Yankees."

Bill came suddenly awake. He reached for two pistols, and with one in each hand rolled onto his belly and followed Jacob's gaze. "Where are the horses?"

"Grazing."

"Where'd they come from?"

"I just woke up. All I can say is what I told you."

"Wake the others."

Jacob crawled through the brush and shook Archie and Haywood awake. His silent expression conveyed what it was meant to convey, and without standing Archie and Haywood fetched their pistols and crawled to where Bill lay, Haywood's good eye wide, his lazy eye rolling blindly. Jacob crawled to his saddle and drew his dragoon pistol from beneath it and lay with it in front of him, his forearm braced on the saddle jockey.

Bill glanced at him. "How many of them do you figure?"

"Thirty, thirty-five."

"We got us a fight?" Archie asked.

Bill snorted. "You got a fight if you want it. Just wait until I'm in the next county."

They waited until the column was gone and the dust behind it was settling. Jacob crawled to the edge of the trees where he could better study both the road and the farm. Nothing seemed to have changed from the morning.

"I think we're all right, Bill."

"They was just out patrolling," Bill said. "Them dumb bastards couldn't find Bill Anderson if he crawled up one of their asses."

"You think they stopped at the farm?" Haywood asked.

"Oh hell." Bill choked. "Oh hell."

They started for the farm, but before they had gone five yards the farmer came around the corner of the house in a heavy jog toward them. By the time he reached them his face was flushed and his forehead beaded and rosy. Some of his hair flared in the breeze and some lay sweat-plastered to his skull. He smelled of the sweat and was gasping.

"What happened?" Bill asked.

"They took them."

"What's that mean?"

The farmer braced his hands on his knees. Sweat rolled from his nose. "They took your sisters. They just come up and took your sisters."

Bill studied the farmer quietly. Suddenly he brought his boot up hard into the man's belly. The farmer whooshed and fell backward and his breath still smelled of the breakfast. Bill kicked him in the side, and when the farmer rolled over onto it, Bill kicked him in the chest. The farmer made frightening little wheezing noises. He passed gas loudly.

"You sold them out, you bastard," Bill said.

"I didn't."

"You sold them out."

"I didn't."

"You waited until we was asleep and then you got hold of the Yankees."

"I didn't, Bill. I didn't."

Bill stood over him with his hands gripping his pistols. He spat on the farmer's cheek. The farmer didn't wipe it off.

"Archie, let me borrow that knife of yours."

"What for?"

"Just let me borrow it."

Archie grinned and loosened his knife in its scabbard. He handed it to Bill. Bill turned it so that the reflection of the sun off of its blade flashed in the farmer's eyes. He crouched and yanked the man's arm away from his chest and knelt with his knee pinning the wrist. He settled the knife blade against the first knuckle on the farmer's smallest finger.

"You tell me you didn't betray them," Bill said.

"I didn't, Bill. Please, Jesus."

"You tell me."

"You know I wouldn't, Bill. You know I wouldn't."

"You a liar?"

"You know I'm not a liar."

"Hell," Bill said. "Everybody's a liar at one time or another." He adjusted the blade and with his free hand held the farmer's arm. He brought up his other knee and brought it down on the back of the knife and the farmer screamed. Blood spurt over the grass. The grass bowed beneath its weight.

Bill released the farmer and stood. The farmer rolled back and forth with his hand clutched to and reddening his chest. The finger lay quietly in the red grass. Bill spat on it, then on the farmer.

"God damned traitor," Bill said.

"Bill," Haywood said.

"Now I'm going to fuck your wife. I'm going to split her cunt open so there's room enough for all of us." The farmer just whimpered. Bill kicked him again.

"Bill," Haywood said again.

"Shut up, Haywood."

"Bill, if he betrayed your sisters, why didn't he betray us, too? We was sleeping not a quarter mile from his house."

Bill looked down at the farmer. His face had been an ugly sneer that now softened. "Oh hell. Roger, are you all right?"

The farmer bit off his whimper in hot little chunks. He stared up at Bill with his face red and tense, his lips pulled back and his features trembling, as if he were trying to lift a great load. Blood covered his shirt and the waist of his pants.

"Oh hell, Roger, I'm sorry. I'll get you a doctor."

"You won't get me nothing."

"I'll ride into Strother and get you a doctor. I'll kidnap him if he won't come."

"You won't get me nothing."

"What do you want me to do?"

"Get off of my property."

"I'm sorry, Roger."

"You're going to burn in hell one day," the farmer said.

Jacob and Haywood helped the farmer to his feet. His whimpers were now sharp little hisses. They led him back toward the house with Jacob's arm bracing his shoulders and Haywood's his hips and blood running in streams and Bill following behind like an embarrassed child. The farmer's wife was standing at the corner of the house, wringing her hands. Tears on her face.

"There was an accident," Jacob said.

"The hell if that was an accident," the farmer said.

"You want us to get him a doctor?"

"You bastards get off of my property," the farmer answered for her. He was crying, too.

As the woman took the farmer in her arms, his knees gave way and she settled him against the side of the house. Jacob and Haywood glanced at each other. Haywood's lazy eye rolled.

"Can I ask you something?" Bill asked. "Can I ask if they said where they're taking the girls?"

"You bastards get off of my property," the farmer said again.

They stood awkwardly for a minute or two. Finally Jacob led Haywood back to the stream with Bill trailing behind. Archie was sitting against a tree and wiping the knife blade off on the grass. He squinted up at the sun.

Bill looked anxiously at him and the others. "He sure is mad."

"He ain't happy."

"It was an accident."

"Hell," Archie said, "he sold them out."

Bill wiped his mouth and studied the house. The wife had run inside and the farmer sat with his hand to his chest, grimacing at the sky. "We best get him a doctor."

"We best get the hell out of here, like he says."

They saddled the horses, mounted, and rode by the house. The wife came out with a towel that became almost instantly sodden. She led the farmer inside. Bill called his apologies through the closed door, but no one came to answer him. They left riding east, taking a cow path into the hills. Flowers bloomed on the side of the path, throwing their scent into the sky. A beautiful summer day. They'd left the finger in the pasture.

"He was a damned Yankee anyway," Archie said.

For two weeks they wandered through the border counties, doing little beyond raiding for food and tearing down the telegraph line running south to Springfield. As they passed by the charred, empty ruins of Osceola, Jacob remembered Jim Buchanan and the jayhawking sergeant and he thought about Lawrence, Kansas. He thought he would ride into Osceola to either check on the storekeeper or kill him, but he could see that no one was living there. The domain of foxes and rats.

The next day they passed a farmer plowing a field with his wife and daughter in harness, their faces drawn, their hunger in their eyes. Archie wanted to kill him, but Bill's heart wasn't in it. He was too worried about his sisters and the farmer he had maimed.

"Where do you suppose they've taken them?" he asked one night. It was the middle of August.

"Don't know," Jacob answered. They were eating a ham they'd taken from an abandoned farm. Chickens had been roosting on its porch. Hogs had been eating the remains of a cur someone had shot through the head. "Kansas City, I expect."

"Where they've got the others. The McCorkles and Harriet."

"I expect."

"How do you suppose Roger is?"

"He ain't picking his nose with his little finger, that's for sure." Archie laughed.

The next morning they rode northwest back into Jackson County. They stopped outside of Strother, and Bill studied the land to the west. "I got to see if he's all right," he said.

"He'll greet us at the door with a shotgun," Archie said.

"I got to see."

"I ain't going with you."

"Then stay here."

"I'm going," Haywood said. "I ain't never seen a cut-off finger before."

"It'll look about like your ears," Archie said.

"I ain't never seen my ears, neither. Not with them like this. I cain't turn my head quick enough."

"I'd keep avoiding mirrors if I was you."

"I got me the mark of Cain."

Bill and Jacob and Haywood rode west toward the farm. Archie stayed back to make camp in a gully south of Strother. Jacob rode with the dragoon pistol across the saddle and worried that someone might have seen them and sent forward word. He thought of that boy lying in front of Dietrich's door with a shotgun blast in his chest. He'd take an unsuspecting Federal soldier anytime.

"You think it's skinned over yet?" Haywood asked.

"What?"

"The finger."

"I don't know."

"I bet it's still got a scab."

They came over a rise and the farm lay below them. A mule grazed in the pasture they had slept in. Bill rode forward with his head down, and Jacob followed uneasily. The Morgan walked beside him with Haywood gripping its mane. His pistols were tucked in his waistband and stuck out on each side of his head.

The farmer stepped out of the door just as they reached the yard. His hand was bound in clean white bandages and he had a shotgun in the crook of his other arm. Jacob and Haywood reined and Bill went forward penitently. Jacob slipped his finger to the dragoon pistol's trigger.

"Hey, Roger," Bill said. The farmer didn't answer. "How's the hand?" The farmer still didn't answer. He studied them quietly.

"Where's the wife?" Bill asked.

"Inside."

"You going to shoot me?"

"I'm not going to shoot you."

"Why not?"

"Because I'm not like you, Bill. I'm not."

"There ain't many like me," Bill said.

"In this country there's too many like you."

Bill nodded. Jacob nudged the piebald forward so it stood beside the gray mare. He put his pistol away. The farmer stared at them impassively with his bandaged hand running up and down the shotgun barrel.

"I'm awful sorry about that, Roger."

"What do you want?" the farmer asked.

"Just to check on you."

"I'm fine, thanks to Betty. No thanks to you."

"I offered to get you a doctor, Roger."

"That isn't what I mean and you know it. Those soldiers could have shot me and they threatened to. They busted up most everything we had in the house and they carted off the rest of it and they threatened to burn it down and all I had to do was tell them where you were and I didn't. Hell, I could have just pointed. And you cut off my finger."

"A fella can only say he's sorry so many times, Roger."

"He can say it until he dies," the farmer said, "which I expect in your case won't be long."

"Well."

"It couldn't be soon enough."

Bill nodded humbly. "It's good to see you're doing all right. We'll be moving on."

"You're wanted on the Blackwater. The Pardee farm."

"I know that."

"You're wanted there again."

"Why is that?" Bill asked.

"You haven't heard?"

"Heard what?"

The farmer sighed through his nose. He switched the shotgun to the other arm and ran his free hand through the hair sticking out on the side of his head. "God damn. I thought you would have heard."

"I ain't heard nothing since the last time I saw you."

The farmer sighed again. "They had the girls up in some building in Kansas City."

"That's about what I figured."

"Two days ago it collapsed."

Bill's eyes went dull, then flamed. "What are you saying?"

"The Yankees, they said the girls were trying to dig a tunnel through the cellar wall."

"Horseshit."

"That's what they said. My opinion is that the Yankees pulled out the supports so that it would fall. Some doctor had looked at the place three days ago and said that he saw them doing it."

"What happened to my sisters, Roger?"

The farmer wiped his hand over his face and glanced back at the door behind him. "This wasn't me, Bill. This was them. I don't want to lose no more fingers."

"It wasn't you, Roger. What happened to my sisters?"

"Armenia Gilvey died. So did one of the Vandiver girls."

"My sisters."

"One of the McCorkle girls and the Swisby woman died, too."

"Harriet?" Jacob asked.

"If that was her name."

"My sisters," Bill said again.

The farmer wiped his mouth again. "Bill, they killed your sister Joe. Mary and Jennie, they're pretty crippled up."

Bill's face was gray, his eyes blazing. His features pulled in different ways, in different expressions, as if he were a different man. "They gonna die?"

"I don't know. Their legs are pretty crippled up. Busted."

"They gonna die?"

"I don't know, Bill."

"I want to see them."

"You can't see them. They're in some Federal military hospital."

Bill nodded. He stared silently at the ground. One eye twitched.

"It's bad news, I know, Bill," the farmer said, "but I got to tell you this, too. If you come back here again I'll kill you. I will. I would have killed you this time, but for your sisters."

"You're a good southern man, Roger," Bill said. One cheek pulled tight, and his mouth shifted. "You got your honor."

"Honor don't have nothing to do with it. I ain't letting no bushwhackers back on this property. No jayhawkers, either. North and south and bad and good, they all run together in a mess like this."

"There's a difference, Roger. There is. We ain't pulling down no buildings."

"So don't come back because I'll shoot you. You've heard it twice. And I'm sorry about your sisters."

Bill nodded. He pulled his mare around and headed back toward Strother. He stopped and looked back at the farmer.

"You picked a bad time to tell me that, Roger. I mean about shooting me. You picked a bad time."

"I had to, Bill. So you knew."

"Well," Bill said. "I'll see you."

"I hope not," the farmer said.

Bill nodded and nudged the mare into a walk. She trudged over the rise. The farmer was standing as he had been before, his bandaged hand caressing the shotgun barrel.

"Tell me what happened," Jacob said.

"I already did."

"That wasn't all of it. You tell me."

The man glanced at Haywood and at the hill Bill had climbed. "I couldn't say it with him here. Even with as much as I hate him now."

"Tell me."

"The building went down and all the Yankees just stood around watching. The dead girls weren't all dead yet and the others, they were in there, too. They were screaming."

"Damn."

"Nannie McCorkle jumped out a window and Jennie tried to follow her, but the Yankees had a ball and chain around her ankle and she didn't make it. The first floor was a liquor store and they had the girls on the second. When it came down, the girls landed on broken bottles. Joe was begging someone to get the bricks off her head and they never did. They never tried. She was all cut up." He glanced at the hill again. "All I'm saying is what I heard."

"You keep telling me."

"That Swisby woman, I guess she was a big woman."

"She was."

"She was lying there in the rubble throwing off blocks of the walls that a man couldn't lift. She had one arm broken at almost right angles with glass sticking out of it and blood pouring down. Crying for somebody, from what I hear."

"And nobody would help her."

"Not a one. When they finally come she grabbed the first by the throat, but her hand wasn't much good anymore."

"Damn them," Jacob said.

"Well, you asked," the farmer said. "Don't tell Bill. He's crazy enough."

"He'll find out somewhere. Sometime." Jacob nodded at the man and reined the horse around. He expected Haywood to follow, but Haywood just stared at the farmer, at his bandaged hand.

"Hay," Jacob said.

"Will you take that bandage off?" Haywood asked.

The farmer stared at him. His hand stopped moving over the barrel.

"I ain't never seen no cut-off finger before," Haywood said. "Is it all scabbed over? My ears, they was all scabbed over. But I didn't see them. I felt the scabs on them."

"Hay," Jacob said again, "you better come along."

"You ought to listen to your friend, son," the farmer said.

"I was just asking." Haywood smiled at the man. He cocked his head to the side while his lazy eye wobbled. "What did you do with the cut-off part?"

"Hay," Jacob said again.

"Can I have it?"

"Listen to your friend, son," the farmer said again.

Finally Jacob rode back and took the Morgan's bridle. He led Haywood up and over the rise. Bill was in the distance, the mare walking slowly. Haywood waved wildly back at the farmer.

"You ain't bright, Hay."

"I didn't mean nothing by it. It ain't like he's ever going to use it again."

"You ain't bright."

"I didn't mean nothing by it," Haywood said.

Chapter Twenty-two

They caught up with Bill and rode silently. The twitch in his eye had spread to his lips, as if he wanted to speak but was unable. He stared straight ahead, never acknowledging them, seeing things beyond. Jacob watched him. Haywood watched him, too, with his head cocked to one side and his breath whistling through the gap in his teeth. Archie had made camp and grinned when they rode into it. Bill rode through without stopping.

"What's with him?" Archie asked Jacob.

"I don't think we'll be making camp here."

"What's with him?"

"His sisters got all smashed up," Haywood said.

"Shut up, Hay," Jacob said.

Bill kept riding, his eyes blind, his lips working. Jacob rode beside him while Haywood waited for Archie. They joined them just beyond Strother. They turned south and rode into Greenwood without Bill looking to either side. The few townspeople remaining gave him a wide berth. Wild people with their memories in their eyes.

They reached Johnson County and headed east, picking up the Blackwater in less than an hour. They followed the headwaters downstream into the deadening sky until campfires speckled the distance, blinking as they passed through the trees. Bill ignored a picket that hailed them.

"It's all right," Jacob shouted. "It's Bill Anderson's bunch."

They rode into camp. More guerrillas had gathered than Jacob had ever seen. Sullen faces reflected in fires, eyes filled with thoughts of dead and crippled women, with Yankee laughter. Jacob and Archie and Haywood dismounted, but Bill rode on, only his lips animated.

Haywood scratched the scar on the back of his head. "He's gone plumb crazy."

"Take care of the piebald, Hay," Jacob said.

"What are you going to do?"

"Follow him around. Make sure he's all right."

"He's gone plumb crazy," Haywood said again.

Jacob followed Bill. A crowd had gathered around a large fire burning in front of the house. Jacob recognized Charlie, Bill Gregg, George Todd, a few others. Not until he reached the fire did Bill dismount.

"Hey, Bill," Charlie said.

"Is this about Lawrence?" Bill asked.

"I sent out Fletch Taylor and Henry Nolan on reconnaissance. It's a plum out there, Bill. All the defenses are down and all the plunder's just waiting." Charlie grinned, his eyes hidden. "Wide streets just right for horses. A plum just sitting on the prairie."

"I don't give a damn about plums," Bill said. "I want to burn it down. I want to shoot all the men in the face and I want to stick a pistol under all the women's petticoats and keep shooting until I've cut them in half." He stared into the fire. One cheek jumped, then the other. "They just stood around laughing while Joe died. While Mary and Jennie got their legs busted up."

Charlie glanced around the fire, glanced at Jacob. "You heard all that?"

"The spirit of my dead sister," Bill said, "has been speaking to me."

Charlie stared at him quietly. Bill Gregg and George threw glances at each other. Jacob waited.

"The spirits of the dead are all around me," Bill said.

The men looked at him and at each other uneasily. Bill stared into the fire while his lips worked. Suddenly he strode away, his silhouette fading. Charlie looked at Jacob.

"You tell him that?" Charlie asked.

"I didn't tell him nothing."

"He isn't right in the head."

"He's a crazy bastard," George said. "I heard he cut Roger Stillwell's finger off."

"He did."

"Bloody Bill."

"He's a god damned lunatic," Bill Gregg said.

"I'll keep watch on him," Jacob said.

Jacob followed Bill into the trees down to the river. Bill stopped, his shadow rigid against the trees, his head back to look up at the sky, his fists clenched at his sides. His shoulders were jumping.

"Why you following me?"

"Just want to make sure you're all right."

"I ain't all right. How am I supposed to be all right? They done took everything I had from me."

"I know."

"First my mother died and then they shot my father and now they killed my sister. Now they crippled my two baby sisters."

"I know."

"How am I supposed to be all right?"

"I don't know, Bill."

Bill turned and dropped his gaze to him. His eyes blazed with something Jacob had never seen. This was a new beginning. "Jake, I'm going to make them a deal."

"What kind?"

"They took everything from me but my life and it ain't worth shit no more. So they can try to take that. I'll give them every chance."

"That don't sound like much of a deal, Bill."

"But if they don't take it, I'm going to take theirs. I'm going to take all of theirs in the ugliest ways that I can. I'm going to burn Lawrence to the ground. I'm going to find Jim Lane and kill him. I'm going to find Jennison and kill him. I'm going to find every one of them and I'm going to kill them all."

"All right."

"And if they don't like that deal, then I'll make it with God. And if he don't like it I'll make it with the devil."

"God will make it with you, Bill. He's done it before."

"He has?"

"Don't you read the Bible?"

"Not in a while."

"You ought to."

"I ain't much of a holy man, Jake. But I've been seeing things." Bill looked again at the sky, at the stars blinking down. "There's things out there, Jake. This world is like a curtain and there's things on the other side. I saw Joe, Jake. She was floating there all white-like, kind of glowing. She told me everything that happened and what I need to do."

Jacob scanned the trees, the sky. Where was McGown? The moon was only a sliver. "She didn't look dead?"

"She's an angel, Jake. She's ascending to the throne of God."

"You didn't see no one that looked dead?"

Bill's eyes flashed. His lips pulled jerkily into a grin that quickly dropped from his face. "I didn't see him. But I felt him. You know what I'm talking about?"

"I know."

"You know him?"

"I know him."

"He ever speak to you?"

"Not as he is now," Jacob said. They stared at each other, at the darkness.

Now McGown was squatting in a branch above Jacob. He stank of his own decay. His lips had rotted off and the bones around his mouth gleamed dully with some kind of internal glow. His eyes stared. Black empty sockets, cold empty sockets, always on Jacob. He dropped full-bodied from the branch, and when his feet hit the ground and some of his rotted sinews gave way his body made a noise like sludge being poured from a bucket.

"Lawrence," Bill said quietly. He took his knotted cord from his pocket and pressed it to his lips. "That's where it starts."

McGown watched Jacob. Black pits for eyes so cold that Jacob could almost see frost forming around the sockets. Fear and knowledge and a strange comfort thrilled him.

"We'll kill them all, Jake," Bill said.

"We will, Bill," Jacob answered.

Bill nodded and walked by Jacob back toward the fires. McGown waddled closer on his rotting, broken, wasting legs, one arm curled to his chest and the other dragging across the ground. Jacob backed away and followed Bill toward the camp. He felt better in the firelight, less cold, and when he turned, McGown had disappeared. He didn't know where he had gone. The fear and comfort lifted, and he felt alone.

Haywood was eating beans beside a cookfire that the mangy redheaded mute was tending.

"Hey, Jake." Haywood shoveled a spoonful of beans into his mouth and worked them with his tongue to his back teeth where he could chew them. "What's with Bill?"

Jacob helped himself to a plate of beans, stared at them, then set them aside. "He's seen his dead sister."

Haywood quit chewing. "You believe in that stuff, Jake?"

"I don't know. I guess."

Haywood's eyes from beneath the bill of his forage cap followed Bill across the camp to the main fire, where he squatted beside Charlie. "Looky here, Jake. We talk about this any more and I'll be spooking."

Jacob spent the night staring up at the darkness, at the slow-moving circle of stars. Just after midnight he found McGown squatting on the peak of the house above Bill and the main fire. Jacob stared at the dead sergeant, and the dead sergeant stared back, his eyes empty and cold.

"What do you want from me?" Jacob asked. But McGown did not answer.

The day dawned bright and hot. The guerrillas waited impatiently, repairing tack and resting, cleaning pistols and loading them. George Todd left early and came back that afternoon leading fifty illiterate Irishmen, loud, harsh voices, eyes as dull and vicious and as full of blood as George's own. Larkin Skaggs rode in alone and explained in theological terms to all who would listen the importance of what was coming. The birds quiet in the heat or in recognition.

Charlie walked through the men, speaking in soft tones, his hand on shoulders, his encouraging smile. He wore an embroidered hunting shirt, a black hat with a gold band and tassels, and he had four Colt Navy revolvers in his belt. The brilliant revengeful fire glowed within his dark-hooded eyes; Lawrence glowed in his eyes. He handed around lists of special targets with Jim Lane and Charles Jennison at the top of it, the Reverend Hugh Fisher, who had raided the church in Osceola, Mayor Callomore, some doctors and others. "Find them all and kill them all, except for Lane," he said. "We'll bring him back to Missouri and hang him."

"You got any chinless sergeants on that list?" Jacob asked.

"Why?"

"I'll be looking for one."

There must have been three hundred guerrillas. Coarse, dirty men, slouch hats and butternut or red embroidered shirts, Federal uniforms grimy with camp grease and dirt. Charlie walked through them to where his brown gelding waited.

"Mount up," he said as he swung up into the saddle.

Jacob patted the piebald, which trembled and nuzzled his shoulder. He climbed onto her back and settled comfortably. Archie mounted beside him, grinning. Haywood mounted the Morgan and worked himself carefully onto the saddle. Bill had been waiting most of the day on the back of his gray mare. He was beyond speaking, beyond seeing, his eyes on the west and his mouth worked silently.

"You ready for this, Jake?" Archie asked.

"Sure. A little tired."

"Too bad you don't got you a ax."

"I'm about sick of that joke, Arch."

"Think any of us will come back?"

"It don't make much difference."

They left the farm in rows of four, hardly talking. Charlie led with Bill Gregg and George Todd behind him, Henry Nolan following, and McGown leading them all, flying clumsily a few yards above Charlie's head, his matted jacket split down the back and in tatters, the stinking flesh on his back in tatters, the ribs it exposed glowing dully. Specks of silver light shone against the red setting sun, like fireflies. The piebald's ears twitched and she neighed nervously.

"What you thinking about, Jake?" Haywood asked.

"Nothing." A pillar of fire leading the Hebrews into the desert. A land to be conquered on the other side.

"You be careful in this, Hay."

"I got me the mark of Cain, Jake. God will look after me."

"You can't trust God. He don't care nothing about us."

"You keep saying that, Jake. I keep never knowing what you mean."

They rode ten miles, then stopped to water the horses. When they mounted, McGown led them southwest. During the night they were joined by a column of around a hundred recruits led by a Confederate officer. Jacob too clearly remembered Independence to like this. With the dawn, Charlie called for a halt on the middle fork of the Grand River four miles east of the border. The men dismounted and Jacob studied McGown perched on a cottonwood branch. He rinsed his mouth with water, swallowed it down. The day was dawning hot and crystalline clear.

Where are you taking me? he asked silently. But McGown only stared and wouldn't answer.

Bill Gregg sent out scouts to search for Federal patrols. The rest of the riders rested all morning until the scouts returned, saying they'd found nothing. They mounted at three with the sun blazing down and rode in a swinging trot into Kansas.

"Jake?" Haywood asked.

"Yeah."

"What are we going to do once we get there?"

"You already know that, Hay."

"We just going to kill those guys on the list?"

"We're going to kill everybody. Every man, anyway."

"I won't have to kill nobody, will I? I already got my revenge."

"Not if you don't want to."

"You think Mam will be satisfied with me just killing that one Dutch? And by accerdent?"

"Let me tell you something about your mam, Hay. She's got no right to tell you to kill anybody. That's something beyond her."

Haywood studied this with his lips pursed. The forage cap kept falling over the stubs of his ears, and he had to keep pushing it up. "Jake?"

"Yeah."

"I don't want to kill nobody."

"Then I'll tell you what you do. You just turn around now and head home."

"I ain't never going home."

"Then when we get to Lawrence, you just ride on through. Then you head north to Nebraska or somewheres. Iowa or Minnesota, maybe."

"It's cold in Minnesoter, Jake."

"Yeah."

"You'll come with me, won't you? I cain't go if you don't."

Jacob studied the head of the column. Charlie was riding with his black hat pulled low and the Confederate officer beside him. McGown looked back over his shoulder at Jacob. Jacob hated him and what he was leading him toward, hated him in a way he imagined every slave hates its master. So that's what this is, he thought.

"I don't know, Hay. I don't know what awaits me."

"Then I don't know neither, Jake." Haywood yanked his father's pants up over his breastbone with finality. One of his pistols slipped loose and he fumbled with it to get it back in place, clubbing himself in the cheek. "But I sure wish I did."

The heat was a blanket that muffled sounds and inhibited talk. The sun fell into a dry, empty land and spit back at them a hot breeze that dried Jacob's throat, that left him almost gagging. Twice they split out of the column to spread their trail to faintness before they regrouped again. The quarter moon was already in the sky, a faint silver that in the growing darkness would soon catch in the blades of the grass. The sunset was a brilliant red fading at its edges into silver and blue and was the most beautiful Jacob had ever seen. To be in that, he thought, with all that red around you. To ride into that. To breathe that into your lungs.

"Hay," he said.

"Yeah?" the boy answered.

"When this is over, me and you will ride west. Or maybe north. We'll do some lumberjacking."

"When what is over, Jake?"

He didn't know. When Lawrence was over? When the war was over? When McGown had rotted away to nothing? When McGown would grant him his freedom? Or could he run away now?

"When all of it is, Hay."

Haywood grinned. His tongue flicked across the gap in his teeth and he scratched at the back of his head. "Sure, Jake. Whatever that means."

They stopped to graze the horses and rest and watch the night come on. The insects danced in the last of the twilight, then settled quietly into the grass. Men and boys rigged up straps across their saddles and hobbled their stirrups in order to sleep on the ride. Jacob ate a Federal hardtack biscuit and watched McGown wait. The black stump of him gazed toward where Jacob guessed Lawrence waited.

Within the hour they mounted again and rode on. They passed a village whose name Jacob didn't know with the dusk thick around them, with the color of the world sucked away into the sunset's final brilliance. Archie and Haywood were dozing and Jacob watched Bill Anderson's lips moving silently, his blazing blue eyes staring. They headed northwest.

"You all right, Bill?"

Bill's voice was soft, his eyes wild. "I'm going to wash my hands in their blood. I'm going to bathe in the blood of their children."

"Jesus, Bill."

Spittle had worked white at the corners of Bill's mouth, had rimed his lips in a thick white paste that made them stick together. "There ain't no Jesus, Jake. There's this world and the one beyond it and Jesus ain't in any of it."

By midnight they had reached Gardner on the Santa Fe Road and were heading straight toward Lawrence. The plodding of hooves, the creak of leather, the swish of grass, the darkness—these were all the world. McGown flew ponderously on before them, dropping almost to the earth, rising into the night, the scraps of his flesh falling back to reveal bones glowing bright enough to cast shadows.

Jacob glanced at Haywood. He could not see him in the darkness, but in his imagination the boy's features came vividly alive, the mangled ears, the broken teeth, the ringworm scar, the blind and lazy eye. How could one boy contain so many faults? How could one boy hold them all in his body, could have suffered, could have seen, could have survived? Jacob thought of Cain, then he thought of Clara with her Bible spread before her and her lips pulled back from her long, glistening teeth tinged red at their cutting edges, reading sacred words in a voice hot with hate and love and anger. Cain had lifted that first stone and brought it down upon the head of his brother. For this he was blessed. Joshua had ridden the dusty plains of Jordan, had left orphans crying upon them, had then cut down the orphans. For this he was blessed. And now, Jacob thought. And now.

He listened to the horses and the muttering of drowsy or sleeping boys and men. He thought of all he had done and what he was doing and what he would do when the sun again rose. God is a God of love and beauty and brother for brother and war and death and murder and blood and blood-soaked screams, of hands clasping in friendship and rising in anger, of souls born into this world and of souls fleeing from it and soulless eyes closing forever. A contradiction that cannot be, but is. Love is war is death is life and it cannot be. He tried to penetrate the darkness and tried to penetrate beyond it; he listened to the men and the horses again; he looked again to McGown. Is this what we are? Is this the dust from which we were formed?

Ahead of him rode a large, bulking shadow that he took to be Larkin Skaggs. Is this what we are? he thought again. He kicked the piebald in the ribs and it protested with an exhausted snort. He kicked it again and it picked up its pace and soon he was riding beside the preacher.

"Reverend," he said.

Larkin Skaggs must have been sleeping, because he did not answer. Jacob tapped the reverend's arm with the back of his hand. The smell of him was heavy and acrid, old sweat, old tobacco, old, rotting smells Jacob could not name.

"Reverend," he said again.

Skaggs cursed and spat. "What, damn it?"

"Tell me about Cain and Abel."

"You woke me up for a god damned story?"

"Tell me about them, Reverend. Tell me about why."

"Why what?"

"Why God would give Cain the mark and let him live."

"Who the hell are you, anyway? I can't even see you."

"Jacob Wilson."

"I'm tired, Jake."

"Please, Reverend."

Skaggs cursed and spat again. His voice swelled with expostulation. "Because Adam brought death into the world and God needed Cain to bring blood into it. Without blood, Jesus can't die when he comes incarnated. If he can't die, then the world is damned because there ain't no blood sacrifice, there ain't no salvation. It all rests in Cain's hands. God needed Cain as much as he needed Jesus."

"Where did you learn this, Reverend?"

"I learned it," Skaggs said, "by using my eyes and mind. You look at a man and you see what he does and there's got to be a reason for it. If there ain't no reason, then God ain't in charge and the devil is, and if the devil is, then the world wouldn't be no more because he'd have us all in hell. So what is, is, because God is in charge and that makes it right. So we got to have killing because that is what man does. And it's got to have a beginning because it wasn't born with us back there with Adam and Eve. And if it's got to have a beginning it's got to have a way of coming into the world and it's got to have God behind it because God's got a plan and he is the beginning of all things. So there had to be a Cain and there had to be an Abel and God had to use Cain to bring killing into this world, to bring this world the chance of salvation. Cain was God's tool just like Jesus was."

"You think Cain had a soul?"

"A soul is eternal and must be a part of God, and if men have souls they are bound to souls, but men can die and that means their souls have to die. If their souls die, then God must, too, and can God die? If God can die, then he would have died when Cain killed Abel. But if he's dead, then the devil has the world, and if he has the world, then the world would have been destroyed a long time ago. So he ain't got the world. No, men don't have souls."

"Some have souls. I've seen them in their eyes."

"Then you have seen an angel. The Good Book says that some men have entertained them unawares."

"Can you kill angels?"

"They don't die."

Jacob looked ahead at McGown guiding the column. "Reverend, if men don't have souls, why do they need salvation?"

"They don't, but the earth does. The earth is birds singing and winds blowing and coyotes howling on hillcrests at night. That needs salvation because it needs protection from the devil. Men need salvation only in that they are part of the world."

"Do you think Jesus is coming again?"

"That's what the Good Book says, Jake," Skaggs said. "I don't know why he'd want to."

Jacob kept his eyes on McGown. He felt a sweep of relief pass through him, a sudden bursting of all bonds, a cleansing. It all made sense. He, like Cain, was lifting a rock, with which he would dash to bits the brains of his brother. He, like Joshua, was crossing the Jordan with reins and a sword in his hand.

He looked gratefully toward McGown. He felt clean and blessed. He lifted a hand to wipe at the wetness tracing his nose's distortion. He wanted to fly. He wanted to bathe in a holy, silver light. There is a reason for everything.

"Thank you, Reverend."

"I don't know why you wanted to bring this up now," Skaggs said.

Jacob dropped back to his place beside Haywood. He reached over and wrapped his arm around Haywood's shoulder. It felt like a dry stick in his grasp. He felt love.

"Hay," he said.

Haywood snuffled. The muscles in the boy's neck tensed against Jacob's wrist as he lifted his head. "What?"

"We are blessed."

"What?"

"We are blessed."

"Hell, Jake. Why is it I never know what you're talking about?"

Jacob laughed. The sound of it flashed like lightning across the sky, like the silver light McGown cast before him. The dead sergeant looked back over his shoulder. His lips were too rotted for him to smile. But Jacob knew. Jacob knew.

Chapter Twenty-three

In the hot, black night, Jacob rode in reverie. A lightness held his spirit with his purpose dancing before him. He was no longer tired. He loosened his pistols in his waistband and watched McGown with laughter on his lips and waited keenly for the morning. He felt as innocent as a child.

Charlie halted the column at the black lump of a farmhouse. George dismounted and banged on the door and a young man answered it, speaking words too distant for Jacob to understand. The man fetched a horse and led them into the darkness. They rode for a mile before a pistol cracked, and a minute later Jacob rode by the man's sprawled body beside the trail, his thin hair feathered out from his skull and his eyes holding the shock of his fate. Jacob smiled. The sky behind the column was growing lighter.

Charlie impressed another guide, then another. They left one blind man groping at his threshold, and Charlie shot two more farmers at the next homestead before they had a chance to mount. One man escaped into a cornfield, but within an hour and with the morning almost breaking behind them Charlie had killed five more. McGown perched on the roof of each house with his arms spread as if in beneficence. Jacob leaned back into the contemplative luxury that his new understanding afforded.

"Day's coming," Bill said as they went by the last house.

In a trot they passed through a hamlet while an old man watched, his mouth gaping. They forded a heavily wooded river and broke into a gallop heading north and west. They left the trees and came up a rise with the clean smell of the new morning, of the dew, surrounding them. Charlie raised his arm and the column halted. Below them lay a town with a population between one and two thousand, still sleeping. Empty battlements skirted its edges and a large hill on its west side rose quietly. The Kansas River on its north side threw mist into the air like a whisper. A cluster of shanties on its far bank was connected to the town by a ferry towline.

Shanties on the near bank and the east side of town were already dotted with a few black faces, some stopping and staring and one sagacious man already sprinting for the river. The morning sun was a brilliant slit on the horizon behind them, God's blessing on the coming day. Jacob wondered what Ai had looked like when Joshua had come thundering in. He felt a warm glow.

"What are we waiting for?" Archie asked.

Charlie, Bill Gregg, George Todd, and the Confederate officer were arguing at the front of the column. Charlie spoke quietly to two guerrillas and they broke in a trot toward the town. The argument continued until the riders came back. Charlie nodded at what they said, then rode down the line of riders.

He looked handsome in the early morning light, thin and well built and dusty, his hat settled firmly on his head, his shirt open, four pistols in the belt of his gray corduroys, cavalry boots in his stirrups. His eyes as alive as the coming morning. The sun caught the gold tassels on his hat.

"What are we waiting for?" Bill asked when he reached them.

"Patience, Bill."

"Damn it, I'm fed up with patience. I'm choking on patience."

"What are we going to do?" Haywood asked.

Charlie smiled. "Kill every man in town. Burn every building."

"Holy rolling thunder," Haywood said.

Charlie rode past them and in a few minutes galloped back to the head of the column. He said something Jacob couldn't hear, then dropped down the face of the hill. Suddenly the horses were galloping wildly and the men were shouting. Jacob waited for the cold nothingness to come, but he felt instead a calm, righteous completeness. He kicked at the ribs of the tired piebald and lifted his eyes to the silver sky. In a rush they dropped over the hill. McGown went before them, his arms spread wide, the tails of his Federal sergeant's coat snapping.

As they burst into town the Confederate officer and his recruits split off from the column and galloped toward the big hill to the west. The remaining riders split into three groups, each taking a different street in a mad rush toward the river. A wizened old man milking a cow to Jacob's left looked up, and Jacob pulled from his trousers his Mexican dragoon pistol. He aimed at the man, but someone else fired, and as the cow hopped away the man fell backward off of his stool. Jacob turned from the man and looked toward the river. Blacks were jumping into the water like rats.

"We got us here some fun!" Archie shouted. "Some fun!"

Charlie ahead of them was firing to his left, with Bill Gregg beside him firing to his right. They rode over a camp of boy soldiers, maybe cadets, and Jacob shot one of them with red hair and freckles while he was still wrapped in his blanket, a sudden hole in the blanket and the rest of it rippling out to its edges in waves like the grass they had spent the night riding through. Someone cried "Kansas City," and someone shouted "The girls." Jacob shouted "Osceola," and someone else took up that cry. He felt a euphoric joy, a reason for being.

The column thundered on with pistol shots and rebel yells and the pounding of hooves an undertone. They roared past a large park, then between two rows of stores lining the street. A three-story stone hotel stood on a corner near the river and Charlie raised his hand in front of it and halted the column. The other two groups swung around on side streets and joined them. The firing and shouting stopped and all eyes scanned the building; all pistol muzzles nervously swept its surface. Somewhere inside the hotel a gong sounded and some of the guerrillas pulled back in fear. Jacob raised the dragoon pistol and pointed it at one of the windows and waited. His breath was hot and strong and sweet on his lips. The piebald quivered joyously beneath him.

A man was trying to crawl over a fence on the far side of the hotel, and Archie leveled his pistol and fired, grinning. The man yelped and fell and caught his arm on the fence and hung there silently. Another man stuck his head out of a window, but withdrew it before Jacob could fire. A few seconds later, hands flung out of the same window the free end of a white bed sheet. The riders cheered.

"You come on out," Charlie called.

"Why have you come to Lawrence?"

"Plunder. You come on out."

"Promise you won't kill no one."

"I won't kill no one in the hotel," Charlie said, "if you'll come out."

The riders waited, pistols drawn, anxious and excited and bloodthirsty looks on their faces. In a few minutes men and women in underclothes began to file out of the building. They stood meekly looking up at the riders, gathered like animals for slaughter, faces gray, mouths quivering.

"Anybody here know where Jim Lane's house is?" Charlie asked.

A man with red wavy hair and a red scruff of beard took a step forward and raised his hand. "I do, Charlie."

Charlie shook his head. "Spicer, you were a kiss-ass when I lived here. You're a kiss-ass now."

"I can show you. Just don't kill me."

"Hell, I can kill you and still find out."

"But don't do it, all right? Remember those times at the north ferry landing? We had some good times, Charlie. Remember?"

Charlie studied him coldly. He looked over his shoulder and sought out Bill Anderson. "Bill, you and a couple of boys follow this piece of shit to Lane's house. If he leads you wrong, you do with him whatever you want. If he doesn't, leave him be."

Bill nodded. Tears traced his face and the foam at the corners of his mouth had grown. An alien smell drifted from him, perhaps the smell of madness. He nodded at Archie and Haywood and Jacob. They waited for Spicer to mount a horse that had been impassively watching, then followed him down the street.

"The rest of you boys," Charlie said. "You know what to do."

Spicer rode west away from the hotel toward the north slope of the hill, glancing nervously over his shoulder. He led them across a bridge spanning a tree-lined ravine with the river to the north beyond a narrow park with a flag-pole boasting a Union flag. The morning was slowly burning away the mist on the river. Behind them came the sound of horses scattering, of curses. Of banging on doors. Of orders given and women pleading and pistols barking. Of the sharp cries of men and the anguished screams of women. A man broke from a house to the south of them and Archie leveled his pistol and fired. The man's arms went up and his knees gave out and he sprawled in the dirt. His fingers clawed the dust until Archie shot him again.

"Mother of mercy," Spicer said. "Holy blessed virgin."

"Get a damn move on," Bill told him.

"Don't shoot me. Don't shoot me."

"I'll do what I damn well please with you," Bill said.

McGown was squatting in a tree along the ravine above where the man Archie had shot was lying. The dead sergeant watched Jacob, then lifted from the tree and flew ponderously toward a house beyond it. Jacob looked up at him reverently.

"Bill," Jacob said.

"Yeah."

"I got to leave you here."

"What about Lane?"

"You take care of Lane. I got to leave you here."

"What about me?" Haywood asked. His good eye was big and round and teary. "I'm gonna do what you said. What about me, Jake?"

Jacob looked from the boy to McGown. "You take care of yourself, Hay."

Jacob followed McGown. He felt within him a calm steadiness, a holy purpose. A joy beyond his experience. McGown propped on the eaves of a porch attached to a clapboard house with rosebushes in bloom in front of it. Jacob dismounted and climbed the steps to bang on the door. No one answered. He banged again and broke a window and finally a woman in a nightdress opened the door. Her hair was loose in auburn tangles around her head.

"Is the man of the house at home, ma'am?" Jacob asked.

She couldn't speak. When Jacob cocked his dragoon pistol and peered around her into the living room she shook her head.

"Where's he at?"

"Leavenworth."

"Business?"

She nodded.

"Do you mind if I have a look around?"

She glanced at a staircase leading up to a second floor. Jacob pushed by her and strode toward it. She screamed and grabbed at his ankles. He kicked her grip loose and climbed the stairs.

He kicked open a bedroom door. Three young girls huddled on a bed in the corner of a darkened room. Dark hair in bangs that fell to their eyebrows, big eyes that shone in the shadows. Though Joshua had spared none, Jacob decided the husband was more important. He went to the next door and kicked it open. Inside was an unmade bed and two pillows lying side by side. He went to the open window. Beside McGown on the porch roof was a naked man scrabbling over the shingles.

"Good morning," Jacob said.

The man looked up. The shingles had scraped his buttocks raw and left them scored with red, seeping lines. "Good morning."

"Nice day."

"A bit warm."

"You going somewhere?"

"Leavenworth."

"That's what your wife told me."

Jacob leveled the dragoon pistol through the window and fired. The man's head jerked back with his neck bones cracking and he pitched off the roof. Jacob listened to him thud in the rosebushes. The woman screamed again. McGown with a bony finger wiped blood from his boot toe, then lifted the finger to stain his teeth and the bone shining around them.

Jacob left the room and walked back down the hall. He stuck his head into the girls' room. They were huddled as they had been before.

"You got any brothers?" Jacob asked.

"Yes," the youngest girl said. "One."

"Where's he at?"

"Under the bed." Her sisters shot her glances.

Jacob walked into the room and lifted the bedcovers. Beneath the bed was a boy who looked about Haywood's age but was larger, huddled in his underdrawers with his thin arms crossed over his naked chest.

"How old are you?" Jacob asked.

"Fifteen," the boy said.

"Guess how old I am."

"I don't know."

"I'm as old as time," Jacob said. "I'm as old as the Bible." He stuck his pistol beneath the bed and fired. The muzzle flash lit up the shadows and the boy bounced off the wall. Jacob stood. The girls huddled as before, except that their eyes were wider. Jacob tipped his hat to them and left the room. He went down the stairs and outside.

Down the street from the direction Jacob had come smoke was rising, and flames licked at windows. Guerrillas were moving from house to house and shooting men and robbing their widows, throwing torches through windows that shattered with sharp crackings, with flames licking up draperies, the low rumble of the new fires mixing with the morning call of a rooster from somewhere in the shantytown east and downriver. Fifteen guerrillas were tearing down the flagpole in the park; ten more were cutting the ferry line crossing the river. The rising sun hot and the air acrid and absolutely still. High above him, a hawk circled. A bright, new day.

The wife of the man he had shot was wailing into the rosebushes. She'd clutched her husband around his chest and was trying to drag him free. His blood soaked her nightdress. Bits of his brains littered it.

"Ma'am?" Jacob asked. She did not answer. "Ma'am?" he asked again.

She looked up at him. Her face was twisted in ways he'd never seen, except on Bill. "Ma'am, I'm looking for this chinless fella who was at Osceola. Do you know who I mean?"

Her voice, when it came, was a blood-filled thunder of rage and shock and hatred. "You'll burn in hell," she said.

"Do you know who I mean?" Jacob asked again.

"You'll burn in hell."

"It ain't possible, ma'am. It just ain't."

She went about her work as Jacob studied the street. A man sprinting down it was shot by five guerrillas at once. The bullets lifted him into the air where he jerked spastically before falling limp into the dirt. Another guerrilla galloped his horse over the body. A low, steady roar of flame now, like the muttering of an audience. The day was hot and bright and clear. The river mist was almost gone, and guerrillas were shooting at men's heads as they bobbed in the water. Occasional shots from the shanties beyond the river echoed across the water, and the guerrillas either fled or dropped into the grass to return them. McGown lifted from the roof and flapped heavily to the next house. He lighted there like a dove and turned to Jacob. Jacob felt a deep satisfaction.

"Ma'am," he told the woman before he left, "they'll come and burn this place any minute. You best get him out of there. Your son and your daughters, too."

"Did you kill them, too?" the woman asked.

"Just one of them," Jacob said.

She screamed again. Jacob smiled at the sun. He crossed to the house where McGown squatted and knocked upon the door.

A man wearing a pair of trousers answered the door. He'd pulled one suspender up over his undershirt; the other looped down to his knee. His thin hair was dirty and gray. He kept his eyes on the floor. He seemed to be melting toward it.

"I'll come out," the man said. "You just leave my family be."

"You saying you're ready to die?"

"I can meet my maker. I have no qualms."

"Let me see your eyes." The man looked up. Jacob shook his head. "I hate to kill a man who has such misguided notions." He looked down the street again. "Why did you come to the door like this? Why don't you come with a gun?"

"I don't have mine here."

"Why not?"

"The mayor's got them all locked up in the blockhouse. He don't like violence."

"When did he do that?"

"A couple of days ago."

"Your mayor's a fool."

The man's eyes fell again. Suddenly very old. How do men change when they know they are going to die? Jacob wondered what this man had looked like a half hour before.

"Will you leave my family be?" the man asked.

"I'll leave them be. You come on out of there."

The man nodded and stepped meekly out. He looked through Mc-Gown to the sky beyond.

"Quite a day," Jacob said.

"Where do you want me?" the man asked.

Jacob pointed with his pistol toward the river. When they reached the bridge spanning the ravine, he pointed north toward a cornfield wrapped in smoke from a house burning. Guerrillas were running across the street and cursing and horses were galloping with wild eyes and foam flecked on their withers and men were dying and their bodies littered the blood soaked ground. A dead man was lying beneath the window of a house spitting flames, and his hair was smoking, his temple blistered. The man Jacob was guiding walked with his head down.

"So you're a family man," Jacob said.

"Two little girls and a four-year-old boy."

"You look too old to have kids that young."

"I got a late start. I was a teamster to Denver for years."

"You ever kill an Indian?"

"Never."

"Where's your wife?"

"She got the consumption and died just after the boy came."

"What's his name?"

"Jacob."

Jacob stopped the man. "What's your last name?"

"Myers."

"That would have been just too much of a coincidence."

Jacob nodded toward the cornfield. Bill Anderson rode a man out of a house in front of them with his hand on the back of his collar. Bill was crying streams and bellowing the names of his sisters and foam dripped from his chin onto the man's shoulder. He drove the man's face into the dirt in front of his door and with his pistol flush against the back of his head shot him. Bill lifted his glistening red face to the sky and shook the gore from his eyes. He howled and ran back into the house.

"Who was that?" the man Jacob was guiding asked.

"A friend of mine."

"The man he just killed was a friend of mine."

"Well," Jacob said, "that's the way of it. Do you know a chinless Federal sergeant who was at Osceola?"

"That sounds like Ehles. He got rich at Osceola."

"You get rich at Osceola?"

"I won't have nothing to do with it."

"Ehles. Do you know where he lives?"

The man glanced back over his shoulder. "It looks like somebody already got him. His house is burning."

"He ain't rich no more," Jacob said.

They were almost to the cornfield now. A woman was trying to drag a smoldering carpet out of the burning house beside it. She had soot on her face. Tears and sweat ran through it.

The man turned to Jacob. His face was as gray as his hair and his lips were trembling. "Please, don't kill me. I got two little girls and my little boy and if you kill me they won't have a thing in this world. They'll end up at some orphanage in Kansas City or somewhere. Please."

"I know someone who just died in Kansas City. They dropped a building on her." Jacob pursed his lips and studied the town. Great billows of smoke were rising; the air carried the stink of burning hair and flesh. He turned back to the man. "You can run," he said.

"Where?"

"Into that cornfield. You can hide in the stalks."

"Can I?"

"Go ahead."

Color came to the man's face and life to his eyes, or the semblance of it. Now Jacob could guess what he had looked like. "I thank you. My children thank you."

"You go on."

The man ran for the field. Jacob leveled the dragoon pistol at his back and fired. The shot threw the man forward, but Jacob had turned to study the town before the corpse landed. He heard cornstalks break.

He ambled back toward the bridge. Archie was forcing a man out of a house at the foot of the hill. He shot the man in the knee, and as the man screamed and lurched, Archie shot him in the other knee. The man fell, scrabbling with his hands, his mouth wide, his eyes wide. Archie pinned one hand beneath his boot and shot the palm. The man screamed again and Archie looked up. He grinned at Jacob and waved his pistol.

"You find a ax yet?" he called.

Jacob didn't answer him. He crossed the bridge, heading toward the hotel. It was burning now, or at least what was flammable in it was burning. Gray stone scorched black. The dead and dying littered the street so that to walk around them he had to weave like a drunken man. Bill Anderson ran out of the house he had earlier run into and sprinted across the street with both arms pinwheeling pistols and foam running back along his cheek to whiten his hair. He was screaming wildly and unseeing and full of the glory of God. He ran into a house. Pistol shots came out of it and women screamed. Jacob stopped in front of the house that had belonged to Ehles and studied it longingly. He remembered Osceola.

The guerrillas who had been shooting into the river had left. Bodies bobbed. McGown was flying bloated above them and the park they were washing up upon, his great, rotting arms flapping, bits of his tattered clothing and whatever they were matted with floating down. A garden patch of sweet corn grew in the park with its ears just beginning to ripen. From within the corn rose the keening cry of a newborn. Jacob traced a line with his eyes from Ehles's house to the sweet corn. He smiled and strode toward it.

He worked his way through the stalks, the knife edges of their leaves cutting finely, the sweet smell of the corn silk and the dust. In the middle of the patch in civilian clothes lay the sergeant from Osceola with the newborn in his arms. Jacob parted the corn, stomped on their stalks to break them down. He stood above the sergeant with his knuckles on his hips and his pistols in his hands. For the first time in the day he felt a wildness coming. Smoke rising, hooves thundering, Mr. Buchanan lying in the street with blood on his face and cradling a broken hand, a whimper whistling in his throat.

Do you hate me? I'll make you hate me.

Jacob felt the strength again coming that he had felt lying on that street in Osceola with his hands digging into the urine-soaked earth, the strength of all the world. The sergeant blinked up at him, still ugly, still chinless, still unshaven, his lips working silently.

"Well well," Jacob said.

"Please," the sergeant said.

"You remember me?"

"I don't remember you."

"You pissed on me."

"I don't remember."

Jacob leveled the dragoon pistol at the sergeant's forehead. The sergeant stared up at him blinking with his teeth chattering as if he were cold. "They tell me your name is Ehles."

"It is. So is the name of this little girl."

Jacob studied the fussing baby, then spat to the side. "I was at Osceola."

The sergeant shifted his head so Jacob's shadow fell across his eyes. His teeth quit chattering. "I remember you."

"You told me I'd never forget." Jacob pulled the trigger. The sergeant's head jerked and split and he quivered not even a moment. The baby cried. Jacob left it with its father.

He strode through the streets for hours, following wherever McGown would lead him. He entered an unmolested house, killed the man who owned it, and set the living room afire, taking nothing because he wanted and needed nothing. On the slope of the hill he shot a boy in the back of the head who was wearing a cut-off Federal uniform, a hand-me-down, probably from his father. Most of the buildings that would burn were burning and as he walked over the bridge on his way back for the piebald he saw that the man who had been lying beneath the flaming window with his temple blistered now had only his blackened skull showing. A fat man who looked like a banker was hiding beneath the bridge, and Jacob shot him in the calf as he tried to crawl away. He yelped like a child and Jacob shot him in the back of his glistening bald head when he quit crawling. A couple of the men lying in the street were still alive and he put a bullet in each of their foreheads. He studied the brilliant blue sky and thanked God for all he had created.

In front of the house with the rosebushes, a short man with cropped, dark hair was trying to mount the piebald. The piebald was flailing her hooves and baring her teeth and the man flopped against her saddle like a side of meat. Jacob shot him. All the houses on the street were burning, and the woman and children gone. The naked husband was lying in the yard. He looked old and soft and vulnerable, ridiculous with his nudity, grotesque with his wounds. The piebald nickered and nuzzled Jacob's shoulder.

He led her by the reins toward the large park on the south side of town and crossed it to the avenue on which he had ridden into town. Black boys too young for even the hint of beards were lying dead on the grass, most trampled to a gummy mush, with a fallen Federal standard trampled among them. All was smoke, choking smoke, strange smells swirling together, even though the day was still. He sat beneath a shady maple on the avenue with the piebald grazing peacefully. McGown lifted and disappeared into the haze. Jacob thanked the dead sergeant. He was tired, and his stomach rumbled. He wiped a speck of blood from the corner of his eye.

Someone had broken into a saloon and the raiders who passed by him were reeling. George Todd had gore clotting on his cheek and was wearing a splendid Federal captain's uniform. He offered Jacob a bottle that Jacob refused. Larkin Skaggs rode by, drunken and tottering in his saddle with blood in swaths on his face and belly and a Union flag trailing on a rope behind him. Henry Nolan was cursing and shooting over and over again into the head of a white man lying beside a milliner's. A gun shop was burning, and a group of guerrillas with Archie and Frank James among them were laughing as they tossed the tied and still living proprietors through the door into the flames. Screams rose with the smoke, with the heat, with the souls if they existed rising, God receiving or rejecting his own. Women screamed maniacally; women stood maniacally dumb. Children wailing and wringing their hands like their mothers. Jacob wished he could find some breakfast.

He sat for two more hours. The guerrillas too drunk or too sated to continue the rapine began gathering around him. Bill sat against a tree on the far side of the park with his elbows propped on his knees and the cylinders of two of his pistols pressed against his temples, blood and foam on his face, in his hair, in his beard, foam and tears and blood dripping from his lips, screaming. Jacob rose and gathered the piebald's reins and walked toward him.

"Bill," he said. Bill kept screaming, just screaming, the muzzles of his pistols pointing into the air and trembling, his face unbelievably wild. Jacob squatted beside him. "Bill."

Bill looked at him still screaming and wiped gore from his forehead with a knuckle and sat again with his pistols against his head. Still screaming. Jacob sat with his back against the same tree and waited. He watched Dave Poole tie a bolt of cloth across the back of a stolen packhorse.

Bill's screaming eased into a rhythmic wail punctuated by gasping, then settled to a grinding gibber. Finally his madness subsided into a hoarse pant. "Bill," Jacob said again.

"Seventeen of the goat fuckers," Bill said. His panting increased and for a second his gibbering came back and then he laughed hysterically. "Seventeen of the goat fuckers. How many you get?"

"You all right, Bill?"

"Vengeance is mine. That is what I truly believe."

"Are you all right?"

"It don't make no difference. How many you get?"

Jacob looked down the avenue at the smoke rising, the litter, the bodies. One man was crawling toward the edge of the street as Mr. Buchanan had done. He'd have been better off to play dead. "I didn't keep count."

"I saw you get one. I know you got at least one." His face was contorted, the foam on his lips dripping, his eyes rolling, his lips working in a discourse separate from his words. "Did you get seventeen?"

"I don't know."

"I got seventeen." He shoved his pistols into his belt and groped wildly in his pocket. He drew out the silk cord and began tying knots, his fingers stumbling over each other.

"Bill," Jacob said.

"Don't make me lose count."

Jacob waited. The piebald grazed beside him, and when he passed his hand over her muzzle she lifted and shook her head. Bill was whispering loudly the number of each knot he tied. Jacob waited.

"I got thirty-eight now," Bill said as he shoved the cord back into his pocket. "If I ain't careful, I'll need another cord." He drew the tithe pouch he had taken at Independence out of his shirt and stuffed a wad of gore-clotted bills into it. He studied it with mad satisfaction and drew the draw-string tight. His fingers jumped wildly.

"You seen Archie?" Jacob asked.

"He was with me for a while, then he wandered off. He got at least five, I know."

"I saw him burn up a couple of guys down the street."

"Then he got at least seven. I got seventeen."

"You seen Haywood?"

"I ain't seen him since we burned Lane's house."

"You kill Lane?"

"The bastard wasn't home. You kill that sergeant?"

"I did."

Bill clapped him warmly on the shoulder. "Good for you, Jake. Good for you."

They watched the men and boys gather around them. It had been a long ride, and some were dozing. "Looks like a god damned picnic," Bill said.

"You all right?"

"Of course I'm all right. Why wouldn't I be all right?"

"I'm going to find Haywood."

"He was heading up that hill, last I saw him."

"Will you look after my horse?"

"Course I will," Bill said.

Jacob nodded and rose. He crossed the rest of the park and walked again by the dead black boys. He went around to the north side of the hill. Women were sitting placidly on piles of belongings in their back yards, watching their houses burn. Dead men lying. He didn't find Haywood. He started up the hill, passing a couple of burning houses. Through the smoke he saw a barn he worked toward. He passed bodies, one of them the boy in the Federal uniform.

Through the haze Jacob could see someone sitting in front of the barn. As he neared and the smoke thinned he saw it was Haywood. The boy was not wearing his forage cap. His saber and pistols were gone.

"Hey, Jake," he said.

"Hey, Hay." Jacob sat beside him. "Where's your pistols? Where's your hat?"

"I give them to a couple of fellas playing picket up the hill."

"You find some new ones? I didn't think you'd ever give up that sword."

"I didn't find no new ones." Haywood kicked at the dirt with a bare heel. "I cain't do it no more."

"What's that mean?"

"Looky down there. I cain't do it no more."

"You can't just be done with it, Hay."

"Why?"

"We got to do what we do."

Haywood studied him with his good eye. His bad one rolled to the sky. "Let's head out west, Jake. We can just walk over this hill and keep walking. Let's find us some gold in California or somewheres. Them picket fellas won't tell nobody because I gave them my stuff and they won't."

"I can't do that, Hay."

"Then let's head up to Ioway and be farmers. Or Nebraska. Let's head up to Minnesoter and cut down trees or something. I don't care nothing about the cold. I don't."

"I can't, Hay."

"Why not?"

Why not. How could that be explained? They were high enough for McGown to be circling the park beneath them. More riders were gathering. Pistols were still being fired.

"We can just walk right over this hill. No one will ever know."

"I can't."

Haywood's lips trembled. He sucked in the snot hanging from his nose and swallowed. He studied the town below them. "Well, let's head back down there, then."

"I can't leave, Hay. That don't mean you can't."

"I ain't got but one friend, Jake. Booger is dead and he wasn't no friend, anyway. If you go down there, I got to go down there. There ain't nothing else."

"You got to understand, Hay. This is bigger than us."

"If we're gonna go down there, let's do it, all right?"

"You ought to get your stuff back."

"I cain't do it no more, Jake," Haywood said again.

They rose and looked down on the ruins of the town. On the loot being tied to stolen horses, on the men reeling in weary drunkenness and derangement. On the bodies lying with heads cocked back over shoulders or elbows jutting, on the bodies roasting in the fires of burning homes. On the incredible, living, rolling, lush sea of green beyond it all. On the silent blue river flecked with silver as the sun caught a wave, a ripple. On the ways of God and men, on the sanity and insanity and truth and lies and right-eousness and the lack of it. On love and hate, on all things necessary. I have come to understand, Jacob thought, like the fiery prophets of old. He felt his knowledge a warm glow within him.

"Well, let's go," Haywood said.

They had just started down the hill when behind them came the pounding of hard soles on grass. A boy was running toward them with a musket, and Jacob raised his dragoon pistol. Haywood stopped him. The boy was wearing Haywood's forage cap.

"Hey, Jared!"

"Hey, Hay." The boy's voice broke.

"You're sure doing you some running."

"Soldiers coming from the west." He was by them, still running. "You seen Colonel Holt?"

"He's down there somewhere."

"It scares me to go down there at all," the boy called, but he kept run-ning.

Jacob and Haywood hurried to the hillcrest. To the west a line of white dust rising. Through gaps in the smoke to the north Jacob could see a sec-ond column.

"Damn," he said.

"So we couldn't have walked away no way."

They reached the park at the same time Charlie did. He was talking to a man and a young woman who stood by numbly watching the riders, no blood on him except in the prideful look in his heavy-lidded eyes. The boy had spread the word and most of the looting and killing had stopped. Jacob took the reins of the piebald from Bill while Haywood chased down his Morgan on the park's southwest corner. Bill Gregg began loading drunken men into a wagon. He found a driver for it from among the townspeople, a man loose in the belly and slack-jowled and probably glad just to be alive. Charlie mounted his brown gelding and formed the raiders into column.

"The ladies of Lawrence were brave," he called back over his shoulder, "but the men were a pack of cowards."

The day's heat was frightening, had a smell in it of fear. Almost every man led a packhorse loaded with cloth bolts and shoes and household goods and money. Toy Union flags were woven into horsetails, quilts and piano covers served as saddle blankets. Bill left with nothing beyond the money in his pouch and Jacob left with nothing at all and Haywood left with less than he had come with. Archie led a mule loaded with cloth and children's toys. On a string around his neck he was wearing someone's ear.

"What the hell you doing with that?" Jacob asked.

Archie grinned. "He didn't need it no more. I thought Haywood might want it."

"I don't want nothing," Haywood said.

They rode in a trot south out of town on the road leading to Fort Scott down on the Arkansas border, Bill Gregg staying behind to gather stragglers. A huge black mass of smoke rose behind them with a low mutter. Now that the killing was done, McGown was gone. Where does he go? Jacob wondered. Where does he hide himself when what must be done is done? Is that paradise?

They left by a different way than they had come. They crossed at a bridge the river they had forded before dawn. Riders reeling drunken and exhausted in their saddles, horses just as exhausted, their heads down, tongues out, legs trembling. Packhorses loaded with coats and boots, with picture frames and mantel clocks, with toys and shoes and old women's shawls. Pockets stuffed with jewelry and money, the bills falling out and settling to the hot, dry grass like snow. Bill Gregg came riding up on an old, flea-bitten gray mare with about twenty stragglers. He had no plunder. They left the bridge and rode south. A fear rippled among them, backward glances at the snakes of dust to the north and west.

"I wish you hadn't given away your firearms, Hay," Jacob said. "They're going to kill you."

"They cain't shoot me no way. But sometimes I wish they could."

The heat was a hammer beating down, a taskmaster driving. A palpable thing riders shook their heads at in wonder. The horses were too tired to do anything but walk and stumble. Riders cut loose packhorses, lightened loads. A cracked mirror thrown to the side of the road caught the sun's brilliance. A dying horse beside it.

"What do you say, Jake?" Archie asked.

"About what?"

"About making it back."

Jacob looked up at the sky, around at the fields, empty blue, empty green. "That ain't in my hands."

"You believe in God?"

"Of course I do," Jacob said.

By noon they had reached a little town on the intersection of the Fort Scott and Santa Fe roads. Word of them must have carried in the smoky smell in the air, in the column of smoke to the north rising. The town was deserted.

"Burn it all down," Charlie ordered.

Some raiders dismounted and set to work, but most were too drunk or tired or sated or frightened to leave their horses. The line of dust behind them had grown and men were watching it and wiping their mouths and looking ahead of them anxiously. They rode on as quickly as the horses would allow, a walk as steady as the passing of the sun, as the heat's slow growing. The Fort Scott road detoured around a farm, and Charlie took a shortcut on a lane through a cornfield. In the middle of the field the lane bottlenecked with the rear of the column crowding into Jacob and Bill and Archie and Haywood. The line of dust behind them had turned to cavalry blue strewn with Indians brandishing knives reflecting the sun. Farmers waving ancient muskets or pepperbox pistols astride broodmares with colts reaching for their dugs. No cursing or shouts. Only a steady, hate-filled silence. A thirst in that dry land for revenge.

"We're in for it now," Haywood said.

"Lighten your loads," Charlie called. "We got to run for it."

The rest of the mules were cut loose; almost all of the plunder dropped. The raiders jostled and swore; the wagon with the drunken creaked as it dropped into and pulled out of ruts. The cornstalks captured the heat, and within it riders swayed and horses stumbled. Jacob held the piebald on her feet with the pressure of his knees and the force of his desire. Suddenly George rode back along the line, gathering riders as he went. The gore had scabbed on his cheek.

"Bill, Jake, Archie? You follow me."

"Can I come?" Haywood asked.

"You ain't got no guns."

"I still want to come."

"You go on, Hay," Jacob said. "We'll catch up with you later."

He wheeled the piebald and followed George. By the time they reached the end of the column they had gathered twenty riders. A horse lay gasping at the edge of the stalks and George shot it in the head. He studied the lane while wiping his mouth.

"Just give them hell when they come," was all he could say.

Jacob and Bill and Archie took their places in the line forming across the lane. From the north side of the field came the rustling of stalks and the whinny of horses. Jacob drew the dragoon pistol in his right hand and a Navy Colt in his left. Just as he lifted them a column of cavalry and Indians came through the corn and he fired. Twenty men fired. Men dropped, horses dropped, horses screamed, the horses behind them stumbling over their bodies and the bodies of their riders. Farmers stood at the edge of the field and fired harmlessly. Jim Lane rode up upon the bare, swayed back of an old farm mule wearing a bed shirt and trousers far too small for him, his parchment skull shiny with sweat, cursing wonderfully. He was too distant for any shot but what Haywood might make. Jacob turned to look for him. Bill's mouth worked around animal sounds as tears streamed from his eyes.

Behind them, the bottleneck had cleared. George broke in a stumbling, sickening gallop for it and Jacob followed. The cavalry and Indians crept on their bellies through the stalks, knives and muskets in their hands, shots and war whoops resounding. Suddenly George's horse tumbled with blood squirting from its nose and George was up and running, leaving the horse behind, stripping off the heavy captain's uniform he had been wearing. He jumped on the back of a horse abandoned in the narrowed lane. Jacob steadied it for him as he kicked off the baby carriage strapped across its back.

They cleared the field. Beyond it lay the road again and a creek the rest of the raiders were wading. The cavalry was breaking from both the lane and the field toward the raiders' rear, the tassels jerking and trembling with their passing, the heads of men still mounted above the corn like ships on a sea. Jacob aimed at a head and fired; it cursed and ducked into the stalks.

Jim Lane rode up on his pathetic mule, his eyes frantic, his dark hair wild, and swung his long leg over its back, dismounting and ripping at the crotch of the trousers he was wearing that must have belonged to his son. He cursed the cavalry for its slowness and the raiders for their evil.

A heavyset cavalry officer with a thick walrus mustache dismounted beside Lane. He ordered his men to dismount in a booming southern voice and they took line at the edge of the field. The raiders watched them; Jacob watched them. The cavalry leveled their guns, and when they fired their shots went high and the horses behind them reared and bolted in fright. Some of the men broke to chase them down.

"Let's give them hell, boys," George said.

The raiders kicked their horses toward the line, screaming and shooting. Their pursuers stampeded back into the field, trampling the corn, trampling each other into the dust, into the blood in the dust from the wounded. Jim Lane was too busy cursing and did not look up until Jacob was almost upon him.

"You remember Osceola?" Jacob asked.

"God will send you to hell, you spawn of the devil!" Lane sneered until he saw he was alone. Fear ripped open his arrogance and dissipated his righteous anger. He broke in a clumsy run into the corn, his hands gripping the waist of his pants and the tail of his oversized nightshirt flying.

"He looks like Haywood!" Archie called.

The raiders laughed. Shots followed Lane, but none hit him and he disappeared into the corn. George pulled up the chase and they worked their way south across the creek with the horses fighting their riders for the time it would take to drink. They had gone about two miles before Jacob could look back and see their pursuers re-forming.

The chase continued all afternoon, murderous heat, plunder abandoned, dying horses gasping and falling, their muscles twitching, horses shot where they fell and exchanged for mounts just as exhausted. The cavalry must have ridden all the way from Leavenworth or Kansas City, because their horses were so jaded that even the mules and broodmares of the farmers outdistanced them. Twice the farmers came upon the raiders and twice George again formed the rear guard. Twice the civilians scattered, though now they left dead raiders behind. Four riders with their brains stewed straggled unknowingly into the pursuing column, and they were instantly killed with rifle reports ending their pleading, with the hoot of Delaware Indians lifting dripping scalps to the sun. They cut across fields and tall grass prairie, heading southwest. The piebald stumbled and Jacob dismounted and led it by the reins until he grew dizzy with the heat. He had to mount and kick the poor horse into a trot that almost killed it. A macabre, creeping chase burned free of its reality by the sun.

The heat didn't break until twilight. Jacob didn't know where he was; he didn't know if anyone did. The cavalry officer with the southern voice was shooting a straggler in the head, not a ten-minute walk behind him. Jacob searched the sky for McGown and guidance.

As darkness grew they climbed a hill and looked down on a village perhaps a mile away. A tree-lined river clung to it. The piebald worked her nostrils and whinnied frantically at the smell of the water. A ford crossed the river, but a line of a hundred men in blue had arrayed on its far side. Jacob was thirsty enough to feel the water pull at his throat, his eyes.

Behind them, the civilian column was working up the hill with the cavalry far to the rear. Charlie looked back and whistled at George, and George nodded. The raiders worked down the slope heading northeast, and as soon as the dark crest of the hill intercepted their sight of the farmers, George pulled up the rear guard.

"We're going to charge," he said.

"I'm too damned tired to charge," Archie answered.

"You're going to do it," George said.

Jacob desperately searched the sky going black and impenetrable. He sensed very near a blackness darker than the night, and when McGown dropped out of it onto the crest of the hill and looked back at him with the flesh on his skull rotted to a few patches, huge, unearthly flies feeding, Jacob was happy. He drew his dragoon pistol with one hand and a Navy Colt with the other.

"Let's do it," he said. "Damn it, let's do it."

George grinned and nodded. They formed a line. Someone at the end of it was gibbering like the crickets, and Jacob turned to see Bill's face a mad mask, the moonlight catching in the tears on his cheeks, the foam on his lips. Such a summation. The raiders beat their horses into the fastest walk they were capable of maintaining. Archie yelled and raider after raider picked it up, a keening, unearthly sound in the darkness. McGown lifted from the crest just as they reached it and dropped like a stone down the other side. Halfway up the slope the farmers and their horses stood, black and featureless, hardly human. Jacob fired the dragoon pistol and felt it leap wildly in his tired hand. He watched a young farmer with a thick, black beard get plucked from his horse as if fingers had reached down out of the sky. He didn't get a chance to fire again. The night sang with revolver reports and the flash from their muzzles. The farmers turned and fled.

"Hold up," George called over the noise. "Let's get on back."

They walked the horses back up the hill. The night was too thick to see by. They followed the trail of the others by the black lumps of dead horses, by the moonlit glint of abandoned plunder, like bog frogs hopping hillock to hillock. They did not catch up to the main body until almost eleven—it had crossed the river at a ford several miles up. It took Jacob two minutes to quench his parched throat and another ten to drag the piebald from the water. Charlie had called for a halt there, not so much a halt as a surrender to exhaustion. Most of the raiders and horses were sleeping. Jacob sought out Haywood and collapsed beside him. He had not slept in over twenty-four hours.

"What did you do?" Haywood asked.

"Why ain't you sleeping?"

"What did you do? I heard shooting."

"Then you can probably guess what we did. Leave that thing in your pants tonight, Hay. I don't need you disturbing me."

"I'm too tired to do that if I wanted to."

Jacob lay back with his head on his saddle. He looked up at the stars. He could taste the smoke on his lips, could smell the flesh burning, could hear the screams as Joshua must have done. God's ways are hard but they are his ways and so they must be ours. He felt sanctified. He could feel blood sticking to his hands.

"You seen the reverend?"

"Not all day," Haywood said.

"I wonder what become of him."

He had just closed his eyes and was drifting into that world at the back of his mind, the farm in the valley, Clara and Cyrus and Tobias and Isaac. Sarah. The glisten of black skin in lantern light. He could feel her within him as if he were pregnant with the need for her. His sorrow and longing a great, gaping wound. When someone kicked his boot, he was almost grateful.

Henry Nolan was walking by, cursing and banging two frying pans together. Jacob groaned and rolled onto his side. He tried to shake the dream from his head. Haywood lay with moonlight reflecting oddly in the lazy rolling of his eye.

"Get up, Hay."

"I'm too tired. My balls are swollen up to the size of punkins."

"Get up."

"I ain't going to."

"They'll kill you."

"Let them try."

"They'll at least lock you up. You'll never get to California or Iowa or Minnesota then."

"I don't care."

"We'll never get to California or Iowa or Minnesota then."

Haywood fell quiet. Around them raiders were groaning and cursing and fumbling with saddles. "We should a gone when we had the chance, Jake."

"We'll go when this is over."

"This cain't never be over."

Jacob rose. For a second his head swam and he tottered and could hear all around him the roar of rushing water. He thought of the Ohio in the spring and wondered if it was possible to ever leave anything behind.

Chapter Twenty-four

The next two weeks were constant running, constant hiding, constant killing, constant dying—Federal soldiers dying, guerrillas dying, men and boys hunted like dogs and with dogs, no quarter given or taken, no mercy, revenge sought and found, the revenge revenged, blood sport that sang in the blood, a game to be played. A pair of guerrillas bayoneted in their bedrolls, Federal patrols ambushed and murdered in minutes, innocent farmers stuck like pigs for stopping in the road to pass the time. Boys hanging by their necks in trees with signs labeled "Lawrence" pinned to their chests, with signs on the trunks beneath their feet warning passersby not to cut them down. The war took its ugliest turn, scalped men, ears and noses and eyes and fingers as trophies, like for like with each like a little closer to the truth of what we all are capable of. Bill added knots to his cord, and kept each scalp of every boy or man he killed hanging from his bridle, stinking of rot until they shriveled in the sun. The mare shied from them until she got used to the wet slap against her neck and withers. The necklace of ears around Archie's neck grew.

Jacob killed only one boy in those two weeks. The boy had come down a cow path riding a mule, so young that his short legs were splayed across its back. Jacob had shot him in the chest before thinking.

"He don't look like no Yankee," Haywood had said.

"He probably ain't. He caught me by surprise."

"Ain't no southerners allowed in this county no more." Archie had kicked the dead boy's cheek. The boy's neck cracked and jerked to the side.

"There ain't no Yankees allowed neither," Haywood had said.

"Damn it, Haywood. You always got to cloud up everything."

The weather was turning cool and the leaves changing. At the end of September, Charlie called the guerrillas to the Pardee farm. By the time Bill, Jacob, Archie, and Haywood rode in, more than four hundred guerrillas had gathered. Dave Poole, Frank James, Henry Nolan, George Todd, and Bill Gregg were there. Larkin Skaggs was not. Jacob had not seen him since Lawrence.

That night he approached Bill Gregg at the fire. Gregg looked at him from his sad eyes. "Hey, Jake."

"You were supposed to gather up the stragglers at Lawrence, weren't you?"

Gregg looked back at the fire. "What do you mean, supposed to? I did."

"Did you get Larkin?"

"I left Larkin."

"Why?"

"Because he's a bloodthirsty son of a bitch. The man had no honor." His eyes didn't leave Jacob's face, and a smile traced across his lips. "Don't you read the papers, Jake?"

"Nothing in them interests me."

"You should read the papers. You know what happened to Larkin? Some Lawrence kid shot him in the shoulder, then some Indian put an arrow in his chest and took his scalp. They dragged him around in the streets until all his clothes were ripped off and most of his skin. They tore him into pieces. Women and everything. Fingernails ripping chunks of him away. I think he finally died then."

"You shouldn't a left him, Bill."

"Then they threw him in a ditch and burned him. He's probably still lying there now."

"You shouldn't a left him. It's hell of a thing for a preacher like that not even getting buried."

"He wasn't no preacher. You can't do what he done and be a preacher."

"You did the same."

"Yeah, well." Gregg stared into the embers. "I ain't a preacher, am I?"

Jacob spent the night with Haywood fitfully tossing in his sleep beside him. Jacob wondered what Larkin Skaggs was doing now, if he was just lying in that ditch or if his soul was in heaven and his body like that of Mc-Gown's, guiding the soulless to do God's bidding. He wished he had paid more attention to the reverend's eyes.

Finally he slept and dreamed of the farm and he was flying above it again and his mother and father were in the field below him. Isaac stood in the river with the water up to his waist, staring across it at Tobias hanging comfortably in the dying cottonwood, smiling up into the sky. Sarah in the yard dancing, one hand raised above her head, dancing and laughing, and he plummeted toward her and she lifted her arms to receive him. He awoke before he reached her. He was cold. The wet sheen of his tears lay like ice upon his scrubby, dirty cheeks, and his breath floated above him, white in the moonlight. Would this be how it always will be? he thought. Am I cursed to remember? To grasp at things beyond my reach?

The gray lay blanketed in a cold mist and the stars were hidden above it. A world collapsed to the fifty feet around him. Jacob rose and shivered and walked to the fire. It was only embers, and Henry Nolan was squatting beside it with a tin cup in his hands.

Henry nodded toward a cup beside the fire. Jacob picked it up and Henry filled it from a coffee pot nestled among the embers at the fire's edge.

"You've changed," Henry said.

"Since when do you speak to me?"

"I'm speaking to you now. You've changed."

"How so?"

"A year ago you come in here all high and mighty with this wild look in your eyes. I kind of liked you then. Now you kill and you like it. I've seen it. There's something wrong with that, Jake. You're losing the meaning."

"What's the meaning?"

"That's different for every man. But there's got to be more to it than just liking it. Bill Anderson likes it. Archie Clement likes it."

"You like it, too. I saw you at Lawrence."

Henry shrugged. "There's a power that comes over a fella, and hell knows niggers don't get to feel power much. But it's also like fucking your best friend's wife. Mighty fun while you do it, but you don't like it after. I don't like killing sitting here now."

"Ain't you got the meaning neither?"

"I got it, and that's the problem." He spat into the fire. "You a religious man, Jake?"

"Sure."

"God's waiting. He's got his big book that he marks all the sins down in and his old pen is scratching away right now."

"We're just doing what we have to do. Me and you."

"You'll come out of this all right."

"You won't?"

"God sees us different."

"How so?"

"Jesus is a white guy. Since when has a white guy ever given a nigger a break?" Henry stared at the embers, then at the mist slowly rolling. "They say everyone comes into the world with nothing, and everyone leaves it with nothing, too. But some folks come in with a hell of a lot more nothing than others."

"That's true enough."

"And some folks are going to leave it carrying more nothing than others, too."

"That's true enough, too."

The sky in the east was turning silver. A new guerrilla, only a boy, walked by the fire. He looked at them sullenly through sleep-filled eyes before relieving himself against a tree. He faded into mist.

"You want some more coffee?" Jacob asked.

"Hell no," Henry said. "It's boiled down so far that it's blacker than I am."

"Where's that mangy redhead of yours?"

"We found him strung up with his tongue cut out last week. I guess they didn't like him not speaking."

"Sorry."

Henry shrugged. "Now or later don't make any difference." He stared at the mist, wiped some of it from his cheeks, his eyes. "You heading south with us, or are you heading back to that girlfriend of yours?"

"South, I guess. Henry, I got to tell you something about Sarah."

"That your girlfriend?"

"She was. I wouldn't say she is no more."

"That why you're heading south?"

"Yeah. She's a slave, Henry. She come across the river with her father when I was living on the Ohio."

"The hell."

"She hid in our barn."

"You loved her?"

"I love her."

"I've heard of that, the love, I mean," Henry said, "but I ain't never seen it. I seen white boys rape black girls all the time. Is that what you're talking about?"

"I tried to rape her the first time," Jacob said. "I couldn't do it."

"Couldn't get the pecker up, or you couldn't do it in your mind?"

"Couldn't in my mind."

"But you could get your pecker up. You end up fucking her anyway?"

"Yeah."

"Then it was rape. If a white boy is fucking a runaway slave girl who's hiding on his farm, it's rape."

"She let me. She wanted me to."

"If she don't let you, you turn her in and she gets sent back. So she's got to let you and she's got to want you to. If there's a got figured into it, it's rape."

"That ain't the way it was."

"You mean it ain't the way you see it. But it sure as hell is the way she seen it."

"She said she loved me."

Henry laughed. "Hell, Jake. What do you think she'd say?"

Jacob stared into the embers. An orange glow, a blue flame crawling over the edges. This couldn't be. He had seen her eyes, and if there was one thing he knew it was eyes. This couldn't be.

"I love her, Henry."

"You love a nigger?"

"That's what I'm saying."

Henry nodded. He swished his cup and threw its grounds into the embers. "When I was your age I knew this girl. I used to work beside her daddy in the hemp fields when there wasn't nothing to do in the corn. Used to lie with her out in the pasture. I thought I loved her then, but I know now that I didn't."

"What happened to her?"

"Nothing. I got sold to Daniels." He shrugged. "It don't matter, no way. I didn't love her."

"You must have loved her, Henry."

"I didn't."

"You must have."

"I didn't."

"You had to."

"What do you know?" Henry laughed. "You're just a kid."

Jacob watched the sun begin to rise, watched the guerrillas awaken. Henry stood and dropped his cup and disappeared into the mist.

When the dawn had completely broken and the guerrillas were awake, they scattered to abandoned farms to search for food. Jacob rode with Haywood. They found a chicken gone wild in the trees that Jacob killed with one of his Navy Colts. They roasted it over the embers, but Jacob couldn't eat. He thought about Sarah and knew this couldn't be.

Just before noon, Charlie formed the guerrillas into four companies led by Bill Gregg, George Todd, Dave Poole, and Bill Anderson. They rode south, hugging the border in the eerie desolation of the burned and empty fields, the burned and empty houses. The land inhabited only by the silence, and a silence within Jacob just as intense and chaotic. He could feel it wanting to burst out like a sweat. He thought of Sarah, of all the times he had spent with her. He thought of those times one by one and in every detail as the column moved south. He didn't know what he knew and what he didn't.

They crossed the border into Kansas just north of Galena and followed the banks of Shoal Creek south toward Baxter Springs. Bill's company rode in the rear. Almost all of the guerrillas were wearing Federal uniforms taken from dead soldiers. Jacob's was frayed, but still fit him well, and he liked it. Dave Poole was scouting out in front with his company. Shriveled scalps slapped against the neck of Bill's mare.

"Shit Jesus," Archie said, "sometimes I get tired of riding."

"So go back to Missouri," Bill said. "Take the oath and tell the Yankees you want a job in an office."

"Sure. I'll write down a number every time a bushwhacker gets killed. Sure, Bill."

"Then stop complaining. You can sit on your ass all winter."

"At least you're not getting your balls squarshed," Haywood said.

"Adjust your god damned stirrups."

"I tried that. It don't do nothing."

"It ain't like you use your balls for anything anyway."

"I use them," Haywood said. "Or I will."

"Sheep don't count."

"I ain't talking about sheep. I'll get me a sweetheart before you know it."

Archie laughed. "A sheep would be prettier than any girl who would take up with you."

"At least I don't hurt them, Arch," Haywood said.

"I don't hurt any of them that don't want to be hurt. If they didn't want to be hurt, they wouldn't drop their knickers in the first place."

"I wouldn't hurt them even then."

"Hell."

"I took that oath," Jacob said.

They approached a rise in the prairie, grass on its slope trying to hold the breeze, the smell of the breeze, the edges of each blade long and yellow and withering. Trees rising beyond it with their crowns dusty and waving. Shots sounded over the crest and the column halted. More shots, many shots. Bill turned to Jacob.

"What do you think?"

"Don't know," Jacob said.

Bill kicked his mare into a trot and rode up the side of the column, his curls bouncing on his shoulders, the scalps bouncing against the mare. Two riders went forward from Charlie and dropped over the hill just as Bill reached him. In a few moments the riders came back and talked to Charlie excitedly, their words jumbled in the breeze. Gregg led his company over the hill. Bill nodded and rode in a gallop back toward Jacob.

"So?" Jacob asked when he reached them.

Bill's eyes were already afire, his lips already wet and working. His face a mass of excited twitches. A madness coming. "So there's a fort."

"There weren't no fort there last year," Archie said.

"There's a fort with a bunch of niggers in it. A hundred of them, maybe. Dave's already attacking it. He already got a couple of them."

"What you going to do with a nigger scalp, Bill?" Archie asked. "How you going to tie that wool around a bridle?"

Bill led the company up the slope. Below them beyond the trees at its foot lay a few log cabins and a tent encampment, all foggy in gunsmoke. Behind the cabins, someone had thrown up dirt and log embankments about four feet high. Dave had his company firing from the grass and the willows lining a creek. Bill Gregg had his in the trees at the foot of the hill and was firing from there. Bits of the logs splintered up and out, and through loopholes in them musket barrels protruded and fired. Barking gunfire, shouts and curses. Screams and moans from the wounded.

"God damn," Archie said. "I hate forts. They can hit you and you can't hit them."

"They cain't hit me," Haywood said.

Jacob studied the fort, the smoke rising. Two black men were lying before its walls in blue Federal uniforms, just like the white soldiers Jacob had seen, just like the guerrillas attacking. He spat and scowled and cursed because this reminded him too much of Independence. He looked at the sun. McGown was flapping away from the fort, a great, stinking, bony vulture, toward the northern horizon. A dust cloud there was rising from a dark blue line. Jacob felt a warm reassurance.

"Bill," he said.

"What?"

"Look behind you."

Bill turned. His face worked wildly, each muscle and tic with its own will, his eyes holding insanity. "Hot damn."

"Who do you suppose they are?" Haywood asked.

Bill's lips worked into a twitching smile. Already a rime of slathering white at the corners of his lips. He kicked the mare in the ribs and rode toward Charlie. Charlie looked over his shoulder, then shouted orders that put the column in a battle line across the road.

As the blue line drew closer, it resolved into a train of eleven wagons escorted by perhaps a hundred cavalry. In one of the wagons rode a band, and its members were busy setting up music. One of the wagons looked like an ambulance. Two sorrels drove a buggy at the front of the column and two more drove another toward the middle. Mules drove all the wagons.

"Looks like a color guard," Bill said. "Who's the head Yankee general now?"

"That nigger-lover Blunt who hanged Perry Hoy," Archie said. "You guessing that's him?"

"Why don't they turn and run?" Haywood asked.

"They probably think we're a welcoming committee from the fort."

"I wish they'd turn and run."

From the column facing them someone shouted an order incomprehensible in the wind and the distance. The column dressed its ranks smartly and moved forward at a trot. Soon they were only two hundred yards away, one hundred, fifty.

Charlie ordered the guerrillas forward in a walk. Jacob pulled his Mexican dragoon pistol free and studied it, then studied the column. McGown was flapping lazily in circles above it. The flesh had rotted off of his good hand completely, was hanging in withered strips from the tattered sleeves of his uniform. His bones glowed in patches.

"Fish in a god damned barrel." Archie grinned.

The column came forward. Jacob smiled and waved, and one of the riders in the front lifted a long, thin arm to return it.

"Give them hell, boys," Charlie said.

Jacob raised his pistol and fired, all the guerrillas in the line but Haywood raised their pistols and fired. In a rush like pumping blood the air turned bright with screams and the horses galloped forward, lurching, blood in their eyes, blood in the grimaces of their pulled-back lips, blood in the smell of their sweat, in the dust, Joshua sweeping across the plains in all God's glory, in all of man's. Jacob fired as he rushed at the line and the soldier who had waved at him jumped backward off of his saddle with his thin, muscular throat reflecting the sunlight. Soldiers stared with wide child's eyes with their horses rearing. The ones at the front of the column were falling and the ones who weren't dead were trampled beneath the clattering hooves of the guerrillas' horses. The cavalry at the back broke and fled. Gunsmoke with its taste like pennies was everywhere and through it Jacob saw three horses galloping toward the west with McGown flying above them. Jacob followed them with Haywood on his right sitting wide-eyed with his lazy eye rolling. He was trying to keep in the saddle. Archie on his left tried to draw a bead on one of the men they were chasing.

When they cleared the smoke Jacob saw they were following two men in officers' uniforms and a dark-haired woman hardly more than a girl, the woman sitting astride the horse with her feet tucked into the straps above the stirrups and her skirts billowing behind her, her knickered behind showing with each bound. Archie screamed and fired and the great gray horse one of the men was riding stumbled and dragged a back leg. Jacob felt within him only a serenity. The three horses leaped a ravine, but the wounded horse couldn't make it and slammed into the far bank, pitching the rider hard into the dirt. Jacob reined in the piebald and waited as Archie rode down the man. The man formally turned over his revolver and Archie accepted it just as formally before shooting him in the forehead. The man's head jerked and his hair leaped as he slammed against the bank. The other man had fallen as his horse cleared the ravine and was clinging to its neck like a monkey with his feet dragging in the grass. Only the woman had grace.

Archie galloped back toward Jacob. "I got him, Jake! I killed Blunt!"

"You sure it was Blunt?"

"I killed him!"

Jacob wheeled the piebald and followed Archie back toward the column in a wild, jouncing, maddening gallop. Haywood followed silently.

This is what they had become. The column when Jacob reached it was an ugly chaos of dying men and killing men and abandoned, fired wagons. Pistols emptied into the heads of the wounded soldiers lying and dying. The band spilled from its wagon amid the clash of brass on brass and all of them dead within a minute. Powder charges packed into ears and set alight. Scalps and other trophies taken. They'd become what others had become before them and what awaited many who would follow. A line is crossed. McGown watched it all from his perch amid the flames of the bandwagon.

Frank James was marching among the bodies, blowing on a trumpet, and Charlie watched him and laughed. He drank whiskey he'd taken from a wagon and it coursed onto his chest. Jacob had never before seen him drunk. Jacob looked down to step over a dead man, then looked up to see Haywood, still mounted on the Morgan.

"Jake," Haywood said.

"Hey, Hay."

"We didn't have to do this, Jake."

"Joshua drew not his hand back, Haywood."

"That's in the Bible, Jake. You ain't in the Bible."

"Why don't you head west, Haywood?" Jacob asked. "Go find some gold. Or go up north and cut down trees or something."

"You know why."

"Then quit your whining. If I got to put up with you, I sure as hell don't got to put up with your whining."

"We just shouldn't a done this, Jake. I'm just saying."

Jacob walked by him, shaking his head. "You don't know, Haywood. You just don't."

"I'm just saying," Haywood called after him.

They celebrated for maybe an hour before riding south around the fort. They followed the old Texas road into Indian Territory, toward Fort Smith on the Arkansas border. The prairie was littered with grazing horses and mules marked with Federal brands. The riders killed what handlers they could find. Most were Creeks or black.

They rode for two days, still carrying their jubilation. McGown had disappeared and that made Jacob uneasy. He didn't like the south, the look of it, the smell of it, the cold prairie wind blowing, the dust in the air, the smell in the air. He wanted guidance. They rode quietly and happily and stopped when they wanted and killed when they could. Eighteen miles north of Fort Smith they crossed the Arkansas River.

They circled around the garrison and worked their way into Confederate territory. On the twelfth of October, six miles south of the Canadian River, they came upon Douglas Cooper and his rebel Choctaw and Chickasaw soldiers. They rested with them for two days, and for Jacob they were two days of pacing and muttering and Haywood staring out over the plains. The last thing Jacob needed and wanted was idleness in which he had too much time to think about Sarah and about what Henry had said he had done. On the second day he found Henry squatting beside the fire. He squatted beside him.

"I love these god damned Indians," Henry said.

"Why?"

"They're the only god damned human beings in creation you white boys let us look down at."

"Henry," Jacob said.

"Them and the Chinamen."

"Henry."

"What?"

"Did you mean what you said back there?"

"Back there where?"

"Back there in Missouri. About Sarah."

"Who's Sarah?"

"My girlfriend."

"Oh," Henry said. "You mean that girl you raped."

"Then you meant it."

"I wouldn't a said it, Jake," Henry said, "if I didn't mean it. You ought to know by now I ain't much on lying."

Jacob nodded and rose. Charlie raced his gelding, and Jacob watched him beat all comers. Some of the Choctaw could pitch a good horseshoe and Jacob played a few games, once with Douglas Cooper as his partner, and Cooper was an ugly, drunken fool. Jacob couldn't keep his mind on the games. Henry watched him from where he sat by the fire.

They left Cooper and rode south across the Indian Territory toward Texas. In four days they crossed the Red River at a place called Colbert's Ferry into a gray world of gray skies and gray wind, a gray landscape and gray water, gray grass and gray dust in the air. Gray faces, the dull, dead smell of gray all around them. Jacob was uneasy being this far south, uneasy contemplating a winter of idleness. They set up camp at a place called Mineral Creek, a few miles from the river. The guerrillas began to build log cabins and hunt the deer that abounded.

Jacob spent his time standing on the north side of the camp, staring across the prairie. Finally he saw in the distance what he thought at first was a vulture, and he stared at it with his eyes burning. His heart leaped within him. He turned quickly on his heels and went back to saddle the piebald.

"Where you going?" Bill Anderson asked him. He lay against a tree, directing a group of guerrillas in a cabin's construction.

Jacob adjusted the cinches eagerly. He looked again north. McGown was tiny, but no tinier than he had been before. He was waiting.

"North."

"Why you doing that?"

"Because this is the south."

"Back to Ohio?"

"Not Ohio. I don't think, anyway, Ohio."

"Then Kentucky, then. That girlfriend of yours."

"I don't know about that, either."

Bill studied him silently. When his madness wasn't upon him he held in his eyes a wisdom that Jacob envied. "Why you leaving, Jake?"

Jacob paused in his saddling. He couldn't tell him the real reasons. "What you going to do down here, Bill?"

"Find me a whore."

"What else?"

"Nothing else."

"Them Confederate officers are going to want you to fight for them."

"Things might get dull if we don't."

"You'll have to fight by their rules. Every time they try to fight the Yankees they get their asses kicked."

"We'll be fighting with them."

"By their rules. And last winter when you fought Blunt with them you got your asses kicked."

"Blunt's dead."

"I ain't so sure, Bill. There's that one that got away with the woman. Or what if the Yankees bring in another like him? Confederate soldiers surrender and they're treated as prisoners of war. You think you will be?"

"No."

"That's why I'm riding north."

"Then I won't fight with them."

"Charlie will."

"I won't. Stay, Jake."

"I can't, Bill." He swung up into the saddle.

"You'll be back in the spring?"

How could he answer that? He looked again to McGown, who hovered on the horizon.

"God willing," Jacob said.

He walked the piebald past the cabin Bill's men were building. Haywood was standing there with a bucket of mud to chink the logs. When he saw Jacob he dropped the bucket on the toe of the man beside him. The man hopped and swore bloody hell. Haywood pulled his father's ragged pants up to his armpits and rubbed the backs of one set of bare toes across the other calf. He cocked his head and studied Jacob, his lazy eye swinging.

"Where you going, Jake?"

"North."

"You heading to California?"

"Don't know."

"Ioway, maybe? Minnesoter?"

"Don't know."

Haywood ran around the base of the cabin. The hopping man tripped on the bucket and wedged his knee in it with mud splattered up on his chest. He shouted for a pistol so he could shoot Haywood.

"Oh, save your breath," Haywood said. "You cain't hit me no way." He grabbed the hem of Jacob's trousers and held him by it. "Can I come with you?"

"I don't even know where I'm going."

"I'm coming with you."

Jacob studied the horizon. He was too anxious for an argument.

"Well, come on then," he said.

Haywood bounded away to look for the Morgan. Jacob waited with the guerrillas stopping work to sullenly watch him.

"Ain't none of you got to stay," Jacob said. No one answered him. "Not a one."

Archie had out his Bowie knife and was playing mumblety-peg in the turf. Bark scraps littered his forearms.

"You going to kill me, Arch?"

"In the spring, Jake."

"Well then, I'll see you."

"See you."

Haywood rode up eagerly, his fingers in the Morgan's mane and his crotch slapping loudly against the saddle, his toes searching for the stirrups. His mutilated face held a grin. His breath whistled.

"You going to ride all the way to Minnesota like that?"

"If I have to."

"You're going to be sore."

"That's all right. Holy rolling thunder, Jake. Let's get going."

Jake looked at the men still staring at him and shook his head. The piebald stepped forward only reluctantly with her eyes wide and on the horizon and Jacob had to kick her into the pace he wanted her to go. Henry Nolan watched Jacob from beside smoldering kindling. He had a new boy gathering firewood.

"You're going back to Ohio, ain't you?" Henry called.

"No."

"I know you is. In your heart, you're already there." The black man laughed.

Jacob set out across the brittle gray prairie toward the river with Haywood riding barefoot and bareheaded beside him. The air was cool and misty, but lightened when they reached Colbert's Ferry and crossed into Indian Territory. McGown was waiting for them on the other side.

They rode north toward the Canadian River. Jacob rode silently with his eyes on McGown and only spoke in answer to Haywood's questions. Haywood asked them often and gaily until he finally saw that Jacob was preoccupied, then he chattered happily to himself. The nights in the heart of the Indian Territory turned colder, and when Haywood crawled out of his filthy bedroll in the mornings he had to hop from one bare foot to the other until they mounted and he could rest his soles in his stirrups or warm them against the Morgan's sides. Jacob shot a white Federal soldier and offered Haywood the soldier's boots, but Haywood wouldn't take them. He quit chattering.

They reached Cooper's camp and found it deserted, scraps of broken tack, trampled grass, fire rings, piles of offal weathering white. They crossed the cold Canadian River and had to wipe down the horses with their bedrolls. It was an achingly cold night beneath the damp blankets. They huddled together for warmth.

They rose the next morning before the dawn with the cold and damp heavy in their joints, teeth chattering, fingers curved and swollen and blue, and mounted. They didn't know the country, so they rode until they saw a Federal patrol heading east, then followed it, keeping low in the grass. When they saw Fort Smith they pulled the horses down on their bellies and waited for nightfall, then skirted the fort and crossed into Arkansas. They slept for most of the next day in a willow-grown gully, then made their way north into Missouri.

"Where we going, Jake?" Haywood asked.

"Don't know," Jacob answered.

They followed McGown into Vernon and Bates and Jackson counties. The burned country; the land completely desolate, hardly even a Federal soldier. Skeletons of char-blackened houses, rats scampering across the foundations, starving dogs watching them with baleful eyes. The riding was easy, and with the chickens and cattle gone wild in the brush they ate well. They passed Osceola and Jacob stopped to study the ruins. He looked to the north and turned his mind to McGown.

They camped for two days on the Sni, picking themselves clean of the gray-backed lice and in the frigid water trying to scrub away the eggs. Jacob shaved off his patchy beard. In an abandoned cabin they found some old denims that fit Jacob and washed them in the river. When they rode into

Kansas City with Jacob's pistols hidden in saddlebags, they looked almost like two upstanding, even Christian, young men. Jacob stopped on Union Street and studied the remains of the building where Harriet had died. He had a yearning for Rocheport, as if that had been an innocent time. With money he'd stolen at Baxter Springs, he bought them each an overcoat and Haywood a pair of boots. Haywood got stares until he pulled a wool cap over the stumps of his ears.

Frost coated the grass in the mornings. By the time they reached the Iowa border the sun didn't have the strength to burn it off until mid-morning. Jacob was tired and cold and he wanted to stop but McGown led them onward.

"Where we going, Jake?" Haywood again asked.

"Don't know."

"To Minnesoter?"

"Maybe."

"Figure we can be lumberjacks? We'll never have to go south next spring at all."

"Maybe," Jacob said.

They followed the Missouri north. By the middle of November they reached Omaha. A thin blanket of snow lay on the ground and the breath of the horses came back over their shoulders in a clinging, minty white mist. Jacob thought that they might stop there, maybe find jobs in dry goods stores, but McGown led them north another day, then up a Missouri tributary a farmer on its banks called the Little Sioux.

"Where you heading?" the farmer asked. A thick man with a straw hat pulled down over a stocking cap and a white goatee that trembled in the frigid breeze. Rheumy blue eyes.

"Don't know."

"Maybe Minnesoter," Haywood said. "To be lumberjacks."

"You don't want to go up there. They're crazy up there. You head up there and your blood'll be flowing."

"Flowing from what?"

The farmer stared at them. "You ain't heard about the uprising? I thought everybody'd heard about the uprising."

"What uprising?"

"The Sioux. A year ago last August they went crazy killing everybody. Killed a thousand of the white folks or so. But it was only them Dutch and Swedes, so it don't make much difference."

Jacob studied the horizon. McGown was waiting in a cottonwood, the bare, glistening joints of his toes clutching a branch like a bird's. He looked back impatiently.

"Is it still going on?" Jacob asked.

"Hell." The farmer wiped the wind from his eyes. "Is anything like that ever over?"

Jacob shrugged and nodded his thanks. "It's getting damned cold."

"It'll be a damn sight colder in Minnesota," the farmer called after them.

Three inches of snow blanketed the northern Iowa prairie, virgin snow unmarked but for gentle wind runnels, an innocent land or a bloody land beneath a façade of innocence. McGown led them north and away from the river, and Jacob rode with his pistols in his waistband and studied the brilliant white and naked horizon. They heard stories from a wanderer of Minnesota farmers castrated and eviscerated and their wives raped until they bled to death and their children pinned to trees by knives through their throats with their little toes quivering three inches from the ground. Of babies with their eyeballs sucked from their sockets. The Sioux, he was told, were savages, and Jacob wished he had a rifle. Why, McGown, why? he thought as he watched the heavy body floating above.

They reached a lake fringed with trees and completely covered with wet, black ice. The temperature was rapidly falling. Haywood sat on the Morgan beside Jacob, huddled in his overcoat, the breeze tugging at the threadbare fabric of his father's trousers. He had his coat collar pulled up over his nose and his breath came out white from beneath the coat's two top buttons.

"We in Minnesoter yet, Jake?"

"I don't know."

"I don't see hardly no trees. Not near enough to do no lumberjacking."

"They must be farther north."

"We heading farther north?"

"Don't know."

"I'm cold, Jake."

"Me, too."

They spent the night in an abandoned cabin on the eastern shore of the lake. A shed leaning against it held hay for the piebald and the Morgan. Inside the cabin hanging by the hearth they found a pitifully small side of bacon. They cooked it on sticks over a fire started with dried cow dung they found in the shed. A mattress lay on a bed frame in one corner, but it was so vermin-ridden that Jacob had to drag it outside. They slept on the floor beside the hearth, faces warm, backsides the temperature of the wind whistling at the windows.

"Will it be this cold all winter, Jake?"

"Probably colder. It ain't even Thanksgiving yet."

"Ain't much to be thankful for."

"We got food. We got a fire."

"We got each other, don't we, Jake?"

"Sure."

"And we ain't in Missouri. I'm thankful for that. I ain't never going back there, Jake, I ain't never. I don't care about Bill or Archie or Charlie and I don't even care about my mam. Not anymore. You ain't going back, is you?"

Jacob looked out of the window. Darkness, complete and sacred darkness. "Don't know, Hay," he said.

They slept late, not waking until the sun was already dazzling on the snow. Jacob stepped outside and pulled his collar tight around his throat and studied the lake, the blackness already hidden beneath more ice and more snow, his teeth aching with the cold. He searched the horizon for the Sioux and felt for his dragoon pistol. The sky was a paler blue than he had ever seen, and on the northern horizon the black dot of McGown was waiting.

"Ain't this enough?" he called to him.

"Who you talking to, Jake?" Haywood asked from inside the cabin.

McGown lifted and fell, lifted and fell. Heavy, bloated, skeletal, hellish, and sacred. Did the Sioux have a McGown? Did they search the sky as Jacob did for dark, empty eyes? "I ain't talking to nobody."

"You got to be talking to somebody. Even if you're talking to yourself you're talking to somebody."

Jacob turned to the door. Haywood was standing in it with his bedroll wrapped around him. It had slipped to reveal a shoulder as white and delicate as a girl's. Jacob spat, watched the spittle make a hole in the snow. He didn't know what he was thinking. "Let's go."

They mounted and rode north again. A shockingly bitter wind blowing, a cold that brought tears to Jacob's eyes, that ached in his deepest bones, that made him press himself into the piebald's warmth. A cold that filled his lungs on the inside and counted each rib from without. They rode north into an empty land with McGown always before them. Why? Jacob asked him, why? But naked, empty houses stood on naked, empty hills, wind-blown ashes and cold cinders, chimneys like pointing fingers. Lumps in bare, flat fields he took to be bodies, twisted and frozen and silently screaming. This is Missouri, he thought. This is Missouri beneath a pale blue sky.

McGown lifted high into the air, drawing Jacob's eyes to the dazzling white sun, as drained of color as the sky around it.

"I understand," Jacob said.

"What?" Haywood asked.

Jacob turned to the boy. He was curled like a question mark over the Morgan, his coat drawn up to the top of his head. He had undone one button and was peeking out.

"I said I understand."

"You understand what?"

"They danced here just like we done, Hay. It's a dance that goes on everywhere. We ain't alone."

"I cain't never understand what you say."

The sun left spots in Jacob's eyes. When he could see the horizon again McGown was truly gone; Jacob couldn't even feel him anymore. He saw only slightly rolling hills, dazzling white, the cold truly alive now, an animal, the temperature not above zero. The wind lifting the snow from hillcrests to dance like ghosts in the sunlight, the ghosts of the bodies lying frozen in the fields that could dance only in a winter like this.

"Where do you want to go, Haywood?" He felt so free now. He felt a part of things.

"I'm just following you."

They found a cabin still intact on the banks of a narrow, lonely stream. Like the cabin on the lake it had a shed built on one side loaded with fodder, and bacon, more of it this time, hanging by the hearth. They put in and fed the animals and went inside to wait out the cold. No trees grew near the cabin beyond a few scraggly willows on the stream bank. The only wood was a small stack beside the hearth. They burned a quarter of it in the first fire.

"What are we going to do, Jake?" Haywood asked. His teeth made an odd, hollow sound when they chattered because of the lack of them. His knees tapped dully against each other.

"Don't know. What do you want to do?"

"I don't want to cut down no trees in weather like this. It's too damned cold."

"There must be towns to the east. We'll put up in one of them for the winter."

"Unless the Injuns get us."

"I thought you had the mark of Cain."

"Unless the Injuns get you. We going to put up in a room?"

"In a shithole. Of course in a room."

"I ain't never had a room of my own before. Mam and Pap had me pull a old mattress up on the table. You ever have a room, Jake?"

"I slept in a loft."

"I'll share my room with you."

"All right."

Haywood smiled. His voice whistled. "That would be fine, Jake. That would be just fine."

They waited one day, two days, three, but the cold did not break. It became ferocious, a wild, crazy thing, as wild and crazy as Bill Anderson's blood madness, as Jacob's own, as cold as his God knowledge. They huddled by the fire throughout the day with the senator's blanket wrapped around both of their shoulders until the fuel was gone, then Jacob struggled down to the river wrapped in his coat and their blankets to break branches from the willows. They burned them and ate the rest of the bacon and brought the horses inside the cabin to keep the cold from killing them. Day after day they waited and the cold did not lessen.

"I'm hungry, Jake," Haywood said.

"Me, too."

"You reckon it's going to be like this until spring?"

"I hope to hell not."

They lived a week on a broth made from the fodder. Jacob tried catching fish from the river by breaking a hole through the ice with a hoe and spearing them with a tripod he made from a willow branch, but he had no luck. He flushed a prairie chicken on his way back to the house and learned to look for their breathing holes. He shot enough of them with the Colt revolvers to keep him and Haywood alive. When the willows were gone, they kept a meager fire alive with the manure from the horses and twisted handfuls of dead grass. At night they slept together for warmth.

Clouds came in a blanket sometime toward the end of the year and the cold lessened. The fear of it returning was too great in both of them to risk traveling. They huddled at night with Haywood's back against Jacob's chest and stared hungrily at the little fire. The horses stomped in the corner and quietly ground the fodder between their teeth and filled the cabin with their rich smell of life.

"Jake," Haywood said.

"Yeah."

"You remember what I told you about Booger?"

"You mean how Jennison's men shot him?"

"The other thing."

"I remember."

"You remember how I told you he wasn't no friend of mine?"

"I remember."

"You're my friend, Jake. I knows it." He paused to snuggle his backside into Jacob. "You can do that to me, if you want."

"Hell, Hay."

"You can."

"I don't want to."

"You're my friend, Jake."

"I still don't want to."

Haywood sighed. He smelled of salt and the horses, and his cropped hair prickled against Jacob's cheek. "Well, if you change your mind."

"The only reason we're sleeping like this is to stay warm, Hay."

"I ain't dumb, Jake," Haywood said.

That night Jacob dreamed of the farm. He was flying over it; everything was tiny but clear. Cyrus behind Buck in the fields, sweat glistening on his brow. Clara sweeping dirt out of the cabin door. Tobias crossing the river, and Isaac standing in the current and watching him. Sarah, sweet Sarah, dancing in the yard with one arm wrapped around her waist and the other above her head and her skirts trailing out and away, her bare, black legs flashing in the sun. He felt an ache in his chest as heavy as the world and he plummeted toward her. She laughed as he dropped and quickened her dance before breaking into a run for the cabin. She was by Clara and through the door before he could reach her.

Now he was a man again, or a boy, and was running from the barn to the house and Clara guarded the doorway. Sarah peeked over her shoulder at him. When he tried to push by his mother, she shook her head and barred his way. He tried to push by her again and suddenly she was red-tinted claws and fangs and blood-dripping eyes. She was tearing at him with blood flying and wounds ripping open from his chest to his crotch from which poured blood but no pain. Cyrus paused to smile and wave as Clara did her work. Tobias was hanging dead in a tree on the riverbank, the tips of his boots resting on Isaac's shoulders. They both smiled and waved. Sarah's laughter rang in the cool spring air.

He awoke staring up at the dark eaves of the cold, cold cabin. A huge empty feeling filled his chest and he knew that he would cry. He breathed the frosty air deeply and felt a mix of warmth and cold on his crotch as curious as his dream wounds had been. He threw off the blanket. In the thin firelight he saw that Haywood was lying across his legs with his cheek pressed against Jacob's naked erection. Jacob kicked him away.

"What the hell are you doing?"

Haywood was crying. "I was lying there and I felt it rising against me while you was sleeping. I just had to, Jake. I had to."

"Archie's right. You're the sorriest bastard I ever knew."

"It ain't being sorry, Jake. It ain't."

"I ain't no god damned sheep, Haywood."

"I don't want to do it to you, Jake. But you can do it to me if you want to."

"The hell if I want to."

Haywood choked on a sob and sucked a load of snot into his throat. He came back to Jacob and lay again across his legs, rubbing his wet cheek across Jacob's privates. "Please, Jake. You can if you want."

"You get the hell off of me or I'll shoot you."

"You can pretend I'm anybody. Your girlfriend, maybe. Just please, Jake."

Jacob lay back on the floor. Haywood lay across him crying and Jacob was too tired and cold and hungry and too full of his dream and Haywood's tears to kick him off again. Oh Sarah, he thought.

"Haywood," he said.

Haywood turned his head. When he spoke, Jacob could feel his lips against him. "Call me Hay."

Oh, Sarah, Jacob thought. Why did you run? He looked down at the boy.

"I ain't making you no promises, Hay."

"I ain't asking for none."

Jacob stared up at the dark eaves. His breath rose cold and bitter, a thing with a life of its own. It was flying as Jacob wished to be. Oh Sarah, he thought again.

"Come up here then," he said.

Chapter Twenty-five

The weather was more forgiving by spring and McGown had not returned. The land remained desolate—they had not seen a single person all winter and did not see one as the snow began to melt, turning black on the stream and shining brightly on the land beneath the raw, new sun. The smell of the earth returned. They moved the horses out to pasture.

Jacob felt happy. He didn't know why. Missouri seemed so far away and the things he had done and the things he had thought seemed the actions and thoughts of a different man. In ways he missed Sarah as much or more, and in ways he no longer missed her at all.

When the land dried enough for the horses to cross the low areas without slogging, they moved to the cabin on the lake. The water there was clear and cold, the grass lush, the earth rich with the smell of fertility. Jacob made fish hooks from bones, and though he searched the horizon for the Sioux as much as he watched his line, the fishing was good. Haywood kept house and did the cooking. He found vegetable seeds in the shed and chattered about planting a garden. Whatever woman had lived there before had left behind a tattered old skirt that was in better shape than his pants. Though the weather was warmer, they still slept together at night.

One morning in what must have been early May Jacob lay naked beneath the covers and watched Haywood dress. The boy had pulled his mother's blouse over his shoulders and was drawing the skirt up around his knees.

"You look god damned silly dressed like that," Jacob said.

"My pap's trousers are about shot."

"They ain't so shot you can't wear them."

"They're shot enough. And yours are, too. You need to go to town and get a needle and thread. I'll darn them for you."

"There ain't no town."

"I'm happy, Jake. I'm happy there ain't no town. Are you happy there ain't no town?"

"Don't know."

"But I guess if there was you could get me a bolt of cloth and I could make you a new pair of trousers."

"You ain't my mother, Hay."

"I know." Haywood grinned. "I'm your wife."

"You ain't my wife, neither."

"I sure is. I used to do dishes back home and listen to my mam and pap in the bedroom. You do everything Pap did but shout holy rolling thunder."

"You ain't my wife, Hay."

"But you can call me your wife if you want to, Jake. Just don't call me late for supper!" Haywood laughed his keening laugh and lifted the skirt to pull on his boots. "Ain't it like none of that other stuff ever happened?"

"It's kind of that way."

"I hope nobody ever comes back here. Then we could live here forever and ever."

"You want to go through another one of them winters?"

"It wasn't so bad, Jake. And we'll have vegetables this time. Taters and things." He grinned his gap-toothed grin. His blind eye rolled to stare at the ceiling. "You know the best thing about skirts and no underwear? You can piss whenever. Just got to tuck it down a little. You going to catch some fish today?"

"Thought I'd try."

"You want a quick one before you set out?"

"No."

"Come on, Jake."

"Maybe I will."

"You can call me your wife if you want to."

"You ain't my wife, Hay."

"Holy rolling thunder," Haywood said as Jacob stood.

They could not live well, just living off of the land, but they could get by. Jacob worried about running out of ammunition and took to snaring prairie chickens and gophers as they came out of their holes rather than wasting balls and powder charges—he missed too often and though Haywood would never miss he would not touch a gun. Gopher meat was wild and stringy but cooked up tolerably well in a stew made with some kind of root Haywood found that he loved to fuss over. They cleared a patch of the prairie for a garden with a broken spade they found in the shed and the hoe they'd taken from the cabin by the stream. They took firewood from the deadfall of trees on the lakeshore. The beginning of summer came and went and high summer came and was going and Missouri was only a dark spot in the back of Jacob's mind, a place where things stuck in the back of his throat. As unbelievable a thing as that dream he had had the first night he had slept with Haywood.

They were sitting in the threshold of the cabin looking out at the new garden. Haywood had lost his boots with the warmth and was now working one set of toes over the other in the dust. Jacob let his eyes sweep the horizon. The setting sun caught the sunlight in shades of silver-tinged scarlet and threw it back pleasantly in his face. He felt as he imagined a man should feel, as he imagined his grandfather had felt when he hewed out the farm on the banks of the Ohio and brought his new wife to it. His grandfather had understood omens. Jacob had been wrong and Larkin Skaggs had been wrong and the things he had now were the ways of God and men—a farm, making a farm, making a life. Having someone to sleep next to at night. And a black spot rose and fell on the horizon. He closed his eyes and felt his breath go cold within him. He opened them again. He hoped that it was a vulture, but everything came back then and he knew that it wasn't.

McGown flew heavily out of the setting sun and dropped into the garden to waddle grotesquely across the furrows toward the cabin. The winter had not been good to the dead sergeant. One arm of his coat was gone and the other hung by threads from the seam at his armpit. One arm was bone to the shoulder and the other bone from the stump of his wrist to just above the elbow with scraggled strips of his biceps hanging. White fingers clicked together hollowly as he dragged his carcass closer. He squatted a few feet from the threshold and studied Jacob from bare-boned sockets in a skull with flesh only in a scrap on the bridge of the cavern of his nose. A dry, mortuary smell had replaced the stink of putrescence. Almost sweet.

It all loomed up within Jacob. He closed his eyes and opened them again. "You," he said. He was suddenly exhausted.

McGown stared. Haywood stared, too. "Who you talking to, Jake?"

"I'm tired," Jacob said.

"Who you talking to?"

McGown raised a bony finger and pointed to the south.

"I'm too tired," Jacob said.

"Tired of what?"

"I can't."

"Tired of what?" Haywood asked again.

McGown kept pointing. Jacob resisted. Finally, McGown flapped his bony arms and flew toward the south. Jacob followed him with his eyes. He remembered the mirror in Dawson Springs, Rachel's reflection behind his own, his face containing those blue and dead and soulless eyes. He remembered his place in this world. He cursed and spat and stood and studied McGown and the southern horizon. God, he thought.

"Get your pants on," he told Haywood.

"Wives don't wear no pants."

"You ain't my wife. Get your pants on, then saddle the Morgan."

Haywood stared up at him with his lazy eye rolling. "I ain't saddled him up since we got here."

"We're heading back south."

"The hell, Jake."

"Well then, don't. But I am."

"Why?"

"Just do it, Hay."

Tears brimmed in Haywood's eyes. "We don't have to go be gorillas. We got it nice here."

"You coming?"

"God damn you, Jake." Haywood rolled his head on the stalk of his neck so that the tears tracked crazily across his face. "We got it so nice."

Jacob went to the shed for his saddle. As he brushed the dust from its jockey and inhaled the leather and sweat and blood smell of it, Missouri came back larger than the life around him. This stint on the Minnesota prairie was nothing, a mistake, a foolish reprieve. He whistled for the piebald and she lifted her head from where she was grazing, and when he threw the saddle blanket over her and tightened the saddle cinches she stamped one hoof impatiently and trembled with excitement, her eyes on the southern horizon. She knew as she had always known and if he had not dissipated the attention she deserved between Haywood's buttocks he would never have made this mistake. She had grown fat in her leisure. My God, Jacob thought, what have I done? He knew his duty now and wished he wasn't so tired.

It felt good to have her between his legs, to feel the way she shifted as she walked and his own movements, once unconscious, to adjust. He rode to the cabin door, dismounted, and went inside for his things. The revolvers felt good again in his waistband, the Mexican dragoon pistol where he could easily reach it. The dead lieutenant's frock coat felt good over his shoulders. He walked outside and mounted again and the piebald pawed impatiently at the turf. McGown waited on the prairie. Haywood was still sitting on the threshold in his skirt.

"You coming?" Jacob asked.

"We got something here, Jake. I ain't giving it up."

"You want me to leave you a pistol?"

"Please, Jake."

"I'll leave you a pistol."

"I don't want your god damned pistol."

"Well then," Jacob said. "I'll see you."

He kicked the piebald in the ribs and she started jauntily across the plains. McGown lifted and led him southward. Within fifteen minutes Jacob heard hooves behind him, and Haywood came riding up on the Morgan. He was wearing his father's pants again, pulled up to his armpits.

"Nobody's going to be around to eat them taters," Haywood said.

"Somebody might be."

"I put a lot of work into them taters."

"You did."

"We can go back, Jake."

"No we can't."

McGown flapped heavily on ahead of them, bony arms catching the last of the sun, lifting him mysteriously, as if he were riding the rays.

"Why, Jake?"

"I see with different eyes."

"I cain't never understand a damn thing you say."

They rode south as the darkness spread across the prairie, the night as full and dark and heavy around them as Jacob's sense of McGown. McGown's bones captured and held the moonlight, the starlight, gave them a beacon. They had not gone ten miles before the dead sergeant settled into the grass and they made camp. But at least they had started.

They had no fuel for a fire, so they lay silently side by side and looked up at the summer sky. Jacob felt good and right and the feeling was warm in his chest, in the hollow place where a soul might have been. Though he was still tired he felt a need to expend the feeling. He rolled on his side toward Haywood and worked the suspenders off the boy's shoulders. He had Haywood's pants down to his waist and his hands inside on his hips working forward before the boy rolled on his belly and with his hands fought Jacob away.

"What?" Jacob asked.

"No more."

"What's that mean?"

"That mean's no more. I ain't your wife. You ain't doing nothing to me no more."

Jacob felt a slow growing anger. "I will."

"Then you're just another Booger."

Jacob rolled onto his back and stared at the stars. "Damn it, Hay. We got to go back."

"There ain't nobody making us."

"You don't understand. You don't know."

"I know I need to take care of them taters."

"Hell, Haywood."

"You call me Hay, unless you're just another Booger."

They lay the rest of the night without speaking. Jacob studied the stars and slept only fitfully. The horses stood over them and once the piebald shied away as McGown waddled across the grass to crouch beside Jacob, the smell of him like ambergris, though his breath was rancid and cold. Jacob felt reverence. He could see now that he just wasn't any good without someone to guide him.

He arose before dawn. Haywood was already waiting moodily in the dewy grass. Jacob saddled the piebald and was tightening the cinches when Haywood finally went to the Morgan. They left the camp just as the sun was rising.

They found and followed the Little Sioux River south. Farmers were cutting and stacking hay in their fields, and Jacob thought about the Germans in Lafayette County. They rode in the mornings and rested during the day's heat; rode at night, rode all day with the sun sucking the sweat from their faces, rode as McGown directed, downriver to the broad, brown banks and broad, brown waters of the Missouri. Jacob felt as if he were almost home. He was anxious.

"We're getting there," he said, but Haywood didn't respond.

Jacob bought a paper when they reached Watson, Missouri, and rode with it spread across the piebald's mane. He skipped the main news concerning Grant's actions in Virginia and Sherman's Georgia terrorism, read the minor news of a stolen cow and a dead and unknown guerrilla, looking for news of Charlie. He found too many stories of dead guerrillas, thirty dead in one skirmish, forty in another, and he wondered what had changed. George Todd and some of the boys had ridden through Johnson County and killed every discharged Federal soldier and Union civilian they found. Bill Anderson had been busy around Rocheport, killing Federal soldiers and shooting at steamboats. No news of Charlie.

"Bill's taken to shooting up sidewheelers," he told Haywood. Haywood didn't respond.

They rode into Kansas City with the revolvers hidden in saddlebags. They had bathed and shaved north of the river and were again two upstanding young Christian men, with Haywood wearing Tobias's slouch hat pulled low over his ears. They rode east toward Independence, reaching it during the hottest part of the afternoon on the second to the last day of August. The stone building they had attacked was pocked with bullet holes; two-year-old wooden crosses in the cemetery had begun to peel. Jacob did not recognize anyone and did not care to. McGown did not stop, and Jacob was glad to leave the town behind.

They spent the night on the river just outside of Wellington in Lafayette County. The night was clear with just a hint of cool, and the early morning wrapped itself in a mist that moved quietly along the water. They rode east and camped the next night in the hills of Saline County. The land was eerily quiet and empty, and what people in it who hadn't fled silently stared from drawn, gray faces. They picked up lice again as they approached Howard County. Jacob grew more anxious. Haywood grew more quiet.

They crossed the river at Glasgow on the first day of September. A new day, a new month. The promise in it leaped in Jacob's heart; his mouth went dry with it and it flickered at the edges of his eyes. McGown danced ponderously in the air.

"Where we heading, Jake?" Haywood asked.

"Rocheport, I guess. Bill always liked Rocheport."

They rode southeast toward Fayette, reaching the little town by noon, but didn't ride in because a Federal cavalry patrol reached it just before them. They rode through the hemp and tobacco fields toward Rocheport without stopping to eat. Jacob thought of Swizz and Harriet.

They kept off the main roads, following streambeds and gullies and stretches of wooded hills humming with insects and slow, late-summer heat, punctuated by the caws of the crows and jays flitting through the branches before them. The going was slower than Jacob expected and he did not smell the river until almost four in the afternoon. When they reached the spot where he'd bathed his feet after he'd left Osceola, gunfire from downriver echoed off of the hills and caught in the trees around them.

They dismounted. Jacob drew the dragoon pistol and stepped back into the willows.

Haywood crouched beside him. "You guessing there's trouble?"

"Don't know."

"There's trouble, Jake. I know there is."

The gunfire mixed with the *huff-huff-huff* of a steamboat. A side-wheeler with the name *Buffington* on her bow came around the bend just up from the dock, and all the firing was coming from it, little puffs of smoke floating along the gunwales from bow to stern. Jacob waited. A few men and a lot of boys in slouch hats and embroidered shirts riding the side-wheeler hooted and laughed. Archie Clement was straddling the prow as if he were having intercourse with it. Jacob stepped out of the willows and smiled, waving the dragoon pistol in the air.

"Arch!" he called.

Archie looked toward shore. When his eyes met Jacob's he dropped his bottle and fumbled for a pistol. He aimed it at Jacob and Jacob stood waiting. Archie's arm swung back slowly to maintain his aim as the boat moved upstream.

"God damn it, Archie," Jacob called.

Archie dropped the muzzle an inch and peered over it. "Who is that?"

"Who the hell you think it is? It's Jake Wilson."

"Well god damn," Archie said.

He didn't put away the revolver. The boat swung around and for a minute Jacob couldn't see the prow, and when it came back into view, Archie was no longer straddling it.

"You stay behind them willows, Hay," Jacob said.

"I knew there was trouble."

"If something happens, you ride out of here as fast as you can."

"I knew it."

Jacob searched the sky for McGown and guidance. The dead sergeant was gone. Damn, Jacob thought, damn, and he tightened his grip on the pistol. The boat churned slowly toward him, with guerrillas leaning on the rails, silent now, and watching him. Jacob still couldn't see Archie.

A white frame door opened on the side of the pilothouse and Bill Anderson stepped out onto the deck, looking as he always had, long hair, wild beard, wild blue eyes. He was wearing a black slouch hat with the brim pinned up with a peacock feather. Archie followed him out. Jacob dropped his pistol to his side and felt his palm slick upon it.

"Hey, Bill."

"Hey, Jake. Have Hay step out where I can see him."

"I don't know if he wants to do that."

"Why?"

"I ain't seen nobody smiling."

Bill nodded and leaned his forearms on the railing, his hands hanging over the water. "So where you been?"

"Minnesota."

"You said you'd be back in the spring."

"Got delayed."

"Why don't you and the boy come on up to the dock?"

"I ain't seen no smiles yet."

Bill laughed. "Hell, Jake. Why would I kill you?"

"I ain't worried about you."

"Why would any of us kill you?"

"Don't know. People get funny reasons."

"Come on up to the dock."

Jacob nodded and watched the boat go by. Most of the guerrillas resumed their drinking and shooting. He stuffed his pistol in his waistband.

"Let's go, Hay."

"I don't like this, Jake."

"They can't shoot you. You got the mark of Cain."

"I didn't think you believed in that stuff."

Jacob didn't answer him. He took the piebald by the reins and walked toward town. Haywood followed.

The boat had docked by the time they reached it. Bill was still leaning on the railing with Archie standing behind him. Jacob couldn't see Archie's hands, but only three pistols were in his belt and the knife sheath was empty. Jacob rested his right hand on his hip, close to the dragoon pistol grip, and edged behind the piebald. A group of guerrillas was filling tin cups from a whiskey barrel on the dock. Bill studied Jacob quietly.

"So why are you back?"

"Missing it."

"Let's go up to the Liberty Bell for a drink."

"Just like old times," Jacob said.

Bill disembarked and Archie followed. Bill shook Jacob's hand. A heat in his grip as if the fire burning in his eyes was consuming him. A twitch in his cheek betrayed his tenuous control.

They walked up the street, leading the horses. Two dead men lay in front of the milliner's with big green bottle flies settling onto their scalped and clotted skulls.

"How you doing, Arch?" Jacob asked.

"All right."

"You going to shoot me?"

"Maybe later."

Drunken guerrillas staggered across the street, and one was puking into a rose bed. Townspeople glanced out of dark windows. The Liberty Bell held nothing but drunken guerrillas and broken bottles and a thick, salty, musty, smoky odor. Bill pulled a whiskey bottle from behind the bar and gathered together four dirty glasses. He filled each one and slid three of them to Jacob and Archie and Haywood. Jacob swallowed his quickly, enjoying the burn of it in his throat, the way it steadied his jumpy nerves. He was surprised to find he was no longer used to this.

"You remember old bucko, the barkeep?" Bill asked.

"Sure do. He's poured me a lot of drinks."

"I shot him."

"What for?"

"I don't remember."

"Because he was a god damned Yankee," Archie said.

Bill and Archie and Jacob finished their drinks. Bill filled all the glasses but Haywood's, which hadn't been touched. Haywood sat silently, his lazy eye rolled up to stare at the ceiling.

"You like my steamboat?" Bill asked.

"Sure."

"I decided I needed a private navy." He drained his glass again. "Minnesota, huh?"

"Yeah, well."

"I figured you was dead, Jake. I was kind of missing you."

"What's been going on?"

"I split with Charlie."

"No."

"He ain't what he was and everybody knows it. The whole thing broke up. Bill Gregg joined Jo Shelby's Iron Brigade in the regular army. Bud Younger headed out to New Mexico. George, he split off and has been having a time of it."

"I read about him."

"And that damned Charlie, he's been lying up in the Perche Hills doing nothing but feeling sorry for himself."

"Henry Nolan with him?"

"Sure. Why do you care about that god damned nigger?"

"I don't know," Jacob said. "I knew him at Osceola."

They drank their whiskey with the smell swimming around them as Bill recounted the spring and the summer, the ride up from Texas in June, the fighting in Lafayette County, the steamboats, the dead boys floating in the water. The awful battle at Flat Rock Ford where they had lost too many.

"What's going on, Bill? I pick up the paper and read about all these bushwhackers dying."

Bill ran a mouthful of whiskey around his mouth and swallowed. "The Yankees brought in twelve hundred of these killers from Colorado that had been fighting the Utes and Arapahoes. God damned devils, they are. They took off Fletch Taylor's arm. They shot Dick Yeager in the head. They scattered us up by Renick and killed five. At Wakenda they shot Frank James's little brother. Sixteen-year-old kid, and they shot and almost killed him. It ain't like the old days anymore; it ain't boys and old men fumbling with muskets that even Haywood there couldn't hit the side of a barn with. God damned devils, they are."

"We ought to move on," Archie said. "Kentucky or Iowa or someplace. It ain't hardly no fun here anymore."

They spent a week drinking and talking and shooting out windows and sleeping in the bar, beneath the tables. At the end of the week a sympathetic farmer rode in with a warning that the Colorado killers were coming, and they finally left Rocheport in a band of a hundred to tear down telegraph lines and kill what Federals they could find. The Second Colorado Cavalry followed them as relentless and silent and pervasive as the dusk each evening settling in the sky. The hundred dropped to ninety, to eighty, hardly ever a battle, but boys who walked off into the trees did not walk out again, boys off to bathe were found lying with their scalps lifted or hanging from branches, silent screams twisting their faces. A fear now. In the middle of the month, the hot dry days of September, word came from one of the few farmers left that George Todd was near Fayette. Bill and his men were just east of Rocheport, and as they rode to join him they came across a twelve-wagon military train just northeast of the town. They killed fifteen. Bill stuffed a few hundred dollars into the bulging pouch he'd taken at Independence.

On their way to Fayette, the Second Colorado killed and scalped five stragglers. A farmer warned them of a command of five hundred Federal Missouri cavalry coming north from Rocheport that they had to circle during the night. When the sun rose the next morning, the piebald was shivering beneath a coat of sweat and dew and her breath was steaming. They were in the hills south of Fayette and looking down at the town. So much like Lawrence.

"I think we ought to take the damn place," Bill said.

Jacob studied him. Something had changed in Bill since the year before that he couldn't define. He felt uneasy and he had not seen McGown. "Let's find George. You know where he'd be?"

"I know," Bill said.

Bill led the column south through the tangled brush, the cornfields wet with dew and either burned or ripening, the valleys and the water and the smell of fresh hay and all of it gaining color beneath the steadily brightening sky. They followed a stream around the base of a hill, then climbed a rise. The town behind them lay hidden. As Jacob tried to place the land around him, a barn loomed out of the morning that he recognized as the barn he and Bill and Archie had slept in when they had first left Rocheport in search of Charlie, so long, it seemed, before.

Perhaps a hundred and fifty guerrillas were lounging in the yard. The farmer, as toothless as Haywood, as twisted and knobby as the trees growing behind the house, was standing among them while his daughter hauled a water bucket from the well. It seemed to Jacob as if it had been a thousand years since he had seen her, the knights and their damsels and their dragons had been born and had died and had passed forgotten into history since he had seen her, but she was still a child, long blond hair in braids, a child's face holding both innocence and the experience Archie had introduced to her that night a thousand years ago. She looked at them as blankly as she must have looked at the others, but her eyes caught on Archie's face, and when Archie smiled she hurried into the house and slammed the door behind her.

"What the hell's with her?" Archie asked.

"You know," Jacob said. He felt for this boy that old distaste and hatred rose again. He thought he might kill him.

Jacob dismounted, keeping his eyes off of Archie. He was working the saddle off of the piebald when Bill crossed the yard to where George Todd and the farmer were standing. George nodded, and Bill returned his greeting. Bill was excited about something. The farmer ran his hand over his head, now almost completely bald.

"You remember me?" Bill asked.

"You're Bill Anderson," the farmer said.

"But do you remember me? I come here back about two years ago. You fed me and a couple of my boys."

"I remember. You wasn't Bill Anderson then. You was just some southern boy."

"I told you I'd pay you back for what the Yankees took from you."

The farmer's hand on his scalp slid down to the back of his neck. "Did you?"

Bill hurried back to his mare. He took from his saddlebag the pouch of coins and bills he had been collecting. He hefted it and grinned at Jacob and strode back to the farmer. "Here you go. I figure there's about two thousand dollars in there."

"That's for me?"

"For you."

The farmer took the pouch. "It's heavy." He loosened the drawstring and peered inside. Bill watched excitedly. "Where'd all this come from?"

"Dead Yankees."

"How many dead Yankees?"

"Hell if I know." Bill jerked his head toward his mare. "I brought some of their scalps. You want to see them?"

"I don't want to see them."

"I'll show them to you if you want me to."

"I don't want to see them." The farmer hefted the pouch, the coins clinking. He stared at it, then stared across the fields. "You're in a bloody business, Mr. Anderson."

"Bloody as hell. But you done us a good turn."

The farmer nodded. He hefted the pouch, then handed it back. "I'm a simple man. Simple ways. I don't know much, but this is blood money."

"Money's money," Bill said.

"No it ain't." A sudden life in the farmer's tired, defeated eyes. "I put you up then because that's what I wanted to do. I'm putting you up now because that's what I got to do. This has become a damned bloody business. I seen what you done. I got to do a lot of things, but I don't have to take your blood money."

Bill looked down at the pouch in his hand. He shrugged and smiled weakly. "I've been saving this for you for a long time."

"Old blood is still blood."

"You could get yourself a new mule. Build up the house. Maybe retire and move into a town somewhere."

"Old blood is still blood."

"I thought maybe that daughter of yours would like a new dress. I wouldn't mind seeing her in one."

"I know what's going to happen to you, Mr. Anderson," the farmer said. "I seen it happen to others like you. You're going to be kneeling in a field surrounded by Federal soldiers. One of them is going to put a gun to the back of your head and blow your brains out of your eyes. You're going to die crying, Mr. Anderson. You're going to die begging for your life. And it's all going to happen before the dress my daughter is wearing now wears out. There's a penalty to pay for what you've done. You and all the boys with you."

Bill stared down at the money. A shadow fell across his face, and Jacob looked up to see McGown pass overhead and settle on the roof of the house. Bill's hand gripped the pouch's drawstring and a snarl worked over his lips and he swung the pouch hard and fast to hit the farmer in the jaw. The farmer's head snapped and cracked and the blow knocked him off of his feet. He fell onto his back, twitching and gasping tight little high-pitched gasps, and he was trembling and all of the guerrillas were staring at him silently. The farmer arched his back hard like Baker's brother-in-law in Council Grove had done with his heels clawing at the earth and making signs, then he relaxed and the last of the air went out of his lungs. He looked younger.

"Hell, Bill," Jacob said.

"You try to do something nice for a guy," Bill said.

"You done killed him, Bill," Haywood said.

"You try to do something nice for a guy and he has to say something like that. Well god damn. What was I supposed to do?"

"You shouldn't a killed him, Bill," Haywood said.

"Oh hell," Archie said, "you heard him. You heard what the bastard was saying."

George shook his head at the dead man lying at his feet. "I suppose we'll have to say he turned Yankee. I'd hate for word to get out that we're killing our own."

"You try to do something nice," Bill said again.

The girl came out of the house. She walked by the guerrillas standing around her dead father into the barn. When she came out she caught a glimpse of her father's boots between their legs, and her face paled as she yelped like a puppy. She stood trembling.

"Get her out of here," George said.

Archie stepped toward her. She did not see who took her arm. When she looked up, she screamed a high-pitched, girlish scream and clawed at Archie's face. Some of the guerrillas laughed, and the attention given the farmer broke.

"Hell, Archie," one of them called. "I think she already knows you."

"God damned Yankees. She's as bad as her old man was." She screamed as he dragged her by the crook of the elbow toward the trees beyond the house. She fell and her thin legs thrashed; one bony hip left a trail in the dust.

"You give her this money," Bill said. He had to raise his voice above the girl's. "I got it for her and her daddy."

"That's a hell of a lot of money to be giving to some damned Yankee."

"You give it to her."

"If I got to give her that much, then she's going to have to earn it."

"You don't hurt her, Archie," Jacob warned him.

The girl had risen on one hand and her knees and she was screaming. Archie cursed her and slapped the side of her head.

"God damn you, Archie. You don't hurt her."

"Jake," Archie shouted, "you mind your own damned business."

The sun was warming the yard, drying the dew clinging to the grass. By the time Archie had gotten the girl into the trees, Jacob had gone back to wipe down the piebald. The girl's cries grit his teeth and he tried to shut his ears against them. The sound of clothing being torn. Jacob looked up at McGown, but McGown was gone as if he had evaporated into the morning. What am I to do? Jacob thought. He felt enough indignation to stride toward the trees, but he stopped when he remembered Henry Nolan's words before they had left for Texas. He remembered Sarah. No sounds at all came from the trees beyond muffled grunts from Archie and faint, animal moaning. Other guerrillas were waiting at the edge of the trees for their turns, glancing shyly at each other. Jacob tried to keep his attention on the piebald.

Haywood had unsaddled the Morgan and was squatting at the edge of the yard, working his bare toes in the dirt, his back to the guerrillas, gently rocking, his hands over the stumps of his ears. Jacob walked over to him. Haywood looked up at him, squinting from his good eye.

"Ain't you going to do nothing?" Haywood asked. "You ought to."

Jacob spat. He looked back toward the trees and felt withered with impotence. Two guerrillas were dragging the farmer's body away. "Ought don't mean nothing, Haywood. It's just a word."

"We didn't have to come back to this, Jake."

"Us not coming back wouldn't have helped her none."

"We could still leave."

"No we can't."

"Why not?"

"We just can't," Jacob said.

Time passed. The sounds in the woods died. Some of the guerrillas went out after food and some slept. The ones waiting for Archie to finish one by one worked into the trees. Jacob found a spot in the back corner of the barn where he couldn't see the woods beyond the house. He lay with his saddle under his head and his Mexican dragoon pistol beneath the saddle. Haywood curled up at the barn's far corner into a ball and fell asleep immediately, whimpering in his dreams. Jacob watched him and strained to hear what sounds might be coming from the trees. The ringworm scar on the back of Haywood's head had taken another turn.

Jacob heard nothing. He lay with the sweet smell of hay around him and the stamp of the mule still in its stall and the steady whistle of Haywood's breath in a mix with his whimpering. Finally Archie came into the barn. His pants were buttoned and all of his weapons in place. Blood flecked his cheek, but no scratches. He nodded at Jacob, then lay beside him with a long, luxurious sigh.

"Wasn't there a cat in here?" he asked. "I seem to remember a cat in here."

"What did you do to her?"

"Nothing she didn't ask me for."

"Where is she?"

Archie smacked his lips. "I got me an appetite. There any food in this place?"

Jacob lay back on the saddle. The hatred in him was tangible. "You know something, Archie?"

"What?"

"At first I hated you and then I liked you and now I hate you again. I'm going to kill you someday, just like that farmer said. I'm going to blow your brains out of your eyes. You're going to die crying."

"There ain't no call for talk like that, Jake."

"I'm going to put the muzzle of my Mexican dragoon to the back of your head, and I ain't going to pull the trigger until that god damned smile drops from your face."

Archie pursed his lips, then grinned. A black, cold gash, inhuman. Something to be feared. "You won't do it, Jake."

"Why not?"

"You know how I been saying every fall that I'm going to kill you when you come back? You know why I never do?"

"Why?"

"Because it would be just like killing myself."

"We ain't the same, Archie."

Archie lay back on the hay, that black slit of a grin still on his face. He pulled his hat over his eyes. "So I can lay here and sleep as long as I want and I don't have to worry about nothing. Because killing me would be just like killing yourself. I've always known that."

"Try to sleep. You won't wake up again."

Archie laughed. "You're funny, Jake. You and me, we got us a sense of humor."

The rim of his hat covered all of his face but for his mouth and chin and his grin. Jacob's hand went beneath the saddle and his fingers tightened around the pistol grip. But he left the pistol where it was as he watched Archie drift off to sleep. Finally he rolled onto his back and stared up at the rafters. Every feeling inside was jumbled, a roil. What is the truth and what isn't?

Swallows darted among their nests upon the rafters, filling them with their gossip. Haywood's breath whistled, and Archie slept with his grin on his face.

Chapter Twenty-six

Jacob slept only fitfully. He dreamed that McGown had taken the girl and was flying high above the farm and that he was flying behind him. The dead sergeant was naked to the waist with nothing but bare bones shining and a few scraps of flesh still clinging to the hollows of his hips. Far below Jacob the farm became the farm in the valley and then became the prairie. The girl's mouth worked frantically as if she was trying to tell him something, but he couldn't hear her. Every time she kicked her legs she changed color. A scream echoed in his head.

He awoke breathing hard with Haywood and Archie still sleeping. He sat up and rubbed his eyes and felt a warm stab of sun across his cheek from a slit in the planking beside him. He looked at Archie again, and his hand went beneath his saddle. He found the pistol, but not the resolve to use it. He hated what he was seeing.

"Fine mule."

He turned. Henry Nolan was standing on the other side of the mule, leaning on its withers. His long face drawn, forehead pulled to the top of his scalp, long spider fingers, long spider hands. He whispered something in the mule's ear, and the mule tossed its head.

"I used to look after mules like this," Henry said. "But I guess you already know that."

"What you doing here?"

"I come with Charlie."

"He's here? I thought he was out of it."

"Once you're in it," Henry Nolan said, "you ain't never out of it." He clucked at the mule. "And I come looking for you."

"Why?"

"Because you still believe. Charlie don't believe no more, not since Lawrence. Poor Little Willie and Georgie are just crazy, murderous bastards who never believed nothing to begin with. Most of these boys are just boys and they don't believe in nothing but funning, and that ain't nothing to believe at all. But you believe. You and me."

"I don't believe a damn thing, Henry."

"The hell you don't."

"What do I believe?"

Henry shook his head. He smiled a broad, tobacco-stained grin. "There's a way to this world, Jake. There is. And a big, white God is sitting on his throne."

Haywood was tossing and had an erection showing through the thin fabric of his father's trousers. Archie's mouth was open and snoring. Henry Nolan watched Jacob silently, one hand caressing the mule's withers. Jacob reached again beneath the saddle and pulled out the pistol. He stood and stuck it in his waistband and walked toward the door.

"So what do you think of that?" Henry asked.

"I don't think nothing of it," Jacob said, "because I know it ain't true. Nothing you say is."

"All right," Henry Nolan said.

Jacob stepped outside. The sun was high and hot, and a dusty smell salted the air. McGown was crouching on the top of the house with the blank sockets of his eyes staring and the sweet rotted smell of him mixing faintly with the dust. He no longer had his boot and his pants were gone and the ligaments holding his genitals rotted away to leave them hanging at an angle. Perhaps the dream had been real, but how could such a dream be real? How could any dream?

Twenty guerrillas were lounging in the shade of the trees behind the house. Others were playing horseshoes by the field. Two boys were wrestling in the dust, giggling like the boys they should have been allowed or should have chosen to be. Jacob watched them. He was nineteen.

Henry Nolan followed him out of the barn. He stood beside Jacob with his hands on his hips, his eyes scanning the field. "So where's Charlie?" Jacob asked him.

"In the house with Poor Little Willie and Georgie and a few others."

"Doing what?"

"Planning."

"Planning what?"

"On taking Fayette, I expect."

"Hell." Jacob spat. "Sounds like they want to play soldier again."

"Crying and dying," Henry said.

Jacob waited throughout the afternoon for whatever was going on in the house to finish. He thought about looking for the girl and decided against it. He thought about killing Archie and decided against it. He and Henry tried to join in the horseshoes, but no one wanted to get beaten by a black man. When the games died they played one alone that Henry won handily, his long arm swinging, his long fingers releasing, the horseshoe catching the sun. Jacob kept thinking about what he had said before they'd left Missouri for the last winter. He longed to see Sarah. He was afraid to see Sarah.

Archie came out of the barn just as the day's heat was breaking. He shook his head at Jacob and smiled at the trees and ambled over to the guerrillas lounging in their shade. One boy asked about the girl. Archie said something Jacob couldn't hear, and they all laughed. Haywood came out and watched two boys building the night's fire, picking his father's trousers from the crack of his ass, his mutilated face holding both a grimace and sorrow. He avoided Archie. He avoided Jacob. He walked to the cornfield and squatted and studied the sun.

"My little nigger," Henry Nolan said.

"Yeah."

"He's your little nigger now."

"No he ain't."

"He used to be. What changed?"

"Hell if I know."

"Then I'll keep him," Henry said.

Guerrillas were mounting to search for supper. Jacob was not hungry enough to bother. He accepted the hardtack Henry offered and sat with his back against the house. Muffled voices seeped from inside, a hint of argument. The crack and snap of the growing fire, the dusty smell of summer, the dusty taste of the hardtack, the smell of the fire burning. Haywood walked into the corn.

"Where's he going?" Henry asked.

"Hell if I know."

"He gone for good?"

"No."

"Why not?"

"He wouldn't leave without me."

Henry worked on a square of hardtack, his thick, red tongue kneading it. He carved a slice of salt pork off of a chunk he had taken from his pocket and offered it to Jacob. Jacob chewed it until all the salt and taste were gone, until most of the fat had melted. He watched the night coming, the blue sky turning silver, turning gray, the stars coming out, the night animals fussing in the trees behind him. He couldn't see McGown crouching on the house peak, but he could see the dull glow of his bones cast into the yard. He could feel him there.

Henry Nolan whittled shavings off of the salt pork and worked them into his mouth. Haywood came out of the field and stood at the edge of the fire, then walked over to the house.

"How's my little nigger?" Henry asked him.

"I'm good."

"Best little nigger I ever had."

Haywood squatted beside Jacob, opposite of Henry. The night came thickly. They waited.

"Gonna get cold soon," Henry said.

"Sure will."

"I got me some relatives in Canada, I think. I bet it's cold up there."

"They tell you that?"

"Don't no slave niggers ever hear from free niggers."

"But you ain't a slave no more."

"Technically I is. I believe that's the word."

"Maybe we could go to Canada," Haywood suggested.

Henry's jaw worked on his pork. "They all speak French up there." He swallowed. "They all parley vou. Maybe that's why I never hear nothing. Probably can't even speak American no more."

They sat for an hour. The guerrillas returned, their horses shadows, their bodies ghosts. Within the house someone lit a lantern, and its light through the window was strong and defined, the campfire flickering, the shadow of the house now only the ubiquitous darkness, a strange, silver glow cast down from where McGown waited. Frank James stepped out of the door, his long, thin face drawn thinner. He shook his head at the night and nodded at Jacob.

"Hey, Frank. What's going on?"

"Hell to pay," Frank said. "Hell to pay."

He crossed the yard. George and Charlie came out without speaking. Bill stood in the door with a wildness in his eyes that nearly outshone the lantern he was carrying. He hung it in the eaves and grinned down at Jacob.

"I outdid him, Jake."

"What do you mean?"

"Charlie's taking orders from me now."

"The Great Little Willie," Henry said.

Bill quit grinning. "God damned niggers. What are you doing here, anyway?"

"The Great Little Willie," Henry repeated, "ain't nothing but a fool."

Bill's cheek twitched. "I ought to slit you open and load you with rocks and dump you in the river."

"No originality, Willie. Georgie already came up with that idea."

"Well, I ought to."

"So do it. Or maybe I'll do it to you."

Bill stared at Henry, his face twitching. Henry's thin fingers slowly pulled the knife blade across the last of the salt pork. A steady calmness in his eyes. Perhaps he knew all that Jacob knew; perhaps he knew it more clearly.

Bill spat to the side. Henry slipped the sliver of salt pork onto his tongue. The crickets had begun to chirp; the mosquitoes whined shrilly. A chill in the air, the warmth of the fire too distant. Finally Bill cursed and stepped off into the darkness.

"Holy rolling thunder," Haywood said. "You done threatened Bill Anderson."

"He's just a shitbird white boy, and not much of one, neither." Henry pursed his lips and pointed with his chin into the darkness. "You two better run along. You don't want to be seen as being friendly with a black man who just challenged the Great Little Willie."

"Bill would never do nothing to us," Jacob said.

"Don't be so sure. He don't believe, and that leaves him free to do anything he wants. Now run along before I stripe your asses."

Jacob shrugged and stood and stepped off into the darkness. His joints ached from sitting so long and though he had slept most of the afternoon he was tired. Too many things troubled his mind. Behind him in the lantern light Henry worked at the salt pork sliver with the knife. It amazed Jacob how long he could make that last. McGown crouched on the roof, watching silently. His naked teeth in his near naked skull gleamed in his own light.

Word had passed about the raid, that they would take Fayette in the morning. The younger guerrillas talked and laughed and the older stared into the darkness or the fire. Some cursed the raid and others the lack of liquor. The boy who'd won the afternoon's wrestling match stood in the center of the yard flexing his farmer boy arms and announced that he would take on all comers. A huge man with thick hair on his chest and shoulders stood. The boy changed his challenge to taking on all comers who could not yet grow a beard. The guerrillas laughed and the hairy man laughed and the boy laughed along with them. On a thong around his neck he was wearing someone's finger.

By the time the moon rose, most of the camp had settled. Men slept rolled in blankets or on their sides in the grass or at the edge of the fire. Hands slapped at mosquitoes. Bill's band had slept most of the afternoon and they stayed by the fire, its puny flames glowing dully on the slats of the weathered barn. They discussed the wisdom of the coming morning. No one spoke of the girl. Haywood sat with his legs crossed, his elbows in the dirt and his chin in his palms, staring into the fire, always silent. Jacob sat beside him and watched the boy or watched McGown. Finally he rose. He tried to find a place in the barn, but it was full. He walked into the corn-field and lay between the rows and stared up at the darkness.

The stars shimmered against their infinite background, and the moon worked steadily among them, near full and bright with the shadows of the stalks moving with it. A chill around him, the sweet smell of the corn around him, the soil hard against his back. Jacob thought about many things. He thought about his life as it was and his place and purpose in this world and he thought about God. He thought about the stories Clara had read out of God's word, about Moses, about Ruth, about Joshua. About Cain and Abel, about God and man. About Jesus hanging and dying and rising again, about a man thrusting his fist into the wound in his side. About the disciples and their bickering and the Holy Spirit coming upon them. Was that a rape, too?

Clara had become a story, too. He could see her sitting there, her hair tied back, her teeth red-rimmed and dripping, long claws turning pages; he could see Cyrus sitting at the table; he could hear the low distant thunder of Isaac's voice, his bald head glowing like polished wood in the light from the hearth, his gentleman's clothes, his daughter, his daughter, his daughter. Jacob cried silently to the sky for a life that had died. As if in epiphanous answer he heard a heavy fluttering and the click of bone and a silver shadow passed over the silver moon. Now a holy light surrounded him and Mc-Gown was settling to the ground between the stalks and the stalks were bowing down to make room for him. He could hardly even be called a corpse anymore. Jacob feared him, not with the icy fear of Dawson Springs but the reverent fear in his mother's stories from the word of God. Perhaps that was the beginning of the wisdom both those stories and Larkin Skaggs had expounded. Jacob studied the naked skull face of the man he had killed and felt toward him as he would toward a father.

"I want to go home," he whispered.

McGown squatted silently. Bare-bone elbows rested on bare-bone knees. The flesh on his handless arm had retreated to a scrap just below his shoulder. What was left of his genitals dropped almost silently to disintegrate in a puff of dust.

"I've done enough," Jacob said. "Will you take me home?"

McGown only stared silently. So little of him remained to rot that he looked purified. His bare-bone fingers hung between his legs and glowed dully.

"Will you take me home?" Jacob asked again.

McGown lifted his good hand and pointed one finger at the sky. It glowed with the same brightness as the stars.

"There ain't no place there for me," Jacob said.

McGown's finger kept pointing. He stared at Jacob and Jacob stared back as they had done the day the sergeant had died. He just couldn't understand.

"Do I have hope, then?" he asked fearfully.

Finally McGown lifted and flew back toward the house. Without the weight of his flesh, he was as graceful and light as the swallows in the barn.

Jacob watched him go until the stalks hid him. He looked again at the stars. He lay in the field for hours, trying to decipher the dead man's actions.

The talk around the fire died as Bill's followers began to doze. Jacob slept only fitfully because he was afraid of his dreams and losing in them the warmth and hope that McGown seemed to offer. He rose before the dawn, shaking the chill from his joints. He studied the spot where McGown's flesh had dropped and found nothing.

He walked from the field to the house. McGown had gone to wherever it was he went when Jacob could no longer find him. He sat with his back against the house and waited for the sun.

When it rose it dazzled him. He closed his eyes and watched the spots of brilliance move across his lids. He saw in his mind that dull, silver finger pointing into the sky. Hope leaped anew within him, a new found faith. He opened his eyes and studied the sky, the slowly growing blue. He was as dazzled by it as he had been by the sun.

They left the farm just after ten in a column with Bill at its head and George and Charlie following. Haywood rode beside Jacob with his hands gripping the mane and a far-away, sorrowful look on his face, a fly buzzing around the stub of his right ear. On the other side of Jacob rode Archie Clement. McGown appeared behind them, and they stopped the column in the timber south of town as if to wait for him to catch up. He dropped from the sky into the branches ahead of the column and looked back at Jacob. He pointed again at the sky and Jacob nodded, not in understanding but in the wish to understand.

Bill kicked his mare into a trot and the column followed. They left the woods and were on a street with a cemetery east of them. At the edge of the buildings they broke into a gallop and Archie yelled as he shot a white man running along the street. He grinned and yelled again and the other riders took it up and the wildness like a wind was coming. Jacob drew the Mexican dragoon pistol. Haywood rode silently with his crotch slapping the leather. Jacob felt only a warm, reverential hope and a holy sanction. He wondered how much this looked like the plains of Jordan.

They dashed in a wild scream into the town square with the horses wild and wide-eyed and the smell of their excitement upon them. A brick courthouse squatted on one side and beyond it and up a hill to the north someone had built a blockhouse out of railroad ties. The guerrillas screamed and Jacob rode straight at the courthouse where McGown was directing him. He could see everything so clearly. He aimed at a courthouse window and fired and saw the glass break, then a line of smoke came out of the windows and bullets whistled and horses screamed in their dying. All around Jacob, riders without faces anymore or with huge red splotches on their chests were falling backward off of their horses, and then there was nothing to see but the white gunpowder smoke and bodies reeking with vomit and urine and feces within it and the tangy smell of spent gunpowder and the horses stumbling over the bodies of their riders. Jacob reined in the piebald beside the cloudy white courthouse wall. Haywood sat quietly by his side. Another volley erupted and a bullet snatched Tobias's hat from Jacob's head to disappear somewhere in the smoke.

"We don't have to be here, Jake," Haywood said. "We could just ride away."

Jacob pulled the piebald around and dashed across the square. When he cleared the smoke another line of it erupted at the blockhouse and a row of guerrillas fell into the dirt in front of it. Dying horses, limping and screaming, and one lying on top of the dying men thrashing its legs at its entrails, its hooves thudding heavily against arms and chests and skulls. Bill was still mounted and was screaming his sisters' names with his eyes wild and foam bleeding heavily back along his beard. He led a mad dash at the courthouse with Henry Nolan cursing beside him. Musket fire erupted in front of them and another line of men fell and another congregated scream rose from the horses. Bill and Henry had survived it and were pointing their pistols at one of the windows. Suddenly Henry dropped his pistol with his dark face twisting in rage and pain and he grabbed at the sudden red-tangled meat at the back of his thigh. He cursed the white God above as his horse reared and that God plucked him from it. He was lost in the smoke and the tangle of horse hooves and Jacob looked for the bastard who had shot him from behind.

Archie was now aiming at the blockhouse. He fired once and galloped wildly north out of the square. Jacob followed him filled with a hatred so hard within him he thought his ribs would crack. He aimed at Archie's back, but in the madness and the smoke and the screaming his shot went wild. He'd emptied the dragoon pistol, and when he reached for his Navy Colts he found that both had fallen free. Now he was out of the square and caught up in the guerrillas' flight. In the screaming behind him and the riders bleeding all over their horses around him, in the smoke and the fear and the panic, he could not find Archie Clement.

The riders slowed as the sounds of the square faded behind them. Too many of them were wounded, too many fell out of the saddle and had to be left behind. Too many rode between friends who had to support them. McGown led them north, his bare-bone feet trailing in the smoke-tinged air behind him.

"God damn it!" Jacob shouted. "What happened?"

"What the hell do you think happened?" Frank James was riding with his kid brother beside him, the kid only a boy, wide eyes, smooth cheeks colored with the fighting. "We got our asses whupped. Were those them Colorado boys?"

"I want to know who the hell shot Henry Nolan," Jacob shouted.

"Forget about Henry Nolan," Frank said.

"Some bastard shot him from behind."

"God damn it, Jake. Guys were getting shot from everywhere."

Jacob reined the piebald around and started back for the square. He had almost reached the end of the riders when he came upon Charlie, who grabbed the piebald's reins. In Charlie's face was a sad wisdom.

"Let it go, Ohio boy."

"Somebody shot Henry Nolan."

"Of course they did. They shot a lot of people. Let it go."

"Not one of them. One of us."

"Let it go," Charlie said again.

Jacob looked at the town. Smoke and cheering rose from its center. Rifle shots rang that he guessed were for the wounded who had fallen. "God damn it," he said. "God damn it."

"This is what I told them would happen," Charlie said. "But nobody listens to poor Charlie Quantrill anymore."

Finally, Jacob turned the piebald and followed the fleeing riders. He wondered which of the rifle reports behind him was meant for Henry Nolan. Not as many horses were screaming now.

"God damn it," Jacob said again.

"He takes them to Lawrence and gets them out, but nobody listens to poor Charlie Quantrill anymore."

When they were safe from the town they stopped to organize the wounded. Curses and cries and threats and more curses. Haywood found Jacob and tried to ride beside him. Jacob found Archie and worked his way toward him with his rage thick in his veins. When the column was organized with scouts in front and pickets behind they moved slowly north, stopping only to leave the wounded with farmers who watched with sad faces from the side of the road. Once Archie turned his head away, and without thinking Jacob pulled free the dragoon pistol and put its muzzle against his skull and pulled the trigger. It clicked impotently, and then Jacob remembered that it was no longer loaded.

Archie turned to look at him. A black slit of a grin. "You can't do it, Jake."

"You shot Henry Nolan."

"You can't do it."

Jacob studied his eyes. God damn it, he thought, god damn it. What is the truth?

"If I ever find out you done it," he said, "I'll kill you."

Archie pushed the pistol away. "God damn, you sure get worked up over a nigger."

"Henry called me his little nigger," Haywood said.

They rode slowly on through the afternoon, always with the sun on their left shoulders, with the fear and the shock and the shame of their defeat within. When dusk began to settle, the column pulled off of the road and over a grassy hill into a gully beyond. Bill and his followers dismounted. Charlie, George, and the others didn't.

"What's going on?" Bill asked. "Ain't we going to make camp?"

"Not with you," Charlie said. "You pull another stunt like that and we'll all be dead. You should have listened to me."

"It was a bad break is all."

"The hell it was." Charlie pulled his brown gelding around.

"You leave and I'll kill you, Charlie."

"No you won't. You never could kill a man better than yourself." Charlie nudged his gelding and a few of the riders followed him back over the hill. Bill watched him go, but did nothing. George shook his head at Bill and spat and led his men north, following the gully.

"You, too?" Bill called after him.

"You're a god damned crazy bastard, Bill," George called back.

Finally the evening settled, a beautiful, clear evening with water whispering faintly in the gully bed and the birds singing their evening song. They bedded down for the night and though none of them were wounded they all were quiet. Haywood sat beneath a tree and drew with his finger in the dust.

"Bill," Jacob said.

"Yeah?"

"We've been through a lot, ain't we?"

"We've been through hell, Jake."

"Did you have Archie kill Henry Nolan?"

"Is that what you think?"

"Did you?"

"I wouldn't do that, Jake."

"I trust you, Bill. I do. But someone shot him from behind."

"Hell. Them Yankees was shooting us from every which way."

They slept on the edge of the trees with the horses hidden in the gully. Haywood took the first picket. Jacob watched him walk to the top of the hill and thought about going up to speak to him, but he was too tired. It had been a hell of a day. Archie slept with the others while Bill leaned against a tree and fingered the silk cord he kept in his pocket.

"Bill," Jacob said.

Bill looked up. "Yeah?"

"What happened?"

"Hell if I know."

"I thought we was going right. I thought I knew we was going right."

"How'd you know?"

"I just knew."

"Then what went wrong?"

Jacob thought of McGown. He wondered where the dead sergeant had gone. He wondered why he had led them into that. "Maybe we just don't understand it is all."

"Maybe."

They spent the next day resting in the gully, only going off to hunt squirrels that they cooked over a fire after the sunset when the darkness would hide the smoke. They listened to Frank's kid brother read from a newspaper he had in his pocket about the war in the east, but he wasn't much of a reader. On the morning of the twenty-sixth of September they mounted and rode over the hill and north on the road toward Audrain County. Just around noon with the sun high and hot, they stumbled across two Federal scouts. They waved to them like good Yankee soldiers and managed to kill one. The other escaped north.

"That other one ain't from Colorado," Archie said as he worked at the dead scout's ears.

"How do you know that?" Jacob asked.

"He's running."

Haywood sat with his bare feet in the stirrups. "Where we heading, then?"

"Not after him," Bill said. "Down south somewheres."

"Down south like in Texas?"

"No, you damned fool. Down south like in by the river."

They left the dead man in the road and followed a cow path into the fields and trees. With Federal patrols so active it took them all afternoon to go ten miles. Just before evening a farmer called them to the side and told them that George was camped on land owned by a man named Singleton just south of a little railroad town called Centralia.

"That's where we'll head then," Bill said.

Archie spat on the farmyard. "George ain't going to be too glad to see us."

"He'll be all right. What's he going to do, kick us out of camp in the middle of the night?"

"I'm more worried about him shooting us."

"He cain't shoot me," Haywood said.

They crossed the tracks of the Northern Missouri just as darkness fell. By the time they reached the Singleton farm the night was complete with the moon not yet risen. Crickets chirping, and from somewhere drifted the smell of bacon. The guerrillas stared at them quietly as they rode into camp. George didn't say anything as they dismounted and unsaddled their horses.

"Hey, George," Bill said.

"Hey, Bill. You going to do something crazy?"

"Is sleeping crazy?"

"Sterling Price is coming north with twelve thousand troops. He come in near Doniphan and he's going to take St. Louis."

"I hope he kills all the damned Dutch there," Archie said. "One thing I can't stand is a god damned Yankee Dutch."

Bill grinned. "Maybe he's coming up just to give us medals."

They slept. Jacob awoke to the clear, cool morning, mist in the valleys, dew on the grass, the smell of it like flowers. He ate the ham and eggs the Singleton woman cooked for him. Bill strode into the kitchen wearing a full Federal uniform with his hat brim pinned up on one side. He took coffee from the woman and sat at the table and grinned.

"What?" Jacob asked.

"I'm going to ask Price to make me a captain."

"You think he will?"

"There ain't one captain in the whole Confederate army that's killed as many Yankees as me."

"How many knots you got?"

"I don't know. Fifty-some."

"You know where Price is at?"

"I figure to ride into Centralia and find out."

"I'll come with you," Jacob said.

He finished his meal and waited as Bill finished his coffee. The Singleton woman stood silently by like a servant. They went outside. Most of the boys were still asleep, their blankets and clothes glistening with dew. Only thirty agreed to ride into Centralia through the fresh morning air, the bright, new day.

They crossed a pasture on the west side of the house to a narrow dirt road, Bill in the front flanked by Archie and Jacob. Haywood had still been sleeping, or pretending to sleep, and Jacob had left him where he lay. Cows in the pasture watching them, slowly chewing their cud. It felt good to leave the boy behind.

The town was only a railroad with a cluster of perhaps twenty-five houses and a depot with a freight house along the side. Two small stores down the street from the depot, both with their shades drawn. It couldn't have held more than one hundred inhabitants, and they all appeared to still be sleeping. Bill pulled free one pistol and raised it as they approached the town. He fired. Archie grinned his black grin and fired and Jacob felt a calm righteousness rise within him. The day was so beautiful he was stunned by it. He pulled the dragoon pistol free and fired through the window of the first house they came to. The shatter of the pane was as sharp and clear and brilliant as the sun on the grass, as the birds singing.

They galloped madly through town, then turned and came back, screaming and shooting. Stunned faces blinked out of windows, men in underdrawers opened and peered out of doors, then quickly shut them. The riders stopped at the depot and dismounted. Jacob kicked open the door and found a little old withered man with an engorged Adam's apple and a paper visor on his bald, pink forehead. He was sleeping with his cheek upon a desk littered with paper and inkwells and blotters, with a Bible at its corner. He could hardly lift his head when Jacob came in.

"Morning," Jacob said.

"What?" The old man's voice was high and cracking and reminded Jacob of that broken windowpane.

"You got anything good in here?"

"What?"

Jacob shook his head and looked back out at the morning. The riders were passing by or milling about. Bill was standing at the edge of the tracks, looking south.

"Hey, Bill."

"What?"

"We got us in here an idiot. All he can say is what."

"Ask him if he's got in there a paper."

Jacob turned back to the man. "You got a paper?"

"What?" the man asked again.

Jacob leaned over the desk and lifted the man's nose with a nudge from the dragoon pistol's muzzle. The man's eyes went wide and watery and fixed on Jacob's face.

"What's your name?" Jacob asked. "Don't tell me it's what."

"Hiram."

"A newspaper, Hiram. You got one?"

Hiram fumbled in a drawer on the side of the desk and took out a folded newspaper. He kept his eyes on Jacob with the pistol muzzle clicking against his teeth. Jacob took the paper in his free hand, keeping his pistol pressed against the man's upper lip.

"What's the matter?" Jacob asked. "You don't like my face?"

"It ain't that," Hiram said.

"You don't like my nose?" Jacob cocked the gun. Hiram swallowed loudly. "You better not tell me you don't like my nose."

"I don't like your nose." Hiram shook his head wildly. Thin tears bled back from the corners of his rheumy old eyes, and his lip pulled from side to side. "I mean I do. I do like your nose."

"A Yankee sergeant busted it up. You know what I done to that sergeant?"

"No."

"I busted the side of his head with an ax. You know where that sergeant is now?"

"No."

"Me neither," Jacob said.

He let down the hammer and shoved the pistol back into his waistband. Hiram sat as he had when the pistol had been under his nose, his back arched, his face pink, tears following the wrinkles down his cheeks, his breath coming in short little whistles. Outside came more shooting and shouting and the sound of breaking glass and splintering doors.

"Oh hell," Jacob said when he looked at the paper. "This is old."

"The train ain't come in yet today," Hiram said.

Bill's heels thudded on the wooden walk outside and he stepped into the depot. He stood with his hands on his hips and studied Hiram. His eyes held just a hint of wildness.

"Say good morning to Hiram," Jacob said.

"Morning, Hiram."

"This paper's old."

"What do you mean, it's old?"

"It's old."

"It ain't got no news of Price?"

"Maybe of his birth. It's old."

Bill studied Hiram. Hiram sat as he had before. "What you doing with such an old paper?"

"The train ain't come in yet."

"You got a telegraph office in this town? You got any dispatches about General Sterling Price, Army of the Confederate States of America?"

"The lines are down. All the lines are down."

Bill grinned at Jacob. "I bet George done that."

"You ever heard of George Todd?" Jacob asked Hiram.

"Oh, God," Hiram said.

"This here's Bill Anderson."

"Oh, God," Hiram said again.

Bill took the paper and looked through it, the pages snapping. "Ain't nothing about the general in here. There's an ad for corsets, though. Hey, Hiram."

"What?"

"You got any corsets in this town?"

"My wife's got one."

"I bet she's a big old fat bitch, ain't she? You got to pull that son of a bitch tight on her? Maybe you hook her up to the mule and let it do the work?"

"What?" Hiram asked.

"You got anything good in this depot?" Jacob asked again.

"Got some boots that just come in," Hiram said.

Jacob sighed. He turned to Bill. "Maybe we ought to just shoot him."

"Got some whiskey, too," Hiram added quickly. "A whole barrel of it."

"He can hear just fine," Bill said.

In the back storeroom they found the boots and the whiskey. They made Hiram haul the boots outside to the walk, then roll out the barrel after them, Bill prodding his ass with a pistol muzzle as he did. Archie ran into one of the stores and came out carrying an ax. He grinned as he handed its haft to Jacob.

"You're supposed to be good with that thing. Open the damn barrel up."

Jacob nodded. It felt good to have an ax again in his hands. He settled the blade on the top of the barrel while the guerrillas gathered around. He swung it back over his shoulder.

When he brought it down he wasn't swinging at a barrel. He was back in the cabin in Ohio, and Archie wasn't there but Klausmann was, Klausmann and Newt and Benjamin Bartels looking down from the loft and Clara, his mother, her swollen-faced, evil-faced, bloody-red-lipped-and-red-fangs-dripping mother, sitting in her chair beside the hearth and smiling. McGown was lying on the floor wrapped again in his flesh and his hand lay twitching by the hearth. Jacob was a boy again and everything within him was bursting because, he thought, sweet Jesus, because this is wrong, this is wrong, all of it is wrong. McGown's eyes went wide as the ax met his skull, and Klausmann and Benjamin Bartels and Newt and Clara laughed with harsh, southern voices. Jacob stood dumbly staring at the haft in his hands, at the ax head against McGown's skull, the sunlight striking upon it, the glow of McGown's broken skull striking upon it. Klausmann and Benjamin Bartels and Newt and his mother reached into that skull with cups and boots to fill them with McGown's blood. They drank. They laughed and drank. Behind him, Teague was sitting at a desk, an old man now, a huge gaping gash just below his jaw, a paper visor shading his dead and winking eyes. The ax jerked loose from Jacob's hand as if it were living and he stumbled back against the cabin wall. Clara's Bible lay open on the floor beside the upturned table. For Joshua drew not his hand back.

Clara was laughing with her lips pulled back from bloodstained teeth. She lowered a tin cup into the blood overflowing. McGown was staring at Jacob from full-of-life eyes, eyes that knew the truth of this world. He was grinning.

"What's the matter, Jake?" McGown asked with Archie Clement's voice. "Ain't you going to have any?"

"Sweet Jesus," Jacob said.

Teague was still sitting behind him and McGown still lay on the floor and Klausmann and Benjamin Bartels and Newt and Clara were drinking the blood from his skull, but the cabin had become the depot again and everything Jacob saw was swimming. His hands groped before him as if in darkness. He could not remember raising them.

"Well, ain't you?" McGown asked again.

Jacob closed his eyes. He felt his hands press into his eyes until he thought they would burst, and he could not remember putting them there. The darkness behind his lids flashed with pain and a red, bloody brilliance. He pulled his hands away and felt his nails dig into his palms. He could see through his eyelids the orange brilliance of the Missouri sun. He could feel it on his face. When he opened his eyes McGown was gone and Klausmann and Benjamin Bartels and Newt were gone and his mother was gone and Bill and Archie were drinking from the whiskey barrel, Archie with a boot and Bill with a tin cup he must have taken from Hiram. Hiram still sat at his desk. The Bible still lay on its corner. The wind had blown open its pages.

"Jesus Christ, Jake," Bill said. "What's the matter?"

"Don't know. Just got a little dizzy for a second."

"Looks like you seen a ghost," Archie said.

"Maybe I did," Jacob answered.

He was numb for the rest of the morning. He was numb when he forced Hiram to drink a bootful of whiskey, numb as Hiram vomited it out in the corner, numb when the train came into town. He was numb when Bill ordered the twenty-five Federal soldiers on furlough off of the train and numb when they stripped them and numb when they shot them all in the foreheads to crumple at the side of the track. He was numb when they scalped them and burned the depot and numb later that afternoon when with George they slaughtered the one hundred and twenty Missouri militia who had been sent to investigate the black, billowing smoke rising above the town. Numb when he cut off their heads and left them grinning blankly from fence posts, from saddles, grinning about the obscenities carved in their foreheads, grinning about their swapped bodies, numb when he cut the genitals from the few still living and stuffed them down their throats. Numb during the scalping, the eviscerating, the taking of trophies. Numb that night at the fire. Numb as he followed the column following McGown, who was wrapped in his flesh again with the soul in his eyes burning brightly. Numb when they found Henry Nolan's body hanging in a tree just north of Fayette, his hands tied behind his back and his ears and nose and eyelids cut off, a warning from the Second Colorado stuck to his chest with a kitchen knife, his belly ripped open and his guts hanging down and the crows feeding. Numb through the following cold, rainy month as Bill received from Price his captain's commission. Numb as they rode through the bone-soaking drizzle into northwest Missouri. Numb with the fear of the relentless pursuit of the Second Colorado as steady as McGown before him. Numb through the gang rapes of two slave girls in Glasgow; numb with the girls weeping beneath him. He'd become what he had become. Numb when they received word that Blunt who they thought was dead and Jennison who had mutilated Haywood defeated Price on the border at Westport. Numb with the news of George Todd's death to the bullet of a Second Colorado sniper. Numb as the last hope was driven south across the Indian Territory.

No one knew what he had become because he did not act differently, but he was only a boy from Ohio who had killed a man with an ax and had killed too many men and too many children, who saw that man and all that he had done floating before his eyes. He was a boy who had murdered horribly, cowering within himself numbly like a boy, closing his eyes to his actions, closing his ears to the cries he had wrung from his victims. He was a boy who had drunk from the blood of McGown, and bathed in that blood and painted with it the sky and the river and the land, but even with all that he was only a boy. He was still only nineteen.

He was sitting quietly with his back against the side of a farmhouse of a man named Blythe a mile north of Orrick, just north of the Missouri and twenty-five miles east of Kansas City. The sun was bright in his eyes, but its heat was absent. Haywood was sitting beside him. Archie in the distance was urinating against a tree and Bill was going into the house to check on the breakfast they had demanded. McGown was squatting on a bench in the garden, full of flesh with his skull caved in and the side of his head wet with the blood everyone had been drinking, the bare bone around the wound Jacob had given him casting his head in a silver glow. He stared at Jacob with his eyes full of his soul, full of his life, and grinned. He held a knowledge Jacob didn't possess.

"Haywood," Jacob said.

"Yeah?"

"How do you do this?"

"How do I do what?"

"How do you keep from going crazy?"

"You ain't crazy, Jake."

Jacob looked at McGown. "You don't know me." He wiped hot tears away with his sleeve. "You don't."

Haywood cocked his head and squinted at him. The hem of his father's pants had worn to the point of shredding. One of his suspenders was gone, and that side of the pants hung down to show the lighter filth of his mother's blouse that had not been as exposed to the dust. His lazy eye rolled obscenely with only the white showing and his breath whistled through his teeth.

"I just keep remembering that it's going to be over someday. That's how I do it."

"I keep thinking about that lake, Hay. In Minnesota. I want to go back."

Haywood's good eye widened. "Do you, Jake? Do you mean that?"

"I wouldn't say it if I didn't mean it."

"Oh, Jacob," Haywood said. "Oh, Jake."

Archie had finished urinating and was walking past McGown toward the house, buttoning up his trousers. "Where's that damned breakfast?" he called.

"Don't know."

"Anyone who don't hurry and give us a damned breakfast we ought to string up."

"You're a bloodthirsty bastard, Arch."

Archie stopped at the threshold and grinned down at Jacob. Black eyes, black hair, a black grin. "You gonna shoot me, Jake? Are you?"

Jacob didn't answer him. Archie stared at him with that god damned grin, then laughed and went inside.

"What's that mean, Jake?" Haywood asked.

"It don't mean nothing."

McGown grinned. He rubbed the stump of his wrist with his fingers, then reached into his pocket and took out his severed hand. Thick fingers which had spent a life bending iron and a death bending a will to his own. The severed hand clenched and unclenched and pointed a finger at Haywood.

Jacob's eyes went from McGown to the boy and back again. "What are you asking me?"

"I ain't asking you nothing, Jake," Haywood said.

McGown offered the pointing hand to Jacob. His smile was wrapped in the glow of his bones.

"I won't do it. This ain't something you can ask."

McGown only stared. The finger pointed. Fear and duty grew like a stone in the pit of Jacob's stomach. He felt trapped sitting there. He felt tired.

"Please," he said.

"Jake?" Haywood asked. "Who you talking to?"

"Please," he said again.

Jacob closed his eyes. He tried to see in his mind his life as he wanted it to be. A life out there on a prairie lake with this boy beside him, with Sarah beside him, out there with only the wind and the snow and the grass and to never see Archie or Bill or McGown again. To never think about them again. He made it as real as he could make it, so real he could see the cabin with the shed on its side and he could smell the wind and he could almost forget all that had happened and the aching numbness of who he was inside. He could almost believe what he felt he needed to believe. But when he opened his eyes McGown was still squatting on the garden chair, his severed hand still pointing a finger at Haywood.

"I'm tired," Jacob said. "I don't have it in me."

"Jake?" Haywood asked.

Jacob turned to him. He ran the back of his fingers down Haywood's cheek. He was so tired of it all.

"All right," he said.

"What do you mean, Jake?"

Jacob looked at McGown. The dead sergeant only smiled. "You still got you the mark of Cain, Hay?"

"Sure I do. Cain't you see that?"

"You think God ever changes his mind?"

"I don't know."

"He changes his mind, Hay. He does."

Haywood grinned. "He can do whatever he wants, as long as he gets us back there to our lake. Them taters are more than ready."

"Good." McGown, Jacob thought. Damn you. "We'll leave today. We'll head north just like we done before."

Haywood's good eye widened. A wondering smile on his lips. "You mean it?"

"I wouldn't say it if I didn't mean it."

McGown had turned to study the road. Jacob imagined Haywood lying in dust, a bullet hole filling the ringworm scar on the back of his head. God was a liar.

"It will be hell all winter. You know that?"

"I know it." Haywood smiled. "That's all right."

"You got to do me a favor once we get there. You got to let me call you Sarah."

"You can call me anything you like. Just don't call me late for supper!"

Haywood laughed, his voice keening, at his old joke. Jacob laughed, too, throwing his laughter at McGown like a curse. McGown put his severed hand back in his pocket and smiled.

"Jake?" Haywood asked. "Is Sarah your girlfriend?"

"Not no more."

"That's because I am."

"No," Jacob said. "You're my wife."

Haywood grinned happily at Jacob, then at the sun. "This is a fine day, Jake. It really is."

Jacob rose because he couldn't sit beside Haywood any longer. He followed the smell of pancakes into the house. A sallow-faced woman with her gray hair in a bun had her back to him and was working at a stove. She wore a faded gray dress printed in little blue flowers and her hips were as wide as a cow. Archie was sitting at the table, carving its edge with his Bowie knife into curling slivers. Haywood followed Jacob in and sat across from Archie.

"Ma'am?" Haywood asked. The woman didn't answer. "Ma'am, you got any molasses for them there pancakes?"

"Applesauce," the woman said hoarsely.

"No molasses?" Haywood scratched at the stump of one ear. "I sure could use some molasses."

"You'll take what you get and be happy for it," Archie said. "Didn't your pap ever teach you no manners?"

"I shot my pap's little toe off," Haywood told him. He turned quickly to the woman. "By accerdent."

"Where's Bill?" Jacob asked.

Archie jerked his head toward a room in the back. "Cleaning up."

Jacob nodded and walked into the back room. A bed stood in the corner with the covers awry. Bill was standing before a wash basin and a mirror, wetting a woman's brush in the water and using it to pull back his long hair. A dead man as gray as the woman was lying in his bedclothes on the mattress with his mouth open and the covers across his chest soaked with blood. His ears stubs like Haywood's. Jacob felt only tired.

"Bill," he said.

"Yeah?"

"I'm going to be heading out. For the winter."

Bill glanced at Jacob's reflection as he brushed his beard. "Haywood going with you?"

"No."

"You told him that?"

"No. Don't you tell him, neither."

"Where to?"

"Don't know."

"It's all different now, Jake. George is dead and Charlie, he ain't nothing. Seems to me that if you stuck around, you'd have your own band by the spring."

"Just the same, I'll be heading out."

Bill brushed his hair. He stopped to pull back his lips and, staring into the mirror, scratch a fingernail down one tooth. "Can I trust you, Jake?"

"You can trust me."

"Can I trust you, Jake?"

"I said you can trust me."

"Seems like we always just get hooked up and you're off again."

"Seems that way."

"Poor Haywood's going to be disappointed. He's taken a shine to you."

"He won't be disappointed. Bill."

"Yeah?"

"Don't tell him nothing."

"I won't. Breakfast ready?"

"About."

"Well then." Bill stepped back from the mirror and examined himself. He pulled down the hem of his jacket to sharpen its military lines. "Good morning, Captain Anderson," he said to the mirror. "How are you this morning?" He grinned at Jacob and then at the mirror. "Damn well, thank you."

Jacob left him and walked back into the kitchen. Pancakes lay piled on a plate on the table. Archie was spooning golden applesauce onto the stack on his plate and Haywood was waiting eagerly for the jar. Bacon sizzled in the frying pan and the woman stood immobile and stared dumbly at it. There was nothing to say. Jacob sat at the table.

Bill came out of the back room and loaded a plate with pancakes. He joked with Archie and Archie joked back and Haywood laughed at all the wrong moments. Jacob sat quietly. He didn't eat. When they finished, they went outside and sat in the sun and waited for the other riders to gather. McGown was squatting in the apple tree the apples for the sauce must have come from. The branch beneath him bent to the ground and creaked with his weight. Jacob was too tired to cry.

Within an hour, seventy riders assembled and Bill gave the order to mount. Before they left, Jacob reined the piebald by the open door and looked in at the woman. The last piece of bacon in the pan at which she was staring was black and had ceased to sizzle. Smoke rose gray around her face.

McGown lifted like a sated buzzard and led them down a narrow dirt lane toward the swale they had spent the night camped beside. The day was as crisp as the fruit in the trees and the dense woods held only the gentle whisper of its leaves falling. Jacob rode half a length behind Haywood with his left hand holding the reins and his right resting heavily on the grip of the dragoon pistol. McGown smiled back over his meaty shoulder. He pointed at Haywood, then at the sky.

What, Jacob thought, does that mean?

They rounded a bend and rode into the heart of a stand of maples. Stretched across the lane on its far side was a thin blue line of Federal soldiers with their Enfield rifles aimed and waiting. McGown was hovering above it with the light around his head so brilliant it could have been a second sun.

Bill pulled up his mare. He turned with the insane wildness within him already twitching on his face and foaming at his lips. It shone in his eyes; all of his life was bursting from his eyes. He did not speak, but drew a pistol and screamed an unearthly wail and suddenly his gray mare leaped forward.

"Looks like some fun!" Archie shouted.

Now all the riders were screaming and kicking their horses into gallops toward the soldiers. McGown grew dazzling bright, his entire head now enveloped in the light. The piebald dashed forward with the battle trembling in her sides and flecked on her withers. Haywood slapped harshly against his saddle.

"This is it, Jake," Haywood shouted. "It's this and then no more!"

Jacob aimed his pistol at Haywood. He wondered again why McGown had pointed at the sky. A line of soldiers rose from the brush on his right and raised their rifles. He could not rein in the piebald to meet them in time. Some of the riders were so close to the muzzles they could have touched them.

All of the soldiers fired at once. The morning broke open with the screams of wounded horses and wounded guerrillas and dying horses and dying guerrillas like a blister discharging. The piebald screamed and stumbled and Jacob had to drop the dragoon pistol and grab for her mane to keep from pitching over her head. All was smoke and the stink of smoke and pain and death and madness. A red maple leaf settled down before Jacob's eyes.

When the smoke lifted, he saw that the soldiers were reloading and he could not find Haywood. The piebald was stumbling over the body of a guerrilla who lay with his face in the dirt and both of his legs twitching violently. Dead guerrillas and thrashing, screaming horses littered the lane and dying guerrillas were trying to crawl into the brush on its left side. The soldiers' youthful cheering filled the air and the sound of ramrods being jammed into barrels and the stink of blood and sweat and evacuated bowels, the stink of pain and of dying. The piebald had a great pumping red swath on her neck and a hole in her withers that bubbled pink and whistled as she breathed. So many riders were down. Bill was still mounted and charging madly toward the soldiers lined across the road. His hat had fallen off; his curls were bouncing upon his shoulders. Haywood was riding beside him, bouncing wildly, his bare feet out of the stirrups and his only anchor on the Morgan was his grip on its mane. The ringworm scar on the back of his head shone like a target.

"Haywood!"

Jacob kicked the piebald as hard as he could. She kicked herself free of the boy at her feet and stumbled forward screaming, her eyes huge and wild, her blood bright in the morning. Bill and Haywood reached the line just as the soldiers beside Jacob raised their rifles. They broke through the line as the soldiers pulled back the hammers. The soldiers in front had turned their backs to Jacob and were firing at Bill and Haywood. Bullets riddled Haywood's blouse beneath his armpits, but he still held to the Morgan. Two rifles cracked and Bill's head jerked madly. He threw up his arms and fell backward off of the mare.

The day was terrifically bright. Jacob looked up to see two suns, the sun in the southeast and McGown rising. The dead sergeant was bathed in a light so bright it hurt Jacob's eyes, his silver legs dragging behind him and his arms stretching upward like wings. Haywood was bouncing on the Morgan's back like a monkey, his legs flailing, the soles of his feet flashing in that light. Jacob desperately kicked the piebald toward him. A heavy thunder rumbled that he could not place, then the huge explosion of the Enfields and a howling, horrible pain ripped through his left shoulder and threw him sideways off of the horse. The piebald screamed and reared with her eyes rolling toward the terrific, blinding sight of McGown above her and Jacob felt his heel slip through the stirrup and heard the bones of his ankle crack. The piebald dashed screaming across the lane, dragging Jacob with her, first over bodies and dirt and blood and then through brush. The silver pain of the hole in Jacob's shoulder overwhelmed him; the silver light of McGown filled the sky. Jacob's ankle glowed with the silver and the brush the piebald dragged him over cut him like knives. He closed his eyes.

Chapter Twenty-seven

The piebald died within a half mile. It coughed hard once spraying blood and collapsed on Jacob's leg. His ankle snapped with a sound like the now sporadic gunfire behind him. He wept both in pain and for the piebald.

To get his foot from beneath her, he had to reach over her body and undo the saddle cinches and pull the saddle jockey beneath her out along with his leg, bracing his good leg against her still quivering back. His ankle flopped loosely within the stirrup, and behind him through the trees filtered the boyish pleading of the guerrillas and the harsh soldier laughter and the pop of revolvers that ended the pleading. His shoulder held a stabbing, brilliant heat, but he had to use both arms and his good leg to drag his bad one and the saddle into cover. Fear was in him like a harsh winter. Every time he moved he heard little whimpers that he couldn't believe were coming from him.

The soldiers were drawing closer—he could hear their cursing distinctly. He crawled through the brush with his clothes and skin in tatters and his shoulder awash with blood. He looked at the red trail he was leaving behind. The saddle scraped up the duff from the forest floor.

Before him lay a huge fallen oak, some of its bark stripped and the exposed wood gray and rotting. He crawled along the trunk until he reached the upturned roots and scuttled into the hollow they had left behind. He worked the saddle into a crevice in the roots and covered himself with debris. The dusty, musty smell of decaying leaves filled his nose. His swollen ankle throbbed tightly against the boot leather, hissed on his ragged breath. His pain filled his mind and he tried to keep from whimpering. He listened with fear to the soldiers pass by.

By nightfall, all was silent but for the crickets, the owls, the moon singing among the stars. He crawled to the edge of the hollow and studied the woods, but was too stiff and weak and frightened to go any farther. He cursed McGown and prayed that he would never see the dead sergeant again. His pant leg was ripped, and in the moonlight the skin above the boot on his broken leg was either black or purple. The skin was hot and felt about to split, like ripe fruit in a late autumn harvest.

With his lip between his teeth he probed his ankle. Silver swam in his head. When he could think again, when he could see again, he found he had bitten his lip and blood was dripping from his chin. When he fingered the ragged scraps of meat at his shoulder, the pain overwhelmed him.

When he awoke he felt he had been sleeping for years, but he was still tired. He was lying on a bed in a shanty with a thin sliver of sunlight edging beneath the door, sunlight filtering dustily through a tiny window. A rusty cookstove stood in one corner with a soot-dusted picture of Jesus on the wall beside it. He was lying beneath a worn woolen blanket, naked except for a bandage on his shoulder and another he could feel around his bad foot. Someone had deloused him. His shoulder was close to numb but his foot pulsed with an ache that ran up his backbone and settled in his nose. When he tried to reach for his ankle, he collapsed with the room spinning. He slept.

When he awoke, the light beneath the door and through the window were gone. A black woman perhaps in her seventies stood with her back to him, feeding kindling into the stove. Heavy hips, a lined neck, a kerchief tied over her head. Beside her sitting on the floor was a black man with a shiny bald spot on the back of his head and a grizzled, woolly mustache. His pants reached only mid-calf and he had a scar around one ankle. One bare big toe worked the other. He looked up at Jacob and with the back of his hand tapped the woman's hip. She turned to look with the kindling in her hands.

"Well, Mother," the man said.

"Maybe he won't die," the woman said. "Bless the good Lord above."

Jacob got to his elbows before he had to lie back down. The man scuttled across the floor and with one callused hand gently helped Jacob to settle his head. The woman crossed the shanty to straighten the blanket.

"Where am I?" Jacob asked.

"You be quiet," the man said.

"I want to know where I am."

"You be quiet, or the whiteys will hear you."

Jacob lay for a time without speaking. The pain in his shoulder was just a small maggot working toward the bone, but he thought his foot might make him scream. "What happened?" he whispered.

The man looked at his wife. "I do believe you're right, Mother. He might just live."

"What happened?"

"We found you all shot up."

"Where am I?"

"Ray County. Three mile out of Orrick. We got you a doctor and he patched everything up. He treats Yankees, but don't you ever tell no one about that around here. They'd string him up for sure."

"Us, too," the woman said.

"Can't he do something about my foot?"

The man and woman looked at each other. "Well, Father," the woman said. She shook her head and ran a hand as heavily callused as the man's down Jacob's cheek. "You ain't got that foot no more, child."

Jacob tried to rise again, but collapsed before his hands had reached his knee. "Jesus," he said. "Sweet Jesus."

The woman pet his face. Rough ridges on her palms pulled at his cheek. "Jesus will take care of you, child." She leaned over him confidentially, her face huge and heavy, the smell of her sweet and strange. Old eyes so wet they seemed ready to slip from their sockets. "But you keep your voice down so them up at the house don't hear you. They'll turn you over to the bushwhackers as sure as they're white and they'll string us all up from the rafters. Even as old as Father and me is."

The man reached beneath the bed and brought out the dead lieutenant's frock coat that Jacob had been wearing. "We got this and your trousers all cleaned up and patched as well as they can be. We boiled them with the whiteys' own clothes."

"As if he'll need them for a while, Father."

"A man likes to know where his clothes is at." He dropped his eyes apologetically. "We had to get rid of that saddle. We ain't got no place to hide it."

The man studied Jacob with bloodshot eyes as the woman hobbled back to the stove to stir a kettle. The smell of chicken in the air. Jacob watched her work because he couldn't look into the man's eyes. "You got in that fight, didn't you? With them bushwhackers?"

Jacob thought about it. "Yeah."

"What regiment you in?"

"The Second Colorado."

"We thought you boys was down in Jackson County. So you're the ones who killed Bill Anderson."

"He's dead?" Jacob asked.

The man laughed quietly, his face a maze of wrinkles. "Dead and stiff. They had his body out and I went and saw it myself. A whole big party over in Richmond. They cut off his head and his privates and dragged his body through the streets. Everybody cheering. They put his head on the top of a telegraph pole with the blackbirds picking his eyes out. Everybody celebrating." The man laughed again, then grew serious. "You didn't shoot him, did you?"

"No."

"God bless the fella who did," the man said. "He sent him off to the hell he was asking for."

Jacob stayed with the slaves for three weeks, with the woman and man sleeping on the floor by the stove. While they were in the fields one day he threw the blanket off, and when he saw the stub of his leg he leaned over the bed and vomited onto the wood slat floor. The woman cleaned it up without a word. At night the man sat beside him fashioning a crutch and Jacob made up lies about all the battles against the guerrillas he had fought in. He had been at Fayette; he had been at Flat Rock Ford. He had ridden into Lawrence after the massacre. He said he had fought for the Union with pride.

He was still too feeble at the end of the second week to cross the shanty alone. On the Sabbath harsh voices passed by outside and he had to crawl beneath the bed with fear leaping within him wildly, his face against the wall and his eyes squeezed shut as if he were a child. He feared staying there any longer.

The woman stole a towel from the house and the man tied it over the crutch to make a cushion, and by the end of the third week Jacob could hobble around on it without bleeding. His shoulder had healed faster.

"I got to leave," Jacob told them one night.

"We know," the man said. "I'm a bit nervous myself."

"I was in the cavalry."

"I know you was. The Second Colorado."

The woman sighed and shook her head. "Father. He's telling you he needs a horse."

The old man scratched the bald spot on his head. His throat worked. "I'd have to steal it. Stealing's a sin."

"God will forgive," the woman said. She glanced at the soot-smoked picture of Christ. "He knows our hearts."

Two nights later the man and the woman were out and Jacob was sitting on the bed with the crutch across his lap and staring at the dull glow coming through the stove's open door. He was wearing the dead lieutenant's frock coat, though he hated the feel of it against his skin. He was trying to understand who he was but he could not work it out. The door creaked open and he cowered on the bed's far corner with the crutch raised before him. A black hand gripped the edge of the door and he relaxed.

"Come on," the old man whispered.

"You go help him, Father," the woman said. "That crutch will make a ruckus."

The man helped Jacob out of the door. The night was clear and cool to the point of almost biting, the first night sky Jacob had seen since that night he spent in the oak's hollow. An ancient, swaybacked sorrel mare was standing by the door with her head down and looking at him dully. She had nothing but a rope bridle and a blanket across her back.

"I figured they wouldn't miss an old horse like this," the black man whispered.

He helped Jacob up onto the blanket. The mare looked over her shoulder at him with tiredness in her eyes. Jacob sat with his stump across her back in order to keep the wound high and the blood from leaking.

"You just tap her behind with your crutch every now and then," the man whispered. "She'll go slow, but she'll go. I farmed with her for years and I know."

"I thank you."

"I suppose they'll send you home, now that you ain't got a foot. Where's home?"

"Around Fort Bent."

"I wish you could stay. With the Second Colorado, I mean. I'd like you to kill that Archie Clement for me. He cut the head off of a friend of mine."

"I'd like to."

"I wouldn't mind if you killed a couple of others I know about."

"You ain't heard nothing about a little stump-eared bushwhacker, have you?"

"Not a word. I wish you could be around to kill him, too." The man glanced at the main house. One light burned in a second-story window. "You go now."

"Go with God," the woman said.

He rode southeast for two miles before he reached the Missouri River, the ridge of the mare's spine pressing painfully into his crotch. He wasn't sure what time it was, but the moon was high and the lanes silent and one farmhouse he passed had no lights in the windows. The air was cold enough for his breath to rise and fog rose in the moonlight from the water. He pulled the dead lieutenant's frock coat together at his throat and followed the river upstream toward Kansas City. He was tired and dizzy and his leg felt odd as if his foot were still there, as ghostly as McGown. Whenever he touched the end of the bandage on his leg it felt a little wetter. But a desperate fear flooded him so that he had to get out of Missouri. The old sorrel plodded on mournfully.

By traveling only at night it took him two days to see beyond the river the lights of Kansas City. Twice during the day the low thunder of beating hooves awakened him. The first time was a Federal patrol that went by at a gallop. The second time was two dark-haired boys on fine blooded mares with pistols stuck in their belts galloping even faster. Jacob lay in the brush so frightened that his breath shook in his throat and his tears wet the weeds. The sorrel mare stood quietly by in her own wisdom.

When he reached Kansas City he rode north up the same road he and Haywood had taken the year before. He didn't make as good time. The old mare was steady but slow, and too often he sat upon her with his eyes closed, wrapped in the dull ache of his wounds or contemplating all he had known and all he only thought he had known, letting her find her own way. He opened his eyes on the second day north of the river to find the mare drinking from a stream in a pasture dotted with frost-laced clover that caught the moonlight, the road nowhere in sight. He tapped her behind with his crutch. She looked at him patiently, then turned to keep drinking. He closed his eyes again, and when she began walking he only opened them long enough to insure she was walking north.

He rode for three days without knowing where he was or where he was going. Plowed fields and burned fields with only black stubble standing. Burned farms with blackened chimneys and once three fresh, white cross graves in the cemetery of a soot-blackened and abandoned church, one of the graves opened and the body thrown carelessly out and to the side. The ways of God and men, he thought. For Joshua drew not his hand back. He set his face against his growing emotion, but tears burned coldly in his eyes. He gave himself up to weeping.

A light brushing of snow fell the fourth night. The mare plodded on resolutely, perhaps knowing what he did not. The land had flattened and held fewer trees and in the distance he could see smoke rising from a series of chimneys. He was cold and tired. A road ran toward the chimneys off to his right and he directed the sorrel onto it. A black carriage was coming down the road, pulled by a black horse. The sun was just rising.

A man stuck his head out of the carriage. On his long, thin face he wore round little glasses that he had to squint through. A strand of thin gray hair lifted and fell weakly on his incredibly high forehead.

"You all right, son?"

"I'm lost," Jacob said.

The man pointed back at the chimneys. "That there's Bedford. Does that help you any?"

"Bedford, Missouri?"

"Boy, you are lost. That's Bedford, Iowa."

Something tight in Jacob's chest relaxed, something that had been tight for so long he had forgotten to notice it. He smiled. "So Missouri's behind me."

"About four miles behind you. Where you heading?"

"Don't know."

The man studied him quietly. Eyes flicking up and down, eyes that looked to have seen much that they had never wished to see. "You deserting?"

"No."

"You come stay with me. They'll shoot you if they catch you."

"I ain't deserting."

"There ain't no shame in it. I've cut open men from the north and from the south and they all look the same inside. This war is a damnable sin."

"I've cut them open, too."

"You a doctor?"

"No. You?"

"I am. You come stay with me. They'll shoot you if they catch you."

"They won't shoot a gimp like me." He gently tapped the stump of his leg.

The doctor squinted at it and adjusted his glasses. He climbed out of his carriage with surprising energy for the hour. "Oh hell, boy."

"It happens."

"You come to my place and let me take a look at that."

"What are you doing out this time of the morning?"

"I'm just coming back from delivering the ugliest baby you ever saw. Its mother wasn't so bad, so its father must have been a toad. He's dead now. The father, I mean. A casualty."

"I'd like to get on. But thanks."

"You come and let me look at that. Those damned military surgeons. It's a wonder you ain't dead, too."

The doctor helped Jacob off of the mare and into the carriage, then tied the mare's rope to the back. He smelled of carbolic. He took Jacob to his home a mile or so east of Bedford on the banks of a narrow river that was beginning to freeze. He awoke his wife, a silent woman with heavy eyes and wrinkles framing the corners of her lips, red hair with a hint of gray tied back severely, and while she fried eggs he and Jacob sat at the table beside a sputtering lantern. Jacob shivered in the warmth coming off of the stove, felt it rise along his spine.

"Who'd you vote for?" the doctor asked.

"I ain't old enough to vote."

"Hell of a thing when you can get maimed for the government but you can't vote for it. God damn this. God damn this." The doctor took off and wiped his glasses with a handkerchief his wife handed to him over his shoulder. He propped Jacob's stump between his legs and began to unwrap the bandage.

"Who won?" Jacob asked.

"The election? You don't know?"

"Who was running?"

The doctor stopped unwrapping and squinted at Jacob's face. "How long you been out wandering, boy?"

"Don't know. A while. Before that they took my foot and I was out of my head."

"Lincoln beat McClellan in a landslide. So you ain't heard nothing, huh? You ain't heard about Sherman taking Atlanta or the battle at Franklin or nothing?"

"Sherman took Atlanta?"

"And Schofield turned back Hood at Franklin south of Nashville and you can call this war just about over."

"You believe that?"

"Of course I believe that. All things come to an end." He concentrated on his work. The stump grew cooler and tingled as he unwrapped it. Jacob saw a flash of dead white skin and had to turn away. The doctor lifted his leg a few inches and clicked his tongue.

"Well now. That don't look so bad."

Jacob stayed in the kitchen with the doctor and his wife through breakfast and into the morning. They let him lie down in a back bedroom and when he awoke it was dark again. He sat up and fumbled for his crutch. With its thump on the floor the door opened and the doctor sidled in. He sat in a straight-backed chair with faded green upholstery and watched Jacob put on the dead lieutenant's frock coat.

"Where were you fighting at?" the doctor asked.

"Missouri."

"Good Lord. Couldn't you have picked a less hellish place?"

"They don't let you pick."

"Where you from?"

"Ohio."

"Ohio boys are fighting in Missouri?"

"I'm from Minnesota."

"Which is it? Ohio or Minnesota?"

"Minnesota."

The doctor leaned forward with his elbows on his knees. Long hands hanging down, fingers growing longer like slowly melting wax. "You don't know where you're from, do you?"

"I'm from Minnesota."

The doctor rested his hand on Jacob's knee. Jacob was still buttoning up the coat. "You listen to me. I'll trade you that old swayback sorrel for a ticket out west somewhere. That's where all the deserting boys are going, and I suspect that's what the government wants them to do. Someone to tame the wilderness."

"I ain't deserting."

"Sure. But a civilian doctor did up your leg because there ain't no military doctor who's got the time to be that careful. And that ain't no military mount you're riding. And you're riding at night."

"I like riding at night."

"I'll trade you that old swayback for a ticket."

"I don't want to go out west."

"Then I'll trade you for a ticket to Minnesota or Ohio or wherever. You just can't stay here because if they find you they'll shoot you. They're shooting everybody." He withdrew his hand and wiped his face with it. "Here you are, sporting a wound like that and they'd shoot you anyway. They have no respect. This god damned war takes away respect. It takes away everything. So where do you want to go?"

"Minnesota."

"It's cold up in Minnesota."

"Ohio, then," Jacob said.

The next morning the doctor hitched up his horse to the carriage while the mare stood silently watching. He and his wife took Jacob into Bedford. They lunched on liver and onions at the hotel as they waited for the coach to arrive. Through the front window, Jacob watched a soldier with an Enfield slung over his shoulder pass by, then come back and stop. He cupped his hands against the pane and peered in at Jacob's meal. Jacob felt the edge of his fork handle press hard against his finger. Its tines clicked hard against china and a piece of liver skittered off of his plate and onto the white tablecloth. He couldn't stop his fingers from trembling. The doctor's hand gripped his knee and didn't release him until the soldier went on.

The stagecoach came just after noon and the doctor bought him a ticket onto it. He gave him enough money so that when he reached Des Moines he could buy a train ticket to Cincinnati. He didn't say anything, and neither did Jacob. Though the doctor's wife had never spoken to him and Jacob could not even remember her looking at him, she hugged him and kissed his cheek and whispered in his ear, "God watch over you."

He got on the coach without saying anything to her. He listened to the driver's hollow whistle and looked out the window as the coach pulled away. The doctor and his wife were walking back toward their carriage, the doctor slouching with his head down. Jacob did not even know their names.

He rode in the carriage all day. A beautiful young woman, ivory skin, perfect features, boarded at a little nameless town he didn't know the name of and sat across from him. She kept smiling at him from under the rim of her hat, but Jacob looked out the window and pretended to study the dull, monotonous scenery. He didn't speak and she didn't speak and Jacob tucked the stump of his bad leg behind the boot on his good one. He felt better when she disembarked at the next town.

The coach spent the night in a little farming town named Lorimor. Jacob didn't have money for a hotel room, but the hotel was nearly empty and the keeper had been a Federal sergeant and he let Jacob have a room for free. He had a scar on his cheek he said he had gotten at Independence. He wanted to spend the evening swapping stories, but Jacob said his leg was bothering him and hobbled up to his room. He lay on the bed, staring up at the ceiling, and tried not to think about Missouri. He managed to think about the girl in the coach, and she made him think of Sarah.

His hand slipped down to his crotch. His mind slipped between Sarah and Haywood, and every time he thought about Haywood he withdrew his hand because he wasn't that way. Finally he returned to thinking about the girl in the coach, but he still had no luck. He withdrew his hand and clasped his fingers behind his head and watched the night on the ceiling. He could smell his own sweat. He hurt inside. He fell asleep after midnight.

When they reached Des Moines, the coach driver gave him part of his money back and told him to buy laudanum for his leg if he needed it. Every time the train stopped on the trip back to Cincinnati and he went in for a meal they refused to take his money. He felt anxious about seeing so many Federal soldiers and awkward when they saluted him. Twice he returned the salute with the wrong hand. One of those times the soldier had to wipe tears from his eyes and apologize for making Jacob salute with his crutch hand. He wondered about the tears, since it seemed as if half the men he met were missing arms or legs or pieces out of their jaws. Perhaps it was because of the look on his face. In his eyes.

He could feel the Ohio River before he saw it. He could smell it and even hear it beneath the steady rumble of the train engine and the thunk of the car wheels on the metal track, its low murmur so familiar it was a part of him. When just before the train reached Cincinnati the current reflected back sunlight through the trees, he felt something clawing deep within as if it were trying to dig through his chest. Silent tears ran down his face and wet the collar of the dead lieutenant's frock coat. Two old women sat across the aisle from him with their eyes turned toward the floor. The thin, bowed conductor stepped to Jacob's seat and mumbled a few words about the train arrival, but let his words drop and stood respectfully beside him for a few minutes before moving quietly on to the other passengers. Jacob sat with his face to the window and his elbow on the sill and the tears coming down. He chewed gently on the pad of his thumb and wiped at one cheek with his knuckles. He couldn't quit crying.

The station in Cincinnati was a bustle of workers and farmers and soldiers and workmen on their way down to the river. Jacob stood uncertainly, then asked at the ticket window the best way to get to Ripley. A farmer who smelled of the earth overheard him and told him he could take him halfway. Jacob rode sitting beside the farmer's mother, who over the course of her life had soaked into her cavernous pores too much lilac water. She related ecstatically and endlessly her trip to Philadelphia to visit her other son, a lawyer who planned on running for Congress. At Georgetown, ten miles from Ripley, Jacob waved them goodbye. He had not hobbled a half mile before another farmer driving a wagon offered to take him the rest of the way.

He stood on the main street of Ripley leaning on the crutch and studying the town. He didn't feel at home and hadn't expected to. He took a meal at the local hotel because he wasn't sure if he yet had the courage to go out to the farm, but he couldn't eat it because across the street was Mc-Gown's blacksmith shop being worked by another man. Fear as palpable as the fear in the shanty leaped within him as he remembered that in this town he was probably wanted for murder. He thought at first that the fear might be the same as the clawing he had been feeling since before Cincinnati, but by the time he had left the hotel and hobbled halfway to the farm he knew he was wrong.

The farm looked much as he remembered it from that winter day two years before. He was exhausted and his crutch arm ached and all of his wounds were throbbing. The night was settling in. He couldn't see the field very well, but he could tell it hadn't been worked and the fence guarding the overgrown pasture was down. Boards were off the side of the barn, and a skeletal cat slunk through the hole they left behind. He couldn't hear any livestock. The cabin looked deserted. He started to go in, but to place his crutch he had to look down upon the spot where he had murdered Teague. He glanced around as if all the eyes of the world were upon him. He hobbled to the barn instead.

The barn was as deserted, no cow, no mule, the buckboard gone, with only swallows in the rafters. He could smell the musky odors of animals, though, and when he checked Buck's stall he found fresh manure. Fear thrilled his chest again. The back corner where Isaac and Sarah had slept looked as if it had never been inhabited, as if none of the things that had happened there really had. He leaned his crutch against Mabel's old stall and collapsed in the straw on his back. He sighed deeply and closed his eyes and tried to capture from what remained of him all that he had been. Those nights with Sarah, her sweet touch, her liquid smoothness, the warmth and the darkness of her skin, her eyes, the warmth of being within her. For a moment he had it and he smiled, but when he opened his eyes he was just a broken-down guerrilla with a shattered nose and a missing foot and a wounded shoulder. He was just a broken-down guerrilla wearing the frock coat of a Federal lieutenant he had killed. He began to cry. The blood on his hands, in his heart. He rolled on his side and curled into a ball like a child and stared out between the barn slats into the trees. The night had almost come.

He couldn't stay there anymore. When he tried to stand he fell and rammed the stump into Mabel's stall and fell back into the straw whimpering with his pain and his loss. He lay there for a half hour before he wiped his eyes and reached for the crutch and crawled on his hands and knees out of the barn. He stood once he reached the yard. No lights were on in the cabin and he felt it safe to enter. In the heavy dusk he could no longer see the spot where Teague had died.

The cabin was as chilly as the yard, but a few orange embers were glowing in the hearth. The bed had been slept in on both sides and bread rinds littered the table. He sat in his mother's rocker and threw a handful of kindling and three split pieces of oak onto the fire. He shuddered as the warmth came and an orange glow crawled up the walls, fell into the darkness where his mother's china cabinet had stood. The picture of Jesus still hung on the wall. A dark stain lay half covered by a rug on the floor where McGown had died. Jacob turned away from it.

Finally he rose and hobbled to the bed. He pulled back the sheets and saw that they were stained, then remembered lying in the loft and listening to the sounds of his parents below him. It had been so long ago. He'd been just a child then.

He thought of climbing again into the loft as if that would grant him something, but with his stump leg he didn't know if he could make it. Finally he just pulled the sheets back up and lay curled upon them, facing the fire. He slept.

He awoke to the sound of a wagon in the yard. Fear leaped within him and he cowered on the bed with the crutch drawn up before him. Someone pushed the door open and he waited, then Sarah came in with a sack of cornmeal over her shoulder. She glanced at the fire but not at the bed and let the sack slide to the table.

"Sarah," he said.

Her back stiffened. Her fingers rested lightly on the sack. She turned her head enough for him to see her profile. No longer the child. My God, he thought. My love.

"You're back," she said.

"I come home."

She turned to him. She was still so lovely that he thought his longing for her would kill him. "What happened to your foot?"

"I lost it."

"Where?"

"Franklin," he said. "In the war."

She turned back to the cornmeal. Everything leaped within him.

"You're a lieutenant," she said.

"Are they looking for me?"

"Who?"

"You know who."

"They were. I don't know if they are now."

"Where's my mother?"

"Dead. She went crazy and she died."

"Where's my father?"

"He reenlisted before Gettysburg and died there in Pickett's charge."

"Isaac?"

"Canada. He and my mother are in Canada."

"Your brother?"

"Already sold off."

Did he know why she had waited? "Why didn't you go?"

She paused. She said nothing.

"What do you got here, Sarah?" He felt panic. "What do you got here?"

She didn't answer him. He struggled to sit. "I love you, Sarah."

Her shoulders tightened again. She pulled a chair away from the table and sat on it with her knees toward the fire. She sighed. She did not look at him.

"Sarah, I love you."

She stared at the flames. All the emotion Jacob was feeling gathered in a hard, cold lump in his throat that he could hardly get his breath around. He knew now.

"Did you love me, Sarah? I knew this fella who told me that you didn't."

"Jacob," she said, "do you have to ask?"

He scrabbled his crutch upon the floor, then stood and clumped heavily toward the table. She wouldn't look at him. At last he let the crutch and his knees go and he collapsed with his face in her lap. He cried for a minute, and for that minute he thought everything would be all right.

"We'll go out west," he said. "I know this place in Minnesota. It's on a lake. You'll love it out there, Sarah. I know you will."

For a moment, she said nothing. "You aren't going anywhere with a black woman. What will you tell them?"

"There ain't nobody out there to tell anything to."

"There will be."

"I'll tell them you're my wife. You will be, won't you?"

She gently lifted his face from her lap and tucked her knees beneath the table and let his face down again until his forehead rested on the edge of the chair. He looked up at her with his hands clasped together at his knees. She was staring at the cornmeal.

"Sarah," and then, "Sarah?"

They stayed as they were without speaking. Finally, he grabbed up his crutch and stood. He felt as numb as he had when he had been a guerrilla and he was a guerrilla again. He saw in his mind Joshua sweeping across the plains and the children in his wake crying, the children in his wake dying. He lifted the crutch over his shoulder with all his anger and all his sorrow and all of what had been his life burning at the edges of his vision.

"Sarah, you look at me. God damn, it, Sarah, you look at me."

She stared at the cornmeal. His balance was failing and he had to release the crutch with one hand to steady himself on the table. Even with that bastion he needed the crutch beneath his arm—he was too weak to hold it. She stared at the cornmeal. He lowered the crutch and braced himself on it and wiped his face with his hand. The numbness was complete, as if all that was left of his life had just burned out of his eyes.

He hobbled past her, the crutch thumping hollowly. He opened the door and looked out at the night and cursed his inability to bring all of this to an end. The stars were bright and the river murmured blackly.

"Is it the bum leg?" he asked.

"It doesn't have anything to do with your leg."

"You let me cry on your lap like that once."

"I remember," she said. "You were raping me."

Jacob hobbled out of the door and closed it behind him. The firelight through the window flickered on the spot where Teague had died and he felt nothing about it. He hobbled down to the river over mud half frozen and stared across the black water to the other side. The bare branches of the old cottonwood, dead now, open wounds in the trunk rotting, clawed the naked sky. Jacob searched the stars for McGown.

"Please," he said.

Someone was rowing a skiff across the water. He was wearing a slouch hat and had wide shoulders and hair that swallowed the darkness. Dark hands gripped the oars.

Jacob stepped back into the shadows and thought he would kill him when he came ashore, but McGown wasn't there and he lacked the will. He hobbled away as the skiff met the bank, passed the livestock pens to the path leading to the McIntyre farm. He stopped to listen to footsteps fade as they went up to the cabin behind him. He imagined the man going into the cabin and closing the door and he would not let himself imagine anything further.

He shut his eyes and wiped his face with his free hand. God damned niggers, he thought. First Isaac then Sarah then Henry and then Sarah again. Now this nigger in the skiff. They're the cause of all of this.

No, he thought, they're not the cause of any of this. He knew the ways of God and men. Like Joshua, he had thundered across rivers and dusty plains. To hell with it all. To the bloody, god damned hell that the bloody, god damned God had created with it all. Now he was finally done with it. He spat at the water and cursed his own soul.

The McIntyre farm looked as desolate as his own had been. A light filtered through the dirty window and when he knocked on the door Mary answered it. The lantern light through her hair made it colorless. Jacob felt nothing toward her.

"Jacob," she said. She was hollow-cheeked and hollow-chested and her eyes were dull and empty.

"Is your father here?"

"He run off out west somewhere to avoid the draft. Jacob?"

"You got any money?"

"Some. Is that really you?"

"We're leaving for Minnesota in the morning."

She hesitated before throwing her arms around him. He tottered. She released him and gasped when she saw the crutch and followed it down to the bandage around his leg.

"I lost it fighting," he said. "Does it make a difference?"

She smiled, showing her yellow teeth. He still felt nothing toward her.

"Oh Jacob, it don't make no difference. Nothing ever made no difference." She led him inside and around the table and helped him onto the bed.

Chapter Twenty-eight

They used Mary's money to buy train tickets to St. Paul. She wanted to marry in Cincinnati, but Jacob said he wanted to get out of Ohio before he was arrested for murder. She wanted to marry in St. Paul, but he said they should use the money to get themselves settled instead of buying a license. He said no one in Minnesota knew they weren't married anyway.

In the spring the snowmelt was great enough for them to take a steamboat up the Minnesota River to Mankato, a bustling town on the edge of the prairie where thirty-eight Sioux had been hanged for the uprising. With the last of their money they bought a mule and plow and wagon and seed and they started west. They found the lake within a week, but the cabin was already inhabited. Jacob's heart leaped until he saw that it was a woman working the garden. He turned the wagon around and headed back to Mankato. Mary didn't protest.

He clerked at a store and Mary took in laundry until they had enough money to put down a payment on their own store that they called Wilson's. Jacob had no problem getting a loan on the balance because though he didn't have an honorable discharge, he said that he had lost it and his polite, calm, serious manner and missing foot placed him in good stead. They sold dry goods. He hired a boy to haul supplies from the railroad until the boy was grown and Jacob and Mary had their own son who could take over the work. They had three sons and three daughters and Jacob lived with Mary on the southern slope of the Minnesota River Valley, and except for the quietest times, except for those times in the night when in the darkness he could see nothing and the only sound was the beat of her heart and the only thing he could feel was her breath on his shoulder, except for those quietest times he believed that he loved her. He knew many things in those times that he would not face when he had distraction. Faces would float in the darkness.

Their children grew. Their two oldest daughters somewhere had found a vitality neither of them possessed. The girls married men in town. The towheaded son went west to Seattle and the redhead east to New York and the nondescript other one took over the store for Jacob just after the turn of the century. Their youngest daughter had always been delicate and died of consumption in a sanatorium on the Canadian border. No blacks lived in Mankato. He had not seen any since the war.

In 1917, Jacob watched two bright-eyed grandsons go off to the Great War with his old wrinkled hands clutching the rail at the train station and trembling. One came home in six months with his lungs burned black and his eyes burned dull by mustard gas; he died a month later. The other died in the influenza epidemic on a transport train without ever having left the country. Their war was as brutal as his war had been and he believed nothing he had believed then, nothing at all about God and souls and the lack or abundance of them. He did not believe in or look for omens. He had been young and foolish and he looked back on that time with the wisdom which perhaps in their cold, murky deaths his grandsons now possessed. All you can hope for in any war is to not die like a dog.

He never thought of Bill or Archie or Charlie beyond hoping that Archie and Charlie had joined Bill in the hell the old black slaves outside of Orrick had spoken of. He only thought of Haywood when he'd see boys cock their heads and squint and a feeling would open inside of him that he did not understand or care to. He wanted to forget. Though he constantly thought of Sarah, he never mentioned her. Sometimes he walked down to the river and stared across it to the bluffs rising on the other side.

Mary died in 1920, and he buried her with his hand resting on her coffin and his eyes painfully dry. Though their surviving daughter wanted him to move in with her, he at first refused. He had come to believe that he had never depended on anyone. The cold, dead numbness within him he now accepted as strength. But his circulation was bad because of his leg, and eventually his blood began to clot and his heart to fail. He couldn't get out of bed anymore. He finally agreed to live with his daughter.

He awoke one morning in the summer of 1922, knowing with calmness that he would not see the night. He called his daughter to his side, an old gray woman who liked to dress stylishly and flaunt her driving skills by buzzing around the town in her Model T. She sat beside him with tears on her dust-colored face and took his hand.

"Papa," she said.

"I loved Sarah," he told her. "Do you believe that?"

"Who's Sarah?" she asked.

He smiled. It took all of his effort. "Your mother."

His daughter looked puzzled. "Mom's name was Mary, Papa."

Jacob just smiled again and faintly shook his head. He could remember everything so clearly. He'd been wounded at Franklin where he'd gained acclaim for shooting a murdering animal named Archie Clement. He'd come home to Ohio and married Sarah and they'd lived on the farm and raised their family and they had loved each other. He'd been a deacon in the local church and he'd worshipped a God with a lazy eye and he believed, God, how he believed. He could see heaven's glorious golden gates open before him.

And now Sarah's daughter could not remember her own mother's name. Well, he thought, she's getting old.

"My grandfather came to this farm," he said. "While he was clearing it he had to live in the hollow of a fallen cottonwood. Then my father was born and he died in the war and I took the farm. I lived in the hollow of a fallen cottonwood, too, but I don't remember where. I was young then."

He could feel her squeezing his hand. It was such a distant thing. "Papa?" she asked.

"And now it's yours. You take it."

His daughter just stared at him. "David's got the store, Papa. Do you mean the house?"

He couldn't remember a David. He was contemplating his daughter's confusion when a shadow passed over the ceiling. He thought it might be a car's headlights, but if so, then the light and the dark were confused, too, because wasn't it the middle of the morning? He watched the shadow take on flesh and stare at him from soulless eyes. He wasn't surprised.

"Damn you," Jacob said. "Damn you to hell."

His daughter was crying. "Don't say that, Papa."

"You've always led me wrong."

"Papa, don't say that."

"But I believe," he said. "I do."

She raised his hand to her cheek and he could feel her tears upon it. He looked from the shadow to this strange feeling and saw all around him the farm. Cyrus was working in the field with Buck, and Clara was standing in the door slim and strong. Isaac stood in front of the barn door and Sarah was running toward Jacob with her skirts gathered up in her hands and her bare legs flashing in the sun. He spread his arms to receive her. He had waited his whole life for this.

Now he was in the air with the river far below him snaking off toward his dreams. Tobias was rowing across it from the other side. Sarah was dancing below him, dancing as she had danced on the senator's mantel, one arm lifted gracefully above her head, with her tears rolling down her face in streams, her lips pulled back in a smile. Someone was flying beside him and he lifted his eyes, but in the brightness he couldn't make anything out. An eagle or angel or demon. The ways of God are beyond men's ways and perhaps in that knowledge he floated. He had never felt so happy before. He looked down for Sarah, but his eyes were too dazzled to find her. Everything is so distant.

He is flying now as he feels he has been always. He has been unburdened, and he burns with a silver light. He is flying now. He believes he will never die.

Afterword

George Todd and William Anderson died in 1864.

William Quantrill left the state for Kentucky in December of that year. He committed his usual raids and had minor skirmishes with the militia. In May of 1865 during a skirmish in a horse yard he was shot in the back. He dropped into mud and manure, paralyzed below the shoulders. He died in a Louisville military hospital in June, after converting to Catholicism. His bones have become collectors' items.

James Lane was charged with cowardice and ineptitude after the Lawrence raid. With his fortunes declining he tried to jump from a St. Louis hotel room window. A doctor took him to a Leavenworth farm, where on July 5, 1866, he shot himself in the mouth with a derringer. It took him ten days to die.

Archie Clement fled to Texas after the war, returning to Lexington, Missouri, in 1866. He surrendered with twenty-six men in December, but died in a gun battle the same day.

After Fletcher Taylor lost his arm, he went on to prosper as the vice president and general superintendent of the Joplin Mining and Smelting Company in Joplin, Missouri.

James G. Blunt settled in Leavenworth and resumed a medical practice. Later he moved to Washington, D.C., where in 1879 he was committed to an insane asylum, diagnosed with softening of the brain. He died in confinement in 1881.

David Poole became one of the first guerrillas to surrender after the war. He was granted amnesty and settled in Lexington, where he led several posses after the James-Younger gang, who always managed to escape, because, Poole said, of the inferiority of his horses.

Charles "Doc" Jennison was court-martialed in 1865 and dishonorably discharged. He prospered in Leavenworth as a saloon and gambling house keeper and breeder of racehorses and cattle. He was elected president of the Leavenworth city council, served two terms in the Kansas House of Representatives and one in the State Senate, consistently opposing black suffrage. As he grew older his health worsened, and he died in 1884 at the age of fifty.

Frank James was able to settle with his brother, Jesse, in Clay County, Missouri, because they had not been guerrilla leaders and were virtually unknown. With Bud Younger, Frank and Jesse robbed a Liberty bank in 1866. A long series of bank and train robberies followed that ended at Northfield, Minnesota, where three members of the gang were killed and all three Younger brothers, Bud, Jim, and Bob, captured. Frank surrendered to the authorities in Missouri after Jesse was killed, and after the statue of limitations had run out on most of his crimes. He was tried twice, once for murder and once for bank robbery, and was twice acquitted. He died on the Clay County family farm in 1915.

Coleman "Bud" Younger moved from New Mexico to California, returning to western Missouri in the fall of 1865. He joined the James brothers in a career of bank robbery. He spent twenty-five years after the Northfield raid as prisoner 699 in the state prison in Stillwater, Minnesota, where he read the law, the Bible, and Shakespeare, not returning to Missouri until after his pardon in 1903. He joined the church on the fifty-first anniversary of the Lawrence massacre. He died in 1916 of a heart attack at Lees Summit, Missouri.

William Gregg settled with his wife first in Jackson County, then in Kansas City. He worked as a handyman, carpenter, teamster, and deputy sheriff until arthritis forced him to retire. He became the unofficial historian of the Quantrill band and died, broken and impoverished, in 1916.